MW01134868

Harrington's Valley

HARRINGTON'S VALLEY

A Novel

Darrel Rachel

Createspace Independent Publishing Platform

Harrington's Valley

Copyright© 2021 by Darrel Rachel

All rights reserved. No part of this book may be used or reproduced by any means, graphic, electronic, or mechanical, including photocopying, recording, taping, or by any information storage retrieval system without the written permission of the author except in the case of brief quotations embodied in critical articles and reviews.

This novel was originally published under the title *The Circling Eagle*.

Certain characters in this work are historical figures, and certain events portrayed did take place. However, this is a work of fiction. All the other characters, names, and events, as well as all places, incidents, organizations, and dialogue in this novel, are either the products of the author's imagination or are used fictitiously.

Printed in the United States of America
October, 2015

To Jesse, Konnor, and Kailynn

To M. Cody Suman, my appreciation for editing the manuscript and providing helpful suggestions.

To Leah Kayajanian for her excellent editing and suggestion.

Chapter 1

Tennessee Homecoming

They blended with the damp, cold Northern Tennessee night—the two weary men. A log caught—the flames flickered. Light from the fire fell across lean, haggard faces. Sunken, tired eyes stared beyond the fire into the darkness. A tattered Confederate cavalry officer's uniform hung on one of the men like rags on a scarecrow. The other wore the twin stripes of a corporal sewn to one frayed sleeve.

Tiny red rockets radiated out from the fire. The officer turned his slender frame, watched the corporal thrusting a small limb into the dying flames. He made no comment, turned back to his own thoughts. After one last poke into the ashes, the limb landed on top of the fire's remnants.

"Cap'n, we must be near to Montgomery County now," the corporal, a short man with red hair, said.

The officer turned, leaned on one elbow. He pondered the remark before answering. "A few hours ride, I believe."

"We'll be there tomorrow then."

"I would expect to."

"Well, Cap'n, what do you think we'll find?"

The captain considered that question. "I hope for the best, but experience tells me we'll find what war tends to leave behind, destruction."

The corporal nodded. "Yep. From what I heard, the Yanks been there for most of four years. I 'spect they've taken about all that's worth taking."

"That could well be. Tomorrow we'll know," the captain said.

"Yes, sir, tomorrow we'll know." The corporal got up and retrieved a dirty blanket from a saddlebag at the edge of the camp. "I believe I'll be turning in now, Cap'n McKane."

"All right, Corporal Hays, splendid idea. We've got a long day ahead of us tomorrow."

Hays lay down on the damp ground and pulled the blanket around him.

1

Soon, he was snoring.

James McKane stared into the dying flames. Tomorrow, he would be home. Home! For four long, bloody years, he had thought of little else. Now, he was just a day's ride away from his family. So, where was the enthusiasm he should be feeling? It was a time for elation; instead, he felt only doubt and fear. It was the hard, cold reality of war staring him in the face. So many times during the past four years, he had seen, had felt, the horrors of war. His experiences left little room for optimism, for hope. Unlike so many of his comrades, he had been spared death, but for what purpose? There was so much to lose, so much that could be taken from him: his wife and children, his mother and father, and the plantation. These thoughts had plagued him so since slipping out of Nashville.

The war—blast the bloody conflict that had brought him to this state. Throughout the campaigns, he had seen so much of the South laid to ruin, battered by artillery fire, trampled under, reduced to ashes. Would it be any better in Clarksville? From what he had been able to learn, the Yankees had occupied it during most of his absence. How had they treated the people?

How different things had been four years earlier. People treated the upcoming conflict like a carnival. Pomp and ceremony ruled. The residents of Clarksville stood on the sidewalks cheering as the military parades passed the town square. "How innocent we were," James mumbled.

Patriotism, the idealism of youth. With the enthusiasm of a young man going on a hunt, he journeyed from Clarksville up to Kentucky in April of 1861 to join a cavalry unit. The thrill of the campaign, a fight for his land, and way of life had been his motto. Standing proud with other men from Clarksville, he watched Captain Blanchard take command of the new unit. "Bravo," they all thought. They'd show those Yanks what proud Southerners were made of.

Idealism faded in the face of reality. There were no bands playing or pompous celebrations on the battlefield. The somber reality of war met them head on in April of 1862. After the Cumberland and Tennessee River Valley campaigns, the glory of war was forever shattered. Bitter retreats followed, first to Shiloh, then further south. Hell on Earth, the battlefields covered with the dead, and the screams of the wounded had replaced their idealism.

The specter of death stared James in the face at Garrettsburg, Kentucky. His horse was shot from under him. For the duration of the battle, he was forced to lie under the dead animal, bleeding from a wound to his side. When the skirmish ended, he worked himself free and wandered for hours to reach the Confederate lines. Then came weeks in a field hospital: it offered no reprieve, just grim reminders of the carnage.

The remaining war years found him in Chicamauga, Columbia, South

2

Carolina, and Bentonville, where his unit was almost decimated. Then there was the humiliating end. In Washington, Georgia, James and what remained of his cavalry unit were captured trying to escort Jefferson Davis, the Confederate president.

James and his comrades were paroled in early May of 1865. The Yanks allowed them to keep their horses for a time. Then, at Chattanooga, the Federals went back on their word and took their horses from them. They were marched to Nashville on foot. Once there, they were forced to take the Oath of Allegiance to the Union.

During his confinement at Nashville, James made the acquaintance of Corporal Arlen Hays, a farm boy from near Clarksville. They stole some horses from the Yanks; as a bonus, James took a Henry repeating rifle and a pistol from a sleeping sentry. The rifle was a weapon he knew well. At Bentonville, the Confederate forces had encountered Yanks armed with these repeaters. The firepower of the 44-caliber rifles left a lasting impression.

They traveled the back roads, often at night, to avoid Yankee patrols. They carried their oaths, but four years of bloody combat left them suspicious of the Federal troops. James also kept the Henry rolled up in a blanket. A Confederate carrying a weapon even few Yanks had been issued invited questions best left unasked, he figured.

Aided by sympathetic farm families and luck, they were poised to enter Montgomery County, back on home soil again. When he thought of home now, how far in the past it seemed. Memories obscured by war, of a summer evening on the balcony with his wife and children, riding his favorite horse across the plantation, Sunday dinners in the dining room of the main house, walking across a tobacco field with his father, days of innocence now lost, perhaps forever.

The guilt—it would not leave him in peace. Most of it was guilt for not communicating with his family. The war, he told himself, the bloody war was to blame. But that would not placate his conscience. He was returning with not a hint of what he would find, a victim of his short-sightedness.

When drowsiness came, he got his blanket, spread it out, and lay down next to the fire. Dreams came, omens of things to come; they were not pleasant.

*   *   *

Mist, thick and gray, greeted them. James pushed aside the damp blanket and stood up. Hays stirred and got to his feet. "I'll fetch some wood, Cap'n."

While the corporal searched for firewood, James poured some water from his canteen into their small coffee pot. Poking around in the ashes, he found a

3

few red coals. He used some damp hickory leaves and bits of grass to start a flame. The wet fuel was slow to catch. He blew on it until a small flame erupted. Smoke spiraled upward. Not a good thing if Yankee patrols were about. The mist was their ally; the smoke couldn't be seen from any great distance.

Corporal Hays stepped out of the woods carrying an arm full of tree limbs. "It ain't much Cap'n, but it's the best I can find."

"They'll do."

Hays dropped the limbs beside the fire. James broke them into pieces before casting them into the flames. The moisture in the wood sizzled; clouds of smoke drifted up into the gray sky. When they caught, he set the coffee pot over the flames using some small rocks to support it. "All we got is a couple of biscuits and a little coffee," James said.

"Well, Cap'n, I've forgotten what it's like to eat regular."

The scant rations from sympathetic families had played out. Hunger had been their constant companion for much of the war, so they were accustomed to living on little. "You know, Cap'n, when I get home, I'm gonna ask my ma to fry up a big skillet of side meat, make some gravy from the drippings, and bake a big pan of biscuits."

"That does sound appetizing, Corporal. Be careful you don't founder yourself."

The corporal laughed. When the coffee was ready, they sat by the fire, wrapped in their blankets, eating the biscuits and sipping the hot liquid. It was weak, tasteless.

The mist thickened into a drizzle. James pulled a rain slicker from his saddlebags; all Corporal Hayes could find was a wool coat. "I'll fetch the horses, Cap'n."

The corporal led the poor, wet horses into camp. In their emaciated condition, would they last the ride into Clarksville? They might have to finish the journey home on foot. But without some grain or hay, there wasn't much the men could do. When the horses were saddled, and their gear packed, they set out for the road. As always, James had the Henry wrapped in a blanket. "Cap'n, what you expect them Yanks might do if they found that rifle on you?"

"Don't know, Corporal. Maybe hang me." The comment wasn't meant for amusement; neither of them took any from it.

They rode out of the woods onto a makeshift road. This morning, gray clouds hung over the tops of the tall oak and hickory trees. The horses plodded through the mud, carrying their wet and tired riders.

Hays wiped water from his forehead with his sleeve. "Cap'n, what do you plan to do now that the war is over?"

James thought. Often, during the past four years, he never expected to

4

have a future. "Can't say, Corporal. My family owned a tobacco and grain plantation. But now, I don't know what's happened to it. There may be nothing left."

"You know, Cap'n, maybe that's one of the advantages of being poor. When you ain't got much to lose, you don't miss it so much when it's gone. All my folks had when the war started was a little dirt farm south of Clarksville, next to the Cumberland. Makes it easier to start over again. You ain't got so far to go to get back to where you were. A man don't miss what he never had."

"I suppose you're right, Corporal."

James lapsed into silence. Worry—more like downright apprehension—was back again. What was he going to find today? Beyond that, what would he do now? The plantation might be gone. First, he had to get back with Kate and the children. With his family beside him, he would find a way to start over. After all, the McKanes had not always been people of means. His grandfather had come to Montgomery County when it was nothing but wilderness.

There were farm houses along the road. But James noticed something peculiar; many of them looked deserted. He pointed it out to the corporal. "Most these folks ain't very trustin', Cap'n. It's the Yanks. These folks try to avoid them as much as possible, so they don't get out much."

"Thank God it's over, Corporal. Maybe the Union troops will soon be gone."

"I hope so, Cap'n, but I ain't countin' on it too much. The Yanks, they wanta punish us for leaving the Union. I 'spect they gonna be around for a while."

"I suppose. They want to make as much profit as they can."

"Yes, sir, I believe they do."

The drizzle continued. The water dripping off the front of James's hat ran in little streams down the front of his rain slicker. The corporal's wool coat became soaked, so he removed it. "I hope I don't come down with pneumonia," he said.

They had endured such as this for most of the war. James recounted the times they had gone without protection against the elements. Confederate forces had shivered in the cold without coats and many without even shoes. Human endurance had been pushed to the limit; how did any of them survive?

In the heavy drizzle, they were close on them before James spotted the men standing next to the road, mere shadows in the gray mist. "Corporal Hays, it seems we have some company ahead," he said.

"I see 'em, Cap'n. What do you reckon they're about?"

"I don't know. I think you better take this." He passed his pistol over to the corporal.

"What 'bout you, Cap'n?"

"I think it's time to get the Henry out." James pulled the blanket concealing the weapon around in front of him. He kept the rifle covered with his hand resting on the trigger.

There were five in the group. They all appeared to be in dire straits. One was stooped, a beard hanging down the front of his tattered gray jacket. A battered cap partially covered his head. He was holding an old muzzle-loading shotgun at his side. The rest were in a similar state and dress. Only one other had a visible firearm, an old muzzle-loading rifle.

They watched James and Corporal Hays approach. James figured he'd try and ride past while keeping a wary eye on them. When they were even, the one with the shotgun spoke. "Mornin'."

"Morning," James replied.

The man spit out a stream of tobacco juice. "You gents wouldn't mind sharing a little something?" he asked.

"If its food you're asking about, we're out ourselves," James said.

"Damn shame when a man ain't got nothin' to eat."

"I can understand your plight," James replied. "We've had to skimp and scrounge ourselves."

More tobacco juice on the ground. "You men coming home from the war?" the man with the shotgun asked.

"We are," James said.

The shotgun barrel came up a few inches. James tightened his finger on the Henry trigger. Damn—the last thing he wanted this close to home was a shootout with a group of desperate men. *Wasn't that the way of things?* He thought. *Survive four bloody years of war and get shot down coming home.*

"The only thing worse than being hungry is being hungry and afoot," the shotgun holder said.

Their horses were tempting these men. James glanced at Corporal Hays. He had the pistol in his right hand, resting on his saddle horn.

"Mister, I don't like the way you keep raising up the barrel of that shotgun."

"Well, how about that? Now, sir, there's a great many things I've encountered these past few years I didn't like. Man don't always get what he likes."

The old shotgun barrel was up to where, with one quick move, it could blast him or the corporal off their horses. The man holding it laughed. "For soldiers coming home, you fellas ain't very well-armed. I 'spect this old gun could take both of you off your horses with one shot. That before you could get a shot off with that old pistol."

"That might be so," James replied. He eased the Henry from under the blanket. "But I wouldn't count on it."

All five of them stared at the rifle in James's hand. The one holding the shotgun wavered, looked at the rifle barrel pointing at him.

"Let me explain to you gentlemen what you're looking at here," James said. "This is a Henry repeating rifle that came to me courtesy of a Yank soldier in Nashville. Forty-four caliber. You've never seen a gun that can match this one. I believe I could bring down the lot of you before you could get a shot off with your old guns."

The man spit out more tobacco juice, swallowed, and lowered the old shotgun until the muzzle was pointed at the ground. "Hellfire, mister. I was just jawing a little. I never had no intention of harming you fellas. We're Southern men, just like you."

"Well, sir, these are desperate times," James replied. "A desperate man is a dangerous man, in my view. Now, I'm afraid we're going to have to take that old scatter gun and that rifle, just to keep you men honest."

"Ain't no damn call for that," the man said. He stared at James's hand on the trigger of the Henry. James urged his horse closer. The rifle pointed at the man's chest.

"It's not a debatable question," James said. "It's not a request either. Me and the corporal here are cold and hungry. We've been through four long years of bloody war. We're close to home. We're not going to be stopped by a band of highwaymen. I don't know what brought you men to the state you're in, and right now, I don't have time to care."

"Hell, mister, these two guns are all that stand between us and starving. We have to live off what we hunt."

"I can sympathize with that. We'll leave both of them a little ways down the road. You can walk down and pick them up. Time you get there, we'll be almost to Clarksville."

All five stared at James, their faces expressionless. "Just lay the old shotgun and that rifle down on the ground and step back away," James commanded.

For an agonizing moment, the men stood motionless, not complying with James's request. "One more time, gents," he said. "Lay 'em down."

The one with the old rifle laid his down first. The one with the shotgun wavered a bit longer, gave the Henry another look, and then put the old gun down next to the rifle. "Corporal Hays, would you please pick up those two weapons."

The corporal dismounted and picked up the rifle and shotgun while James held the Henry on the other five. "Your arms will be about two miles down the road," he said. They rode off, leaving the five men to watch them go.

"Cap'n, I don't mind telling you I thought it was going to come to shooting it out with that bunch." He handed the pistol back to James.

"So did I, Corporal. Let's put some distance between them and us."

"Who you reckon they are?" James asked after they had ridden away from the men.

"Hard to say, Cap'n. Some of the irregulars that operated around here during the war, I 'spect. I figure they might have slipped down from Kentucky. Lot of guerrilla bunches up there. Old Nathan Forrest raised a lot of havoc there during the war. Now it's over, the Union folks are going to be out looking for revenge. So some of the Southern bands have to scatter."

James sought to put the incident out of his mind. It was just another reminder of the war and its aftermath. Home—perhaps there, he would put it all behind him. The rain eased. They stopped, leaned the old shotgun and rifle against a tree, and then rode on. The muddy road took them to the Port Royal Road—the route to Clarksville.

Traveling was easier on the macadamized road than the muddy back roads, but it came with a price. Now they were sure to encounter Union patrols. Would the papers he and the corporal were carrying get them past the Federals? James hoped they didn't have to find out.

They had the road to themselves much of the time. There would be an occasional rider or farm wagon; otherwise, the busy thoroughfare that James remembered had no travelers. For thirty minutes, they eased along, and then they could see the outline of Clarksville in the distance. Emotions swept over James. His bitter memories of war eased. Kate and the children, his mother and father, and the plantation all danced around in his mind. His happy thoughts couldn't take hold. They were replaced by apprehension and doubts. He had been gone so long, would they remember him? Kate had been pregnant when he left for war. His homecoming would be the first time to see his latest child.

"Corporal, I'll be leaving you just ahead. I want to ride out to the plantation first."

"Sure, Cap'n. I hope you find everything in order."

At the edge of Clarksville, where the tollbooth once stood, the road came to an end. There, James stopped his horse. He looked toward Clarksville, then turned his gaze northward, toward home. Hays stopped his horse nearby. "Cap'n, been my pleasure to ride home with you. We sure gave them Yanks back in Nashville the slip."

"That we did, Corporal. It's been my pleasure as well." James urged his horse over and extended his hand. "We're home Corporal Hays; not under the best of circumstances, but we're here."

"Yes, sir, that's so. I hope your family is in good health."

"And I wish the same for yours."

8

They shook hands. Hays rode on toward Clarksville; James turned his horse north toward the family plantation. His heart was beating fast. Surrounded by death and destruction the past four years, he often felt this day would never come. So many of his comrades had fallen; they would never come home. Widows and fatherless children with no means of support was their legacy.

In the distance, through the very light rain, James could see the gate to the plantation. Hope, worry, guilt all tugged at him. The moment of truth was almost at hand. He urged the horse forward.

Chapter 2

The War's Aftermath

When the main house was in view, hope arose. At last—it was behind him, the bloody war with all its suffering. Then he was at the gate. Hope took flight. James sat on his horse, frozen at the sight before him. Since leaving Nashville, he had tried to prepare for the worst. But he had hoped for better, which his concerns were for naught. But they were not. The chance of a pleasant homecoming vanished like mist on a hot stove. The front yard was riddled with the ashes of campfires. The grounds that had been the envy of Northern Tennessee had been trampled under, now resembling a barnyard. The war had followed him home.

He shook off his paralysis and rode up the drive. He felt anger, heartbreak, a sickening feeling in his stomach. He tried to remember the good times spent here, but they would not come. They were all hidden under the devastation. He stopped in front of the porch, dismounted, and tied the reins to one of the railings.

He paused to look at the house. Above the large porch with the white circular columns was the balcony, still intact from what he could surmise from below. But the paint had peeled away from the porch columns. Glass from the large picture window lay in pieces on the porch and flowerbeds below. James's father would never have allowed this. Albert McKane took great pride in his estate.

He stepped up on the porch. Through the open door, he could see more devastation inside the house. The furniture was overturned and scattered around the large living room. The large red settee imported from Nashville was turned up on its side and pushed against the far wall. Only the piano was left intact. It sat in its usual corner, unscratched. James let out a bitter laugh. Had the Yanks who wrought such destruction on the house been music lovers?

Trying to render the heart-wrenching scene out of mind, James now could

10

recall many of the grand events played out here. McKane Plantation had been one of the social hubs of Montgomery County. To be invited to a formal gathering here was considered a feather in the cap to those aspiring for social recognition. But the Yanks had come in without an invitation and brought it to ruin.

Prepared for more despair, James walked inside and through the main hallway that separated the living room from the dining area. Grandfather Buford McKane's portrait hung in its usual place, but all others had been removed. The large oak table was gone from the dining room. A master craftsman in Nashville had made the table and chairs and shipped it all down the Cumberland by steamboat. Now all that remained of the ensemble were two overturned chairs.

James was tempted to end his inspection to spare himself further heartbreak. But that was a coward's way of thinking. He had to face the bitter truth. He went back to the main room and up the stairs. His family, what had happened to them? There was no sign of life around the house. By all appearances, no one had lived here since the Yanks departed.

At the top of the stairs, James turned and walked to the suite of rooms he had shared with Kate and the children. He despaired over the mud stains and rips in what had been the lush, blue hall carpet. *What else am I going to find? How much worse can it get?*

Muddier boot prints, he fumed when he was in the suite. Didn't these bastards have enough sense to wipe the mud off their feet before coming inside? It was as if they had declared war on the house itself. The large chest was overturned, and the drawers scattered across the room. The bed in the master bedroom was in place, but the sheets and bedspread were gone. Some Yank was sleeping under them now, he figured.

James sat on the bed and buried his head in his hands. The ruination of the family estate stabbed at his heart. He started to weep for the destruction of the estate and his missing family. What fate had they suffered? He felt both sorrow and guilt. Why had he not tried harder to keep in touch with those dear to him?

He pulled himself together. There was a missing family to find. He walked back down the stairs, through the hallway, past the dining room, into the kitchen to the back door. Maybe on the grounds there would be some clue as to his family. He stepped out and looked toward the slave cabins. They were deserted. Of course, the Union Army had allowed them their freedom.

The cabins were built of unpainted pine lumber. The roofs were pine shingles, the chimneys of red brick. A few had small porches in front covered by overhanging planks resting on oak posts.

Before he turned his eyes away, James saw someone sitting in front of

11

one of the cabins in a rocking chair. This puzzled him. He walked toward the cabin. Old Williams, a house servant who had cared for James when he was a young boy, sat in the chair, rocking slowly back and forth.

The old man was a master storyteller; oh, how he loved to scare the young children with chilling ghost stories. He saved his most spine-tingling episodes for James and the young visitors to the plantation. His eyes would open wide, and a devilish grin would spread across his face as he spun tales of shadowy aberrations stealing about in the night. At the story's climax, a roar of deep laughter would leave the children quaking in fright.

At the sound of James's boots on the muddy ground, the old man turned. The rocking stopped. He got out of the chair and reeled backwards, his eyes wide open as if he had just encountered a ghost. Williams staggered back until he was leaning against the cabin.

James stopped. He studied the old man. Williams had aged during the past four years. His short hair was white, his shoulders stooped, and there were deep lines across his dark face. He was wearing a white cotton shirt and baggy cotton pants. But what had scared him so?

By nature, many of the slaves were superstitious. But James's presence seemed to scare the wits out of the old man. After four years, had he forgotten him? It was possible, but Williams had been here all his life. He had known all the McKanes going back to Grandfather Buford. The frightened look in the man's eyes indicated more than just a lack of recognition.

Williams' lips trembled. "Dear Lord, why the spirit of a man I done no harm in life done come back to haunt me?"

Now, James was more confused. "Williams, what are you talking about? You been out in the sun too long?"

"Naw, sir. I been sittin' here just fine, livin' easy, then I see the spirit of the young master walking toward me, and now he stand here talking to me."

"Me, a spirit? I grant you I've seen many leave this world the past four years, Yank and Southerner as well, but as for me being a spirit, I don't know what you're talking about."

The man stared at him, unconvinced. James walked closer; the old man cowered in front of him. He thrust out his arm. "Feel my arm. That should tell you I'm in the flesh and not a spirit."

Williams held back, but James kept insisting. With a trembling hand, he touched James's arm. "You convinced I'm alive and not from the spirit world?"

Some of the fear in Williams' eyes vanished. He walked back over to the chair but with his eyes still focused on James.

"What happened to my family?" James asked.

At first, Williams did not respond. He stared down at the ground. James pressed the issue. "The trouble—it start some time ago after you leave for the war. Some men, they come to the house with some news. They say you been killed up in Kentucky."

James tried to process the words Williams had spoken. His emotions went from disbelief to anger. "What? I killed! Who brought this false news?"

"Two men. Master know them, but I don't."

"What did my family do when they heard this?"

"They take to grieving. Missy Kate she take to her room and stay most of the time. The Master, he just set around and not say much to anybody. Things done gone bad by then. The Mistress, she just up and pass away."

Somewhere in the distance, there were the sounds of crows. James heard them, but his mind filtered them out. Across the unplowed fields beyond the cabins, the grass was pushing up; he saw it, but it reminded him of nothing. His mind went blank, his body frozen rigid. The words Williams had just spoken were incoherent echoes, reverberating away from him. "What's that you said about Mama?" he mumbled.

"She just pass away in her sleep."

James' knees shook; his body was numb and hollow inside. He had to sit down on the porch. He shook his head a few times; then, the tears came. A picture of his mother formed in his mind. Martha McKane was a strong woman; it was hard to imagine her being felled by any misfortune. *My Mama's gone, and I wasn't here to share her final hours on earth. It's just so hard to believe,* he told himself. "When did she pass?"

"Be late this past fall," Williams said. "Just 'fore the Yankee soldiers came."

He knew that some people considered his mother to be rude and arrogant. But she never faltered in her duties as Mistress of McKane Plantation. All her duties were tended with a serious nature, and that included his rearing. As a boy, James had received a great deal of attention from both his mother and father. His father's attention was more material in nature, but his mother did her best to ensure her only son was reared as a young gentleman. When he was lax in his behavior, she would remind him of his obligations as the heir apparent to the family estate.

Now, he would never see her again. With Williams looking on, he fought back the tears. When his composure returned, he looked at the old man in the rocker. "What about Kate and the children?"

Williams again was hesitant, a deep sigh his initial response. Then he spoke softly. "When Missy Kate hear the news about you, she stay in her room until everybody worried about her. She don't seem to care about life no more. And her with a newborn baby boy to tend, healthy boy she named Drew. One of the house servants take care of the children."

13

A son—he had another son. This fueled James's impatience for more news about his family. "What happened to Kate and the children?"

"About this time, an uncle show up. Nobody know him, but he start talking to Missy Kate, and soon she back out of her room. Everybody happy for a time. Then one day, she says she and her children leaving with her uncle. Mistress, she have a big fit about it; old Master ain't so pleased hisself. But Missy Kate stubborn about it. She up and leave with her uncle."

"Where did they go?"

"Don't know for sho. Missy Kate tell Mistress they going west to a place called Oregon."

Kate and the children going off with an uncle nobody seemed to know, James found that hard to comprehend. Incredulous! Well, if she believed him to be dead, she might not want to stay at the plantation. But going off into the frontier—that was another matter altogether.

"You sure about all this, Williams?"

"Yessah. Missy Kate up and gone with this uncle."

"Where is my father?"

Williams' face took on a pained look. "Last I hear, the old Master is in Clarksville, living with his sister, Mistress Mary. They say he sick in bed most of the time."

The bad news was pouring like the rain—an unrelenting downpour with no end. "It's hard to imagine my father in a sickbed."

"Times they been hard for the old Master. When the bluecoats came the first time, they say he can keep the place if he sign the oath. Master, he say no. He ain't gonna sign no oath. They come back again and say they take his place if he don't sign the oath. This time, he sign the paper. They leave him alone for a time, then they come back and say they need the house and he had to leave. He already sick by that time. He went to Clarksville. He ain't been back no more."

"How long were the Union soldiers here?"

"They here until near spring. They told all the slaves they free now. They say Mr. Lincoln set them free. Most of them leave when they hear the news. Some come back for a time, but they all gone now."

James felt crushed—buried under the mountain of despair resting on his shoulders. What the war had not taken from him, the distressing news about his family was draining what remained of his spirit. Dreams of being reunited with his wife and children had sustained him for the past four years; now, he had come home to find them gone off into the wilderness. What was left for him now other than the memories of what once was?

There was still his father, by accounts now a sick man. James had to pull himself together and get on to Clarksville. As he started to leave, he looked at the old man sitting in the rocking chair. "Williams, you're a free man now. Why didn't you leave with the others?"

The old man closed his eyes and leaned back in the chair. James thought he wasn't going to answer. Then he sat back up and opened his eyes. "Freedom. For as long as I can remember, I dreamed about being free. All us black folks did. We all wanted to know what it was like to walk this earth as free men and woman.

"When the blue coats came, I helped them with their cookin' and chores. One of them gave me some money. He say I should be paid for my work. That be the first time I been paid for my work." His voice trailed off. James thought he was finished.

"But I'm too old to enjoy my freedom. I was born here on this plantation; I guess I die here."

James thought about what Williams had said. In truth, he had always taken the slaves for granted. Servitude was their fate, he had assumed, just as being a gentleman of means was his. But the war had changed it all. He was no longer a gentleman of means, and the slaves were free. With that, he left Williams sitting in the rocker and walked toward the family cemetery.

Had Union troops sunk so low as to desecrate cemeteries? All he could do was hope they had not. He found it still intact. In front of the large marble headstone marking his mother's grave, he paused. *What kind of epithet would she have wanted?* he wondered.

His mother was a person of feeling, he knew. Some might have disagreed, but James knew otherwise. She was not happy with his choice of a wife. In time, she accepted Kate in order to cherish her grandchildren. He stood there as light rain started falling, trying to figure out what broke her health and took her life. No answer came. He mumbled a soft goodbye and took his leave.

He was left faced with a dreaded chore—seeing his father in a sickbed. After all, he had experienced today; it could be more than he could bear. But it had to be done. He had come back from the dead, at least to those of his family that remained. That would bring some good news. He mounted, set his horse into a slow trot down the drive, still feeling the weight of his return crushing down on his shoulders.

Kate. What was he going to do about her and the children? That thought ate at him as he rode out to the road and turned south. If there was one thing he could not give up on all he had when the war started, it was Kate and his children. He struggled with thoughts of his wife and children all the way to Clarksville.

At the outskirts of town, the rain stopped. It didn't help his low spirits. He reached Third Street and started toward Main. His first impression was that Clarksville, from a physical standpoint, had changed little the past four years.

The most noticeable difference was the near-empty streets and sidewalks. At the intersection with Main, he started to turn his horse. "Hey, you there!" The voice startled him.

James turned around and saw a Union officer riding toward him. Behind the officer was an enlisted man. The officer, a captain, was heavyset with dark receding hair and lamb chop whiskers. The corporal riding behind was a young, clean-shaven man with sandy brown hair. The Federals stopped just behind James. "Don't you know it's illegal to wear a gray uniform?" the captain asked.

"I just got home from the war. I don't have anything else to wear at the moment," James replied.

The captain looked him over. "That a sidearm you're carrying there?"

"General Grant said officers could keep their sidearms." He hoped the officer didn't realize it was a Union issue.

"You don't say. That's a foolhardy idea, letting rebs run around armed," the captain replied. "You had the oath?"

"And a pardon," James replied. He reached into his pocket and pulled out his papers. The captain took them, glanced them over, and then handed the papers back. "You get out of that gray uniform. If I see you out in it again, you'll be arrested. There's a bunch of rebel riff-raff running around that ain't surrendered yet." The officer turned his horse and started down the street with the corporal following.

The Henry, James thought. What if the Yanks had found it? He was on dangerous ground here. The first thing to do was get some different clothes. With haste, he rode down Main and turned onto Franklin Street toward the home of his aunt, Mary McAlliston.

His aunt's husband, Harry McAlliston, had amassed a huge fortune as a tobacco packer and exporter. Since they were childless, all his wealth passed to his wife upon his death.

Losing her husband turned Aunt Mary into something of a recluse. She sent her servants out to do the shopping and other errands. Aside from occasional visits to church on Sunday, her neighbors saw little of her.

The war's impact was noticeable along the once fashionable street. Many of the elegant homes had deteriorated. He supposed it was because so many of the men had gone away to war, leaving no one to care for the estates. Or maybe with the Yanks in control, there was no way to acquire the needed materials. The white picket fences, always freshly whitewashed as James remembered, were weather-beaten; many were lying on the ground. The yards tended to be overgrown with weeds or barren.

Near the end of the street, he could see his aunt's two-story house. Like many of the others, it was rundown. To anyone that had known his aunt, this was hard to picture. She was fussy, near to excessive, about the house and grounds. Now, litter was strewn about the sidewalk in front. Shoots of grass and weeds poked up through the cement walk. James shook his head and rode around to the wide driveway. It led to a large carriage house and stable. Beyond those buildings were the slave cabins.

James rode down to the stable and dismounted. Straw covered the floor, but there were no horses inside. He secured his mount in one of the stalls and looked for some hay or grain. A small bag half-filled with moldy oats was all he could find. He dumped them into a trough in the stall. Into a rusting bucket, he pumped some water from the well behind the stable.

After doing what he could for his tired horse, James left the stable and went up to the front door. The outside of the house needed paint; a shutter hung loosely from a front window. A loose gutter hung from the front of the house. He banged the heavy door knocker several times. He had reached the conclusion no one was home when the door cracked open. A face, hidden in part by the door, peered at him. "Aunt Mary," he called.

The door and the eyes behind it did not move. "Aunt Mary, is that you?" he called again.

The crack in the door widened until his aunt's face was more visible. "Aunt Mary, are you going to leave me standing out here?"

The door opened wider, revealing more of the woman behind it. If this was not her home, James felt he might not have recognized his aunt. Her uncombed hair contained not a hint of its former dark luster; it was now snow white. The brown apron could not hide the shabbiness of her white dress. Aunt Mary had always dressed in accordance with her station. She had never permitted shabbiness in herself or those around her. Moreover, the once sharp, penetrating green eyes were now dull and listless.

"Boy, if you've come for a handout, I can't help you," she said.

"Handout! Aunt Mary, I was told my father was here."

She pulled the door open further and stepped closer to him. "I have to say you look a lot like my late nephew, James. But James is dead."

"Wrong account, Auntie. I am James, and I'm very much alive."

"If that's a line you're trying to use to worm your way in, it won't work. And it's in poor taste. Imagine—trying to pass yourself off as my late nephew."

James bent his head down close to her. "Take a good look at me. Forget the whiskers and just look at my face."

She looked into his eyes, then over the rest of his face. "Oh, my goodness," she whimpered. Steadying herself by holding onto the door, her frightened eyes beheld him. "I don't understand this," she mumbled.

He reached out to steady her. "That report about my demise was false. I was wounded in Kentucky, but I survived."

His aunt gave up her hold on the door and embraced him. "For a time, I felt it might not be true, but after a while, I accepted it. It's a miracle; that's all I can say."

After Aunt Mary unwrapped her frail arms from around him, they walked into the house. The interior, too, had lost much of its elegance. The expensive furniture remained but was showing signs of wear and tear. The settee in the middle of the room was frayed. The mahogany cabinet with the glass door where many of her prized possessions were housed was scratched. Recent times had not been good to Mary McAlliston. In the past, she would have thrown such things out of her home.

When James seated himself on the settee, he looked at his aunt and detected tears in her eyes. This was new. Aunt Mary was not a person disposed to showing much feeling or emotion. "James, you do look a fright," she managed to utter.

"Four years of war took a lot out of me," he replied. "It takes your strength, your willpower, and most everything else."

"Yes, I know. Lord knows we had our struggles here also. The Yankees took over in 1862. Except for one short period, they've been here since that time. They went around making people take the oath. If you refused, you stood to lose your property, and in some cases, were arrested."

"I know. I just came from the plantation."

"Your father and the Yankees went around and around. You know, he's not one that's prone to bend under threats and intimidation. With his only son fighting for the Confederates, he didn't feel it would be right to take an oath to the Union. But, to save the plantation, he reached a point where he felt there was no other option, so he relented and signed the paper. A lot of good it did. The Federals came out and turned it into a troop garrison, forcing your father to leave."

"Low life bastards. The worst of it was hearing about Mother. Old Williams told me."

"Poor thing. It all got to be too much for her. Doctor Lynch came out, but there was nothing he could do."

"Doctor Lynch. Why wasn't the family doctor, Layton, summoned?"

"He wasn't here. He was pressed into military duty. Most of the doctors here were. Old Doctor Lynch was the only one available. There wasn't much anyone could have done. In the end, it was a broken heart that done her in."

"I can understand that. Now, I hear that Father is in poor health as well."

"Yes, he is. Oh my gosh! How am I going to break the news to him that you're alive?"

"Maybe some good news will be good for him."

18

"For certain it will. I just hope the strain won't be too much. It's his heart."

"I have to tell you, Auntie, I feel much of this is my fault."

"What makes you feel that way? You didn't start this crazy war."

"I didn't try to keep in touch with any of you. If I had, things might have been better here."

"No, you had enough to worry about just staying alive. It's just unfortunate that we received some false information."

"Who were those men who brought you the report about me?" James asked.

"Major Whitten was one. You remember the Whitten Family? Before the war, they owned a tobacco stemmery down on River Street. The major came out with a Captain Melcher. They had just been mustered out of their regiment up in Kentucky. Medical discharges, I think. Anyway, Major Whitten said he saw you killed in a battle."

"I was wounded, but I survived. The major should have gotten his facts in order. I can just imagine how everyone here felt, especially Kate and the children."

"Not to mention your father. But you can't blame the major. He felt he was providing a service to our family. The Yankees shut down our newspapers, so unless someone from the fighting passed through, it was rare for us to get any war news."

"The Yanks shut down both newspapers?"

"That they did. I guess they wanted to keep us ignorant about everything. Before the war, we had some of the best newspapers in the South."

"Aunt Mary, I think it's best I go and talk to Father."

"Let me get him prepared first. His health has been on the decline for some time. He had a stroke that made it difficult to get around, and his heart is weak. There's not much else that can be done for him. Doctor Lynch comes out from time to time to check on him."

"I find it hard to imagine my father in such a condition," James said.

"Yes, I find it hard myself. He was always a very strong man. But he's changed in other ways as well. His losses have made him humble. He used to feel that he was in control of all around him, but no longer. He spends his time lying in bed, thinking about his life."

"Can I go and see him now?"

"He's upstairs. You better let me go up and break the news gently. The excitement might be too much if we're not careful."

"I understand," James said.

He stood at the bottom and watched his aunt climb the stairs. There was a soft rap, then the sound of the door opening. While waiting, he tried to gather his own strength. In a few minutes, his aunt stood at the top of the stairs and motioned for him to come up.

Climbing the stairs, James's legs felt like lead. All the tragedies of his family he had been made privy to today, and now he had one more to face: the final agony of his homecoming.

Chapter 3

Oregon

Kate McKane stepped out onto the porch. A beautiful spring afternoon greeted her, but it brought her no joy. Instead, all she could think about was Uncle Lewis. What had happened to the cheerful, witty, and confident man she had come to know? For the past two months, he had been distant—preoccupied. Worse, he would not share his burden with her.

Now, the seeds of doubt were being sown. Was her decision to pull up stakes and come here a wise one? Her uncle's woes, whatever they were, could affect her and the children. So much had been lost in the South. Would there be more suffering? A deep sigh escaped her lips; a chill ran down her spine.

Until recent times, her uncle had seemed to be a man in control of his destiny. No task seemed to daunt him. If anything went wrong, he would step up, take control, and save the day. That had changed. Now, she would find him staring off into space, lost to his surroundings. If anyone spoke to him, his reply would be shrugs and incoherent mumbles. The truth of it was, she met him for the first time just a year ago—perhaps not enough time to really know this man who had been her refuge from a war-torn land.

She seated herself in a hardback chair. How her world had changed. Uncle Lewis had come into her life during a time of despair. James's death in Kentucky had taken away her will to live. After the news, Kate became a recluse, rarely leaving her room. Life at McKane Plantation had been near insufferable from the beginning. The worst of it was being forced to deal with the disappointment of her in-laws. Martha McKane, her mother-in-law, was beside herself over James marrying a woman they thought of as being below their class. The McKanes were given to expressing their disappointment whenever the opportunity arose, and it frequently did.

When James Junior was born, Martha McKane's attitude softened a bit. But her disappointment lay just below the surface. The slightest provocation would bring it out. And if James's mother wasn't enough, there was his Aunt Mary to contend with. She would rail on and on about Kate's perceived social shortcomings. Kate reacted in kind. The more they tried to berate her, the more she loathed them.

Uncle Lewis, undaunted by the war, had traveled to Missouri and Kentucky on business. While there, he decided to visit his relatives in Clarksville. When he learned of Kate's fate, he paid a visit to the plantation. She was soon taken in by this relative she had never known. He possessed none of the aloofness and snobbery of the McKanes.

Lewis Harrington was in his sixties, spry, and full of energy. He was tall in stature, standing well over six feet, with a ruddy complexion and a full head of dark hair mixed with gray. He had the manner of an independent man—full of confidence, yet compassionate and down to earth.

The glowing stories her uncle told of the North Country rekindled Kate's zest for life. In her mind, she could picture the snow-covered mountains he so eloquently described. When he spoke of clear running streams meandering through green forests, her grief eased. She pictured herself relaxing beside a tranquil little brook. It was so much different than the war-devastated South. There, she would be free of the contemptuous nagging and criticism of the McKanes. She emerged from her self-imposed prison with an idea in her head. Kate fell in love with the land her uncle described. "You feel closer to your maker up there," he told her. With nothing to look forward to in Tennessee, Kate decided she and the children would accompany Uncle Lewis to Oregon.

Kate's decision caused an uproar with the McKanes and her family. Martha McKane, true to form, was beside herself at the news. "I'll not have my grandchildren out in the wilderness surrounded by savages," she bitterly said. Albert McKane said very little about it, but that was his way. Her mother-in-law was driven by selfishness and snobbery, Kate concluded. Her parents were heartbroken as well. Deep down, she felt sadness, but without James in her life, there was nothing left for her in Tennessee.

The Union occupation presented an obstacle. Travel was not allowed without a permit from the Federal authorities. This worried Kate, but Uncle Lewis told her not to be concerned. As a citizen of Oregon, a Union state, he had no trouble dealing with the Federals. Kate was astonished when he produced travel permits for both her and the children.

The farewell with the McKanes was a solemn one; the one with her family was filled with emotion. They left Clarksville by boat and traveled down the Cumberland River to Nashville; there, they boarded a train for Lexington, Kentucky. Waiting for them in Lexington were more than thirty families Uncle Lewis had recruited in Missouri and Kentucky, joined by a few from Tennessee who slipped through the Union lines. The entire entourage traveled by rail to Independence, Missouri, where they assembled a wagon train for the trip over the Oregon Trail.

The trip turned out to be a harrowing experience. The Sioux were at war, making travel across Nebraska Territory hazardous. At Fort Kearney, Uncle Lewis joined forces with a larger party to afford them some advantage against the dangers. Even that didn't provide total protection. A few days after leaving the fort, they were attacked. The men in the party fired back, and the Indians broke off the attack, leaving two men from the wagon train wounded. During the skirmish, Kate huddled in the wagon with the children, praying they would not all be killed. There was another attack before they reached Fort Laramie, but this time they suffered no injuries. Even her war experiences in the South had not prepared Kate for the fear she felt during those first few weeks on the trail.

Things improved after Fort Laramie. A contingent of soldiers accompanied them for a time, and there were no more attacks. They arrived at Uncle Lewis's home on the west side of the Grande Ronde Valley, east of the Blue Mountains and the Grande Ronde River, in early October 1864.

Upon arrival, Kate and the children settled into her uncle's home. It was a two-story affair built from logs cut in the nearby forests. The road to the front yard led across a large meadow, which in the spring bloomed with brightly colored wildflowers and camas. Behind the main house was a smaller home for the overseer and his wife; beyond the houses was a barn made of pine logs. Encircling the homestead was a split-rail fence made of oak. A herd of milk cows grazed in a pasture beyond the barn.

During the trip, Uncle Lewis had seemed impervious to danger. If some of the settlers expressed doubt or concerns, he would smile, tell a humorous story, and assure them all was well. In the face of the Sioux threats, he remained calm, never showing any fear. He had been a man capable of dealing with any adversity during that time.

Until spring, Uncle Lewis continued to be his confident self. Then, he changed. At home, he appeared to be preoccupied most of the time. He no longer displayed the humor and wit Kate had come to expect from him. Often, he would be gone for long periods of time, never telling anyone where he was going.

One morning, Kate was cleaning the area around the roll-top desk where her uncle did most of his work. On the desk was a stack of papers; the one on top caught her eye. She started to pick it up but immediately felt guilty. This was Uncle Lewis's business. She had no right to snoop in his affairs. But worry overruled her concerns. The fate of herself and the children might be at stake.

Kate picked up the top paper and looked it over. It was a charter for a business issued by the State of Oregon referred to as the Northeast Oregon

Agricultural Cooperative. There was a list of names:

Lewis Harrington

John McDonald

E. G. Covington

Walter Krenshaw

Preston Banks

The names meant nothing to Kate. Associates of her uncle, she assumed. He seldom talked about his business; she never felt it was her place to ask. What she did know was he brought the families here to settle on the public land in the vicinity. He said he wanted to see the area grow and prosper. To do that, more people were needed to work the land. An honorable purpose, it seemed to her.

In retrospect, Kate had been so anxious to escape her unhappy life in Tennessee that she never gave much thought to what might await her in Oregon. The beautiful land her uncle described had been the icing on the cake. Beyond that, in her eyes, life anywhere would have been an improvement over the McKanes.

Kate stood and watched a rider crossing the meadow. It was her uncle riding his white mare. When he rode through the gate into the yard, she stepped off the porch to meet him. Perhaps today, his demeanor had improved.

Uncle Lewis was hunched over the saddle as if he was studying the ground under him: another sign of his troubled nature. Ignoring Kate, he dismounted and handed the reins to Olaf, the Swedish foreman, who had come out from the barn. "Good day, Mr. Lewis."

"Good day, Olaf," Uncle Lewis mumbled. He walked toward the house. His shoulders stooped, worry lines crossed his brow, and he looked spent. Kate felt pity for him.

"Hello, Uncle."

He looked up as if startled. "Oh, hello, Kate."

Whatever business he had tended to today, it hadn't improved his outlook. *What brought him to this state?* Kate wondered. How she wished he would share his problems with her. Perhaps, if he wouldn't open up on his own, she might nudge him into talking. "Uncle Lewis, you seem to be disturbed by something."

"Oh. Just business."

24

Kate thought for a moment. "Please forgive me, Uncle, but the other day I was cleaning up around your desk, and I noticed a paper with some names. Does that paper have anything to do with whatever has been bothering you?"

He smiled slightly. "No, Kate. What you saw was a business charter granted to me and a group of people by the State of Oregon. The names on that list are the founders of our co-op."

Her snooping didn't seem to bother him. That didn't dispel the disappointment she felt over his reluctance to open up about his problems. Without further word, he went into the house. Not ready to give up, Kate followed him.

The interior of the house wasn't fancy. After all, Uncle Lewis had been a bachelor his entire life. The front room had a hand-hewn wood floor and a large fireplace. There were deer and elk heads on the walls, which Kate didn't fancy.

In the middle of the room was a large brown settee surrounded by several chairs. On the floor in front of the fireplace was a large bearskin rug. There were two windows in the front room covered by heavy drapes. A stairway led to the upstairs rooms where Kate and the children were quartered. Over the fireplace mantle was a rack with several rifles.

Uncle Lewis removed his felt hat, hung it on a rack near the front door, and seated himself on the settee. Hoping for further conversation, Kate sat down on the opposite end. To her surprise, he spoke to her.

"I should have told you more about our business," Uncle Lewis said. "When I came up here several years ago, I met a man named John McDonald. John was a botanist from Scotland who came here when the British shared ownership of Oregon. He had a keen interest in the agricultural potential of the area. For several years, he experimented with crops he thought might thrive in this climate.

"When I ran across John, he convinced me the area had potential if the right crops were introduced. At that time, this area was unsettled, although a number of people had already recognized its potential. John Fremont himself, back in '43, commented on the possibilities this place had for agriculture, but no one took him serious. We each acquired some land, but due to lack of any markets, we didn't establish ourselves at that time. We went our separate ways: John back to Scotland, I to California. I didn't come back up here until '61. I spent the first year back building this house.

"As luck would have it, I got a letter from a friend of mine in Missouri. I served in the Mexican war with this man, Benjamin Prather. After the war, we worked a gold claim in California. In the early '50s, he married and went back to Missouri to take over his family's farm. He did well until the war came along and left him and his family nearly destitute. In his letter, Benjamin asked

25

if there were any opportunities up here for him and several others he knew. That set me off on another idea, the idea of bringing settlers up here to grow the crops we needed for the local markets.

"In the early '60s, people began to settle here; in addition to homesteading, gold was discovered south of here. That would have opened up markets if we could get enough people to work the land. I talked to some of the local settlers, but they didn't offer a great deal of interest in our proposal. By '62, much of the land had been settled, but there were a few tracts still left, and some of the original settlers wound up abandoning their claims. There was still enough land available to accommodate about thirty claims, enough for a start. I figured once we were successful more of the local settlers would be interested. I wrote to John in Scotland that we might now be able to carry on with our plans. In late 1862, Mr. McDonald and his son arrived. Feeling that everything was in place, we went about setting up our farming operation. We found suppliers for fruit trees and seed stock in Portland, but the quality was low.

"John and I put our heads together. We hit on a plan. We would start a farming co-op here in the valley. John and I would use our land as a nursery and seed growing facility. We would stock the settlers; they, in turn, would raise crops for the local market. And that would give us an additional incentive to get people up here."

The glow in his eyes was the first Kate had seen in months. Talking about his business seemed to cheer him a little.

"Now, you see, we had most of what we needed except the growers. That was my purpose for coming down to Missouri and Kentucky. There were people down there made destitute by the war. I knew they would jump at a chance to start over again.

"Now, as to the names you saw, we needed capital and some other help to get started. Some of the names on the charter are businessmen from Portland who invested in our venture. Crops need transportation to market, so we enlisted the aid of a local freight owner named E. G. Covington. Covington owns freight lines in La Grande and Pendleton, so we asked him to join our enterprise. He was the only freight owner in the area with enough wagons and teams for what we needed; the others were too small. Besides, most of them concentrated on freighting supplies to the mines further south. That's the story of the charter you saw."

An interesting story, Kate concluded, but it did not explain his actions of late. Uncle Lewis's sudden change in attitude had to be because of something serious in nature to affect him this way. The more she worried about her uncle, the more Kate became concerned about the welfare of herself and the children. Had they been drawn into something that might prove disastrous to them?

Uncle Lewis lapsed back into silence. He sat with his hands folded in his lap, staring at the floor. It was his way of saying the conversation was over. She got up and went into the kitchen to help Helga, Olaf's wife, with the evening meal.

Helga was a large woman with short, blond hair and a broad, plain face. She wore a long, cotton dress and a white apron. Her face was red and sweaty from working around the cookstove.

The large kitchen had a big wood-burning stove sitting at one end. There was a long, wooden table in the middle, surrounded by high-backed wooden chairs. Against one wall was a large cupboard, and on another a china cabinet.

"Supper will be ready soon," Helga said in a slow, thick accent.

Helga's sweaty face made Kate feel guilty. She should have been helping in the kitchen. She blamed it on the long winter months. Being cooped up in the house had left her restless. With the arrival of warm weather, she wanted to spend as much time as possible outside.

Helga was well along with the meal, so Kate set out the plates, silverware, and drinking glasses. Then she went out to find the children. Her oldest, James Junior, was helping Olaf with the evening chores. He was a skinny boy of eight, tall for his age, with brown hair down to his shoulders and a few freckles around his nose. His most striking feature was a strong resemblance to his grandfather, Albert McKane. Kate didn't mind her son having his grandfather's looks, but his personality—that worried her.

Little Drew was playing next to the house with a wooden horse Olaf had made for him. A boy of near four, he had more of his daddy's features, including an agile frame and mischievous brown eyes. His sandy hair constantly hung over his eyes.

Her five-year-old daughter, Alice, was sitting under a tree near the house playing with a doll she brought from Tennessee. She had Kate's black hair, creamy skin, fine facial features, and also the agile movements of her father. Helga had made her some doll dresses; Alice could sit for hours changing the doll from one dress to another.

Alice and Drew came in immediately, but Kate had to call James Junior and Olaf a second time. When the children were washed and seated, Kate walked over to Uncle Lewis's quarters just off the main floor and knocked. "Uncle Lewis, supper is ready."

"All right, in a minute."

Kate shook her head and returned to the table. She seated herself next to James Junior. Uncle Lewis emerged from his room and took a seat at the end. He was silent for most of the meal. He would nod as they passed him food, but he made no effort at conversation.

With talking to her uncle out of the question, Kate turned her attention to chatting with the others. "I'm helping Olaf with the milking," James Junior announced.

That brought a smile to Kate's face. Her oldest son had endured some difficult times. He was the only child old enough to remember their father. Then there was the ordeal of leaving their home in Tennessee and moving to an unfamiliar land. She knew that deep down, the boy was still suffering. Uncle Lewis spent time with him until his change in attitude. Now, he hardly seemed to notice any of the children. She was grateful that Olaf, a kind man with an abundance of patience, had taken her eldest son under his wing.

Without comment, Uncle Lewis finished eating, got up from the table, and returned to his quarters. Kate watched helplessly. Why wouldn't he confide in her? She let it go and went to help Helga with the dishes. Afterward, she sent the children off to bed. James Junior protested. "I'm doing a man's work now, so I should be allowed to stay up with the older people."

"Sorry," Kate replied as she urged him up the stairs.

After all three children were in bed, Kate went back downstairs. Olaf and Helga had retired to their quarters, leaving the front room deserted. She looked at Uncle Lewis's room and considered going over and knocking on the door. When he answered, she would demand he explain what was bothering him. No, that wouldn't do. She had no right to make demands of him. Her uncle would not appreciate being nagged. He would tell her when he was ready.

After checking the front door, Kate put out the downstairs lamp and went up to her own room. By the light of a candle, she sat in front of her mirror and combed her dark hair.

Her reflection staring back at her prompted Kate to remember a remark her uncle had made. "Kate, you are a beautiful young woman. You need to think about finding you a good man."

She blushed at the remark. Uncle Lewis had good intentions, but since losing James, other men held little interest. For now, all she could concentrate on was the welfare of the children. She blew out the candle and went to bed.

*   *   *

Kate arose early to help Helga with breakfast. She was frying bacon when her uncle emerged from his room, carrying a valise. He looked toward the kitchen, then walked toward the front door. "Uncle, breakfast is almost ready."

"Sorry, Kate, I've got to be in La Grande as soon as possible." Without further word, he stepped out the front door. From the kitchen window, Kate watched him walk toward the barn. A few minutes later, he came out leading his saddled horse. In the front yard, he mounted and rode toward the meadow.

Kate watched until he disappeared from sight. "Helga, do you and Olaf know what's bothering Uncle Lewis?"

"No, dear, we don't. Olaf and I have noticed he seems to be in deep thought most of the time, and that's not like him. He's been our employer for three years now. We've never seen him like this."

The thought disturbed Kate. Helga and Olaf knew her uncle better than anyone. In the short time she had known him; Kate had come to trust and respect Uncle Lewis. She felt he was an honest, caring, and upright man. There was no malice behind his secrecy, she believed. But that didn't stop her from worrying.

After breakfast, Kate was cleaning the main room when James Junior burst through the front door. "There's a buggy coming through the meadow."

"I wonder who it could be." Kate stepped out on the porch and watched a carriage, pulled by a large, black draft horse, coming through the front gate. An elderly man with thin, white hair and stooped shoulders was driving. The carriage stopped at the edge of the yard.

"A good morning to you, miss." The driver stepped down from the carriage. "I'm looking for Mr. Lewis Harrington."

"I'm sorry. He left for La Grande early this morning."

"Blast! If I'd known that, I could have saved myself a trip out here. I got some survey records that Mr. Harrington has been asking about. It took some time to find these logbooks. My name is Duncan Pratt."

He pulled two books with worn covers from the back of the carriage. Kate was confused. What would her uncle want with these old books? She walked out and took them. "Would you care for some coffee, Mr. Pratt?"

"Thank you kindly, but I would like to get on my way back to La Grande. Give Mr. Harrington my regards."

Duncan Pratt considered his business concluded. He climbed into the carriage and untied the reins. He flicked them over the horse's back. When the carriage reached the end of the meadow, he waved.

She took the books to her uncle's room. Temptation tugged at her. This was his business, and she had no right to pry. But her curiosity wouldn't let the matter rest. She opened one up. It was titled:

Surveyor's Log for Northeast Oregon Territory; Everett Skoll,

Surveyor, 1818

Commissioned by his Majesty King George III

The other book was labeled:

Baker County Surveyor's Log 1858

Her curiosity urged her on. Uncle Lewis had mentioned once that Union County, where they lived, had once been part of Baker County. Kate took the books to the settee and scanned through both of them. For the most part, they just contributed to her confusion. They were old survey records of this area; why would her uncle be interested in them? Was the key to his distress somewhere in these books? They told her nothing, so she placed them on the desk in his room.

*   *   *

Uncle Lewis returned late that afternoon. Kate watched from the front door as he dismounted and handed the reins to Olaf. "Hello, Uncle," Kate said when he reached the porch.

"Hello, Kate."

"There was a man here this morning. He left some books for you. I put them on the desk in your room."

He picked up his stride and bounded up the steps and into the house. Kate watched, still confused about the old logbooks. Perhaps they did hold the key to what was bothering him.

The confusing actions of her uncle intensified her fears. She was here in Oregon, far removed from her roots, trying to cope with the harsh climate, and now these problems with Uncle Lewis. She and the children were dependent on him for their well-being—any problem that threatened him was also a threat to them.

Helga yelled from the kitchen that supper was ready. Helga never complained. She was in the employ of Uncle Lewis to take care of the house and meals, but Kate felt guilty that she wasn't helping more.

Kate rounded up Olaf and the children and got them seated at the table. Only Uncle Lewis was absent; she knocked on his door. "Supper, Uncle."

All she got for her efforts was an incoherent mumble. The logbooks seemed to interest him more than food. She gave up and went back to the table. A minute later, he came out and sat down at his usual place at the end. Olaf said grace, and then they got down to enjoying Helga's baked chicken. "I take it the information in the books is related to your business," Kate said while they were eating.

"I don't know yet," he replied. Kate flinched at the sharpness in his voice.

It wasn't like Uncle Lewis to be short with any of them. Since the matter was so touchy, she decided to let it drop for the time being. Still, she remained

30

determined to get the truth from him.

After supper, Kate helped with the dishes then herded the children off to bed. Alone in her room, she felt lonely and a little helpless. Fear had taken hold. Something was eating away at Uncle Lewis. Only something of a deeply serious nature could affect him so. If she asked him directly, it would do no good. She would try a more gradual approach. Maybe then she could get at the root of his problems, and if need be, find a way to protect herself and the children. That night, she tossed and turned.

$$*\qquad*\qquad*$$

Kate arose the next morning. After dressing, she went downstairs and knocked on her uncle's door, but there was no answer.

"He left early this morning," Helga yelled from the kitchen.

Kate was disappointed. She went into the kitchen to help Helga with breakfast. When it was ready, she went upstairs to wake the children. They protested. Kate prodded until they shuffled downstairs to the table.

"Olaf, can you saddle a horse for me before you start working?" Kate asked while they were eating.

Olaf answered in his thick accent, "Of course, missy. You going for a ride today?"

"Yes. I feel like getting away from the house for a little while. I want to enjoy some of this nice spring weather."

"Well, you best be careful. Better you don't ride too far from the house."

Kate had two reasons for wanting to ride today: first of all, she enjoyed riding in the cool spring air with the breeze blowing through her hair. She also wanted to visit some of the settlers who lived nearby, thinking they might know something about Uncle Lewis's problems.

While Olaf was getting her horse ready, Kate went up to her room and changed into some riding pants she had brought from Tennessee. Her mother had always scolded her for wearing them. "They're not ladylike," she would say. Kate, never the one to play the part of a proper Southern belle, did not take to sidesaddles and riding skirts; they were not practical.

One of the older mares was saddled and waiting for her in the front yard. Olaf knew the horses well. Kate had ridden the mare before and found her gentle and reliable. She untied the reins and swung up into the saddle. She felt at home on the back of a horse. Riding had been a passion of hers since early childhood.

It was a peaceful spring morning. The valley lay under a clear, blue, cloudless sky. Kate was still getting to know the land. Behind her were the Blue Mountains, and to the northeast were the Wallowa Mountains. In the distance, Eagle Peak stood against the early morning sun, its snow-covered summit glistening. At the edge of the meadow, a small herd of deer grazed. The country was breathtaking, just as Uncle Lewis had described it.

When Kate was across the meadow and on the road, she turned the horse due north. The road reminded her of one thing she missed about Tennessee: the melting snow had turned it into a muddy bog. Oh, for the macadamized roads she remembered so fondly, she sighed.

Her destination was the cabin of a couple from Missouri named Hiram and Nancy Grigg. The Griggs were part of the contingent Uncle Lewis had brought up over the Oregon Trail. During the trip, Kate had become acquainted with Mrs. Grigg. Nancy had helped care for Drew and Alice during the long days on the trail. Despite being from different backgrounds, the two of them became good friends.

The wagon ruts cut through the grass and cama fields from the main road up to the Grigg homestead. After a short ride, Kate could see the little cabin.

The settlers had arrived late in the year, leaving them only a short time to prepare for the coming winter. Their cabins were hastily built with provisions for few comforts. Four walls, a roof, fireplace, and chimney were the rule. Dirt floors and whatever they had brought along had to do. Many had come from much the same, so they were accustomed to doing with so little. Still, Kate felt pity for them.

Nancy Grigg was hanging clothes on a line that stretched from the cabin to a small tree. She was tall and slender, in her late forties, with mostly gray hair, and her face was tanned and deeply lined. She wore a dingy apron over her faded brown dress.

Like many of the new arrivals, Hiram and Nancy had been victims of the war. Their farm in Missouri had been burned to the ground by Jayhawkers from Kansas. During the raid, they managed to save themselves by hiding in a cellar. The attack also cost them their livestock and farm equipment, leaving them with nothing.

Nancy Grigg paused with her laundry when she saw Kate approaching. "Mrs. McKane."

"Mrs. Grigg. How are you and Hiram faring? And how is the farm coming along?"

"We're trying our best, but there's not much time with spring already here and planting time so near. It's hard work up here, but Hiram is determined to make a go of things. Those Jayhawkers took our property but couldn't take our spirit, he always says. How are the youngins these days?"

"Just fine." Kate dismounted and tied the reins to a small sapling.

They chatted while Kate helped Nancy finish hanging up her washing. Most of the conversation centered on the trip up from Missouri and the long, cold winter. When the last of the clothes were on the line, they went inside the cabin. It was only one room with a dirt floor and a small fireplace they had fashioned out of rocks from the nearby mountains, using mortar Uncle Lewis provided. In one corner was a small bed, and in the middle was a small oak table they had bought in Missouri.

"Lordy be, I thought we would freeze in here during the winter," Nancy said. "We got low on firewood, and poor Hiram had to get out in the cold and cut more. I was afraid he would come down with the fever before spring."

It was such a tragedy for all the poor settlers that had come north to start over again. Many had lost everything in the war. Now they were far from their roots, trying to cope with the harsh climate. For many of them, their only possessions were determination and a willingness to work.

Nancy cleared away some dishes and made room for them to sit down at the table. "There's some coffee left over from breakfast."

"Thank you, but I can only stay for a short while. I wanted to ask if you and Mr. Grigg had seen Uncle Lewis recently."

Nancy's brow rolled up into a confused wrinkle. "Oh yes, he comes by from time to time to see about us."

"Does Uncle Lewis ever talk to your husband about any problems he might be having?"

"They talk mostly about farming up here. Hiram is new to this kind of farming and isn't sure on how to go about it. Mr. Harrington assures him he can do it."

"Do they ever talk about anything else?"

Nancy thought for a moment. "Come to think of it; there was something kinda unusual a few days back. Your uncle was here, and there was Mr. Kenton and two people from Reynolds County, back in Missouri. They were all standing out a ways from the cabin, talking."

"Any idea what they were talking about?"

"They were talking low, but once in a while when I was outside, I could hear them mentioning a man named Covington, or something like that."

The name was familiar. Kate thought about it. The list of names on the business charter—that's where she had seen it. Could it be Uncle Lewis's problems were related to this man, Covington?

Nancy didn't have any additional news concerning Uncle Lewis. They talked for a short time. Then Kate announced she had to leave. Mrs. Grigg followed her outside and watched as Kate untied the reins and climbed into the saddle.

"Please come again," Nancy said. "It gets lonesome here at times."

"I will. You and your husband must come to our house for a visit. Maybe you can have Sunday dinner with us sometime."

"That would be nice."

Kate gave her a wave and then turned the horse toward the road. This man Covington kept invading her thoughts. Had something gone wrong with Uncle Lewis's business? The idea chilled her. More trouble was something she didn't need. There had been enough in her life already.

She rode into the front yard and dismounted. After turning the reins over to Olaf, she went inside to help Helga. Late that afternoon, Uncle Lewis returned.

At supper, Uncle Lewis said without any emotion, "I have to leave this Sunday for Salem. I will probably be gone for about ten days."

"Business?" Kate asked.

"Yes. I'm afraid so."

From the corner of her eye, Kate watched her uncle. He appeared to be emotionally drained. His usually cheerful face was taut and drawn, and there were bags under his eyes. He was clearly a man tormented, which did nothing to relieve her anxiety.

Chapter 4

Clarksville

Aunt Mary was waiting for him at the top of the stairs. "He didn't believe me when I told him you had come back. 'Go on—don't torment a sick man with such a ridiculous story,' he said. Your father can be the most stubborn man at times."

"When he sees me in the flesh, it'll be all right," James assured her.

"I just hope he can stand the excitement when he sees you really are back. It's been such a long time since he's had any good news. I just hope his heart is up to it."

"I know, Auntie. I'll do my best to keep him calm."

She touched his arm. "I know you will. You go down and see him."

He walked to a door that was ajar. Summoning up his courage, he stepped into the room. Inside, he had to wait for his eyes to adjust to the darkness. The one window was covered with heavy black drapes. Inside the room, there was a large dresser sitting next to the wall, a small table with some books and an unlit candle on top, a couple of chairs, and a bed. Next to the bed was a small stand with a glass of water and medicine bottles on top.

Lying on the bed was a skin and bones caricature of the father James remembered. His hair was thin and white, and the taut skin milky pale. The sight of him brought tears to James's eyes.

His father stared at him. *Surely he hasn't forgotten me*, James thought.

When he spoke, the voice was just above that of a whisper. "Boy, you do look a lot like my son, James, but he's dead. I have that on good authority. If you came here expecting something, you're out of luck."

"Father, it is me, James."

"What's that you said?"

"Those men who came to the house got it wrong. I was wounded in Kentucky and nearly killed, but I survived."

His father's eyes flickered. "Step over closer so I can get a better look at you."

James complied.

Albert McKane reached out and touched James's arm. "I must be dreaming. Mary came in and told me you were downstairs in the flesh, but I didn't believe her. As I look at you, by damn, I'm starting to believe you really have come back from the dead. Praise the Almighty, I never believed in miracles, but if I'm awake and not dreaming, this truly is one."

"I was never dead, Father."

Tears were rolling down the pale cheeks. James bent down and embraced the frail figure on the bed. "I'm just so glad to be home, Father."

"The thing is, our home is in shambles now."

"Yes, I went by the plantation today. Old Williams was there. He told me about the Yanks…and about Mother."

"Yes, your poor mother reached the point where she couldn't cope with it all anymore. We thought we had lost you; the war was destroying our way of life, nothing but strife and turmoil all around."

"The war took its toll. I think it's a miracle any of us made it back alive. On top of it all, I keep hearing about everything that happened here," James said.

"The Yanks did their best to make life miserable for us, but they found out the Southern spirit isn't so easy to crush. We will survive and put this terrible war behind us."

His father still had some of his spirit left. He labored to a sitting position, wincing with pain. "Mary, open those damn drapes and let some light in. We need some life in this house again."

James had not noticed his aunt standing in the doorway. "Albert, this is a glorious day for all of us, but don't get yourself all worked up; remember what the doctor told you about your heart."

"Fraud, the old fool, he couldn't cure a sick horse. Besides, my only son is back again—back from the dead. I'm entitled to a little excitement. Pull up one of those chairs, Son, and let's talk."

His aunt opened the drapes. Then James pulled a chair up close to the bed and sat down. "It was heart-wrenching, seeing what happened to the plantation."

"Yes. You see, the Union authorities had it in for me. They came out and wanted me to sign the oath, but I refused. I felt it would be treason for me to sign an oath to the Union when my only son was fighting for the Confederacy. They threatened to arrest me for crimes against the United States, but I held my ground."

That was the Albert McKane he remembered—a man not easily

36

intimidated. "They left me alone for a while, then they came back," his father said. "This time, they were adamant. I guess some of the fight had gone out of me. I didn't want to lose our home after all the other losses we suffered. I gave in and signed the oath. I thought that would be the end of it, but they came back again. The Yanks wanted to use the house as a troop garrison."

"Lowlife bastards," James said.

His father nodded.

"I still can't get over Mama being gone," James said. "When Williams was giving me the news, I had a hard time accepting it, and I still do. She was always so strong."

"That she was. But everyone has their breaking point, and your mother finally reached hers. So many losses took their toll. The worst of all was hearing about you. From that point on, her health went on the decline. There was just nothing anyone could do. We lost her last fall."

"Major Whitten should have gotten his facts straight. I feel like using my pistol on him."

"No. There's no need for that. He felt he was doing the family a service by letting us know. His intentions were honorable. There are so many that haven't heard a word about their family members who went off to war."

James realized his father was probably right, but he found it difficult to accept. "You know, I'm now faced with a very pressing problem. Since I've been back, I haven't been able to find out for certain what happened to Kate and my children. I hear that she went off to Oregon with some uncle. I find that hard to believe."

"She did leave with a man named Lewis Harrington. I believe he was the brother of her father. He came out to the plantation a few times. To me, he seemed like a drifter, full of ideas."

"But why would she just up and leave with a man like that?"

"The news of your death left her devastated. For such a long time, she stayed in her room and seldom came out. One day, this Harrington just showed up out of nowhere. He was a fast, smooth talker, and soon he had her out and about again. At first, we were delighted, but then she announced she was leaving with this man. We tried to talk her out of it, but she would not listen to any of us. Martha was beside herself. You know how she felt about the grandchildren, but Kate just would not listen. Later, I wished that I had run this Harrington off the first time he showed up at the house."

All James could do was shake his head in disbelief. Why would Kate go off into the wilderness with a relative she had just met? She was no pioneer woman. How would she cope out on the frontier?

James talked to his father until well into the afternoon. Periodically, his aunt would stick her head in the room. Each time she inquired if her brother was tired. Each time he sent her away. "Let a man talk to his son. I haven't seen him in four years. You know I never expected to see him again, so let us be."

As the afternoon wore on, James realized his father was getting tired and needed some rest. "Father, I'm going for a while, but I'll be back up soon."

"Son, I have so many things to talk to you about, but for now, I just want to thank the Almighty for bringing you back home again. We'll talk again tomorrow."

After embracing his father, James left the room. His aunt was waiting at the top of the stairs. "There's a hot meal for you on the kitchen table."

This was welcome news; he was hungry. His stomach growled in anticipation. "It's hard to believe that Father's health has declined so much since I last saw him," James said as they walked down the stairs.

"Yes. It is hard to believe. I'm afraid he won't last much longer, but I hope your return will help. So much we held dear to us has been taken away by this terrible war."

"I know. Like Kate and the children. I can't believe she left with an uncle she had just met. Do you know anything about where they went?"

"I could never keep up with that wife of yours. I don't understand how she could just up and leave her duties at the plantation. She was the most ungrateful person I ever met. We took her in and made her part of the family, but how did she repay us? I'll tell you how, by running off with some drifter uncle who wandered in and filled her with foolish ideas about life in the west."

His aunt continued with her tirade about Kate until they reached the bottom of the stairs. James had heard it all before; it was old news he didn't want to hear again.

"You know, she broke poor Martha's heart by taking the children away," his aunt said. "Your father wasn't too pleased about it either, but you know your father; he keeps things to himself, especially his feelings."

"I feel somewhat responsible for what happened. I never made any effort to keep any of you posted as to my welfare. Getting news back to you here would have been difficult, but I should have tried. If I had done so, maybe Kate and the children would still be here, and life would have been better for all of us."

His aunt put her hand lightly on his shoulder. "You had enough to worry about just staying alive so you could come back home again."

His guilt would not yield. It conspired with the long ride and the state of his home to pull him down into a deep depression.

Aunt Mary took notice of his mood. "Boy, you looked starved. Come into the dining room and enjoy the food I prepared for you. That'll cheer you up."

James followed his aunt into the large dining room, remembering the many lavish meals he had enjoyed there. On those occasions, the large oak table would be covered with an expensive linen tablecloth, but today there was an old frayed cotton affair over it. The large chandelier still hung in place, and the mahogany cabinets still filled the walls, but many of the shelves were empty.

Starved as he was, James felt the need to wash himself before eating. He excused himself, walked out to the back of the house, and found a basin and a pitcher of water. He filled the basin and scrubbed away some of the accumulated dirt and grime from days on the back of a horse. Properly washed, he went back to have his meal.

On the table was a platter of sliced ham, boiled potatoes, vegetables, and a loaf of homemade bread. This was a surprise. Aunt Mary had always relied on her servants to tend to the cooking. If this meal was any indication, the departure of her slaves had not left her helpless. She seated herself at the end of the table. "I know you're hungry. Help yourself."

He picked up the silverware and started eating.

"I expect you're surprised to see that I can cook. But, you see, I always knew a great deal about cooking. I had to watch the kitchen help all the time, or they would burn everything to a crisp or make no end of messes to clean up."

"What happened to your slaves?"

"Ungrateful misfits all left when the Union soldiers came around. We always treated them well, but they just took off."

James had no comment about her slaves. While eating, he looked up and noticed his aunt watching him. He supposed his table manners were rusty. "I'm sorry about my manners," he said. "In the war, you tend to forget about such things."

She smiled. "Don't fret about it. It's good to see someone at the table again. Your father usually isn't up to coming down for meals, so I have only myself for company. It's so lonesome here in the house that I'm beside myself at times."

This was not the woman he remembered. When he was a small boy, his parents often visited his aunt and uncle. Both his mother and aunt would scold him for any breach of manners or conduct. "A young gentleman doesn't conduct himself in that manner," one of them would say.

They would pick at James until his father would intervene. "Leave the boy alone for a spell," Albert would tell them.

"What are your plans?" she asked.

"I don't know yet. I need to think about everything. I know I have to do something about Kate and the children, but I don't know what."

"You know, your father will want you to take over the plantation. I don't know how you will operate it with all the help gone, but now that the Union troops have left, your father will want to get it back in operation. He can't do it himself, so he'll turn to you."

"I know, Auntie. If Kate and the children were here, I would be honored to do so."

"Well, I don't know what you expect to do about her. She's out on the frontier somewhere, that is if the Indians didn't get them."

Her remarks stung him. They were inconsiderate and in poor taste, but that was her way. He knew from experience there was no point in arguing with his aunt. He couldn't bring himself to be angry at Kate for leaving; it was the welfare of her and the children that concerned him. What kind of dangers were they facing on the frontier? Would her uncle be able to protect them?

Aunt Mary dropped her criticism of Kate. James stuffed himself until he was afr aid he might burst. He wiped his face with a large napkin. "What a delicious meal, Aunt Mary."

"Thank you, James. I've managed to keep up with most of the household chores without any help. It's amazing what we can learn to live with. I'm just happy to still have a house. The Yankees took some people's homes."

"I can't figure out who suffered the most the soldiers on the battlefields or those we left behind," James said.

"Oh, I don't think the suffering we endured here was anything compared to what our poor men went through on the battlefield. They say that men from Montgomery County are buried throughout the South. I find it ironic that we supplied so many men for the war, yet we couldn't defend ourselves."

James nodded his agreement with her. They adjourned to the main room and sat and talked until it was dark outside. His thoughts turned to a comfortable bed. But he didn't want to be rude. It had been a shocking day for all of them, and there was much to catch up on. When the conversation lulled, he dropped off. "Sorry, Aunt Mary. It's been a long day."

"It's all right, James. I've heated some water for you. I don't know where you plan to stay; you've been to the plantation and seen the condition it's in. You're welcome to stay here until you decide what you want to do. There's a room in the basement that's not in use. Your father is using the main guest room upstairs, and the other two are in need of repair."

"That's kind of you, Auntie. I've forgotten what it's like to sleep in a real bed."

"I found one of your uncle's razors and some clothes that I hope will fit you. You better get out of that gray uniform before you get into trouble with the Union authorities."

"I know. I was warned on the way here."

"I'm going to bed now, so I'll wish you a good night."

James stood up. Aunt Mary gave him an embrace then walked from the room.

For the first time in recent memory, he enjoyed a warm bath and a shave. As he lay in the tub of water, he could feel some of the tension and bitterness slowly ebbing away. He closed his eyes and tried to remember the last time he had felt at peace. It was a futile effort. The reality of the war and his homecoming would not long permit thoughts of peace. He retired to the bed and thought about his family. There was one inescapable conclusion. He needed them; he couldn't go on until he was reunited with Kate and his children.

Chapter 5

The Preparation

James awoke. He felt for a moment he might be dreaming. He was in a bed surrounded by four walls. After so long, he had forgotten the comforts of home. Like the rest of his aunt's house, the spare room had little of its former elegance. The headboard was scarred, the wallpaper starting to fade, and there were worn spots in the carpet. But it was still so comfortable.

Comfort would be a passing thing anyway. Kate and the children—what was he going to do about his family? He had to be with them again. There was only one way that could happen. He had to go to Oregon. The idea intimidated him. After all, he was no frontiersman. There were mountains and rivers to cross, Indians, and many other dangers he didn't know about. And there were his father and aunt. To them, he had come back from the dead. They would be beside themselves if he left again. What an agonizing dilemma he faced.

James crawled out of bed and washed his face in a basin. Then he dressed in his late uncle's silk shirt and pants. They were a good fit. For a moment, he felt like a gentleman again. Well, there was no time for that. After breakfast, he had a full day ahead of him. He could smell bacon frying as he ascended the stairs. Aunt Mary called out, "Come and have some breakfast!"

He found her in the kitchen, removing bacon from a skillet. "I hope your room was satisfactory," she said.

"Best night's sleep I've had in years."

"I'm glad. Now sit down and enjoy your breakfast." James didn't need any urging. He pulled out a chair and seated himself. His aunt set a plate in front of him filled with bacon, scrambled eggs, and several pieces of toast. "Your father is still sleeping," she added.

"What a contrast to days past," James said. He remembered his father rising at the crack of dawn to oversee the plantation's operation. He would ride out to the fields on his favorite horse or into Clarksville to check on the grain mills and warehouses.

When he was stuffed and could eat no more, James excused himself and got up from the table. "I'll be up to see Father later after he's had his rest. I have so many things I must get done today."

"Don't take too long. Albert will want to see you as soon as possible."

"If Father asks for me, tell him I'll be back as soon as I can."

She nodded her head. "You got any money?"

"A few dollars."

"If it's Confederate, it's no good."

"I'm afraid I don't have any Yank dollars."

"I got a few. Wait here for a moment."

Aunt Mary walked into her bedroom and returned with some money. "Here's twenty dollars, Union money. It's the only thing you can spend here, except gold."

"I feel guilty about taking your money, Auntie."

"Go ahead and take it. You can repay me when you can."

James thanked her and took the money. He opened the door and went outside. For a moment, he stood on the porch. Peace, how endearing it was, no sounds of artillery, no screams of the wounded, just a quiet, tranquil morning. He had forgotten what it was like to stand and enjoy a simple sunrise. Now, he had to get on with his business. The first thing he had to do today was find some feed for his poor horse. He went to the stable, saddled up, and rode out into the street.

The rain of yesterday had departed. The early morning air was cool. The sun was rising in a clear sky. It was going to be a beautiful spring day. How James wished he had time to enjoy it. As he rode down the street, a few people waved; others only stared. A Union army colonel was standing on the porch of a two-story house that had belonged to a Clarksville banker. An enlisted man was holding the reins of a large, black horse. The colonel took the reins and started to mount. Then James, riding by, caught his attention. He held the reins and watched. James looked straight ahead. The last thing he needed was a confrontation with the Federals. He couldn't help wondering why a Union officer was using the house. *Greedy bastards probably confiscated it*, he concluded.

James remembered there was a stable at the end of Franklin, near the Cumberland River. It was still there but under a different name. The sign above the door of the weather-beaten building read:

Canfield Stable and Blacksmith

Another Yankee opportunist, no doubt. James dismounted and went inside.

The odor of manure and rotting hay assaulted his senses. Only two of the small stalls were in use. "You need something?" a voice asked.

James turned. The man facing him was short with muscular arms and a dark complexion. His face was covered with sweat. He was wearing a large, heavy apron over his soiled shirt and pants.

"I want to leave my horse here for the day. He hasn't been fed since yesterday."

"Three dollars for the whole day. That includes hay and oats."

An excessive price, but with the Yanks in control, what could you expect? He pulled the money from his pocket. "Where's Bordick, the man who used to own this stable?"

"Don't know. I bought this place two years ago."

"Do you have a horse that I might rent for today?" James asked. "I need to take a short ride, but mine isn't up to the trip."

"I got a couple in the corral behind the stable. Cost you another two dollars."

Money he hated to spend, but he needed transportation. Reluctantly, James agreed to the price.

The man collected the fee then led James down the rows of stalls to the back of the stable. He pushed open the door and pointed to a small corral containing two horses. "Take your pick."

These two were not in the best of condition but were better than the one he was riding. A black mare seemed the best of the lot. He led her inside. To save additional rental costs for tack, he transferred the saddle and bridle from his horse to the mare. She was a little skittish until they were out on the street, but then she settled down.

He followed Franklin back to Second Street, then to Main. As he rode, James noticed that most of Clarksville was still standing. Well, at least the Yanks didn't burn it to the ground.

The thing that continued to amaze him was the near-deserted commercial district. Only a handful of people were on the sidewalks, and just a few riders and wagons were on the street. The war—it had affected everything.

Approaching Main Street, James saw the building that housed the dry goods store owned by Kate's parents. It was a two-story building made of red brick. The second floor extended out over the sidewalk, providing pedestrians some protection from the elements. To his consternation, the windows were boarded, and there was a padlock on the door. He stopped in front of the store and looked around. There was no sign of any recent commerce. Moreover, there was trash on the sidewalk in front of the door, something Kate's father would not have tolerated.

Disappointed that he couldn't find his in-laws, James rode down Main Street toward the Cumberland River. In front of a red brick building by the town square was a large sign that read UNION BOARD OF TRADE. *What kind of Yankee foolishness is this?* He wondered.

Across the square was the brick Bank of America building with the ornate ironwork. Now Union sentries stood on both sides of the door. In front of the building was a sign that read PROVOST MARSHAL.

Just down the street was a large brick building with a sign that read WINES & BREED MERCHANDISE. On the other side of the street was another sign that read MATTIL, LONDON & COMPANY. These were new businesses. Most of the businesses he remembered were gone. Northern interests had taken over.

James turned his attention to a small delivery wagon coming up the street. The driver looked familiar. James waited until the wagon was even. Handling the reins was a downcast young man staring straight ahead, eyes transfixed on the team. "Herman's Market" was painted on the side of the wagon. James found it hard to believe the driver was a boyhood friend, Packy Walters. How out of place he looked. The shaggy brown hair hanging from the straw hat and the faded cotton shirt and pants were out of character for the friend James remembered. The driver started to pass on by without even a glance in James's direction.

"Packy! Packy Walters!" James yelled.

The wagon stopped. The driver toyed with the reins. "Mister, you know you look a lot like my late friend, James McKane. But from what I heard, he was killed up in Kentucky."

"Now, Packy, you shouldn't listen to rumors. I am James."

Packy took off his hat and wiped at his forehead with the sleeve of his shirt. "You're not making a bit of sport with me, are you? I heard that story from a good authority."

"Your authority was misinformed. I don't look like a ghost, do I?"

The wagon driver gave James a long look. A grin spread over the sad face. "Damn, I do believe it is you. I certainly never expected to see you again—at least, not in this life."

"What happened to you and your family?"

"I was in the Fourteenth that went off to Virginia. Got my leg shot up at Fredericksburg, and I could barely walk after that. I finally made it back home, only to learn that my family had lost the plantation. Early this past spring, my folks went off to Nashville. I've been driving this wagon trying to stay alive."

The fate of Packy and his family saddened James. He could still remember the good times the two of them had: riding horses, flirting with the young ladies of Clarksville, living the life of young men of privilege. It was difficult to imagine this forlorn young man sitting in the wagon was his carefree friend from the past.

"There seem to be a lot of new establishments here on Main Street," James said.

"Yeah. The Union Board of Trade decides who can have a business and who can't. Most of the new ones are Yankee owned."

"I figured as much. I was looking for the Harrington's, but I see their business is no longer open."

"I heard that Walter Harrington lives down in Palmyra. He lost a son during the war."

They spent a few minutes talking about old times and the war. Before leaving, James promised his old friend he would come around for a visit. Now aware of where his father-in-law lived, he wanted to get over there and find what he could about Kate and the children.

James crossed the Cumberland River and rode south out of Clarksville. The road was filled with holes full of muddy water from the rain of the previous day. Before the war, the Clarksville area had been noted for its hard-surfaced roads. They had deteriorated during the war. Now, he had to guide the horse carefully to avoid stepping into one of the holes and breaking the animal's leg.

Along the road, he met groups of Negros carrying their belongings in small carts and on their backs. Some glanced up at him. Most just looked straight ahead; none spoke.

In Palmyra, he rode down the muddy main street until he reached a blacksmith's shop near the end. The weathered brick and battered tin roof were not bellwethers of prosperity. Neither was the broken front window and weed-filled yard.

Inside the shop, a large, sweaty man was working at a forge, using bellows to heat a horseshoe. The sweat was running down his tanned face causing him to frequently reach up to wipe at his eyes with the sleeve of his soiled cotton shirt. Without pausing his work, he gave James a quick glance.

The bellows made a sucking sound as the man pumped the handles. James waited until the blacksmith paused and stood back from the fire. "I'm looking for Walter Harrington. I was told he lived here."

"Straight down the road 'bout a mile," the man replied without looking at James.

James resumed his ride. At the edge of town, he had to stop and wait for two teenage boys to herd a flock of sheep across the road. After getting the animals across, the boys waved and then prodded the sheep into a small pen.

When he judged he had traveled a good mile, there was a small house next to the road. Kate's parents, though not wealthy, had always been of a comfortable middle class. The little shack of unpainted lumber and wood shingles was a comedown. On the porch was his father-in-law sitting in a rocking chair.

Walter Harrington gave him little notice at first. As James drew close, his father-in-law sat up in his chair and stared at him. As James was dismounting and tying the reins to a small bush, Walter got up and walked to the edge of the porch. He was near six feet in height, now gaunt with a slightly ruddy face, graying hair, and a bald spot on top of his head. As James walked toward the porch, Walter's gaze remained fixed on him.

"Are my eyes deceiving me, or is that James McKane walking across my yard?"

"Your eyes are doing fine, Walter. It's me."

"Well now, boy, you were supposed to have been killed, or so I was told."

"The Yanks did their best in that regard, but they failed." James extended his hand.

"My poor daughter never knew that. She up and left us over your reported demise," Walter said after releasing James's hand.

"I know. I'm going to try and set that straight." James sat down on the edge of the porch while Walter went back to his rocker.

"Boy, it's good that you made it home. I lost my oldest son down in Mississippi."

"I'm sorry to hear that. Seems like the war took something from all of us."

"That it did. We lost the store soon after the Union took over. The Union Board of Trade was set up to control the business activity in Clarksville. To start with, you had to take the oath. If you had relatives in the Confederate Army, there was no way to get a permit, so we lost all we had."

"Where's the rest of your family?"

"The missus and youngest son are in Nashville. Took them almost a year to get a travel permit. My wife finally convinced the Union authorities her sick mother in Nashville needed her help. Soon as she got their papers, they left."

"I'm sorry to hear about your family. I also heard that Kate and the children went up to Oregon with her uncle."

"That's the straight of it. My brother, Lewis, came by one day. When he found out about Kate, Lewis went to McKane Plantation for a visit. Kate was laid up with grief at that time, but my brother is a smooth talker and can put on the charm. He soon had her out and about again."

"But why did Kate leave with him?"

"Grief, I think—hard to say. Like I said, Lewis can talk with the best of them. He got her convinced life in Oregon is the best thing on earth, so she left. The missus and I tried to talk her out of it, but you know how stubborn

Kate can be. The McKanes tried to keep her from going, but they didn't have any better luck than we did."

"Have you heard anything from them?"

"Not a word. All I can do is hope they are safe. They've been gone for almost a year."

"You know where they went up there?"

"Not for sure. Lewis talked about a place he had near the Blue Mountains, but I don't know much about that country. I wrote her a letter but haven't received a reply. Guess it never made it up there. I moved here after she left with Lewis. So she doesn't know I don't live in Clarksville anymore. She doesn't know her mother is in Nashville, either."

"What kind of man is your brother?" James hated to be so blunt about Walter's kin, but concern for Kate and his kids drove him to it.

"I don't know that much about him. He left home when he was a very young man. He went out west, and we rarely heard anything from him. When he showed up here last year, it was the first time we'd seen him in years. Up until that time, we didn't know if he was still alive or not."

"What about the character of the man? Can he be trusted?" He hoped Walter wasn't offended by these probes into his brother's character.

"I think Lewis is something of a dreamer and probably a little irresponsible."

There it was, right from the man's own brother. And Kate and the children were out in the wilderness with this man.

They talked until James realized it was getting into the afternoon. What was his father going to think? He would be upset James had not been up to see him yet today. "Walter, I hate to leave, but my father will be expecting me," he said.

Walter stood up. "I'm going up to Oregon and to find Kate and the children," James said.

"I admire your spirit, but do you think you're up to it? It's dangerous out on the frontier."

"I just came home from four years of war. I'm used to danger."

Walter shook his hand. "I wish you the best, boy. Be careful out there. I hope you find Kate and the kids and bring them back here where they belong."

"I will."

James had never been close to Kate's family. Like his family, the Harrington's had never approved of the marriage. They felt Kate would not be happy at McKane Plantation. After the children started coming, Kate and James would occasionally take them to the store in Clarksville, but they rarely visited the Harrington home. Likewise, Kate's parents seldom visited the plantation.

The decision was made; now came the difficult part—getting to Oregon. James was no frontiersman. He would have to cross the Rocky Mountains. From what he had heard, crossing the Rockies in winter was near impossible. Here it was, well into spring, leaving him no time to waste.

The consequences of his decision weighed on him. His family had thought him dead, had grieved for him, rejoiced at his miraculous return—now they had to face his leaving. Most of all, how would he break the news to his father? His father's days were nearing the end. If James left now, would he ever see him again? The trip to Oregon would be long. If he found Kate and persuaded her to return, chances are his father would be gone by then. The agony of it all, would he ever be free of it? But it had to be; there was no other way. Painful as it was, Kate and the children came first.

It was mid-afternoon when he reached Clarksville. He retrieved his own horse and a small bag of oats from the livery and rode back to his aunt's house. She was in the front room, knitting. "Your father has been asking for you."

"Yes. I'm sorry I took so long, but I had to ride over to Palmyra and talk to Walter Harrington."

Aunt Mary ignored his remarks about Kate's father.

"After you go up for a visit, you can come back down for your meal."

James started to go up. At the bottom of the stairway, he paused. "I'm going to Oregon to find my family."

She looked at him. "I hope you know what you're getting yourself into."

"I know it won't be easy, but I've got to do it."

"I assume your father doesn't know about this."

"No. I just made the decision today."

"You better tell him as soon as possible before he gets used to having you around again. Once that happens, he'll have a hard time living with it."

"I plan to tell him today."

She turned back to her knitting. Seeing Aunt Mary had nothing else to say, James climbed the stairs, walked to his father's room, and knocked on the door.

"Come in."

James opened the door and stepped inside. His father was sitting up in the bed. "I've been waiting all day to talk to you."

"I know, Father. I'm sorry for being so late in getting up here, but I had to ride over to Palmyra to see Walter Harrington."

His father thought for a moment. "Any news?"

"Nothing beyond the fact Kate went off to Oregon with her uncle, Lewis Harrington. The troubling thing is it seems Lewis Harrington might not be a reliable person, and that worries me. Walter told me his brother is something of a dreamer and maybe a little irresponsible."

"That's rather the impression I had when he came to the plantation. I'm sorry to hear the news wasn't any better."

James pulled a chair up to the bed.

"I've wanted to talk to you about your future plans," his father said. "You know the plantation is out of production right now and has been for some time. It'll take some work to get it going again. First, there's the problem of labor. With the slaves gone, we've got to find another source. We'll have to hire men to do the work."

How was he going to give his father the bad news, the worst he had ever been forced to give? Yesterday, he had brightened his father's day with his unexpected return. Today, he was preparing for the final goodbye. Watching the anticipation on the taut, drawn face, James knew the news could not be put off. "Father, it would be my greatest honor to help rebuild our family home and business, but there is something I have to do first."

James's sadness deepened at the disappointment on his father's face.

"I must find Kate and my children before I can do anything else. I know you're disappointed, and that saddens me to no end. I wish I could stay and rebuild the plantation, but this is something I have to do. Kate will never return here on her own, and her family has lost contact with her. There's only one thing I can do, and that is go and find her. I could never live with myself otherwise."

"Yes. I know how you feel. It would be my greatest joy for you to stay and help rebuild the family fortune, but any man worth his salt would feel the same way you do. Being laid up in this bed has given me time to reflect on a great many things about life. I used to care only about material things and neglected those around me. Now, I've come to know what's really important. Don't make the same mistakes I've made. Do what you must do as a husband and father."

His father's courage, his humble words, left James feeling small by comparison. The strength and determination had always been a hallmark of the man, but the humbleness that was something James had never seen before. His father had truly changed.

"Father, when I find Kate and my children, I would be honored to come back and help rebuild the plantation."

"I'm happy to hear that. I probably won't be here, but the land will be. There's opportunity for you here. The Union cannot survive without us back in it. The South will be in for some rough times, but in the end, we will survive. I hear that in some places, Southern whites can't vote now, but that won't last. They need us too much." They talked for a short time, then his father asked, "You got any funds to finance your trip? It will require some money, you know."

50

"I know. I'm afraid I don't have much of anything right now. The army wasn't able to pay us for the last several months."

"In the top drawer of the bureau, there is a key. Get it for me, please."

James complied with his father's request. He took a key from the drawer and handed it to his father.

"Under the bed is a large metal box. Get it out for me."

James found the box and pulled it out. After dusting off the top, he set it down on the bed next to his father.

His father handed him the key. "Open it, please."

James inserted the key in the gray metal box. He found several cloth bags inside.

"Before the war started, I realized the South would be in for a hard time both from a military and economic standpoint. I converted a portion of our family fortune into gold. I knew that Confederate money would be worthless, but gold always has value. Take out one of those bags."

James did as his father instructed and pulled one of the bags out of the box.

"There's about three thousand dollars in gold coins in that bag and some Union money as well. It's yours."

"Father, I can't take money that you and Auntie will need."

"We got enough for our needs. Besides, won't neither one of us be around much longer anyway. Go ahead and take it. Use it to do what's required of you."

James embraced his father. "I don't know how I can ever repay you."

"Just be careful and come back home as soon as you can."

They talked until his father grew weary. With a promise that he would be back early the next day, James excused himself. His aunt was waiting for him downstairs.

"Did you tell him?" she asked.

"Yes."

"Come and eat."

When the gold coins and money were secured in the spare room, James washed up and went into the kitchen. His aunt served him baked ham with all the trimmings. Over the meal, James described his visit with his father.

"That doesn't sound much like my brother, but as I told you earlier, he has changed a great deal. When do you plan to leave?"

"As soon as I can make all the arrangements. I need to get to the mountains before winter."

"Do you know what you're doing out there? You may have been a great cavalry officer, but what do you know about the frontier?"

"Not much, I admit," he replied. "On the other hand, I survived some of the bloodiest fighting of the war. I know a few things about taking care of myself."

"I do hope your wife appreciates what you're doing for her. She was so ungrateful to the rest of us."

Here it came again, another tirade about Kate. That didn't do anything for his appetite. It was history he didn't want to rehash. He knew his family was disappointed that he married Kate; he had heard all the speeches before. "I think Kate was unhappy because she felt she didn't have a place here."

"I don't know why she felt that way. We did our best to help her out. Did it matter? She repaid us by running off the first chance she got."

When Aunt Mary got her nose up about something, bringing it down again was difficult. "I remember one time we were getting ready to entertain some of your father's business associates. I was trying to rehearse her on some of the social graces that were required, but what reward did I get? She got up and called me a snob and a phony. I'll never forget that."

James, being as subtle as possible, tried to ignore her assessment of Kate. He held a great fondness for Aunt Mary, but there were times when the woman was insufferable. She did, after a time, seem to pick up that he wasn't paying attention and dropped the matter.

He thanked Aunt Mary for the meal then retired to his room to go over his plans. This was a daunting task he faced; every risk had to be considered. James knew he was ill-prepared. He could only hope the survival skills learned during the war would carry him through. He also had to hope that Kate and the children had arrived in Oregon safely. That worried him more than his own welfare. He fretted over his undertaking until weariness took over. Then, he crawled into the bed and dozed off to a troubled sleep.

*   *   *

The next morning, James sat down to a breakfast of ham, thick toast, and blackberry jam. His aunt was spoiling him. He would be on the trail in a day or so, roughing it. For that, the war had prepared him well. *Just don't get used to the luxuries of home*, he advised himself.

Today, there was much to do. After breakfast, he saddled his horse. The sun was spreading an orange glow across the eastern sky as he rode down a nearly deserted Franklin Street to Third Street, then north toward the plantation. At the edge of town, a small group of Union soldiers was congregated. They ignored him. The early morning air felt cool as he rode down the still muddy road.

The devastation was still unbearable. He tried to put it aside and focus on why he was here, but the ruins of his way of life were buried under the ashes in the front yard and the ransacked house. Feeling hollow, he rode up the drive to the porch and tied the reins to a small bush.

He endured the heartbreaking state of his home one more time for the sake of his upcoming trip. Inside the house, James walked through the debris of the front room over to the stairs. His father was a learned man who always maintained a well-stocked library. Had the Union troops left it intact?

The library was located down the hallway from the quarters he had shared with Kate and the children. He discovered the facility had been partially ransacked, but there were still some books on the shelves. Others were lying about on the floor with pages torn out. He guessed the Union troops had needed something to start their fires.

In the library was a large atlas, still intact. He sat down on the floor and paged through it until he found a map of the Pacific Northwest. The information was limited. At the time of the book's publishing, the Oregon Territory had not been completely explored. It did show the general location of the Blue Mountains.

James took the atlas with him out to his horse and stored it in one of the saddlebags. He felt the pressure rising. He needed supplies for his trip, and time was precious. Tomorrow, he had to be on his way.

How he cursed the bloody war that was forcing him to leave his sick father for a dangerous journey across the frontier. Four years of fighting and near dying, and all there was to show for it was misery and torment.

Yankees now controlled the commerce of Clarksville. He hated the idea, but he would have to buy his supplies from the profiteers. He picked one of the stores, secured his horse in front, and went inside.

He was amazed. There was little the Wines & Breed Store didn't carry. The bottom floor was one large spacious room filled with an assortment of goods, including both men's and women's clothing. He started to walk up to the second floor when a clerk dressed in a white shirt, dark suspenders, and pants approached him. The man had short, black hair that was slicked down and combed straight back and a thin, dark mustache. The expression in the clerk's eyes carried a hint of contempt. "Can I help you?"

"I hope so. I need a raincoat and some oilcloth."

The man wrinkled his nose. "We have apparel for laborers in back."

Ignoring the man's condescending manner, James followed him to the back of the store. The prices were high, much more so than before the war. That explained why there were so few customers, Yankees trying so hard to get rich they priced themselves out of the market. Served them right, James felt.

In the back, James found a raincoat to replace his worn-out Confederate issue and replacements for his worn-out boots. On the second floor, he found some cooking utensils and some oilcloth. He paid the clerk with what remained of the money his aunt had provided and one of the gold coins his father had given him. The clerk eyed the coin. *How did a poor Reb get hold of this?* he was probably wondering.

"Don't see many of these," the clerk commented.

James did not reply.

Due to the war, ammunition of any sort was in short supply. For the Henry, it was out of the question. He made some inquiries among some of the families he knew and found some hunting friends from days past who provided him some rounds for the pistol. From another merchant, he bought some bacon, salt pork, coffee, sugar, hardtack, and flour. A stable sold him a bag of oats. While at the stable, he inquired about a horse. The one he was riding was in no shape for a long trip.

"Don't have much to offer," the stable owner replied. "Man named Enoch Mitchell south of town keeps a few. I suggest you give him a try. You'll have to be careful dealing with him or any others out there. The Union army comes through and takes their property, so they tend to keep their stock hid most of the time."

The saddlebags were full, so James took them back to his aunt's house and stored them in the stable. Aunt Mary fed him a lunch of ham sandwiches and cool milk. After eating, he went up to have a word with his father, who he found sitting up in bed. "I assume you're getting ready to leave," his father said.

The anguish took away James's voice. The best he could do was a whisper. "Yes. If I can find a suitable saddle horse for the journey, I'll be leaving in the morning. I wish with all my heart it didn't have to be that way."

"Life doesn't always leave us with easy choices," his father replied.

James understood what his father was doing; he appreciated it. His father was trying to make his departure a little easier with his understanding. But deep down, he was feeling the disappointment of losing his son after such a short time. Even worse, James couldn't even spend the rest of the day with him. The best he could do was promise to come back later.

Following directions from the stable owner, James rode toward the edge of Clarksville and took the river road. Birds singing in the oaks and hickories along the road and insects buzzing from the river provided most of his company. Other than two boys fishing along the riverbank, using lines tied to thin willow poles, he saw no other people. The boys glanced at him as he passed but turned quickly back to their fishing. After a thirty-minute ride, there was a muddy side road that led eastward. He slogged his way through the quiet countryside to a small farmhouse.

It was a rundown affair made partially of logs and clapboard lumber. The back of the log portion had a chimney made of rock and mortar. The clapboard portion had wooden shutters that closed over screen wire-covered openings, which sufficed for windows. Beyond the house, there was an empty corral made of oak poles surrounding a barn made of logs.

A woman wearing a long cotton dress and large bonnet was behind the house, hanging clothes on a line stretched between two tall oak trees. She was a large woman with long, brown hair hanging below her head cover.

Next to the house, a pair of motley-colored hounds was sleeping. They stirred, raised their heads and eyed James, lost interest, and lowered their noses between their front paws.

The woman looked weary; she paused with her wash, looked around, and watched James tie the reins of his horse to a bush and walk toward her. She sat the wash down as if ready to take flight.

"Afternoon, ma'am."

"Afternoon."

"I'm looking for Mr. Mitchell. Is he about?"

The woman eyed him harder. A stranger asking about her husband had aroused her suspicions and evoked caution. He had to ease her fears before any business could be conducted. "Please, ma'am, I mean no harm to anyone. I'm just a recently returned Confederate soldier looking for a horse to buy."

She studied James. "Confederate soldier, you say. You be from around here?"

"Yes, ma'am. I'm James McKane, the past four years in service of the Confederacy. My Father is Albert McKane of Clarksville. Perhaps you've heard of him."

"Can't say that I have. Don't get up to Clarksville much." Then she pointed toward a grove of scrub oaks in the distance. "Husband's down by the crik."

"Thank you, ma'am." James walked over to the trees. On the edge of the scrub oaks was a small creek. Inside the stand of oaks, in a small clearing, a man and a young boy were shoeing a horse.

"Afternoon!" James yelled out as he approached.

The man looked up toward James, then toward a shotgun leaning against a nearby tree.

"No need for alarm, Mr. Mitchell. I'm just looking for a horse to buy. I was told you might have something."

The man looked James over. Mr. Mitchell was stout in appearance and had a deeply tanned face and thin, graying hair. His cotton shirt was wet with sweat, and his pants were caked with mud. The teenage boy had long, stringy brown hair, and some of his front teeth were missing. He wore a dirty cotton shirt and pants that were held up by a single homemade suspender.

"You a Union man?" Enoch Mitchell asked.

"No. I'm just a recently returned rebel soldier in need of a good mount."

Enoch spit a stream of tobacco on the ground. "Rebel soldier, are ye?"

"Was until it ended," James replied.

"You plan to pay for a horse with Confederate money?"

"No, sir. I got gold."

The man's head shot up. Gold—that got his attention. He pointed downstream. "I got a couple staked out further down the crik. They done been broke ta ride."

James followed the man and boy a short distance down the brushy creek bank. At times, they had to wade out into the shallow water to get around the thick bushes. Further downstream in another clump of oak trees was a small corral made of poles. Inside were two horses.

"The blasted Union army comes through the countryside looking for horses and anything else they can get their hands on. We keep our stock hid out in the woods. The black gelding is a little skittish, but he's got a lot of spirit. Make a man a fine saddle horse."

James studied the horse; it seemed to be in reasonable condition. "How much?"

"Sixty Yank dollars," the farmer replied without hesitation.

"I need to ride him first," James said.

Enoch agreed, so James went back to the house and got his own mount. When he returned, he transferred the saddle and bridle from his horse to the black gelding. It stood patiently while being saddled but fought the reins when James mounted. After a spirited ride down the creek and back, he felt the gelding would serve his purpose. Besides, he was short on time.

They negotiated for a time. Enoch Mitchell was a true Tennessee horse trader. James wound up with the gelding, a shotgun, and a few more rounds that he could use in his pistol. As part of the deal, James threw in the horse he currently owned. Well, actually, it was stolen from the Yanks in Nashville, but that was a fine point he would not belabor.

With the deal sealed, James transferred the rest of his property to his new horse. He shook hands with Enoch Mitchell then started home. The headstrong gelding tried to fight the reins, but James was an experienced horseman; he had dealt with spirited mounts before. Since he was a small boy, he had spent much of his life on the back of a horse; handling them was second nature. He patiently worked the gelding until they reached town. Horse and rider had come to an understanding; now, he had reliable transportation.

It was dark when James reached his aunt's house. He secured his horse in the stable, pumped a bucket of water, and filled the feed through with oats. He made a final check of his supplies before going into the house.

His aunt was in the kitchen, cooking supper. A roasted chicken was sitting on the table, and she was taking a pie out of the oven. "Blackberry, one of your favorites," she said.

The rumbling in his stomach embarrassed him. "Auntie, I'm going to miss your cooking when I'm out on the trail."

"We're going to miss you, boy. After you eat, you had better go and say goodbye to your father. You won't ever see him again."

Of that, he was painfully aware. "I know."

James washed up, then sat down at the table and stuffed himself. When he was finished, he excused himself and walked over to the stairway.

Climbing the stairs, James felt himself a condemned man walking to the gallows. If only there was some other way, but he could think of none. Time was short, and somewhere out there was his family. As a man, a husband, and a father, he had a duty. But it was a duty that came with a terrible price. He stopped in front of his father's door and knocked.

"Come in."

He found his father sitting up in bed. "Have a seat, son."

James pulled a chair up next to the bed and sat down.

"I guess you're ready to leave us."

"Yes. I'm afraid I have to leave early in the morning. I need to get to the mountains before the winter snows, so that doesn't give me much time. I also have to find a guide in Independence."

"Well, son, whatever happens out there, I want you to remember the McKanes are a proud people. Your grandfather came here when this place was nothing but wilderness. With hard work, he built it into one of the finest estates in the entire South. We never back down from our duty no matter how difficult it may be, so never forget your heritage. Set your mind on what you have to do, and don't let any obstacle stand in your way."

Some of his father's strength and determination had returned. Beyond the frail body racked by illness, there still remained a strong and proud man. Albert McKane had always been a man who charted his own destiny. How it must pain him to be in his current state. James could only hope he had inherited enough of his father's mettle to carry out the task he was undertaking.

They talked for several hours about their family, politics, and the future of the South. James didn't want to stop, but he realized it was getting late. He said good-night to his father, promising to be up in the morning to say goodbye.

Before going to bed, James went out and checked his gear one more time. Satisfied everything was in order, he went back inside and got out the atlas to check his planned route. He would go straight west, crossing the Cumberland and Tennessee Rivers, then into Kentucky, and from there west to the

Mississippi River, where he would cross over into Missouri. Once in Missouri, he would head northwest until reaching Independence. There, he would hire a guide to take him up the Oregon Trail to Oregon.

That night, James had a dream. In the dream, he was standing on the edge of a lake, and Kate and the children were on the other side. James called out to them, but they turned their backs and walked away, disappearing into a cloud of mist. He called and called to them, but they did not return, leaving him to stand on the bank and cry for his lost family.

Chapter 6

The Confrontation

Olaf came in from his morning chores as Helga was removing strips of bacon from a large iron skillet. Kate herded the sleepy, protesting children to the breakfast table. "Has anyone seen Uncle Lewis?" she asked.

"I knocked on his door," Helga said. "He said to start without him."

In a few minutes, Uncle Lewis came out of his room carrying a valise. The dour look on his face discouraged the rest of them from asking questions. He stopped at the table just long enough to swallow a cup of coffee Helga had set down. "Olaf, please hitch the buggy for me," he said.

"Yaw, right away."

This was a departure in character for Kate's uncle. She would have expected him to wait until Olaf had eaten before sending him on a chore. All the more reason, her concerns were growing.

While waiting for his transportation, Uncle Lewis sat on the front room settee and pulled some papers from the valise. He was still sorting through them when Olaf appeared in the door. "The buggy is ready."

"Thank you, Olaf. I'm off to Salem," Uncle Lewis replied. He got up and walked to the door. Kate followed him. She expected him to at least bid them goodbye. He shuffled across the porch, then stopped and turned around. "Kate, I know I've been a grouch the past few weeks. Please forgive me. I hope when I get back from Salem, things will be better."

"I hope so, too, Uncle. Don't worry about anything here. We'll help Olaf and Helga keep the farm running. I understand you have a lot of weight on your shoulders, helping the new settlers and managing your own farm."

"Thank you for your understanding, Kate. I'll be back in a few days."

He walked out to the waiting buggy. After depositing the valise in the back, he climbed into the driver's seat. With a tap on the horse's flank, the buggy lurched forward. At the front gate, he turned and waved.

59

With apprehension eating away at her, Kate stood in the yard and watched her uncle drive away. Worry—downright fear tugged at her. Her mettle was wearing down. With Uncle Lewis away, she felt compelled to do some snooping on her own. The idea of spying on the man who had done so much for them brought her shame. But concerns for the welfare of herself and the children trumped guilt in this case.

Since her conversation with Nancy Grigg, the man named Covington had gnawed at her. She had to talk with this Mr. Covington and see if he could shed some light on her uncle's woes. That meant a trip to La Grande, which posed a problem. She didn't want to ride there on her own, and Olaf was busy with the farm. The next morning at breakfast, the problem solved itself. Olaf announced he had to go to La Grande to pick up some farming supplies. "I'd like to come with you," Kate said.

"Yes, missy. It might be a little rough riding in the wagon."

"I don't mind," Kate replied.

Kate helped Helga with the breakfast dishes while waiting for Olaf. When the wagon drove into the yard, Kate promised the children some candy, dried her hands, and went outside. Olaf was a busy man; she didn't want to keep him waiting. He helped her up into the front seat. Then he got into the wagon and tapped the team with the reins; the wagon rumbled across the yard and through the gate.

It was a pleasant spring day. A few fleecy white clouds hung below a bright blue sky. The meadow was abuzz with activity. A pair of rabbits scrambled across the road in front of the team. A large buck deer stood at the edge of the meadow. "It's nice here in the spring," Kate remarked.

"Yaw. It is nice."

The high peaks of the Blue and Wallowa Mountains were still white with snow. The most prominent were Mount Emily rising up out of the Blues and Mount Fanny nestled in the Wallowas. The early morning sun glistened off the white peaks.

"Olaf, do you know this man Covington?" she asked.

"Yaw. He's well known here. He owns a freight line that operates in La Grande and Pendleton. I don't have much use for him myself. He charges high freight rates because he knows the people don't have much choice. The other freighters haul mostly for the mines down south. The rest here have to depend on Covington; he takes advantage."

Why would Uncle Lewis get involved with such a man? Kate wondered. He didn't sound like a good business partner. This Mr. Covington sounded like a greedy man, and a greedy man couldn't be trusted. Perhaps this business deal was at the root of Uncle Lewis's problems.

To the south of La Grande, they passed a steam-driven sawmill. Pine logs and finished lumber were stacked in front. They passed a gristmill and a blacksmith's shop that advertised itself as a manufacturer of plow shears. Kate hadn't noticed it on her previous visits, but there was a flour mill. On the outskirts of town was a settlement of tents and flimsy shacks made of pine and tar paper. Clothes hung on makeshift lines strung up between the dwellings and trees. Children were playing around the muddy grounds. "Miner's families," Olaf pointed out.

In La Grande proper, there was a livery stable next to a tavern. On the other side of the street were several businesses, including a general store, butcher shop, barbershop, an eatery, and blacksmith shop. Next to the blacksmith shop was an emporium that sold everything from housewares to farming supplies.

The building fronts were made of rough pine siding, the roofs of wooden shingles. There were sidewalks of rough-cut pine in front of the businesses. In places, the wood had rotted away, leaving pockets of mud oozing up through the boards. Behind the businesses were the homes of the town's residents. The Union County courthouse was just off Main Street. It was newly built, two stories, and, in contrast with most of La Grande, it was painted.

Olaf parked the wagon in front of the emporium. He got off the wagon and helped Kate down. "Olaf, can you tell me where Mr. Covington's freight business is located?" she asked.

Olaf raised his eyebrows at her request. "Down the street and to the right," he replied.

"Thank you."

"You going to see Covington, missy?"

"Yes, I am."

Olaf thought about it. "You want me to come with you?"

"No, that's all right. I don't want to keep you from your work. I'll be fine."

Kate started down the sidewalk, holding her skirt up to keep the hem out of the mud. She was starting to miss Clarksville with its paved streets and well-maintained sidewalks. She had no qualms about La Grande; it had a frontier charm, she supposed. It was just different than what she was accustomed to.

At the end of the street, there was a large lot filled with empty wagons. Next to the lot was a corral filled with draft horses and mules. At the end of the lot was a building, the office, she assumed.

Watching where she was stepping, Kate wove her way through the throng of wagons to the building. It was made of stone, somewhat out of step with the rest of the town. The single front window was covered with dark curtains. The sign on the door read:

COVINGTON FREIGHT COMPANY

E. G. COVINGTON, OWNER

She knocked.

"Come in," a voice yelled from inside.

Kate pushed the door opened and stepped inside. The furnishings were sparse. There was a large cabinet in the corner, in the back was a wood stove, and in front of the stove was a brown settee. In the middle of the room, a large man with graying hair, a broad face, fleshy jaws, bushy eyebrows, and long sideburns was sitting behind an oak desk. He looked up; surprise registered on his face. "Can I assist you with something, miss?"

"I'm looking for Mr. Covington," Kate said.

"Well, you've found him. If I may ask, who are you?"

"I'm Kate, Lewis Harrington's niece."

"Oh, yes, I heard Harrington brought some family back with him. Please have a seat." His voice was flat and dry.

She sat down in a wooden chair in front of the desk. "What brings you here, miss? I didn't get your last name."

"McKane, Kate McKane. Mr. Covington, I take it you and my uncle have a business arrangement of some sort."

"Yes, we do. Your uncle and I, with some other men, entered into a business association. For my part, I agreed to provide freight services to the settlers he brought up here. It's just a standard business agreement. Your uncle and a man named John McDonald came to me with a proposal to start a farm co-op here. You see, they needed a way to get their crops to market. The deal had some merit, so I agreed to come in with them. We drew up the necessary paperwork. That's all there is to it."

His brow rolled up into a puzzled furrow. "Why are you asking me about your uncle's business? Why don't you ask him?"

"Uncle Lewis has been distant recently. I can't get anything out of him."

"Well, as far as I'm concerned, we have a deal; the deal stands."

His sharp tone startled her. All of a sudden, Mr. Covington had become defensive, indicating the business agreement was a sore point. Maybe she was getting at the heart of the matter. "Mr. Covington, I hope this business agreement isn't going to become a source of trouble. I came up from Tennessee last year. The last thing I want to see is conflict."

"I assure you, Mrs. McKane, any trouble will be the results of your uncle's actions, not mine. I'm just a businessman trying to earn a living. That's all I'm prepared to tell you."

Mr. Covington didn't' appear willing to go any further with the discussion. No matter their short conversation had been an eye-opener. He had been polite, but there was something disturbing about him. He had confirmed, at least indirectly, there was a conflict between him and Uncle Lewis. That was enough; the alarm bells were going off in her mind.

She stood. "Thank you for your time, Mr. Covington."

"Anytime. Don't get many young ladies in here."

The conversation with the freight owner had added to her worries. *How did Uncle Lewis get mixed up with such a man?* She kept wondering. The man reeked of distrust; couldn't her uncle see that? Kate fretted all the way back to the wagon.

Olaf and a young man were loading bags of seed into the wagon. Kate stood on the sidewalk out of the way until they were done. When the last bag was loaded, Olaf started into the emporium behind the young man. "I'll be ready in a minute, missy," he yelled.

Kate started to get into the wagon then remembered her promise to bring back some sweets. She went into the store and bought a bag of rock candy.

The conversation with E. G. Covington took center stage in her mind on the ride home. If only she knew what the source of contention was between her uncle and the freight owner, maybe she could get some peace of mind. Whatever it was, it seemed to be a sore point for both men.

Olaf's voice interrupted her thoughts. "I'm sorry, Olaf, what did you say?"

"Did you find the freight yard, missy?"

"Yes. I didn't like the owner very much."

"Yaw. Many people feel that way about Mr. Covington."

When they were home, Olaf stopped the wagon in the front yard and helped her down. Kate went into the house to assist Helga. The children inquired about their candy. "After your noon meal," she replied.

After eating, Kate kept her promise to the children then started sweeping the floor. She was filled with distress. *Could this situation lead to violence?* she wondered. Maybe they were in danger. She would come to understand the seriousness of the situation all too soon.

*   *   *

Late the following afternoon, Kate joined Olaf and Helga on the porch. It was a warm spring afternoon without a cloud in the bright blue sky. The younger children were playing in the front yard. James Junior was pitching horseshoes at a peg Olaf had driven into the ground. The boy glanced toward the road. "There's some riders coming toward the house," he yelled.

Kate got up from her seat. "I wonder who it could be." Her first thought was some of the settlers were paying a call.

"Probably just someone passing through," Olaf replied.

From the edge of the porch, Kate watched the riders approach. They were riding single file across the meadow. Nobody she knew; they were strangers. The lead rider was a dark-haired man wearing a faded cotton shirt and what looked like buckskin pants. When he was close, the dark piercing eyes caught her attention. He wore a pistol strapped to his belt, and a rifle was sheathed in his saddle.

There were seven riders following the leader, all heavily armed. The lead rider stopped his horse just inside the gate; his companions stopped behind him. "We're looking for Lewis Harrington," the leader said.

"He's not here," Kate replied. "He's away on business."

The one just behind the leader urged his horse forward. He had a broad, clean-shaven face and stringy hair hanging down to his shoulders. A twisted smile played on his face. "You want me to take a look around the place?" he asked.

The dark-haired man looked around the house and yard before answering. "I reckon not. The lady says he's not here. We'll take her word for it, this time." He urged his horse forward until he was directly in front of Kate. The dark eyes seemed to stare through her, driving Kate's heart up into her throat. "When Harrington gets home, you tell him we was by. He'll know who we are. You tell him we'll be back. He can't avoid us forever."

He turned and rode back toward the others. His companions urged their horses to one side so he could pass. They fell in behind the leader and rode across the meadow to the road.

Kate held onto the porch to support her trembling legs. The dark-haired man, the piercing eyes, drove chills down her spine. "Did you know them, Olaf?"

"No, missy. I've never seen them before. Gunmen or highwaymen would be my guess. They were armed to the teeth and spoiling for a fight."

Kate's fears had now reached the breaking point. When her uncle returned, she would confront him and demand the truth. He had brought her and the children up here; they deserved to know what was happening. Their future—their very lives might be at stake; she would not let up on her uncle until he told her everything.

Chapter 7

The Journey Begins

James awoke. The dreaded departure was at hand. He sat on the edge of the bed, agonizing over what he had to do. Why had fate placed this heavy burden on his shoulders?

Well, it couldn't be put off. He got up, dressed, and started his last journey up his aunt's stairs, feeling broken and disillusioned. He could hear her in the kitchen, making him one final breakfast. He slipped out the back and went to the stable. He fed his horse, then after one final check of his supplies, he placed them all in his saddlebags.

As a precaution, he wrapped the Henry in a blanket. Union troops would be about. He saddled his horse and secured all his gear.

He was so distraught over leaving his father and aunt, for a moment, James considered just riding away without saying goodbye. But that was a coward's way of thinking. It would be cruel and insensitive to slip away like some thief. No, however painful, he had to face up to this. His hands trembled as he led the gelding around to the front of the house and tied the reins to the picket fence.

From the front room, he could smell bacon cooking. In the kitchen, his aunt was tending the wood stove—to his astonishment; there sat his father at the kitchen table drinking coffee.

James was quick to realize why his father had managed his way down to the breakfast table. He wanted his son to remember him as a strong and determined man, not as one laid up in a sick bed. Remember him as he was, not as what he had become; James knew and understood this, felt humbled by it.

"I trust you have everything ready," his father said.

"Yes. All saddled up and ready to go."

"Sit for some breakfast before you leave," his aunt said.

The best thing for him was to be on his way. The longer he remained, the more difficult it would be to leave. But he owed this to his father and aunt. He put his wishes aside and sat down at the table. Aunt Mary filled their plates with strips of crisp bacon, scrambled eggs, and thick slices of toasted homemade bread. *How long would it be before he had another meal like this?* James had to wonder. "Auntie, I wish I could bring you along to cook for me."

"Sorry. I'm a bit too old to be riding a horse across the country."

They lapsed into silence. James's broken heart prevented him from speaking. When he tried, his lips trembled—the sadness threatened to spill out of him. His father and aunt seemed also at a loss for words. He struggled for some words that might ease everyone's sorrow, but none came. His father sipped at his coffee, ignoring the food on his plate. His aunt, whom he remembered as rarely ever being without anything to say, sat and stared at her plate.

All James could do was try to mitigate the pain of his departure as much as possible. A few attempts at conversation failed to lift the gloom that hung over the table. It was just what had to be—he left it at that. James ate, finished his coffee, and then got up from the table. Making an effort not to choke up, he said, "It's time for me to go."

His aunt got up and embraced him. "Boy, you be careful out there in the wilderness. Try to keep in touch if you can."

"I will," he promised.

Aunt Mary released him. James turned to embrace his father but was in for another surprise. Albert McKane had labored to his feet and was extending his hand for a handshake. James extended his own hand and felt his father's grip, which was like that of a bear trap, not a man who spent most of his time in a sickbed.

"Do what you have to do and try to come back home," his father said.

"I will," James said through tear-filled eyes.

James could feel their eyes on his back as he walked to his horse. He dared not turn around—if he did, it might be impossible for him to leave. He stored some biscuit and bacon sandwiches Aunt Mary provided for him in the saddlebags, then he mounted. He urged the gelding into a slow trot, never looking back at his aunt's house.

He rode slowly past darkened houses while struggling with his emotions. He fought for control, to get focused on what lay ahead. But the sad faces of his father and aunt tormented him, urged him to turn around and go back. That he could not do—there was a long and dangerous task facing him, so he had to get his mind on what must be done. At Third Street, he turned and rode to Commerce, then to Water Street.

The waters of the Cumberland slipped along its banks. The Nashville

Queen was at the dock taking on cargo. He rode past the McKane family tobacco stemmery and grain warehouses where in days past they stored oats and wheat from the plantation. At the end of the street, he stopped. The drab gray buildings were mere shadows in the darkness. James looked at them for a few minutes as if to say goodbye to this segment of his life, one that would probably be no more. Then he rode on.

At the end of Water Street, he hesitated. The Dover Road would take him out of town, but before leaving, he had an urge to see the plantation one more time. He wanted to say goodbye to the plantation, goodbye to his home and way of life. The urge wouldn't yield. He swung his horse around to the right and rode along the west edge of Clarksville to the road that would take him home one more time.

The sun was just announcing its presence in the east when he reached the gate to the plantation. He rode up the drive past the main house and slave cabins out to the fields. There, he sat on his horse and remembered his life on the plantation.

The unplowed fields were covered with weeds. In years past, spring planting would have been in full swing. He could picture his father sitting on his favorite horse, overseeing the entire operation. As he watched, James could hear the sounds of the slaves as they toiled in the warm, spring sun. A lump formed in his throat; this life was gone, maybe forever.

James finished his reminiscence then rode back to the house. He tied his horse to the porch of one of the slave cabins and walked to the family cemetery. In the early morning silence, he felt a presence around him—not threatening in any way but calming and peaceful. In front of each of the headstones, he paused and remembered. In front of his mother's grave, he stood for some time and grieved for her, for the pain and suffering the war had brought down on their family and for those, he was leaving behind. Then he said his goodbyes and went back to his horse.

There was no sign of Williams or anyone else around the slave cabins. He put aside going into the house again; all it brought him was anguish. Time was wasting, so he mounted and rode back out to the road.

When he was back in Clarksville, he crossed the bridge at the confluence of the Red and Cumberland Rivers and struck the Dover Road heading west. As ever since slipping out of Nashville, he worried about Union patrols. His papers were safely secured in his saddlebags, but with the Federals, that was no guarantee. Feelings from four years of bitter fighting were not erased overnight. Soldiers dressed in blue he still could not trust.

There were no Union patrols on the road this morning. In fact, there were few travelers of any sort. There would be an occasional rider or wagon; otherwise, he had the road to himself. The birds singing in the trees and the steady clop, clop, clop of the horse's hooves on the road surface nearly lulled him to sleep. By midmorning, the sweat was running down into his face, and mosquitoes and gnats were buzzing around his ears.

When James got hungry, he pulled one of his aunt's sandwiches out of the saddlebag. These morsels were the last pleasures of home he would be able to enjoy. He munched while swatting at the insects and tried to ignore the hot sun.

He rode through a little village called Oakwood without stopping. It was nothing more than a few buildings housing a small post office, a general store, a stable, some churches, and a few houses. A few people paused to stare at him as he rode past.

Before noon, just as the heat and pesky insects were becoming unbearable, James reached a bridge over a creek. The clear water winding slowly along the banks looked so inviting. He turned the horse off the road and followed the banks until he was out of sight of any passersby. He watered his horse, then tied the reins to a small tree, stripped off his clothes, and waded into the creek.

The cool water, only knee-deep in the middle, helped soothe the pain and itch brought about by multiple insect bites. He sat down in the middle of the stream and let the water flow past. When he started to drowse, he got up and climbed out of the creek. After drying himself with a rag from his saddlebag, he got back into his clothes.

Now, he faced another temptation. The relaxing interlude in the creek left him feeling sleepy. He just couldn't resist the urge. In the soft grass of the creek bank, he lay down and dozed off.

James awoke from the short nap and cursed himself for being so lazy. How would he ever get to Oregon if he lay around sleeping all day? He got up and untied the reins, watered his horse again, and climbed back in the saddle.

The delay at the creek was not a total loss. The bath in the creek and short nap improved James's outlook. He rode down the road filled with a new resolve. So anxious he was to get on with the journey, he didn't bother to stop for a noon meal. Instead, he pulled out another of his aunt's sandwiches and pushed on. The hot sun bore down on him, and the pesky insects kept up their assault, but he did his best to ignore it all.

By mid-afternoon, the drowsiness was back; on one occasion, he dozed and almost fell off his horse. Every so often, he had to remove the felt hat and wipe his brow with his sleeve to keep the sweat out of his eyes.

Try as he might, while he rode, the emotional departure from Clarksville would not let him be. His father laboring to be strong, his aunt's fussing left him feeling numb inside. If only he could quickly find Kate and bring her and the children back to Tennessee, then they would all be together as a family again. Maybe he would still have the opportunity to spend some more time with his father and aunt. But that was a long shot. He knew nothing at all about Oregon; he might never find Kate. After the difficult life she had had at the plantation, would she want to come back? The only certain thing in his future at the moment was the long and perilous journey ahead of him.

As night was falling over the countryside, James reached the Cumberland River. There was no bridge, leaving the Dover Ferry as the only means of crossing. And that meant waiting until morning, as the ferry was shut down for the evening. A short distance down the river, there was a clearing in the woods that lined the bank. It would do for a campsite.

James pulled his gear out of the saddlebags then hobbled the gelding so it could graze during the night. In the dark, he fumbled around, almost tripping a few times, until he had enough dry limbs to make a fire. He brewed some coffee and had the last of Aunt Mary's sandwiches for his supper.

James fashioned himself a place to sleep by spreading his bedroll on the ground and putting a mosquito net over it. He lay in bed for a time, listening to the night sounds. From deep in the woods came the sound of an owl, intermingled with the sounds of frogs and night insects. He fell asleep listening to the night symphony.

*   *   *

The warbling of birds flittering among the trees awakened James. Sunlight filtered through the canopy above him. He roused himself, found his blanket was wet from the dew. No matter—he had slept soundly and was ready for another day on the trail. He packed the mosquito net and bedroll with his gear and then stirred the remains of the fire. Over a small flame, he brewed a pot of coffee and fried some bacon. Not being much of a hand with a skillet, he fried it nearly to charcoal but ate it anyway. Though with little taste, it was filling and would get him started on another day.

The gelding was grazing nearby. When the horse was saddled, he put out the fire, washed the frying pan in the river, and packed it with the rest of his gear. As a precaution, he put his papers in his pocket.

The second day started out as a repeat of the first. The insects resumed their assault on his neck and ears. To be rid of them, he would take off his hat and fan the air. It was, for the most part, futile; as soon as he stopped fanning, they were back.

In a few minutes, he was at the Dover Ferry Station. The ferry was currently in the middle of the river, working its way to the dock after depositing passengers on the other side. His apprehension kicked in at the sight of a contingent of Union troops gathered near the dock. Before proceeding, he felt in his pocket to ensure his papers were handy. With the Henry secured out of sight in the bedroll, he rode forward. Mingling around the dock were people waiting to cross the river. The soldiers stood back a distance from the others, talking among themselves.

James thought it best to appear nonchalant. *Appear to be calm, and the Union troops would have no reason to be suspicious,* he felt. It must have worked—the soldiers took no notice of him. He paid the attendant fifteen cents.

When the boat was against the pier, a crew member swung a rope over the side to a man who slipped it over a mooring post. The gangplank opened, and the travelers scrambled up on the deck. Some were on horseback, and a few were on foot. James stood back and waited until the others were on board.

"Pleasant day for traveling," came a voice from behind him.

"I suppose so," James replied without looking around.

"Where you bound for?"

"Missouri," he replied. The man's questions annoyed James.

"I'm bound for Memphis myself."

James turned around. The man addressing him was short, balding, and wearing a white suit and large red necktie over a blue vest. He had small beady eyes, a thin face, and a few strands of brown hair. The sun glared off his pink scalp. *Yankee opportunist,* James thought to himself.

The line was released, and the boat lurched from the dock into the deep water. The front of the boat swung around, and smoke billowed from the large smokestack as the paddles churned the muddy water. The river current slammed against the hull, nearly twisting the boat sideways. It held sway.

The bow of the ship nudged into the dock, and the mooring line was slipped over a post. The gate opened, and the passengers made their way down the gangplank. James held onto his horse until the foot passengers were offloaded, and then he led his mount down from the deck.

"Enjoy yourself in Missouri," the stranger said.

James gave the man a quick nod, did not speak. There was something about the Yankee that he did not trust. He mounted and rode quickly away, looking back over his shoulder from time to time.

It was the first of two crossings. A short distance to the west, in his path, was the Tennessee River. He rode around Dover and started west, hoping to make Paris Landing before nightfall.

Ahead of him to the west, clouds were building, indicative of a spring storm brewing. Soon, he was riding into a cool breeze, a relief from the heat, and it drove away the pesky gnats and mosquitoes.

When hunger hit, he tried some of the hardtack. It was like biting down on iron. Concerned for his teeth, he threw it away.

Lightning streaked across the darkening sky. What he needed now was shelter from the storm, but where was he going to find any out here? James urged the gelding forward, looking for a place where he might find refuge. He saw nothing at first, then, just ahead, was a small house next to the road. He raced the horse forward and reached the front yard as the first drops of rain fell.

The house was made of rough pine and appeared abandoned. One front window was missing, knee-high weeds grew in abundance in the yard, loose shingles on the roof rattled in the wind, and there was no smoke coming from the chimney. It would have to do. James jumped from the saddle and tied the reins to a small tree. After removing his saddle and gear from the gelding, he slipped on the hobbles and untied the reins. The wind drove the rain into his back as he raced into the house with his belongings.

The house was empty, save for some old magazines and newspapers piled in one corner. The only other sign the dwelling had been inhabited were the ashes in the fireplace.

Rain water dripped from the ceiling onto the hand-hewn oak floor. The only dry spot of sufficient size was near the fireplace. James seated himself there on the floor and leaned back against the wall. Rain hammered down on the flimsy roof, leaving James fearful the entire thing might come crashing down on him.

The rain eased in intensity, making a soft pattering on the roof. The sound of it lulled him to doze off. He awoke and could still hear the rain on the roof. The delay annoyed him. He considered just ignoring the storm and riding on, but that could be dangerous. Better to stay inside where it was a little safer until the storm eased. To pass the time, he reached over and picked up one of the newspapers that had escaped the water from the leaking roof. It was from Union City, Tennessee. In the dim light, the print was hard to read. He started to toss it aside when a headline caught his attention.

MISSOURI REBELS SPOTTED NEAR UNION CITY

Late yesterday, April 14, a patrol under the command of Lt. Hoskin, encountered a group of men near Latham. The men are believed to be part of the Tannahill gang from Missouri. In the ensuing shootout, the rebels escaped and were believed to be headed toward Kentucky.

Interesting—he was headed to Kentucky. It was a reminder that the aftereffects of the war lingered, making travel risky. Lee's surrender had not put a total stop to the madness. Hatreds, passions for this cause, or that, they still remained to fuel more violence. If that wasn't enough, there were the

71

profiteers, such as those mentioned in the paper. James had survived the war itself, and now he faced the task of surviving the bloody remnants.

When the rain subsided, James found his horse grazing a short distance from the house. The hour's delay from the storm left him with some hard riding to reach the Tennessee River by nightfall. He saddled and pushed on.

When darkness came, James had not reached the river. *But it was close*, he felt. He could camp here tonight and reach the river early tomorrow. He camped in a copse of oaks just off the road. After tending his horse, he tried to build a fire. The wet wood at his disposal would not catch. Determined to have at least some hot coffee, he stumbled around in the dark woods until he found a log. The underside was reasonably dry. With a small hatchet, he hacked away at the dry wood until he had enough for a fire.

After the long day in the saddle, James didn't feel up to cooking. He brewed a pot of coffee then got out some more hardtack. How could he eat these hard biscuits without destroying his teeth? The coffee—maybe they would soften up if they soaked in the coffee. He dropped a couple into a cup of the hot liquid. In time, they softened until he could chew them without breaking a tooth.

Remembering the dew of the previous night, James covered his bed with the rain slicker. He awoke the next morning dry and rested. A little optimism came his way. The trip to Oregon seemed a little less daunting this morning. That was the spirit. Now, if he could find a way to keep his spirits up, he could well be reunited with Kate and the children in a few months.

This morning, to keep up his strength, he needed more sustenance than hardtack could provide. He poked around in the ashes and found a few embers. With a few twigs and leaves, he got a small blaze going. He let the iron skillet get too hot, again burning his bacon. At that, it was chewable, preferable to hardtack.

He gathered his supplies, saddled up, and found Paris Landing after a short ride. He also found a large contingent of Federal troops at the dock. And they weren't standing idly by as those at the Cumberland crossing had been doing; they were checking the passengers. Well, sooner or later, the Union authorities would test him, and this was it. James took his papers out of his pocket, checked them one more time, and placed them back in his pocket. He gave the blanket holding the Henry a quick check, found the weapon concealed. "Let's get this over with," he mumbled under his breath.

In front of the gate that opened to the gangplank, a Union captain and two noncommissioned officers were checking each passenger. The sight of blue-clad soldiers, men he had been fighting for the past four years, brought out the anger, the torment, and the anguish of his experiences. With a nervous hand, he grasped the reins and led the gelding forward.

Ahead of James was an elderly man riding a large, gray mare. His face was covered with white whiskers, and there was a dark patch over one eye. On his head was a battered felt hat stained with sweat, and his pants were tucked down into his boots. The captain motioned to the man; he dismounted and led the gray horse up to the waiting soldiers.

The captain was a young, clean-shaven man, save for long sideburns and sandy hair. Both the non-coms were older men. One was tall, gaunt with a trimmed white beard and mustache. The other had dark whiskers and was short and heavyset.

"Where are you from?" the captain asked.

"Paris, Tennessee," the man replied.

"You a loyal Union citizen?"

"I reckon so."

The captain looked at him for a moment. "What are you doing over here?"

"Horse trading. That's how I make my living, trading horses."

"More like stealing horses," one of the non-coms remarked.

The old man bristled. Few things could rile a Tennessee man more than being referred to as a horse thief. "Where I'm from, a man can get killed with such talk as that."

"Is that so?" The non-com put his hand down on his pistol and walked up to the old man. "You threatening a Union soldier?"

"Nope. Just stating a fact."

"Sounded threatening to me," the non-com said.

"Never mind, Sergeant," the captain said. "I'll handle this."

The non-com took his hand from his pistol and stepped away from the old man.

"You ever take the Oath of Allegiance?" the captain asked.

"Can't say that I have."

"Would you be willing to take it now?"

"What fer?" the old man asked. Anger was starting to show in his voice. "The war is over. What else do you want?"

"To make sure you're a loyal citizen of these United States," the captain said. "You willin' to take the oath?"

"What if I don't?"

"You might find yourself under arrest for treason. If that happens, your property is subject to being confiscated."

The old man took off his hat and rubbed his brow, then put the hat back on. He looked at the captain and non-coms, then at the larger contingent of troops behind them. "Hell. I guess you Yanks won the war. Let's get it over with."

The captain turned toward the troops behind him and yelled, "Lieutenant

Hastings, give this man the oath. Make sure he signs it with his name or makes his mark."

A young, clean-shaven officer walked out away from the other troops and motioned the old man over. The old horse trader hesitated for a moment, looked at the Federal troops again. If he had second thoughts, he wisely put them aside. He led his horse to where the Union officer was waiting.

With the old man out of the line, James led his horse up to the captain.

The officer regarded him. "You're a reb soldier if I ever saw one."

"I was, but I've had the oath." He pulled his papers from his back pocket and handed them over.

The captain studied the papers for a few minutes before handing them back; then, he laughed. "You must be a part of that bunch that tried to sneak old Jeff Davis out of the country."

"I was part of the escort detail."

"I heard that Jeff Davis was dressed up like a woman when they caught up with him," the captain said. "You rebs had a sissy for a leader. No wonder you got your rear-ends whipped."

James swallowed hard to push back his anger but said nothing.

"Hell, maybe this one wears women's clothes as well," one of the non-coms said. "You got any woman's clothes in the saddlebags?"

"No!"

"Now, maybe I'll just take a look." The soldier reached for one of James's saddlebags.

"No. You will not look in my saddlebags," James said. He reached out and caught the soldier's arm.

"Boy, you want a good horse whipping this morning?" the non-com said. "You puttin' your hands on a Union soldier."

"I'm a citizen of the United States, and I just showed you the papers to prove it. You're trying to make an illegal search of my property."

James's initial reaction had been on instinct. Having a little time to think, he realized he should have swallowed his pride and let it be.

"All right, Sergeant," the captain said. "I'll handle this."

James released his grip on the sergeant's arm and stepped back.

"We were just having a little fun," the captain said. "In the future, I advise you not to get so uppity about it; such an attitude might land you in some serious trouble. Be on your way now."

Anger and relief: James felt both as he led his horse to the gangplank. He survived a close call with the Federals, but the humiliation was still eating at him. When he glanced back, one of the Union non-coms was watching him closely. In the future, he had to be more careful and keep his feelings in check.

James stood on deck and held the reins of the skittish gelding as the boat steamed across the Tennessee River. Two days of travel, and he was still in Tennessee. How far away Oregon seemed; would he even make it? But the longest journey started with the first step.

Getting out of the occupied South would make the going a little easier, he hoped. His next stop was Kentucky, a Union state. And then there was Missouri, a Union state, but one bitterly divided by the conflict. What would he find there? The bloody aftermath, he feared.

With the smokestacks belching out dark clouds of smoke, the boat steamed into the dock. James led his horse down the gangplank. There were Union troops on this side of the river as well. He mounted and started riding away, watching the troops out of the corner of his eye. They showed no interest in him. A short ride and he was at the Kentucky border.

Would he ever see Tennessee again? Four years of bloody fighting for the land he loved, and now he was leaving it, maybe forever.

Having decided it would be best to avoid the populated areas, James stayed south of Murray; less chance of trouble that way, he figured.

That night, he camped in a clump of trees near the road. Over a small fire, he brewed a pot of coffee and fried a piece of salt pork. Chewing on the greasy meat, he thought of his aunt's cooking. Well, that was a luxury he would have no more. Such as this would be his sustenance until Independence.

The next morning, James was up before sunrise. After having his coffee and bacon, he saddled and was on his way. It was cool in the early morning, so he let the horse set its own pace while he enjoyed the solitude. His only company was the birds congregated in the trees along the road. For nearly an hour, he continued to let the horse jog along in the early quietness of the calm Kentucky countryside.

A column of smoke just ahead ended the peaceful lull. Highwaymen, guerillas hanging around from the war, or scoundrels of all sorts could be camped out here. He, on the other hand, was alone with considerable gold. He thought about all his options—there weren't many. He could try riding on past or turning around and going back. James chided his lack of nerve. Hell, after four years of combat, here he was, his nerves in a pinch over a campfire. He rode forward.

A man with a shaggy beard stepped out into the road just a few feet in front of him. He was dressed in a tattered gray coat and shabby hat with part of the brim missing, the remnants of a rebel soldier's uniform.

"Morning," he said when he saw James.

"Morning," James replied.

"Come down and sit a spell if you're a mind. I and my comrades got a little camp set up back in the woods there."

Although leery of this stranger, the man was a fellow comrade-in-arms,

75

so James felt obliged to be courteous. He followed the rebel into the camp, keeping his hand close to his pistol.

There were six gaunt, ex-confederate soldiers, wearing ragged gray uniforms, seated around a fire. They were unshaven and unwashed, representative of what remained of the Confederate Army at the end of the war.

"Name's Nash Fuller," the one he had met in the road said.

"James McKane."

"I take you to be a rebel soldier from the recent war," Nash said. "Just like the six of us."

"Tennessee Cavalry."

"Like us," Nash said. "We were members of the Eleventh Tennessee Volunteers. We're on our way down to the Indian Nations and maybe on to Texas. We hear that Jeb Stuart's down in Mexico putting together another army."

Now, James knew for a fact Jeb Stuart had been lost in a battle in 1864. But he kept silent about it. *Don't take these men's hope away from them,* he felt. From their looks, hope was about all they had. But if anyone was in Mexico or anywhere else putting together an army, he wanted no part of it. No sir—no more wars. The one just concluded had taken too much from him.

"You been to breakfast yet?" Nash asked.

"Yes," James replied.

"Get down and sit while we have ours if you wish," Nash said.

James dismounted. There was a rabbit roasting over a campfire. One of the men was cooking pan bread over the fire in a blackened skillet. Scenes from the war: the army rarely had food for the troops, so they scrounged the countryside to survive.

"Where you off to?" Nash asked.

"Missouri and on to Oregon from there," James replied.

"If you'd like some company, we're headed toward the big river ourselves," Nash said. "Once we reach the Mississippi, we'll be headin' over toward Indian Territory."

Did he want to ride with these men? James thought about it. The company would take some of the boredom out of the long days in the saddle. But being soldiers from the South didn't automatically make them trustworthy. They were in dire straits. If they learned of his gold and money, would they try to take it? He compromised; he would ride with them a day or two but keep his eyes open for trouble. "I guess a little company would be a relief," he said.

The men finished their meager meal, then they mounted and started west. Nash and his companions gabbed constantly about their exploits during the war. "We'd fire a few shots in the air, and them Yanks would run like a bunch of scared rabbits," they would say. James might have found some amusement in their tales had it not served up his unpleasant memories of the conflict. To him, there were no heroic stories or self-promoting exploits to muse over—there were just the reminders of suffering and death. But he kept it to himself and let his companions carry on.

"How you men manage to evade the Yank patrols?" James asked. "Those gray uniforms are outlawed in most places."

"We manage to sneak past them most of the time," Nash said. "Besides, most of the folks around here supported the South during the war, so they ain't so likely to bother us."

"Kentucky was a Union State," James said.

"That it was, but a lot of the people here were Southern supporters," Nash replied. "A lot of men from around here rode with Nathan Forrest."

The road through the rolling Kentucky countryside was rough and filled with mud holes. During the day, they kept to the back roads to reduce the odds of being stopped by Federal troops. They passed a few farmhouses. Some of the occupants would nod a simple greeting, but most seemed to prefer to ignore them.

Late one evening, they found a clearing just beyond the road. "Good place to camp," Nash said.

James secured his horse and started into the woods when he was startled by a voice behind him. He turned around. Three riders were stopped at the edge of the road. One rode forward. He was tall and slender with a black mustache and dark, thin eyebrows, wearing a long black coat, a black hat with a white hatband, and a string necktie. Around his waist, he wore a belt with a holster and pistol. A Confederate flag was draped over his saddlebags. "You men look like Sons of the South," he said.

The others had spotted the three men. "That we are," Nash replied. "What you have here is a passel of veterans of the Confederacy from the State of Tennessee. I and my boys here were infantrymen from the Eleventh, and our friend here was a cavalryman."

"Sounds like the kind of folks we like to associate with. If you gentlemen don't mind, we'd like to join you for a toast to our glorious land."

"That's a splendid idea," Nash said.

The man turned to his companions and motioned for them to join the others. One of them was dark-headed with a clean-shaven face. He carried a pistol strapped to his waist and a rifle in his saddle. The third one looked a little older. He had sandy red hair; like his companions, he was heavily armed.

When the men dismounted, the leader got a ham from one of his saddlebags and handed it to Nash. "Some fine eatin' there. You can't beat a good cured ham."

One of Nash's companions took the ham and soon had it roasting on a spit over the fire.

The newcomer got a bottle from his saddlebag. "Fine Kentucky Bourbon. After we eat, I suggest we drink a toast to our land."

James found these three men troublesome; he seated himself out away from them. They had not given their names, and there was a look of trouble about them. He quickly concluded they were outlaws on the run, probably what was left of some of the guerilla bands that had operated here during the war.

"When I got back from the war, they had taken our family farm for taxes," Nash said. "Can you believe that? While I was away fighting for them, they up and took my family's land. When I saw what they had done, I packed up and took off again. Still, I'd rather live under the Confederate flag than the damn Yankees."

"Me and my friends are carrying on the war in our own way," one of the strangers said. "We hit the Yanks where it hurts the most, in their pocket books. We're on our way south to have another go at them."

No surprise to James, the three were highwaymen carrying on their private war in the name of profit. Such men could not be trusted.

They swapped war stories until the meat was ready, then they stuffed themselves on the ham. Afterward, one of the strangers passed around the bottle of whisky. James took a quick sip when it was handed to him, then passed it on. Afterward, he got out his bedroll.

"Looks like the cavalry is surrendering," Nash said.

"Long day tomorrow," James replied. He picked up his gear and carried it a short distance from the camp. For sure, he did not trust the strangers, and he still wasn't sure about Nash and his companions. Most of all, he didn't want to wind up drunk among a group of men with unknown intentions. Before going to sleep, he glanced toward the camp to make sure no one was watching. Seeing the others were busy drinking whisky and swapping war stores, he put the gold stash and money under his blanket. As he was drifting off to sleep, James could hear Nash and the others talking and laughing as they passed the whisky back and forth.

*　　*　　*

At dawn, James awoke and found Nash and the others snoring heavily around what remained of the fire. He had no intention of waiting around for them to sober up. There was the matter of his distrust toward the lot of them, and time was short. As he was getting his gear ready, he noticed the remaining portion of the ham lying near the fire, wrapped in a cloth. He cut off a bit of it. So much better it was than hardtack and salt pork; he could have a decent meal or two before going back to trail food. He saddled his horse, packed his saddlebags, and then led the gelding out to the road before mounting and riding away.

For his breakfast, he ate a piece of ham while riding. There was one thing he had to give the strangers credit for; they might be bandits, but they had good taste in food.

James tried to cover as much ground as possible. His only stops were at small streams, where he let his horse drink and rest a bit. Like breakfast, his noon meal was another piece of ham, eaten while in the saddle. Mid-afternoon, he reached a small town called Pilot Oak.

He much preferred to just ride on past the town, but he needed supplies. At a livery stable, he bought a small bag of oats and some more bacon and salt pork from a little establishment on the other side of the dusty street. The people of Pilot Oak gave James suspicious looks but left him alone. He quickly stored his supplies in his saddlebags and rode out of town. Southern supporters during the war or not, he didn't feel comfortable around them. It turned out to be an omen of trouble to come.

Just after riding out of Pilot Oak, up the road, James spotted a group of riders coming toward him. They stopped their horses and waited for him to approach.

This didn't bode well. Now, he wished Nash and the others were with him. The men were all armed. One held up his hand and motioned for James to stop. The man had a scar across his forehead and was wearing a blue hat and tunic similar to those worn by Union Army troops; shaggy brown hair hung below his hat.

James stopped his horse.

"You're a stranger," the man said.

"Just passing through. Who are you gents?"

"Fulton County Vigilantes. We're watching for rebel raiders that's been attacking our farms and homes. Some come over from Missouri, and some are local."

"I'm from Tennessee and have never been to Missouri," James said. "I'm heading that way now on my way to Oregon."

"Is that so?" the man said. "We'll see about that. Rebel guerillas were thicker than flies around here during the war. Our job is to protect the interest of the loyal Union folks who've been at the mercy of these cutthroats for years."

Another of the group rode up close—eyed James's gear. He was reaching for one of the saddlebags when James shouted, "Keep out of my property!"

"It's our business to know what's going on around here," the man said. "Maybe you got something hidden in there."

"No, but I don't want anybody fooling around in my gear."

The man kept looking at James. "I swear there's something wrapped up in that blanket."

That prompted James to reach for his pistol. "Keep away from my property," he repeated.

Before he could retrieve his side arm, James felt the barrel of a gun against his neck.

"Just sit still," the man holding the pistol said. "Take a look at what he's got in that blanket."

The other rider reached down, grabbed the blanket, and pulled it away from James's saddle. As he did, the Henry fell out on the ground.

"Look at that fancy rifle," one of them said. "How come a broke down rebel like you is carrying around a fancy piece like that?"

"Brought it back from the war. It's my property."

Another vigilante joined them. "That's a Henry repeater. Those were not Confederate issue. Not many Union troops had one. You stole it from a Yank soldier, I'd guess."

"Don't matter how he got it," the man with the pistol said. "It's ours now."

James studied the men and concluded the odds were against him. There were a total of eight in the group, leaving him outmatched; a fight was out of the question. If he put up too much of a fuss, they might go through the rest of his stuff and find his valuables. The best he could do was keep his losses to a minimum. He would have to sacrifice the Henry and try to hold on to the rest of his belongings—especially his gold and money.

One of the vigilantes got down, picked the Henry up, and handed it to the leader.

"Maybe we need to look at the rest of his stuff," the leader said. "Maybe you got more fancy things down in the saddlebags. Maybe you've been over here stealin' from these good Kentucky folks."

The situation was growing more desperate. Losing the rifle was a loss, but one he could survive. His traveling funds—that was different. With his funds gone, the trip to Oregon to find his family would be in jeopardy. He entertained the idea of going for his pistol and making a fight of it. But with the odds, he stood little chance. He was bemoaning his fate when one of the vigilantes yelled, "Riders coming up the road!"

The leader looked at James. "All right, mister, but you watch your step. If I catch you up here again, I'm going to have you locked up. Old Nathan Forrest and his lot aren't around to protect you rebels anymore."

James watched the vigilantes until they were out of sight. Then he rode over to the side of the road and dismounted. What a mess he had made of things. Losing the Henry made him feel dejected. With its firepower, it would give him some advantage out on the frontier. Now, all he had left was the pistol and shotgun. "Damn the luck," he swore under his breath. He looked up and saw a group approaching, maybe more vigilantes looking for some easy pickings. Then he heard a familiar voice. "There he is."

Nash, his companions, and the three strangers were riding toward him. "You have some trouble here?" one of the strangers asked.

"Bunch claiming to be vigilantes took some of my property."

"Fulton County Vigilantes by any chance?" the stranger asked.

"That's what they introduced themselves as," James replied.

"We've dealt with that bunch before," the stranger said.

"What did they take?" Nash asked.

"A rifle that I brought home from the war."

"We were wondering why you left so suddenly," the tall stranger said. "Figured you didn't trust us; under the same circumstances, I might have felt the same way. I assure you that we don't rob Southern people, only rich Yankees."

"I regret losing that rifle. I may need it before I get to Oregon."

The stranger looked down at him. "You want it back?"

"Of course, but how?"

"We know where that bunch hangs out," he said. "Best we wait until after dark, so we can catch them drunk. They'll be over at a nearby tavern, spending what they've took off folks. Union folks are outnumbered around here, so they have to stay low most of the time."

He didn't fancy taking on a group of vigilantes, but he needed that rifle. That made it worth the risk.

Chapter 8

The Night Visitor

L ate in the afternoon, Kate and the children were seated on the front porch when Uncle Lewis' buggy rolled through the gate and stopped. He waved, then pulled his valise out of the buggy and stepped down. Olaf came out from the barn to meet him. "Good day, Mr. Lewis."

"Good day, Olaf."

Kate stood up and walked to the edge of the porch. "How was your trip, Uncle?" she asked.

"Hopefully, what happened will help my case?"

His mood seemed to have improved a bit, giving Kate cause for hope that he might offer an explanation for his actions of late. He greeted the children then walked into the house. Kate followed, hoping for a conversation. He offered none. Instead, he hung up his hat and started for his room.

"Uncle Lewis, can we talk for a moment?"

"Can it wait? I'm rather tired from the trip."

She was stunned for a moment by his sharp retort. But of course, he would be tired after an arduous journey. She felt a little embarrassed—more like ashamed for imposing on him before he had a chance to rest. "Of course. I'll talk to you at supper."

Tired or not, her uncle was still trying to put her off. She and the children were part of his life now; it hurt that he wouldn't share his burdens with them. His actions of late were so out of character from the man she thought she knew. Could she have been wrong about him? That thought had been popping into her mind recently. But she fought any inclination to believe her uncle was not trustworthy. Though his actions of late confused her, even pained she at times, Kate still held to her belief that Uncle Lewis was an honorable man with honest intentions.

With talking to him out of the question, Kate went into the kitchen to help

82

Helga with supper. When the meal was ready and the table set, she knocked on Uncle Lewis's door. "Supper, Uncle." There was no response.

Olaf and the children came to the table; in a few minutes, Uncle Lewis joined them. "There were some men by asking for you, Uncle," Kate said.

His head jerked up. "Who?"

Kate described the dark-haired man and his companions. He listened intently. His facial expression remained calm, but Kate detected a slight shaking of his hand.

"Do you know these men?"

"They are just business associates. Nothing to worry about."

Where was it going to end? She felt helpless. There had to be a way to get him to open up. Maybe another approach would work. "How is the farm doing?" she asked.

"Well, from what Olaf tells me, everything is going as expected. With the new settlers, we're under more pressure, but I feel we can make it."

He didn't seem worried about the farm; that tended to rule out money problems. Bringing the settlers up here had been costly—she had thought maybe financial troubles could be at the root of his worries, but apparently not. Whatever it was, he wasn't going to volunteer anything. The best she could do was keep her eyes and ears open and hope he would let his guard down.

*   *   *

Life at the farm settled back to normal. Olaf and Uncle Lewis spent their days in the fields. Kate helped Helga with the household; all the time, she fretted. Her uncle went through his daily routine, but up close, the worry lines across his brow, the bags under his eyes, and the hint of pain in his eyes, all were signs of a man tormented. This left Kate with a feeling of dread that they were on a course toward some calamity.

Wednesday the following week, Kate found her uncle sitting on the front porch after supper. Drew and Alice were playing in the front yard. Olaf was in the corral next to the barn, teaching James Junior how to ride.

"Uncle Lewis, do you regret living up here so far away from your roots?" she asked.

He looked at her. "I never cared for the aristocracy of the South. I came to have a deep disdain for the landed gentry and their gangs of slaves. The poor whites in the South were not much better off than slaves themselves. In some ways, we were probably worse off because the aristocrats realized their way of life was built on the backs of the blacks. They never felt any need for people like us."

Kate understood what he was saying.

"No, ma'am. I fell in love with this land the first time I saw it. It's wild and untamed, but up here, there is no social snobbery to contend with. I can sit here and look at the mountains all around me and feel totally free. I can envision I'm on top of one of those peaks looking down at everything below me, and it gives me a feeling that I'm on top of the world. At times, it makes you feel you're closer to your maker up here in the high country. You know, the Indians used to call this valley Cop Copi, the place where cottonwoods grow. Every spring, tribes from all around would come here to the valley and have a peaceful get-together, enjoying all the land had to offer. I wouldn't trade what I got here for anything in Tennessee."

Some vestiges of the man she knew were returning. It had been weeks since he had opened up about anything.

"Just look at your father, Walter. He was a good man, but did he ever get anywhere? The war was all about preserving the aristocrats' way of life, the same ones who wouldn't give him or others like him the time of day. Your father lost his store and one of his sons trying to help preserve a way of life that excluded him."

"I experienced some of what you're talking about," Kate said. "The McKanes, especially Martha, were nothing but snobs. Martha just never had any understanding of anyone or anything outside her own social circle. Her husband, Albert, wasn't much better. He was so aloof most of the time; I don't think he realized that some of the people around him even existed."

"Exactly what I was talking about," he said.

"Along with Martha, there was Albert's sister, Mary. I never had any peace of mind when she was around. She criticized everything I did, saying it was the fault of my upbringing. That made my blood boil. My mother and father devoted themselves to the rearing of me and my brothers, so who was she to pass judgment on my upbringing?"

Her uncle's disdain for Southern society struck a nerve with Kate as well. It reminded her of her in-laws—a sore spot for her. She hadn't meant to get so worked up, but it didn't take much encouragement to get her started on the McKanes.

"I remember one time at the plantation. They were getting ready for a visit from one of Albert's business associates. I think he was a banker from Nashville. Anyway, they were making a big fuss. Mary started drilling me about proper behavior around influential people. The thing that really got to me was when she told me I shouldn't mention that my father was a merchant in Clarksville. I really flew off the handle when she said that about my daddy. I replied that my father was a hardworking, honest man, and I had no reason to be ashamed of him. I also told her such actions amounted to nothing but snobbery and that anyone who resorted to such behavior was nothing but a phony."

"Yes. I knew that plantation life wasn't for you the first time I saw you. Every time I saw that place, it reminded me of all the things I dislike about Southern society. The McKanes are typical of what Southern aristocracy is all about. I wanted to take you out of there after the first visit, but I didn't feel it was my place to do so. I was overjoyed when you decided to leave on your own; I hope you don't regret your decision to come up here."

"No. Not at all."

Kate was pushing the truth. It wasn't the decision to leave Tennessee that was raising doubts—it was her uncle's actions of late that worried her. How she hoped his problems wouldn't cause her to regret coming up here.

Uncle Lewis said no more. He excused himself and went into the house. Kate remained on the porch thinking. Was coming up here the best thing for her? The winter had been tough, forcing her to spend most of the time in the house. The children soon became irritated at being confined for long periods of time, adding to the problem. By winter's end, Uncle Lewis's attitude began changing, taking much of the thrill out of spring.

Kate had come up here to put the pain of the past behind and find happiness for her and the children. Perhaps all she had done was trade one set of problems for another. Until Uncle Lewis's woes were behind him, there would be no joy for her. These thoughts plunged her into depression. When darkness fell, she sighed, got up, and went into the house.

*   *   *

For a time, life stayed on a normal course. Uncle Lewis reestablished himself with the children. He whittled a small bird out of pine and gave it to Drew. He would chat with Alice about her doll and pitch horseshoes with James Junior. Often, he would make jokes with the adults. He was becoming more like the man they met in Tennessee, but beneath it all, Kate wondered. Had his problems vanished, or did they lay in wait? Was this just the lull before the storm?

*   *   *

Two weeks after Uncle Lewis's return, Kate was helping Helga in the kitchen. She looked out the window and saw a group of men coming through the meadow toward the house. Two of the men were on horseback, and two more were riding in a wagon. She recognized them. They were from the contingent of settlers that accompanied them from Independence. The passenger in the wagon was Mr. Grigg, their neighbor.

85

Kate went out to welcome them, but from the porch, she saw Olaf and Uncle Lewis come out of the barn. Her uncle greeted the visitors at the edge of the yard. Then, the men all assembled in a group near the fence. She wanted so much to join in the conversation but felt it was not her place. Instead, she would try to eavesdrop and hope the men wouldn't notice.

From the porch, she could only pick up bits and pieces of what was being said. If she moved closer, the men might take notice. It was, after all, men's business. By staying very still, she was able to make out the general drift of the conversation. "What do you know about this Covington fella?" one asked. Her uncle's response was not clear.

In general, they seemed to be talking about an agreement. *The business agreement, was that what they were discussing*? She wondered. Uncle Lewis looked in her direction, making her feel embarrassed—and a little ashamed. But worry trumped shame and embarrassment. Uncle Lewis wouldn't come clean with her, so she would do whatever it took to find out what was at the root of his problem and those of the settlers.

The conversation came to an end. The men started back to where their horses and wagon were waiting. Kate heard her uncle tell them he would continue looking into the matter.

Uncle Lewis watched the men ride away. When they were out of sight, he turned and walked up to the porch.

"I see we had some company," Kate said. "You should have asked them in."

"I don't think they intended their visit to be a social one."

Still not a clue from him about what was happening. The settlers were involved. This man Covington was in the picture that she had already suspected. The business agreement with Covington, the settlers, how did it all fit together?

Kate followed Uncle Lewis into the house; Helga announced supper was ready.

While they were eating, Kate asked, "Uncle Lewis, if there was any serious trouble, you would let me and the children know about it, wouldn't you?"

"Of course, Kate. I'm responsible for you and the children. I'll do whatever has to be done to take care of you."

His answer was somewhat reassuring but not enough. Her concerns lingered.

Uncle Lewis changed the subject. "It looks like we are going to need more help with the spring planting," he said to Olaf.

"Yaw. We are getting behind."

"Part of that was because of the time I spent in Salem. I need to go find us some temporary help. I'll start looking tomorrow. There's usually not much in the way of reliable laborers in La Grande. I might ride over to Pendleton and see if there are any willing workers over there. I should be back in two or three days."

*   *   *

Next morning, Kate was helping Helga with breakfast. Through the kitchen window, she saw Uncle Lewis in the yard with his saddled horse.

"Can't you wait until after breakfast?" she called from the porch.

"I had a quick meal. I want to get an early start," he replied.

Kate watched as he mounted then rode toward the gate. Once in the meadow, he turned in the saddle and waved, then urged his horse into a gallop. When he was out of sight, she turned and went back into the house and got the children up.

When breakfast was over and the dishes washed, Kate went outside to work in the yard. Being a bachelor, her uncle never put much effort into the house and grounds. She took it on herself to spruce up the place. During the cold winter months, she had worked on the inside. With the arrival of spring, her attention turned to the yard.

Helga had planted some flowers around her and Olaf's quarters. Her busy schedule didn't leave time for the main house. Olaf's time was devoted to the farm. That left it up to Kate to beautify the homestead.

She was down on her hands and knees, pulling up dead weeds and grass from around the house, when she glanced toward the meadow. A chill ran down her back. At the edge of the meadow, a man was sitting on a horse staring at the house. From this distance, she couldn't tell much about him except that he was wearing buckskins. He wasn't one of the settlers—of that, she was sure. Maybe an acquaintance of Uncle Lewis? But if that was the case, why didn't he ride on up to the house? Someone up to no good—her fears intensified.

Trembling, Kate got to her feet. The rider, realizing he had been seen, turned his horse and rode toward the road. She watched until he disappeared. *Why was he watching the house?* she wondered. The encounter left her puzzled and scared.

The rest of the morning, she was too jumpy to get much done. Every few minutes, she would pause and look toward the meadow. She saw no further sign of the rider. When Helga came to cook the noon meal, Kate told her about the incident.

"Yaw. Probably just someone passing through. He was sitting out there trying to get up the nerve to ride in and ask for a handout. We get those every now and then."

87

Kate hoped Helga was right. She mentioned it again when Olaf came in for his noon meal. He repeated what his wife had already said. "Just somebody traveling through. I wouldn't worry about it."

Kate tried to take Olaf's and Helga's advice, but the mysterious rider and the actions of her uncle left her with a sense of foreboding as if there was something sinister going on around them. Until she had a better idea about Uncle Lewis' problems, the fears and doubts would not leave her alone.

*   *   *

The next evening after supper, Kate was in her room reading by the light of an oil lamp. The children were in bed, and Uncle Lewis had not returned from his search for laborers. She was reading *The House of Seven Gables*. Weariness overcame her, so she decided to go to sleep. She started to put out the lamp and get into bed. Had the front door been locked? There was so much on her mind; she couldn't remember for sure. She would have to go down and check. Olaf and Helga had retired to their own quarters, leaving her and the children alone in the house.

Kate picked up the lamp and made her way downstairs to the kitchen. The shutters rattled, the bushes outside the house rustled, and the wind was picking up, indicating a storm.

She went into the kitchen and sat the lamp on the table. Kate froze in fear. The lamp light fell on one of the kitchen windows—staring through the glass was a man with a shaggy beard. He watched for a moment, then disappeared into the darkness.

When her paralysis receded, she screamed. James Junior came running down the stairs. "What's wrong, Mama?"

"There was a man looking through the kitchen window," she shrieked. Now, Alice and Drew were scrambling down the stairs.

"I'm going outside to look for him," James Junior said.

"No, you won't," Kate replied. "You stay in here with your brother and sister while I go and get Olaf."

"But he might still be out there."

"I'll have to take that chance. As soon as I get outside, you put the bar back in place."

Before going out, Kate pulled her robe up around her. When she lifted up the heavy wooden bar and stepped outside, tiny dust particles pelted her face. "Put the bar back in place," she yelled to her son.

Kate listened until she heard James Junior put the bar in place, then started across the porch. In the distant sky to the west, there were flashes of lightning. She pulled her robe up around her to ward off the chill carried by wind blowing across the yard. She swallowed, took a deep breath to raise her courage, and then walked down the steps.

The bushes, driven by the wind, swayed over the wooden walkway between the main house and Olaf's and Helga's quarters. The limbs seemed to reach out and grab at her. She jumped at every sound. When a branch from one of the bushes brushed her shoulder, Kate froze. The man staring in the kitchen window was behind her. When she turned and realized it was only a bush, she felt like a child afraid of the dark.

After what seemed like an eternity, Kate reached the front door of Olaf's and Helga's quarters. She knocked frantically.

"What's wrong, missy?" Olaf asked.

Kate trembled as she explained to him about the face in the kitchen window. Olaf got a lantern and walked back to the house with her. He shined the light under the kitchen window.

"Yaw, there was somebody here," Olaf said. "There're fresh boot tracks in the dirt."

He accompanied her to the main house and waited while she got the children, then they spent the night with Olaf and Helga.

*   *   *

Kate waited in the yard the next morning while Olaf followed the mysterious visitor's tracks.

"Well, it looks like someone was camping out just beyond the meadow," Olaf said when he returned. "I think we need to keep a guard around the house from now on."

The rider watching the house, the night prowler, Kate had a sinking feeling they were all related to Uncle Lewis's problems. She had endured enough of this. It was time to quit beating around the bush and demand some answers.

Chapter 9

The Retrieval

Beside the road, they waited for darkness—James and the others. One of the strangers leaned his back against the trunk of an oak tree and entertained himself with a game of solitaire. Nash fried salt pork and brewed some coffee over a small fire. "Too bad we ain't got no ham left," he remarked to no one in particular. The rest lounged about.

How much it was like the war, James thought. Before a battle, he would sit and worry. *Would this be my last battle?* He would wonder. *Or would fate will him to survive one more time?* Just like those times, butterflies flittered around in his stomach—it was the waiting. "Where are we going to find these men?" he asked no one in particular. Talking, experience had taught him, helped ease his mind a bit.

The stranger paused his card game. "They usually hole up at a small tavern just north a ways," he said.

When darkness began settling over the Kentucky countryside, they gathered their gear and got the horses ready.

"The gentlemen we seek should be liquored up good by now," the stranger with the black hat said. "The whiskey will be our ally this evening."

"You expect they'll put up much of a fight?" James asked.

The stranger grinned. "Not much. They won't like the odds."

They mounted and rode single file along a narrow trail. The strangers, James noticed, seemed at home with this sort of thing. They moved through the dark like cats. He, on the other hand, still had left-over jitters from the war. There always seemed to be another battle to fight. Tonight, he was taking up arms to retrieve what was rightly his. But he had taken the rifle from a Union soldier, so maybe he couldn't rightfully call it his. He compromised with his conscience over that issue by reasoning the Henry represented the spoils of war. The vigilantes were just common thieves.

They rode through the dark night until the stranger in the lead stopped his horse. He called out in a low voice; the others gathered around him. "The tavern is just over the hill in front of us. Nash, I think if a couple of your boys went around to the back with my brother and cousin, the rest of us can handle the front. We'll give you a few minutes; then we can come in the front and back at the same time and catch them off guard."

Nash nodded at two of his companions; they broke away into the night with two of the strangers.

It was back to waiting again. For solace, James gripped the handle of his pistol. "They should be in place now," the remaining stranger said a short time later.

They eased up the hill. From below, light from the tavern windows illuminated the horses hitched in front. James swallowed, took a deep breath to steady his nerves.

The stranger motioned for them to follow. "Keep away from the light," he whispered. "Looks like they're having a good time in there, so we'll just walk in the front door. They won't know what we're about until it's too late."

At the bottom of the hill, they dismounted and tied the horses to some small trees a short distance away. Keeping in the dark shadows, they edged up to the tavern. James recognized a spotted mare tied in front as belonging to one of the vigilantes.

The tavern was a long affair with a low roof and a porch that ran the width of the building. Lantern light from inside illuminated the porch. Laughter rang out from the revelers.

The stranger turned to Nash. "Better leave someone to watch the horses while we tend to business inside."

Nash pointed to one of his group; the man stepped back toward the horses.

They held their pistols ready. The stranger stepped up to the door with the others close behind. He turned the knob and gave the door a hard push with his foot. They rushed in, catching the carousing men off guard. The startled patrons stared at the armed intruders; none moved.

Most of the tables were occupied. Behind a makeshift bar of large planks lying across barrels, a fat bartender was drawing whisky from a wooden barrel. He looked at the contingent of armed men, then reached toward a shotgun leaning against the bar. The stranger's pistol being cocked next to his head halted his reach. "Bad choice, my friend."

James recognized several faces among the tavern patrons. The vigilante leader was seated near the door; his companions were seated around the other tables. He didn't see any sign of his rifle.

A large woman with fat cheeks and long, dark hair, wearing a red dress, sat on a stool near the bar. "What cause do you have for bursting into our establishment like this?" the woman demanded.

The stranger pointed at James. "We're just some weary travelers looking for some property that was taken from our friend here. Property that was wrongfully taken by the Union vigilantes of your county."

The vigilante leader stood up. He stumbled, had to grab the table to steady himself. "Rebel thieves, you'll hang for this."

"You may be right about the hanging part," the stranger said. "I may hang someday, but I doubt you'll be present when it happens."

The stranger stood before the revelers and again pointed toward James. "We're looking for a Henry repeating rifle that was taken from this man earlier today. Which one of you gentleman has it?"

The back door opened; the two strangers and Nash's other companions entered. Their entrance was a little late, but it didn't matter. The drunken tavern patrons were in no condition to put up a fight.

The revelers remained silent. The stranger pushed back his hat with the barrel of his pistol. "I'm losing my patience. You gentlemen better start talkin'."

"We ain't got nothing that belongs to any of you," one said.

"We'll see about that." The stranger motioned to James. "Take one of the lanterns outside and look at what they've got in their saddles."

James retrieved one of the lanterns from the bar and stepped out on the porch. He remembered the leader of the vigilantes had been riding a black horse with a white spot on its forehead. He walked along the horses, shining the lantern light on each one. He found the one in question near the end; his Henry was sheathed on the saddle. He grabbed the rifle, stepped back into the tavern, and held it up in the air. "Here it is."

"That's mine," the vigilante leader yelled.

"I don't think so," the stranger replied. "Now that we've got the rifle back, what other valuables you men carrying tonight?"

"Nothin'. We ain't got nothing," one of the men yelled.

"Let's see," the stranger said. He waved his pistol from table to table. "Each one of you men reach into your pockets and empty 'em on the table."

One of the revelers staggered to his feet, brandishing a pistol. "The hell I will!" he yelled. One of the strangers was upon the man before he could fire. The pistol fell to the floor, and the man followed. "The next man that tries something like that will get more than a whack on the head," the stranger said. "For the last time, start emptying those pockets."

"Thievin' rebels, we'll hunt ever'one of you down!" the vigilante leader yelled. "You'll never get far enough from here to escape us."

"You men couldn't find your way out of Fulton County," the stranger replied.

When all the valuables had been collected from the tavern patrons, the stranger turned his attention to the bar. "Let's see what you got in that money box."

"Ain't hardly nothin' in that box," the bartender said. The woman nodded her head in agreement.

"With the profits you make from this watered-down whisky; you bound to have a small fortune in there. Now open it up."

The barkeeper hesitated; the stranger waved his pistol. That convinced him to comply. He set the box on the bar. Then, his glance wandered to the shotgun.

"You're entertaining dangerous thoughts, my friend," the stranger said. He looked back at the others. "One of you boys get that scattergun before our friend does a stupid thing. Let's take temptation out of his way."

One of Nash's companions walked behind the bar and picked up the shotgun.

"Gentlemen, it's been a pleasure doing business with you," the stranger said. "We're going to leave you now, but we're going to take your horses and weapons with us. We'll leave the horses a few miles from here, and I guess we'll keep the weapons. Time you gents catch up with your horses; we'll be nothing but a memory."

The stranger collected the cash box, and then they went through the tavern picking up the men's weapons. "Nash, I suggest that you and some of your boys go out and take charge of these gentlemen's horses. We'll be out shortly."

Nash gathered two of his companions, and they disappeared out the front door. The stranger handed the cash box to one of his companions. Then he pointed his pistol at the whisky barrel behind the bar.

"Damned Yankee profiteers," he shouted. He fired into the barrel. It shattered, spilling whisky all over the floor. "I detest cheap liquor."

"You men stay put until we're gone. I'll be watching the door. If anyone steps out, he'll get shot." The stranger turned and hurried to the door with the rest of them following.

Nash and the others were waiting with the tavern patron's horses in hand. With the extra horses in tow, they collected their own mounts and rode off into the night. Several miles down the road, they released the vigilante's horses and rode until daybreak.

*   *   *

The tavern raid haunted James—the night had not gone to his liking. Of course, he appreciated having the Henry back. But robbing people—that was another matter. It left him feeling guilty and worried. Now, they might all be wanted men.

The older stranger riding next to James seemed to pick up on his concern. "They likely stole that stuff from some other poor souls," he said. "It wasn't really their property to begin with. These scoundrels have been robbing poor folks for some time now; tonight, they got some of what they deserve in return."

This didn't relieve James much. He had come west to look for his wife and children, not to become a highwayman.

Shortly after daybreak, they found a grove of locust trees back from the road. The night of hard riding left them weary; they stopped and made camp. Nash started a fire. The strangers sorted out the money and other valuables taken from the tavern. There was cash, an assortment of pistols, a few watches, and a large jackknife.

"There's nearly two hundred dollars in cash and goods here," the older stranger said. "That's a good night's work. You gentlemen helped earn it, so we'll split it here and now."

"The rifle was my share," James said. He didn't feel entitled to any of the rest, didn't want it, even if it came from crooked vigilantes that had robbed him.

"If that's your pleasure," the stranger said.

The rest of them divided the spoils of the tavern raid. Afterward, Nash fried a skillet of bacon and brewed a pot of coffee.

"The Mississippi is just a mile west of here," one of the strangers said. "After we get a little sleep, we'll be riding on south."

"We'll be heading on down to the Indian Nations," Nash said. "Once we get in Missouri, we'll head straight west."

"I'll be making my way up to Independence," James said.

"We've been up in Missouri," one of the strangers said. "There's plenty of trouble there; the state militia is trying to round up those people they blame for the ruckus during the war. You'd be advised to watch your step until you get out of there."

James nodded. He intended to do just that.

After eating, James got out his bedroll. After a short sleep, he awoke to find the strangers gone and Nash and the others saddling their horses. Seeing James was awake, Nash said, "The best thing to do is ride up to Cairo where there's a bridge across the river."

James, still shaken by the tavern incident, got up and saddled his horse. For the moment, all he wanted was to be out of Kentucky. He took one last look around, then mounted and rode away with Nash and the others.

Chapter 10

The Business Deal

The shaggy beard, the terrifying face—the images would not leave Kate's mind. The man had only been in the window for a brief moment, but it was enough. Each time she remembered the encounter, a chill went down her spine.

The next morning, she tried to clean the house, but she couldn't focus on her task. Worry—pure dread kept her from doing anything. She would start sweeping the floor, stop, lean on the handle, and fret. The doubts plagued her. Again, she was questioning her decision to come to Oregon. She was starting to reach the conclusion she and the children were better off with their roots. The war was over; things would get better in the South when the Union troops left. But her in-laws would still be there, and her husband would not. For the entire morning, she brooded, torn over what she should do.

She was helping Helga with the noon meal when Alice yelled from the front yard. "Uncle Lewis is coming!"

She dried her hands and stepped out on the porch. She could see Uncle Lewis riding across the meadow on the white mare followed by two men in a wagon.

They rode through the gate and stopped in front of the house. Uncle Lewis dismounted and walked to the porch; the two men remained in the wagon.

"Kate, I found some hands to help us."

"That's good news, Uncle."

From their appearances, it seemed prosperity had passed the two men by. The driver was a young man wearing a baggy cotton shirt and pants. There was a dirty bandanna around his neck and a sweat-stained hat on his head that might have once been white. The passenger was a teenage boy with a toothy grin, wearing baggy clothes and a black hat with part of the brim missing.

Kate knew it wasn't her place to question her uncle's judgment, but these two men didn't look like reliable help. Uncle Lewis motioned to the men. The driver snapped the reins, and the wagon lurched forward toward the barn. Olaf came out of the barn and took the white mare.

"Where did you find them, Uncle?"

"They were living in a shack just outside of La Grande. Their folks came up the Oregon Trail planning to go to the coast, but their luck ran out in La Grande. Their team took sick and died. That left them stuck here with very little to live on. Their daddy agreed to let them work for us. I bought them that team as partial payment for their services."

"That's sad." Her hasty judgment of the young men now left her feeling a bit ashamed.

Helga announced dinner was ready. Kate yelled for everyone to come in for the noon meal. Drew and Alice came from the backyard, and Olaf and James Junior came from the corral. The two new arrivals came up from the barn and stood at the edge of the yard.

"Come in and eat," Kate yelled.

The young men were poor in the social graces as well. They looked around, then walked slowly up to the porch and stood with sheepish looks on their faces. "Come on in," Kate said. "Don't be bashful."

They all sat down at the table. Helga served fried chicken and thick gravy, topped off with cherry pie. The new hands held back at first, but Helga would have none of it. "Eat up," she urged. She had no tolerance for hunger and would not let anyone leave her table on an empty stomach. At her urging, the young men put aside their shyness and filled their plates. They dug into the food without regard for table manners, causing the children to stare. But the adults, in part out of pity, let it be.

Kate had not yet told her uncle about the night visitor. "Uncle Lewis, we had some trouble recently."

He looked up. Apprehension was in his eyes. "What kind of trouble?"

Kate explained about the prowler and the tracks Olaf followed across the meadow.

"That is disturbing. We better start keeping a closer eye on the house. The boys can take turns staying here and keeping watch while the rest of us men are in the fields."

Of course, the farm work had to go on—Kate understood that. But leaving the safety of the house up to these young men, mere boys actually, that didn't provide her with much assurance.

With Uncle Lewis back, Kate hoped life would get back to normal. It was not to be.

*   *   *

The next evening, they were relaxing on the porch. Kate was talking to Helga about a shirt she was sewing for Drew. The children were playing in the backyard. Uncle Lewis was discussing spring grain planting with Olaf. He paused and looked toward the meadow. "Olaf, you better go and get your scattergun while I get my rifle."

"What's the matter?" Kate asked.

"Just a precaution. There's some riders coming across the meadow. It's best to be cautious until we see what their intentions are."

Uncle Lewis went into the house, got his rifle, and stepped back out on the porch.

Kate walked down to the end of the porch and watched the riders approach. A chill ran down her spine. The dark-haired man and his companions had returned; just like last time, they were armed to the teeth. They rode single file through the gate into the yard.

Uncle Lewis sat back down in his chair with the rifle across his lap. "What do you want here, Palmer?" he asked.

The dark-haired man stopped his horse just beyond the porch. He had a cold, evil look on his face. "We were just wondering when you was going to get up enough nerve to come back home, Harrington," Palmer said.

"Go back to your employer and tell him I'm not afraid of his threats," Uncle Lewis said.

"You better think about that, Harrington. You know what you have to do and what will happen if you don't."

Uncle Lewis took the rifle in hand and stood up from his chair. "I'm going to tell you something, Palmer. You and your gang of cutthroats can go back to California, where you came from. The problem here is between Covington and me. I don't want or need your gang of saddle bums buttin' in."

Palmer's eyes narrowed. His hand slid down toward the pistol he was carrying. "You listen to me, Harrington." His voice had a chilling tone. "I don't take orders or threats from the likes of you or that bunch of dirt farmers you brought up here. I never take a threat from any man, but I can give you the names of plenty who tried."

Kate looked on in horror—her heart was pounding against her chest, and her legs trembled. Palmer and his companions now all had their hands on their pistols. Were they going to be shot down here on their own porch? If there had ever been any doubt concerning the magnitude of her uncle's problems, it could now be put to rest.

Uncle Lewis stood in front of the armed men. Kate hoped his good senses wouldn't allow him to act foolishly. She and Helga were in the line of fire. And oh my God! The children were in the backyard.

97

Uncle Lewis and Palmer glared at each other. Then Olaf suddenly stepped out from behind the house, shotgun in hand. "Best get your hands from those guns. This scattergun is mighty nasty at this range."

Palmer looked at the shotgun pointing at him, then at Uncle Lewis. After an agonizing moment, he pulled his hand away from his pistol and motioned for the others to do the same. "All right, Harrington, you got lucky this time, but don't count on it again."

Palmer turned his horse and rode back out the gate with the rest of his group following. Uncle Lewis stood with the rest of them and watched Palmer and his companions ride across the meadow toward the road.

Kate turned to her uncle and said, "Uncle Lewis, it seems that our lives are in danger, so don't put me off again. I deserve to know what's going on here. All of us do."

Lewis leaned his rifle against the house and sat down; he motioned for Kate to do the same. "You're right, Kate. I didn't have any right to keep you in the dark about all this. I hoped it would be resolved without going this far."

He leaned back in his chair and closed his eyes like he was lost in thought. When he opened them again, he let out a deep sigh. "You remember me telling you about John McDonald, the botanist from Scotland?"

"Yes. I remember you talking about him."

"Well, after we reached a place where we could put some of our ideas to work, we needed to find people willing to help us. Only a handful of the people living here at that time had expressed any interest in our plan. That's when I made the decision to go back to Missouri and try to find more people willing to settle up here. There were still a few sections of homestead land in the area."

"That sounds reasonable," Kate said. He was rehashing what he had told her before, but she listened patiently.

"We needed a number of things if we were going to be successful with our venture. The biggest problem is getting our crops to market. There's a large potential market to the west in places like Portland and Salem and the mines to the south, but that requires shipping. There is only one freight hauler in the area with enough wagons and teams to handle the amount of cargo we're talking about. That line is owned by E. G. Covington."

"That all seems like a legitimate business. Why all the problems?"

"It is a legitimate idea. We approached Covington about the idea, and at first, he seemed enthused about it. He even introduced us to some other businessmen from Portland and Salem who were also interested. We put together an organization called the Northeast Oregon Agricultural Cooperative."

"That was the charter I saw with your papers."

"Yes. Before I left for Missouri, everything seemed to be in order. We had all agreed the new settlers would require help in getting started, so John and I would supply them with seed and farming supplies for the first three years. Covington agreed to provide lower freight rates for the first two years as well. At that time, it seemed we had a plan that everyone would benefit from. I knew there would be people down south who would jump at a chance to get a new start."

"And you found plenty."

"That I did. Before I left, we put together an agreement each of the settlers would sign when they arrived. This agreement covered the things I mentioned concerning freight requirements and rates. After they were established, Harrington Farms would provide seed stock and other essentials at a fair price, and we would continue to develop new crops as well. That was the plan. After the business got established, we would sell seed stock, Covington would have the freight business, and the new farmers would have a market for their crops."

"That all sounds like a good plan," Kate said. "What's the cause of all the threats and violence?"

Lewis rubbed his temples as if he was trying to ward off a headache. "Greed. While I was away, some things happened. John McDonald died, and his son returned to Scotland, leaving me with the responsibility for the entire operation, but the biggest problem has turned out to be Covington."

"I've met Mr. Covington. What's he up to?"

"Grabbing these people's land is what it amounts to. There's a provision in the homestead law that allows settlers to buy their land after they have been on it for fourteen months. That way, they don't have to wait five years and make all the improvements before getting the title. He uses that as a lure. Covington has another agreement that he's trying to get them to sign, one that will leave them indebted to him so he can take their land."

"How can he do that?"

"Most of these people have no money. His agreement offers them shipping payments at prices he sets and binds them to his services. And he is promising them loans to buy their land after fourteen months. Even if they choose not to buy at fourteen months, they will still be heavily indebted to him when they get their land due to the high freight costs. They won't be able to pay him and will be forced to sell their land, which he will be able to buy. For those who do accept his loan to buy their land, he will hold a mortgage they can't pay, and he can foreclose on them. Since early this spring, he has been going around with this new agreement, trying to get the new settlers to sign it, and some have."

Kate shook her head. "Why is he doing this?"

"Like I said—greed. He recognizes this area has potential, just like what happened in the Willamette Valley; this will put him in a position to own a

99

good portion of it. To top it off, there is now talk of a railroad coming through here. The War Department has sent out a survey party to find a route for a railroad. It seems the route they are looking at will go through some of the homestead lands."

"He's a wealthy man. Why does he have to resort to taking land away from other people?"

"With public land, ownership can only be acquired by homesteading. There is a limit of one hundred sixty acres per homesteader, and it is only available to people who don't currently own any land. This gives Covington a way to get around the laws and grab a good portion of this area. It means money and power to him, and it looks like he'll stop at nothing to get it."

"I agree it sounds like nothing but pure greed. How can he resort to taking what little these poor people have? The man must have no conscience."

"That he doesn't. "

"What do you plan to do, Uncle?"

Uncle Lewis sighed. "I'm afraid some of the settlers have already signed or made their mark on the agreements with Covington. I'm trying to get word out to the other settlers so they won't make the same mistake, but there's still a problem."

"What's that?"

"Freight. The settlers don't have any way to market their crops without Covington. They'll still wind up broke and lose their land."

The magnitude of her uncle's problems was hitting home. "So far, only a few of them have agreed to Covington's scheme," he said. "Hopefully, I can warn the rest so they won't make the same mistake. He's working on the others, and I'm afraid soon he'll have most of them on the hook. I've got people out all over the valley explaining what Covington is trying to do, but I'm afraid some of them won't listen. The war took just about everything these people had. The prospect of owning their own land is very appealing."

"I didn't realize things were so bad."

"Yes. I regret I didn't tell you sooner, but I didn't want to worry you. My mind has been on this constantly ever since I found out about it. They're going after me also. They tried to contest the title to my land as well; that's why I had to make the trip to Salem. I needed a way to fight back."

"How can they question the validity of your title?"

"It seems the government put some of this land up for sale before they had legally acquired it from the Indian owners. They tried to challenge it on those grounds, but they failed. The courts have already upheld these titles. That's also why Duncan Pratt came to the house that day. He was one of the original surveyors. I wanted to check the records to make sure my property was within the approved boundaries. They failed in their legal attempts, so now they're resorting to threats to try and force me out. If I go, the settlers won't have anyone to support them, and they'll likely go under."

"It's hard to believe the settlers would agree to Covington's terms."

"Like I said, these people have been left with nothing, so the idea of owning their own land clouds their judgment. They jumped at the proposal without realizing what they were doing. Many of these people can't read or write, so they're easily fooled. They made their mark on the paper, believing everything was okay."

"Have you found a way to fight back?"

"I'm still working on it, but it's a tough battle. John and I made a mistake with the freight agreements. At the time, we thought having the settlers make individual freight agreements would allow us more flexibility. We were wrong. It gave Covington and edge. I could sever my ties with him, but that would leave us without a way to market our crops. Most of the settlers don't own any transportation. Unless we find another way to get our crops to market without using Covington's services, then our survival is in question. The freight agreements will destroy the settlers and leave us in peril as well. I've tried talking to the other freight owners, but they don't have the teams and wagons to take on something like this. I'm giving the matter most of my attention, but now my only chance is to stop as many of the settlers as possible from signing the new agreements, and then I have to find another freight source."

"It's your dream, Uncle," Kate said.

"I know, but it's going to turn into a nightmare if I don't find a way out of this. I've thought of starting my own freight line. I think that's what worries Covington the most and why he wants me out of the way. That and the fact the rest of the settlers might listen to me and not sign his agreement."

"You'll come up with something to stop this greedy scheme."

"It'll have to be soon. Covington is pressing the others for an agreement. That's why the settlers came to me that day. They had heard there were problems with Covington, and they wanted to know what to do. I'm thinking about calling a meeting and trying to convince them before it's too late. That also makes Covington nervous, and it's why he's sending Palmer and his henchmen out to scare me. It's also why some of his bunch was hanging around the house."

Pity for her uncle overrode Kate's anger at him for keeping her in the dark. What he was attempting was a good thing, an honorable thing. Now, it was falling apart before his eyes.

"There's something else that worries me," he said.

"What's that?"

"Some of the settlers may think I'm to blame for this. I was the one that talked them into coming up here. That may lead them to believe I'm in on this with Covington."

"Surely, no one would think that of you."

"Well, Covington is threatening to do that very thing. He's threatening to tell the settlers I was the one who wanted to swindle them; some might believe him."

"I just can't believe anyone would take Covington's word about this."

"I don't know, Kate," he said in a low voice. "People are easily swayed by a good story. I encouraged them to get into this. I was careless by getting Covington involved and by not keeping a closer eye on what he was asking people to sign; in a way, I am partially to blame."

"Don't feel that way, Uncle. You did your best, and we'll stand behind you no matter what happens. We're part of your life, and you are part of ours. We'll defend you to the bitter end."

"I see that you've got some of that Harrington spunk. I appreciate your support, and I'm sorry I didn't let you in from the first. I just never realized how far they would go with this."

"Uncle Lewis, you helped me escape an unhappy life in Tennessee, and I'm grateful for that. When it comes to danger, remember we lived through much of the war. We left of our own free will; we will share the hardships and risks of this place. The only thing I ask, in fact, I demand, is that you don't keep me in the dark from now on."

"You've got my word on it."

Uncle Lewis sighed deeply. When he stood up, Kate could see the worry in his face. She wished there was more she could do. Seeing the state, he was in filled her with sadness. His life, his dreams were in jeopardy. Not only did he have business problems to worry about, there were her and the children. It was such a heavy burden for him to carry.

*   *   *

When darkness fell, Kate was still sitting on the porch, feeling the weight of her uncle's problems on her shoulders. She sat there until the cool night air drove her in. After checking on the children, she went to her room. In front of the mirror, tears started forming in her eyes. So much had gone wrong in her life. James was gone, and there was danger here in Oregon; would there ever be peace in her life again?

*   *   *

The next morning, during breakfast, Uncle Lewis asked Kate to accompany him to see the sheriff in La Grande. "Likely won't do much good, but I want him to know about the problems we're having."

Kate helped with the dishes then left the children in Helga's care. Uncle Lewis was waiting in the front yard with the wagon. He got down and helped her up, and they got on their way. A few fleecy white clouds hung from a bright blue sky. Colorful wildflowers were sprinkled about the meadow. Insects buzzed among the plants. Overhead, a large eagle was circling; its sharp eyes focused on the ground.

Uncle Lewis pointed at the bird. "That's always an amazing sight," he said. "It can float along on the air currents until it finds what it wants."

"It certainly is," Kate replied. "If only life were that easy for people."

Uncle Lewis nodded. The road had dried. Kate kept her hand over her face to keep back the dust stirred up by the wagon wheels and the horses. Just up the road, they met a group of men riding single file. Her uncle raised his hand in greeting, and the lead rider did likewise. "You know them?" Kate asked.

"They're from a cattle operation up on Catherine Creek. They aren't overly friendly to those of us who till the soil, but so far, we've managed to tolerate each other."

In La Grande, Uncle Lewis stopped the wagon at the courthouse. He tied the reins to a hitching rail before helping Kate down. At the entrance, he held the front door open for her. "The courthouse is on the second floor," he explained.

"What's the first floor used for?" she asked.

"Newspaper offices. On one side is a paper that caters to the Democrats in this area. On the other side is a paper that represents the Republican point of view. Around here, you can get both sides of the story, or at least each side's version of the story."

An unusual arrangement, Kate thought.

A long hallway ran the width of the first floor. On the right was a door with a sign reading GRANDE RONDE SENTINEL. Across the hall was another door with a sign reading BLUE MOUNTAIN TIMES.

A young man came out of the Times office. He was thin, almost frail, wearing a black bow tie, striped gray suit, and horn-rimmed glasses not typical of a local resident. "Mr. Harrington," the man said.

"Morning, Howard."

The young man nodded, then made his way down the hallway to the door.

"Who was that?" Kate asked.

"Howard Klaspell, a newspaper man from back east. He came out here two years ago to make a name for himself here on the frontier."

103

They took the stairs to the second floor. A door at the top opened into the small suite of county offices. In a narrow hallway past a door labeled County Court of Union County was the county sheriff's office. A small sign on the door read:

Avery Benton - Union County Sheriff

Inside the cramped office, the sheriff was sitting behind a makeshift desk piled high with papers. In one corner was a pot-bellied stove with a coffee pot sitting on top. In the rear were four empty jail cells.

The sheriff was a short, balding man with a ruddy complexion and a sour disposition. Annoyance was written across his face as he watched Kate and Uncle Lewis enter the office. "You folks have some business with me?"

"Yes, we do," Uncle Lewis said. "We're having problems with prowlers around our farm."

"Prowlers!"

Uncle Lewis explained about the rider Kate saw watching the house and the man looking in the window. To her surprise, he failed to mention the riders from the previous day.

The sheriff listened until Uncle Lewis finished talking. The annoyance remained on his face. "I believe your farm is located out toward the west side of the valley. You should realize this is a frontier settlement. People are always passing through here. What you probably saw was some traveler passing by your place heading somewhere else. I don't have enough deputies to patrol this entire county. We do well to keep the peace here in town. I can't do much about what goes on around your place that is unless it gets more serious."

"Well, when folks come around scaring people, that is serious to me," Uncle Lewis said.

"To you, that may be, but there are more important things I have to worry about."

They pressed their case to the sheriff, but it fell on deaf ears. Feeling exasperation at getting nowhere with the lawman, they left the office and went back downstairs.

"It seems the law doesn't extend much beyond the boundaries of the town," Kate said.

"There's more to it than that. E. G. Covington is a local businessman and has considerable influence. He's probably already talked to the sheriff about the problems between him and me. It's obvious which side he's on."

"What are you going to do, Uncle?"

"I don't see anything else to do except get all the settlers together and explain everything. I'll give them a true account of what happened. Some have heard it already, but now it's time for all of them to know. It looks like that's the only chance I have to stop Covington."

"I hope it works. One more thing, Uncle, why didn't you tell the sheriff about the men who came to the house and made threats against you?"

"Wasn't any need. The sheriff had no intention of acting on our complaints. I don't know where Palmer is hiding out, so it wouldn't do any good."

Uncle Lewis bought a slab of bacon, salt, and flour. While he was buying supplies, Kate looked at dresses in the emporium. There was nothing that interested her among the store's meager selections.

They started home. Uncle Lewis was silent for most of the return trip. Kate left him to his thoughts.

When they were close to home, Kate tried to comfort him by saying, "Don't worry, Uncle. Things will work out."

"I hope so, Kate, but these are greedy and ruthless men that I'm up against."

"Greedy men like Covington can be beaten."

Uncle Lewis stared straight ahead at the horses and said nothing.

Chapter 11

Mississippi Crossing

James couldn't get the notion that they were all now wanted men out of his head as he rode west with Nash and his men. Word of the tavern raid had probably spread by now. He imagined vigilantes, militia, the local lawmen, and Union authorities all hot on their trail. He periodically looked over his shoulder and down the road ahead, expecting at any moment to be waylaid by angry men itching to hang all of them. They struck the banks of the Mississippi and rode upstream; his nerves were raw from worry.

"You think we'll find any Yank soldiers around Cairo?" James asked Nash.

"Could be, but this is a Union state, so maybe they won't be so concerned about it," Nash replied. "'Sides, the war is over."

"I know, but some of the Yanks don't seem to realize it."

Every time James looked at Nash and those with him, his irritation grew. Those damn gray uniforms—they were a sure invitation to trouble. The last thing they needed right now was the attention of the Union authorities; the sight of those uniforms would do just that. Why didn't they have sense enough to get some more suitable clothes?

Paddleboats, clouds of black smoke belching from the smoke stacks, churned their way downstream. On the decks of some were men elegantly dressed in expensive wool suits and ladies in velvet dresses carrying brightly colored parasols?

"Damn Yankee opportunists on their way south," Nash said. "They can't wait to get down there and line their pockets. Profiteering bastards, the whole lot."

"Taking advantage of folks who've already lost most everything they had," James replied.

They rode around Wickliffe, crossed into Illinois, and reached the edge of Cairo in late afternoon.

"I'm thinking maybe one of us should go over and check on the bridge," Nash said. "In these reb uniforms, we kinda stand out. If you're willing, me and the boys will set up a camp here and wait for you to get back. That willow thicket over there looks like a good place."

James agreed. The less Nash and the others were seen, the better. He rode along the river bank toward Cairo, trying to stay out of sight as much as possible. Along a row of warehouses, a steamboat was docked, taking on cargo. Laborers, the sun glistening off their sweaty, tanned backs, pushed heavy barrels up the steep gang plank. More profit for folks from the north, he surmised.

He expected a bridge just past the warehouses but didn't find one. Where was it? *Had Nash been mistaken about a bridge?* he wondered. As he was about to turn back, James saw a column of Union soldiers approaching. The worst bit of luck: perhaps they were aware of the tavern raid. No matter it was too late to hide. He urged his horse off the road and hoped the troops would pass.

The young lieutenant in the lead glanced at him as he passed. A couple of enlisted men did the same. They showed no interest in him.

After the last soldier had passed, James watched until the troop column was out of sight. Encountering Union soldiers inspired him to look anew for the bridge. This was dangerous country. Sooner or later, word of the tavern confrontation would be out. It was to their advantage to be out of this country when that happened. Another mile up the river, and there it was; the wooden trestle stood highlighted against the setting sun. He rode up to the bridge, found there was no one about.

Now, he had to round up Nash and the others and take their leave. Tonight after dark would be the best time. He rode back south past the streamer still loading at the dock. It was dark when he reached the thicket.

James expected to see a campfire in the thicket, but it was pitch dark. Feeling uneasy, he dismounted and tied the reins to one of the trees. With his pistol in hand, he eased his way through the thicket. There was no sign of Nash or his companions. Now the question was, had they abandoned him, or was there a more sinister reason for them not being here? "Don't move!" The voice came from behind.

James could not see anyone. He heard the voice again.

"Who are you?"

This time he recognized the voice. It was Nash.

"It's me, James. Why are you hiding back there in the dark?"

Figures emerged out of the shadows—Nash and his companions. "Shortly after you left, there was a group of riders by here," Nash said. "A couple of them looked like men we saw at the tavern last night. Damn scary, I tell you. We put out the fire and hid back here in the woods. There was a bunch of them all in a foul mood, ready to hang somebody."

"I found the bridge. I think it best we get across tonight. Once we're in Missouri, I hope these folks here in Kentucky will forget about us."

"I reckon you're right, but we gotta be careful. That bunch is still out there somewhere."

Nash and his companions retrieved their horses from the woods. In the dim light of a partial moon, they followed the river. Behind every tree and bush, imaginary Kentucky Vigilantes were lying in wait. For comfort, James would reach down and grasp the handle of his pistol, pointless since, in the dark, he couldn't see anything to shoot.

The whistle of a steamship bellowed, startling them. James let his nerves settle, then checked that the others were still with him.

They rode past the now darkened warehouses and the deserted pier.

The bridge trestle appeared against the backdrop of the night sky. They rode up and found it deserted.

The horses were skittish about the bridge. They urged the horses until they were up on the wooden planks. The dull clump, clump, clump of their hooves resonated in the night air. Aside from the noise of the horses, it was eerily quiet, too much for James's liking. Something was amiss. By the end of the bridge, he had a lump up in his throat. He turned around. Shadowy figures of the others were riding single file behind him. They followed him down from the bridge onto a muddy road.

At last, they were across the river. There turned out to be no time for celebration. A voice sprang out of the darkness: "Where you fellas off to this evening?"

They started to reach for their pistols; the voice yelled out again. "I wouldn't do that if I was you. There's twenty guns pointed at you."

A rider emerged from the dark shadows; several more joined him. One of them lit a lantern and handed it to the one in front. Some of the light fell on Nash and his companions. "Rebel uniforms. You planning to fight the war some more here in Missouri?"

"Naw. We was just planning to pass through Missouri on our way somewhere else," Nash said.

"Is that a fact?"

From the lantern light, James was able to get a look at the man holding the lantern. He had a short, dark beard and a wide face with a small scar on one cheek. His white hat had a blue insignia on the front. On the shoulders of his blue tunic, he wore the twin bar insignia of a captain. "I'm Captain Roy Hooks, Eleventh Missouri Militia," he said.

"James McKane, late of the Confederate army, but carrying a full pardon and oath of loyalty in my pocket."

The captain spit a wad of tobacco on the ground. "Man might wonder about your loyalty if you ride around with men still wearing gray."

"I assure you, sir, none of us had any intention of carrying out any aggression in your state," Nash said.

"That's a comforting bit of news," the captain said, "seein' as how we still got a bunch of lowlifes running around, causing havoc. Some of them ride across the bridge into Kentucky and Illinois when things get a little hot over here. That wouldn't concern you fellas now, would it?"

"No, sir," James replied.

"That's a mighty fine bit of news as well," the captain said. "The governor decided we should stop suspicious folks from coming over here into Missouri. We're supposed to arrest those known or suspected of having committed unlawful acts here and to turn back those who look suspicious. You fellas look suspicious to me, wearing those gray uniforms and all."

James silently cursed Nash and the others. Their gray uniforms were putting them in jeopardy.

"I just told you, Captain, me and the boys are just passing through on our way down to the Nations," Nash said.

"That's what you say. Trouble is, I don't know what you're gonna do once you get out of sight. You fellas in them gray uniforms ride up here to the light one at a time and let me see if you're anyone I know."

The captain completed his inspection. "I ain't ever seen any of you before, but there were some gentlemen by here just before dark. They were from down in Kentucky. They were looking for a bunch who robbed some people in a tavern over there last night. As it turns out, some of those robbers were wearing gray uniforms. Not only that, there were three gunmen with them that are quite well known here in Missouri. You fellas wouldn't happen to be part of that bunch, would you?"

The captain's question left James in a dilemma. He knew who they were. Lying would gain them nothing. "We were with the group that robbed those folks over in Kentucky," he said.

Nash let out a start.

"There was a reason behind that," James added. "That same bunch robbed us earlier in the day. We were just trying to get our property back."

The captain spat on the ground. "Is zat so? Was the other three riding with you?"

"There were three men that we met on the road. They never told us their names. They were the ones that took the other folks' valuables in the tavern. The rest of us just wanted our own property back." A stretch of the truth: would it be convincing?

"I wouldn't give a jar of spit for the Fulton County Vigilantes. They're good at filling their own pockets and not much else, but that leaves me in a bit of a spot. I don't care much what you folks did over in Kentucky, but I have to care about what you do here in Missouri."

"We just plan to pass on through," James said.

The captain shined his lantern in James's face. "Let me see them papers you say you got."

James got out the papers and handed them to the captain. He scanned them in the lantern light and gave them back.

"I reckon I'm gonna let you men ride on out of here, but there's a catch. If I find any of you in them gray uniforms again, you'll be arrested. If I catch any of you breaking the law here in this state, I'll hang you on the spot. That clear to all of you?"

"Yes, sir, Captain," James replied.

"Man who'll admit to what you did is either an honest man or a pure fool," the captain said. "The whole lot of you get on out of here before I change my mind, haul you back over the bridge, and turn you over to those Kentucky vigilantes."

Whatever fate had intervened on their behalf, James felt grateful.

When they had some distance between them and the militia, Nash rode up beside James. "I reckon that took some quick thinking," he said. "I don't know how I would have done it. I was just sittin' there sweatin', not knowing what to do."

"It was a long shot," James replied. "That captain already knew who we were, so lying wouldn't have done any good."

"I have to tell you, I had my hand on my pistol ready to make a fight of it if they tried to arrest us or send us back over the river," Nash said.

A foolish thought was all James could conclude. They would have been killed or locked up to await a hangman's rope.

Anxious to be away from the Missouri Militia, they rode until midnight. By then, men and horses were exhausted. They camped near the road and tried to get some rest.

James curled up in his blankets under a small tree. Near morning, his light sleep was disturbed by movement near his bed. In the darkness, he could make out the outline of a man near his saddlebags. He thanked the good sense that compelled him to place his gold and other valuables underneath his blankets. His hand grasped the pistol. "You looking for something, Nash?"

"Now, don't take it personal. Me and the boys were just getting ready to leave, and we're traveling kinda light. We just wanted something to tide us over until we get down to the Nations. What we got from that tavern didn't

110

amount to much. The other fellas got most of what was valuable."

"Well now, Nash, I don't mind sharing with fellow comrades in arms, but stealin' that's a different matter. A man that steals from his friends ain't much of a man."

"I reckon you're right, James. I feel plumb ashamed of myself. I and the boys will ride on now. No hard feelings."

Nash moved toward his companions, who were waiting nearby. James reached into his pocket and pulled out a couple of gold coins. "You men use this gold to buy some decent clothes. You're gonna get arrested running around in them gray rags."

Nash walked back over and took the money. "That's mighty generous of you, helping a man that just tried to steal from you."

"These are desperate times, Nash. They make men do things they wouldn't ordinarily resort to. You folks, be careful out there."

"We plan to."

In the early dawn, James watched as Nash and his companions rode away and disappeared in the faint light. It troubled him that after all they had been through, Nash had tried to steal from him. Well, that was that. It was unlikely he would ever see them again. What's done is done. They had helped get the Henry back from the vigilantes; he owed them for that.

James had a breakfast of bacon and coffee. The sun was rising in the east when he mounted and started down the road.

The prairie country was sparsely populated. *Fewer people, less trouble,* he figured. With the Union in control, anyone associated with the Confederacy was in a predicament. They were viewed with distrust by the Federals. Only when he was further away from the South would the situation improve. And Oregon seemed so far away.

Chapter 12

The Disappearance

To keep her mind off the problems faced by Uncle Lewis, Kate spruced up the house. She worked with vigor, but thoughts of her uncle and his dilemma kept creeping into her mind. What was going to happen if he didn't find a way to thwart Covington's scheme? Could these problems with Covington impact her and the children? Worry was with her constantly.

Now, one of the hired hands remained behind at the house each day. *What good would it do*? Kate wondered. Neither of the boys seemed capable of dealing with ruthless men like Palmer and his gang.

One morning, Uncle Lewis remained behind after Olaf and the other hired hand left for the fields. Kate found him sitting on the settee in the front room, going through a stack of papers.

"Problems, Uncle?"

He looked up. "I've got some visitors coming out today." He turned back to his papers, a signal that he had nothing further to say.

Later in the morning, a buggy pulled into the yard. Uncle Lewis went out to greet the visitors. The driver of the buggy was wearing a black bowler hat and a black suit, carrying a valise. His companion was the young newspaperman Kate had met at the courthouse.

Uncle Lewis greeted the two men. After exchanging pleasantries in the front yard, they walked into the house. Her uncle introduced the older man as Elliot Parkwood, an attorney from La Grande. After the introductions, they seated themselves on the settee, and the attorney took some papers from his valise. Kate's curiosity arose. She stood on the other side of the room, trying to be inconspicuous. With an interest of her own in what was going on, she hoped the men wouldn't mind her listening in on the conversation. Uncle Lewis was so engrossed with his visitors; he took no notice of her.

"I've been going over what you told me about the agreement between

112

your organization and E. G. Covington," Parkwood said. "I'm sorry to say I can't find anything in the agreement that constitutes illegal action under the laws of this state. As you know, Oregon only became a state in 1859. We've got a ways to go in getting our statutes up to standard.

"The emphasis here has been on settlement and encouraging people to come up here. As a result, our laws are lax in some areas. The fact that Covington changed the wording in the agreement from the original wording makes no difference as long as the parties involved knew, or had the opportunity to know, what they were signing."

"Is there any legal recourse for me?" Uncle Lewis asked.

"I'm afraid not much other than what we've already talked about. You can advise the homesteaders not to sign the new agreement if they haven't already done so. For those that borrow money from Covington, they will have to honor the terms of the loan agreement. And those who incur debts to Mr. Covington must make payment or face possible legal action. On that, the law is clear."

"Did you look closely at the new freight agreement Covington is asking them to sign?" Uncle Lewis asked.

"Yes, I did. It's not standard business practice, but I could find nothing illegal about it in the Oregon Statutes. If the settlers agree to this, they must comply with the terms."

"And that includes the use of another freighter," Uncle Lewis said.

"I'm afraid so," the attorney replied. "Unless they get a release from Mr. Covington, they are required to use his services; otherwise, he would be in a position to take legal action against them, possibly sue them for damages. Again, the best chance you have in this matter is to persuade as many as possible not to sign the new freight agreements."

"I'm working on that, but that will leave them without freight service of any kind," Uncle Lewis said.

Howard Klaspell had been sitting at the end of the settee listening as the attorney talked. "You know, the press can be a powerful ally in cases like this," he said.

"I would certainly appreciate any help you can give me," Uncle Lewis said. "I'm aware of the power of the printed word."

How could a thin, frail young man be of any help? Kate wondered. He looked to be almost helpless.

The young newspaper man gave her a glance. As if he had read her mind, he said, "I know that folks must wonder what someone like me can do out here, but don't underestimate the power of newspapers. The importance of the press has been recognized ever since Thomas Jefferson; it has been instrumental in our democracy."

"Well, again, thank you for your offer," Uncle Lewis said. "I look forward to having you and your paper on our side."

The conversation continued. Kate felt guilty about not helping Helga, so she left the men to their business and went in to assist with the noon meal. When dinner was ready, she went to summon the men. The front room was empty. She found Uncle Lewis in his room looking at more papers.

"Dinner, Uncle."

"Thanks, Kate." He put down the papers and joined them at the table.

"Do you think this can be settled peacefully?" Kate asked.

"I hope so. I certainly hope so."

That afternoon after Uncle Lewis went to the fields with Olaf; Kate planted flowers in the front yard. When she would pause and look toward the meadow, she remembered the rider watching the house a chilling omen, she suspected.

*   *   *

"I'm setting up a meeting of all the new settlers," Uncle Lewis said the next morning at breakfast. "I've already put out the word to some, and I'm going to go around and talk to all of them; maybe if they hear it from me personally, they'll be more inclined to listen. I've got to try and stop Covington from carrying out his plans; I can't let him ruin these people. I know the settlers are going to be disappointed, and some may not want to go along with what I'm advising, but at least I'll make them aware of what they're facing."

"How do you think Covington will react to this?" Kate asked.

"I don't think he will like it very much," he replied.

That reminded Kate of Palmer and his henchmen. "Uncle Lewis, promise me you'll be careful."

"Don't worry. I've lived in this country for some time now; I'm accustomed to the risks."

When breakfast was over, Uncle Lewis got his things together. Olaf brought his saddled horse to the front yard. As he was leaving the house, Kate followed him out. "I'll be back in a day or two," he said. He put his supplies in the saddlebags, mounted, and rode through the gate and across the meadow to the road.

*   *   *

While Uncle Lewis was gone, life at the farm settled into a daily routine. Each day, Olaf took one of the hired hands to the fields while the other remained at the house. They were working in a field on the other side of the

114

farm, roughly two miles away. With the safety of Helga, the children, and herself in the hands of one young farm boy, Kate was deeply concerned. Olaf left early in the morning, and often it was after dark when he returned. He listened when Kate explained her concerns. "Well, maybe we should hire some more help, but I can't do it without Mr. Harrington's approval."

Things remained normal until Uncle Lewis returned three days later. Kate watched from the porch as he dismounted in the front yard.

After Olaf took his horse, Uncle Lewis walked up to the porch and removed his hat. "I've got the news out to everyone. They'll be here in three weeks to discuss the situation," he said.

"I hope that will be the end of it," Kate replied.

"So do I."

Uncle Lewis's return kept the farm on a normal course. He joined Olaf and the hired help in the fields, still leaving one behind to guard the house.

*   *   *

James Junior was now going with the men to the fields. Kate appreciated the men taking him along; maybe it would raise the boy's spirits. Since their arrival in Oregon, Kate had noticed changes in her son. He was growing distant and didn't talk to anyone much except Olaf. When Kate would ask him a question, he would often shrug and say nothing. She hated to admit it, but her son was taking on some of his grandfather Albert McKane's personality.

At the onset, he had tried to be the man of the family. Kate, still reeling from her problems, was prone to break down at times. She labored to keep her emotions under control in the children's presence; when alone, she would let loose with the tears.

On one occasion, James Junior found her crying. The boy walked over to her and put his hand on her shoulder. "Don't worry, Mama; I'll take care of you and Alice and Drew."

In time, the magnitude of all that had happened started to overwhelm James Junior. Worst of it, he was the only child old enough to remember their father. Alice was too young, and Drew not yet born when their father rode off to war.

When the news came about their father, James Junior had shown little outward emotion. But Kate was afraid he was bottling up the remorse over his loss and the trauma of packing up and moving to Oregon. She tried to speak with him about losing his father but got no response. The boy had built up a wall that she couldn't penetrate.

*   *   *

115

The closer it got to the day of the settler's meeting, the more Kate's worries intensified. The word would be out by now, so Covington would have heard of it as well. How would he react? She feared another encounter with Palmer and his henchmen would be forthcoming.

To keep it out of her mind, she concentrated on helping Helga with the cooking and chores. As hard as she tried, Kate found it hard to keep up with Helga; the woman was a bundle of energy, always on the go. No task seemed to daunt the woman's spirits. She would go from cooking a meal over the hot stove to scrubbing clothes on a large washboard without slowing down.

*   *   *

Uncle Lewis returned from the fields with the other men. Kate was helping in the kitchen when she heard voices on the porch. Curious, she went to the front door. A young man with long, bushy blond hair, wearing a baggy cotton shirt and wool pants, was standing on the bottom step, talking to her uncle. Olaf was watching from the edge of the yard. "There was some trouble over at the Kenton place," the young man said.

"What kind of trouble?" Uncle Lewis asked.

The young man rubbed at his forehead before answering. "It seems that some men took a shot at Mr. Kenton earlier today. One of his neighbors asked me to come and get you. They sent for the sheriff, but he never came out."

Kate was troubled, felt something wasn't right. She did not know the young man; Uncle Lewis did not appear to be acquainted with him either.

"All right. Olaf, please saddle me a horse."

Uncle Lewis turned and looked at Kate. "I've got to get over to the Kenton place and see what happened. I'll be back as soon as I can."

The young man leaned against the porch and waited. When Olaf came back with the white mare, Uncle Lewis took the reins and waited while the young man walked out to the yard fence where his horse was tied.

As she watched the two of them ride away, Kate felt the uneasiness building. Her uncle was riding away with a stranger. Aside from all the problems they had been having, it was getting late in the day. She didn't like the idea of him riding around after dark. After Uncle Lewis and the young man were out of sight, Kate walked out to the barn where Olaf was now tending to the milking. "Olaf, did you know that young man that Uncle Lewis went off with?"

"No, missy, I never saw him before."

Kate was so consumed with worry that she hardly ate any supper that evening. After the dishes were washed and put away, she put the children to bed, then sat down on the settee and waited for her uncle. Midnight came, but Uncle Lewis did not return.

Kate dozed off but woke up shortly after one in the morning. Thinking that Uncle Lewis might have returned while she was asleep, she went over and knocked on his door. There was no answer. She kept up her vigil for the entire night, but her uncle never came home.

*   *   *

Early the next morning, Kate went down to Olaf's and Helga's quarters and knocked on the door. "Uncle Lewis did not return last night," she told Olaf.

"Maybe best I go and look for him."

"I'll go with you."

Olaf shook his head. "I think it's best you wait here in case he returns. Besides, you need to look after the children."

She reluctantly agreed. After Olaf saddled his horse and rode out of the yard, she went inside and got the children up for breakfast. They seemed to sense her uneasiness.

"What's the matter, Mama?" Alice asked.

"I'm just a little worried about something." Kate did not want the children to know she was concerned about Uncle Lewis.

Kate was unable to eat breakfast. All she could force down were a few swallows of coffee. Worrying about the stranger, Uncle Lewis had ridden away with took away her appetite. After making sure the children were fed, she took a seat on the porch and waited. Olaf returned at about noon. Hoping for good news, she rushed out to meet him. "You find anything?"

"Sorry, missy, nothing. I went all the way to the Kenton place, but they didn't know anything about it. They didn't know anything about a shooting. They didn't know the young man, and they haven't seen Mr. Lewis."

Kate's heart sank. "We've got to start searching for him."

"I'll get the word out to as many as I can."

*   *   *

That afternoon, Olaf spread the word throughout the valley that Lewis Harrington was missing. The settlers organized search parties and combed as much of the area as possible. The search continued until darkness overtook them.

From the front porch, Kate watched Olaf ride into the yard. "Did you find any sign of him?" she asked in a quivering voice.

117

"They found his horse over near the edge of the Blue Mountains, but no sign of Mr. Lewis yet. We're going back at first light in the morning."

There was no sleep for her that night. Fear for her uncle kept her nerves on edge. All she could do was toss around on the bed.

*   *   *

Kate came downstairs before sunrise. Olaf was in the front yard with a saddled horse, getting ready to ride out and help with the search. From the front porch, Kate said, "I'm going with you. Helga can look after the children."

Olaf tried to protest, but Kate would not be denied. He went to the barn and saddled her a horse. As they prepared to leave, Helga stood in the door and watched; like all of them, her face was etched with worry. As the sun was rising in the east, they rode across the yard toward the meadow.

A group of searchers were waiting near the Grigg farm. With Olaf in the lead, they started toward the Blue Mountains. Today, Kate could not see the breathtaking beauty the mountains usually held for her. There was something ominous about the blue haze that gave the mountains their name.

They rode to the Grande Ronde River, where Uncle Lewis's horse had been found just across the stream. They had to ford the river. Kate dismounted and waited on the bank. The country beyond the river was rugged with low, rocky peaks and treacherous to travel by horseback, so the searchers left their mounts and walked. Kate sat on the ground feeling numb and fearful as she watched Olaf and the others disappear into the foothills.

For two hours, Kate sat with her back against a large boulder, waiting for the men to return. When they emerged from the hills with Olaf in the lead, she ran up to the edge of the river. When the searchers were across, the look on Olaf's face told the dreadful story.

"Is he…?"

"Yaw."

Kate dropped to the ground. She sobbed softly at first, then hysterically. The men stood back from her and looked down at the ground. After a time, Olaf reached down and got her back to her feet. As they walked toward her horse, she continued to cry, softly at times, then in a loud, wailing voice. When she was mounted, Olaf said, "They found him at the bottom of a canyon. Maybe his horse threw him."

"They killed him. They killed him so he wouldn't talk to the settlers."

Olaf could say little more; he was fighting back his own tears. "He was my employer and a good man."

They sent one man to find the sheriff while Olaf and the others took Kate

118

home. During the ride, she was hardly cognizant of anything around her. All she could think about was her uncle and what he had done for her and the children. Memories flooded her mind; tears ran down her cheeks.

At the house, Kate called the children together and told them about Uncle Lewis. Alice and Drew sat on the settee and stared down at the floor. James Junior jumped up and ran out the door into the yard. Kate followed behind him. He stopped and leaned against the fence. Kate could see tears in his eyes. "Why did he die, Mama?"

"I don't know for sure, Son. I think it was because he was trying to help the settlers."

He turned his face away. "Somebody is always dying."

Kate walked over to him and placed her arm on his shoulder. She tried to console him; he just looked away, paying her no heed. Kate searched, couldn't find the words to ease his sorrow. At an early age, he had lost two men who were important in his life.

*   *   *

Later that night, some of the settlers brought Uncle Lewis's body to the house, draped over the back of a horse. Behind the horse, carrying Uncle Lewis were Sheriff Avery Benton and a young deputy. While the other men were taking her uncle's body inside, the sheriff dismounted and walked up to the porch where Kate and the rest were gathered. He took off his hat. "I'm sorry, miss."

Kate looked back at the sheriff through red, swollen eyes. "This was a case of murder, you know."

"Now, ma'am, we don't know that for a fact. That's rough country out where he was found. More likely, his horse threw him, or he fell off into the canyon."

"There was a young man that came to the farm talking about a problem over at the Kenton place. Uncle Lewis rode off with this man, but he was found several hours ride from the Kenton farm. Mr. Kenton didn't know anything about any of this."

"I heard about this young man. We'll look around for him, but don't get your hopes up. Could be your uncle got lost or just up and decided to go somewhere else."

"I don't think so. I think that man came here with that story about a shooting over at the Kenton's just to lure Uncle Lewis away from the house so they could kill him."

"Now, there'd have to be a reason for somebody to do that."

"Uncle Lewis was involved in some business problems with a man named

E. G. Covington. He was in the process of trying to stop Mr. Covington from swindling the settlers out of their land. That's why they killed him."

The sheriff wiped his brow with the back of his hand. "That's a strong accusation, and I'd be careful about repeating it. You got to have some powerful evidence to back up something like that."

"Find that young man who came over here, and you'll have your evidence."

"I'm going to look into that, but I've never heard of this man. I'll look into it, but I think your uncle's death was an accident, pure and simple."

Kate was too near exhaustion to argue with the sheriff. What did it matter? He had his mind already made. He had as much as said he wasn't going to do anything about it.

The sheriff turned and started back to his horse. Before the lawman reached his horse, Kate stood up. "Sheriff Benton, I know that E. G. Covington is a man with some influence here, but he can't get away with murder."

The sheriff looked back. "Miss, I know you're powerful upset, but there's no need for unsupported accusations. Like I told you, I'm right, sorry about what happened to your uncle, and I'll look into it. Right now, I don't know if there's anything else I can do."

Without further word, the sheriff walked to his horse with the young deputy following. They mounted and rode out of the yard toward the road.

After the sheriff's departure, Kate sat on the porch with her children. Her mind and her entire body were numb. She had grieved for her husband, James. Now, she grieved again. A war she did not understand took James from her. A group of greedy men took Uncle Lewis from them. *Where was the justice?* she had to wonder. She sat on the porch with her arms around the children until Helga stepped out and took the young ones inside for bed.

After tending to the children, Helga came back out to the porch. "You need some rest, too, dear." Kate looked up at Helga. Around the large woman's eyes, tears were forming. Kate stood up; the two women embraced. "I'm not going to rest until they pay for this."

*   *   *

Most of the settlers attended Uncle Lewis's funeral. Other people came from La Grande and the surrounding area. They buried him on a small hill that overlooked his house and the land he loved.

After the funeral, Kate stood beside the grave and mourned for the man that had come into her life and taken her away from a depressing existence in Tennessee. She again vowed his death would not go unpunished.

After a time, Kate walked down to the house and sat on the porch. Helga came out and offered her a glass of cool milk, but she declined. At the moment, neither food nor drink had much appeal.

Several of the settlers had congregated near the barn, talking to Olaf. When they saw Kate on the porch, some walked over. Hiram Grigg did the talking.

"Mrs. McKane, most of us understand why Mr. Harrington was calling the meeting. We know that Covington wasn't doing what he promised. Instead, he was planning to take our land away from us. One thing that maybe he doesn't know he's not going to do it without a fight. Most of us came up here with nothing. We came from a land torn with war, and we're not going to give up what we've started here, not without a fight."

Amos Gather, a short, stocky man with sandy, red hair, was standing behind Hiram. "We need your help to survive here, Mrs. McKane. Mr. Harrington was the one with the know-how to farm here. He's already shown us a great deal, but we need the support he promised us when we came up here."

"I don't know how I can help you," Kate said. "I'm not a farmer."

"We'll have to learn farming here by experience," another settler said. "The thing we still need is the support that Mr. Harrington promised us."

At the moment, Kate did not know what the future would hold for her. With Uncle Lewis gone, she didn't know if she even wanted to stay in Oregon. There were so many issues remaining to be resolved. Until then, her life was at a standstill.

"I'll keep your needs in mind and do what I can do for you," she replied.

When the last of them were gone, Kate went into her room and cried. No matter how hard she tried, life would not work out for her. She cried herself to sleep, wondering what was to become of her.

Chapter 13

Missouri Raid

The open prairie teemed with colorful wildflowers and tall grass. James avoided the scattered small towns and villages to lower the risk of encountering Union troops or militia. For the first two days, his caution paid off. He encountered no troops—few people at all. At the end of the second day, he set up camp beside a small stream.

Along the creek bank was an abundance of cottonwoods and willows. The branches of the tallest trees were teeming with squirrels. That, he saw, was an opportunity to bring some variety into his diet. A good mess of squirrel meat would be just the thing. He unsaddled and hobbled the horse, got out the shotgun, and started down the creek.

As a boy, James had hunted for sport and with some success. Out here on the prairie, whatever skills he had seemed to have vanished. The little critters scattered before he was in range to get off a shot. When he did get close, he missed on his first two shots. He walked for what seemed like a mile and came up empty. On the way back to camp, his luck improved a bit, and he managed to bag two.

He skinned them then built a fire with dead cottonwood limbs. A gourmet delight they were not. He burned them to a crisp, and the meat was tough as leather. But even burnt and tough, James had to conclude the squirrel meat was better than hardtack.

*　　　*　　　*

By noon the next day, the country gave way to rock outcrops and low, rough hills. By early afternoon, the road was nonexistent in places. In the rough terrain, James was afraid his horse might throw a shoe leaving him afoot. Often, when the going was at its worst, he would dismount and lead the gelding

122

to reduce the risk of an injury.

Later in the afternoon, he reached a pine forest. The tall trees blocked out much of the sun, and insects worked at his neck and ears. Worst of all, the dense undergrowth slowed his progress. Being able to see only a few feet in any direction, he soon became paranoid. "Give me the open country where I can see what's around me," he said to himself. For a little reassurance, he kept his hand close to his pistol.

The sun was sinking in the west when he emerged from the forest onto the banks of a large river. The water was running swift and filled with debris. Fording here would be too risky. The chances were high on losing his supplies and maybe drowning himself and his horse. The best he could do was camp for the night and look for a better place to cross tomorrow.

The river bank was infested with mosquitoes. He covered his bed with the net, but that didn't stop the stinging little pests. They found openings in the net and buzzed around his face and neck. By morning, he was covered with itchy red welts.

After a dip in the shallow water next to the bank that took away some of the misery brought on by the mosquito bites, James made a small fire and cooked the last of his bacon. Low on rations, he had to find a town where he could restock. But first, he had to find a crossing over the high-running stream. He ate his meal, saddled his horse, and started up the bank. The going was slow due to the brush along the river until mid-morning when he struck a road that led into a small settlement.

There was a red brick courthouse on the right side of the street. On the other side was a livery stable and dry goods store. And most, fortunately, up the street was a bridge over the river.

Best of all, there were no federal troops or militia in sight. A handful of people were on the street. Some men were sitting on a bench in front of the courthouse. They watched him, which he did not appreciate. His preference would be to ride on, but he needed supplies.

Near the end of Main Street was a small store housed in a pine log building. There was a door made of pine planks, holding a crudely written sign that read:

Granny's Trading Post

James stopped in front of the log building and tied the reins to a small hitching rail. Inside the store, an elderly woman was sitting in a rocking chair near a fireplace. At the woman's feet, two large, white dogs were lying with their heads between their front paws, sleeping. The dogs opened their eyes for a moment. They found no interest in him and went back to their sleep.

The store was well stocked. There were two leather saddles mounted on a pine rail extending from the wall. Sides of salt pork hung from the ceiling. There was salted bacon on a shelf next to the door. In the middle were racks of coats, men's trousers, and women's dresses and shoes.

"Morning," James said as he closed the door.

"Morning," the woman replied. She continued to rock. "Something fer ye this morning?"

"Some bacon. And I'll take some coffee if you got any."

The woman got up out of the rocking chair and walked over to the shelf next to the door. She pulled a slab of bacon down to a makeshift counter of pine planks then a large knife from beneath the counter. Her hand waved over the meat to drive away the flies. "How much you be needin'?"

James walked over to the counter and measured off a portion with his hands. "Cut it off right here."

The woman raised the knife and brought it down, lopping off the portion that James had measured out. From under the counter, she brought up a roll of brown paper. She measured a strip, tore it off, and wrapped the bacon. From a wooden keg, she drew out a scoop filled with coffee and poured it on a strip of brown paper. "How much coffee you figure to need?"

"Put in a couple more scoops."

She scooped out the coffee, then wrapped it and laid it next to the bacon. "How much?" James asked.

She studied the bacon and coffee. "I reckon a dollar will do."

James fished a dollar out of his pocket and placed it on the counter. "Thank you, ma'am."

The woman picked up the money and dropped it in the pocket of her apron. "Heading north, air ye?"

"Independence."

"Best stay away from Washington and Crawford Counties. Two companies of militia are up there right now. Be advised to watch your step, especially at night. Some folks around are still fighting the war."

"Thank you again."

James picked up his purchases. The woman settled back to her rocker. When he went out the door, she was rocking slowly, her eyes closed.

He loaded his supplies in the saddlebags. At the bridge, an elderly man was fishing. He looked up but did not speak or acknowledge James. It was customary for these Missouri folks, James noticed. The war—that was the cause of their distrust. Jayhawkers, guerrillas: this state had seen its share. And it left the people suspicious of outsiders.

Across the bridge, a narrow winding road cut through the dense forest. There was an eerie silence surrounding the tall pines and scrub oaks. *Ghosts from some of the bloody battles fought here*, James thought. Well, he didn't believe in ghosts, but with all the bloodshed during the violent guerilla battles, if they did exist, this would be the place for them. It left him with the jitters. He breathed a sigh of relief when the trees gave way to open country late in the afternoon.

Being out in the open came with a price: others could also see him. Shortly after leaving the forest behind, he saw a group of riders in the distance, and they had seen him. James entertained the idea of trying to outrun them. Bad idea, he concluded. Both he and his horse were tired. He set the gelding into a slow walk and waited for the riders to reach him. When they were close, he could see they were wearing Missouri Militia uniforms. Men in blue—damn, how he hated the sight of them. Perhaps with a little luck, they might ride on by and not bother him. Wishful thinking. The officer in the lead motioned for him to stop. James complied.

The young officer was not much more than a boy. There were silver bars on his shoulders: a lieutenant. The young man had short hair, a boyish-looking face, and was clean-shaven. The blue tunic and pants were sweat-stained. On his belt, he wore a saber and a pistol. Behind the officer were a dozen enlisted men.

The young lieutenant pulled off his hat and wiped the sweat from his brow. Then he sized James up. "Are you from here, mister?"

"No. Just a poor traveler passing through."

The officer put his hat back on. "Where are you from, and where are you going?" There was a hint of irritation in his voice.

"I just came up from Tennessee. I'm on my way to Oregon."

"Going west to strike it rich, I guess."

"No. I'm going west to find my family."

"You're Confederate, I judge."

"Was," James replied.

"To some people here, Confederate supporters aren't exactly welcome, you know."

James wanted to be careful with his answer. A confrontation with the militia was not in his best interest. "The war's over for me, and I guess for the whole country. The only thing I want to do is get on to Oregon and find my family, that's all."

The lieutenant turned around and motioned to a noncommissioned officer. The large burly man with long whiskers, a sweat-stained hat, and a blue tunic urged his horse up.

"Sergeant, have you ever seen this man before?" the lieutenant asked.

The man gazed at James for a moment. "No, sir. Can't say that I have."

"Thank you, Sergeant. All right. You can be off now, but I'm going to warn you, if you get caught doing anything illegal here in Missouri, you'll be arrested and jailed, and who knows, maybe hanged. Now, good day, sir."

The arrogance of the Federal troops and militias ate at James. But there wasn't much he could do except hold his anger in check and ride on. Get some distance between these troops and himself and hope he didn't encounter any more bluecoats. The resentment burned at him as he rode away. Abe Lincoln had promised the South fair treatment—why couldn't the Union troops abide by it? The sooner he was out of Missouri and its lingering effects of the war, the better off he would be.

James rode until both he and his horse were exhausted, then camped for the night.

*   *   *

The rocky cliffs and outcrops were back the next day. On the rocky surfaces, the going was slow and treacherous. For much of the time, James was out of the saddle leading his horse around nearly impassable rock formations.

Getting through the rocky hills took up most of the day. He took frequent drinks from his canteen as the hot sun beat down on him. Late in the afternoon, he took a drink and noticed he was nearly out of water. Tired and exhausted, he reached the Black River late in the afternoon. A fortunate thing—his canteen was now empty. The water at this point in the river was shallow enough to afford a crossing. When his and the gelding's thirst had been replenished and the canteen filled, they started across.

James underestimated the river. The current was swift in the middle of the stream, causing the horse to panic. Now, James had two struggles on his hands: keeping the skittish horse under control and saving his supplies. Muddy water swirled around them, reaching up to the stirrups. He urged the animal forward; its hooves found purchase in the shallower water, carrying them to the bank.

They rested a few minutes. Hating to waste daylight, James mounted and rode on. After an hour, weariness forced him to stop. He set up camp beside a small rock outcrop. Firewood was scarce. All he could find were a few limbs from a scrub oak. With them, he made do. His supper was the customary trail fare of salt pork and coffee. Tired from the arduous day of riding and walking, he spread his bedroll on the ground. Small rocks poked into his back, interrupting his rest and forcing him to get up and rake away handfuls of tiny stones.

*   *   *

The next day, there were new challenges to confront. The country now was more populated. James got mostly stares from the people he passed, except one. In front of a farmhouse, a man stood in the road and demanded he identify himself. The farmer was thin and gaunt, his face covered by a thick growth of whiskers. An old muzzle-loading shotgun hung from his arm.

The last thing James wanted or needed was a confrontation with an irate local. But the man was striking a threatening pose; he couldn't just ride past him.

"We've had several raids through here," the man said. "They say the war's over, but that don't seem to mean much to some of those bastards that come over here from Kansas."

James advised himself to talk his way around the man. "I understand your concerns, but I just came up from Tennessee. I recently came home from four years of war. I don't have anything to do with Kansas or making raids. All I have on my mind is passing through."

As a precaution, James eased his hand down to his pistol. The man's shotgun was pointed down at the ground. But the danger was still there. From this range, a shot from the old muzzle loader would rip him apart. If diplomacy failed, he had to act first. He had no intentions of being gunned down here in the middle of the road.

The man looked at James, then the pistol. Without a word, he turned and started toward the farmhouse. James started the horse into a slow walk, keeping his eyes on the man and his hand close to the pistol.

Back on the porch of the house, some of the man's bravado returned. He yelled out, "You best not come back though here again!"

Tempting as it was to yell back, James ignored the man and kept on riding. The episode reminded him he had to be very careful here in Missouri. The lingering aftermath of the war had these folks on edge. They distrusted anyone they did not know.

By afternoon, the heat was near intolerable. He and the gelding were exhausted. Worse, his water supply was running out. There was no recourse but to stop at one of the houses and bargain for some water. They wouldn't trust him, but maybe they would sell him some water. Up ahead, just off the road, was a farmhouse. He rode into the yard.

The house was in two parts: a front of logs and a back room of pine lumber. A small boy, shirtless, wearing a pair of homespun pants held up by a single suspender, was playing in front of the house. Several dogs were lying nearby. A few raised their heads. One stood and let out a low growl; James kept his eye on it. "Your daddy around?"

The boy jumped up and ran toward the house. "Papa!" he yelled. A tall, lanky man appeared at the front door, wearing a dirty undershirt and tattered cotton pants. He was clean-shaven, and some of his front teeth were missing. The boy pointed out James.

The man stepped out on the porch. "What do you want, mister?"

"Just a little water for me and my tired horse."

"I don't like having strangers around. Makes me nervous."

"I'd be happy to pay for the water. It's been a long, hard day."

Talk of money perked the man's interest. "Fifty cents for you and the horse. There's a well out back. Get your water. I'll send one of the youngins out for the money. Then you get on out."

"Thank you."

James led his horse to a well behind the cabin. He untied the bucket and dropped it down the well. Splash! He pulled on the rope. At the top, he managed to spill a portion of it back down the well. He salvaged only enough for a good swallow. Snickering behind caught his attention. He turned around. Some children were amusing themselves at his expense. There was the small boy from the front yard plus an older boy and girl. All were ragged and had appearances of malnutrition. The older boy stood up. "For ten cents, I'll draw that water for you," he said.

James was inclined to say no. But a wave of pity changed his mind. Poverty was new to him. War, however, had opened his eyes to suffering and want. He relented and accepted the boy's offer.

What he didn't anticipate was a chain reaction. "How about me?" the girl asked.

"How about me?" the younger boy asked.

He couldn't refuse any of them. "Coins for each of you."

The oldest boy disappeared into the house. Soon, he returned with a wooden bucket. "Don't worry, mister; I'll water your horse good."

The boy dropped the bucket into the well and drew it back out filled with water. He dumped the water into the wooden bucket and repeated the process until it was full, then let James's horse drink. When he and his horse had been watered, James gave each of the children coins. He also gave the oldest boy the fifty cents he had promised their father for the water.

While the boy had been drawing water, James took the opportunity to look around. The house sat on a hill that sloped down to a small barn and split rail corral. The slope was covered with green grass, making it a promising campsite. As the boy started to the house with the money, James asked, "You suppose your daddy would let me camp here for the night?"

"I'll ask Pa."

The children went into the house. James waited by the well until the farmer stepped out the back door.

"I told you before, I ain't very partial to having strangers about the place. We've had considerable trouble these past few years, but you did treat my youngins fairly. You can camp back here, but at first light, I want you gone."

"That's agreeable. I'll be gone at sunup."

The farmer went back into the house. James set up his camp. Some greasy leftover salt pork was his supper. He didn't have the energy or inclination to mess with a cook fire. After eating, he lay down on his blanket and fell asleep.

*   *   *

James awoke. Dogs were barking, and someone was shouting. He listened. The sounds were coming from the front of the house. "Shut up them damn mutts, or I'll shoot the whole lot!" a voice yelled.

"We ain't got nothing worth taking!" a voice yelled back. "Go on and leave us alone."

James retrieved his pistol and inched forward in the pitch dark night. At the back of the house, he paused to let his eyes adjust to the darkness. There was a clump of bushes that would afford him a view of the front if he could get to it unseen. He got down low and angled toward the bushes. He made it undetected. He could see a group of riders in the yard; the farmer and a woman, the man's wife he assumed, were on the porch.

Two of the riders were carrying lanterns. The light illuminated them and some of the others. The man issuing orders, the leader it seemed, had stringy, black hair and a long scar down his face. He turned to a rider behind him. "Go through the house and see what they got."

"Hell, these dirt farmers ain't got nothing worth troubling ourselves about. Why don't we just burn the place and be done with it?"

"Look it over first. They might have a gun or maybe some food we can use."

The rider got down from his horse and stepped up on the porch. "Please, mister," the woman pleaded. "Don't take what little we have."

Her pleas gained her no compassion. The man pushed his way past her into the house. James could hear him rummaging around. Then, he came out carrying a side of bacon.

The woman pleaded again. "That's all the food we got." She reached for the bacon. The man pushed her back and stepped off the porch.

War had familiarized James with inhumanity. But that was war. These were just poor farm people. *Did these men have any feelings?* He found it to be beyond his understanding.

The man tied the side of bacon to his saddlebags then mounted.

The leader then turned to one of the men with the lanterns. "Burn it to the ground."

James could tolerate no more. First, he cursed his lack of forethought. He needed the Henry, not the pistol. It was too late to rectify his mistake. The man was swinging his arm back to toss the lantern. He raised the pistol and fired. The lantern dropped; the rider slumped over in the saddle.

"Damn!" the leader yelled. "Where did that shot come from?"

Another one pointed toward the bushes. "From over there."

"Spread out and make a swing around the yard!" the leader yelled. "We'll flush them out."

That left him in a fix. His hiding place was in jeopardy; he was outnumbered and outgunned. But he had been in battles against superior forces before. *Use that experience*, he told himself.

With the raider's attention diverted, the farmer and his wife lunged for the door. One of the riders turned and fired. The wife let out a loud scream.

"We'll deal with them later," the leader yelled. "Find whoever shot at us first."

They were close. Against the night sky, James could see the outline of a rider in front of his hiding place. The rider listened, then yelled, "I think there's something in these bushes!"

Two more rode over, upping the odds against him. Being cornered, all he had left was the element of surprise. James raised the pistol and fired. The rider next to him fell out of the saddle.

Above the commotion, there was another blast from behind the house, answered by a yelp of pain. "Bill's been hit!" someone yelled.

"There's more around here, so let's clear out!" the leader yelled. "We'll come back and finish this."

The first rider James shot was slumped over in the saddle. The leader rode up, grabbed the reins, and rode off into the darkness with the remainder of the group following.

With the raiders gone, James turned his attention to the family. Inside the house, there was a trail of blood across the floor. The farmer was lying on a bed, the woman sobbing as she attended him. The oldest boy was sitting in a chair by the window with a shotgun lying across his lap; tears were streaming down his cheeks.

The woman was tall and slender with slightly reddish hair. An old robe covered her nightgown. "Please, mister, leave us alone," she pleaded.

"I'm not with them," James replied. "I was camping out back when all this started. I got a few shots at them, but they got away. Let me take a look at your husband."

"I'm sorry; I forgot you were camped out there. Please help me with Clarence. He's hurt bad. He's got a wound in his side."

James bent down and looked at the man. "The first thing we got to do is stop the bleeding. Give me some rags, anything that you can find."

The woman grabbed up a petticoat and tore it into strips. James applied the rags to the wound. "I think he's still got a chance if we can stop the bleeding," he said.

The woman handed James the rest of the cloth strips. Then she dried her tears with the back of her hand. "I'm grateful for what you did for us. They would have burned us out and probably killed us as well."

"Who were those men?"

"One of the rebel groups that roams around the countryside, making raids. They still think the war's going on. Like Bloody Bill and the others that were here during the war, they won't forgive those that supported the Union."

Even being a Southern man, James couldn't understand such hatred. For now, all he could do was tend the wounded man. He listened and concluded the farmer was breathing a little easier: a good sign. Using another old petticoat, the woman made some bandages.

When the wound was bandaged, James stood and felt the exhaustion settle over him. He had done all he could for the man. If the bleeding stayed under control, perhaps the farmer might survive. At least it was cause for hope.

The woman hung her head. "I want to apologize for my husband's behavior earlier," she said. "He's a good man, but life has been hard for us with all that happened during the war. Now we just don't know who we can trust. My name is Josephine Hanks."

"I'm James McKane. I understand how you feel. I served almost four years in the war, so I know the hardships it brings. My family lost nearly everything."

James turned his attention to the farmer's children. The boy with the shotgun was still sitting by the window with his head bowed. The other children were huddled in the corner.

"Did the boy fire the shotgun?"

"Yes. He's a good boy and has been taught that killing another person is wrong, but he was scared for all of us. Now he feels guilty about what he did."

Reflecting on his war experiences, James understood how the young man felt. He walked over to him. The boy looked up at him with tear-filled eyes.

"You probably saved all our lives tonight," James said.

"Is that man dead?"

Drat! The two outlaws outside—he had forgotten them. Were they capable of further violence? Wounded men could still be dangerous.

"Son, I don't know what condition that man is in," James replied. "I just returned home from the war, and I seen men killed by the thousands. It never made any sense to me, but what these men were trying to do to your family was the lowest sort of thing anyone could do. You had a right to protect your family. No one can fault you for that."

There was now a bit of relief in the boy's eyes. James gave him a pat on the shoulder. Now, he had to tend to the other two. He borrowed a lantern from Mrs. Hanks and went outside.

The one the boy had shot was lying just beyond the house. James looked him over. A full load from the shotgun had ended his raiding days. Where was the one he had shot? He found the raider leaning against the wall of the house, holding a pistol in his hand. At James's approach, he tried to raise the Colt but was too weak. He was barely conscious.

James pulled the pistol from the man's hand. "Better let me take a look at that wound."

"I don't need any dirty Yankee farmer looking at me."

"You'll likely bleed to death if that wound isn't tended to. Besides, I'm not a Yankee farmer. I'm a late soldier of the Confederacy, passing through on my way to Oregon."

The man looked up at him. "If I was you, I wouldn't pass through too slow. Elias will hunt you down like a dog for shooting up his band, especially his brother."

"Brother!"

"Yeah. The one with the lantern was Lem Farley, Elias's younger brother."

That was why the leader took the other one with them. James didn't take the time to reflect very long about shooting the brother of a Missouri raider. He had never heard of this Elias. But he did know something about the bloody history of Missouri and Kansas. Quantrill, Bloody Bill—those he had heard of. He considered them all to be of the same lot: killers and thieves, masquerading as men fighting for a cause. He covered the wounded man with a blanket.

James stood watch the rest of the night. He didn't expect the raiders to come back. Instead, they would go somewhere and lick their wounds. Tonight, these men had a new experience, dealing with someone capable of shooting back. They were cowards in the true sense, preying on the weak. The rest of the night passed without incident.

*   *   *

The next morning, James found Mrs. Hanks tending to her injured husband. The young girl was stirring a boiling pot on the woodstove. The two boys were sitting at a small table, eating what appeared to be some type of stew. The younger boy glanced at James. The older one kept his head down.

"How is your husband?" James asked.

"He seems to be resting. Do you think he'll mend proper?"

James wasn't a doctor—all he could do was speculate. He had seen many wounds during the war, had suffered a near fatal one himself. It was hard to tell sometimes if a wound would heal or not. Infection was the problem; an infected wound could turn fatal.

"I think his chances are good if you can get a doctor to clean the wound properly," he told the woman.

"The nearest doctor is nearly a day's travel from here."

"Just the same, I suggest we take him. Do you have a wagon and team that we can use?"

"Down at the bottom of the hill by the barn. First, you sit down and have some breakfast. It ain't much, but it's fillin'."

"I appreciate that, but I think we shouldn't waste any time getting your husband to a doctor. I can eat later."

In truth, James didn't want to take the family's food. The raiders hadn't left much behind. These people needed what was left for themselves.

James excused himself and left the house. At the bottom of the slope, he found a wagon beside the split rail corral. He inspected the wagon and found it to be sturdy. In the barn was a set of harnesses; down next to a creek, a pair of mules grazed. He started for the mules when he heard one of the boys yell, "Some riders are coming!"

He didn't expect the raiders to come back in daylight, but revenge might have driven them to it. He hurried back up the slope, pistol in hand. From the side of the road, he watched a column of riders approaching. Militia or Union troops, he thought. They were preferable to the night visitors was all he could think. When the column was close, he recognized the one in the lead, the young lieutenant from a few days ago.

He put away the pistol and stepped out into the road. The officer commanded the troop to a halt. Then, he rode up to James. "What are you doing out here in the road? If my memory is correct, we encountered you not long ago."

"Yes. These folks need help. A bunch of men rode in and attacked them last night. The man was shot and needs a doctor. The raiders took most of their food. Three of them got shot for their efforts. One's in back, filled with a full load from a shotgun. He's done for. There's another one still alive up there next to the house; the other one got away with the rest of the bunch."

"Sounds like the work of Elias Farley and his gang. We've been trying to track that old bastard down for some time now. We knew he was in this area somewhere."

The officer turned around. "Sergeant, take a detail and look around the house. Check on the wounded."

The burly sergeant dismounted. He selected a detail and led it toward the house. At the officer's order, the remaining militia took up positions around the yard. James led the lieutenant into the house.

"These are Missouri militia," James explained to Mrs. Hanks. "They can provide you the help you need."

She showed James and the lieutenant over to her husband.

The lieutenant studied Clarence Hanks. "We've got some dressing for that wound. Afterward, we'll take him over to a doctor in Reynolds County. Wound like that needs to be treated proper, or he'll die."

The prognosis jolted her to tears.

"There's a wagon and team of mules down by the barn," James said.

"My men will fetch it. We'll haul him and the wounded man outside to the doctor. We'll take the body of the other one with us."

Outside, the sergeant reported. "Sir Looks like what we got is part of the Farley gang. Behind the house is what's left of Bill Straggs, and over next to the house is old Pratt Henderson. Straggs is dead, and old Pratt ain't feelin' to frisky hisself."

"Like I said, I suspected this was Elias Farley's doings," the lieutenant replied. "Too bad old Elias ain't one of them lying out there in the yard."

"Who is this Elias Farley?" James asked.

"Leads a bunch of cutthroats who spent their time during the war raiding folks suspected of being Union supporters. Old Elias can't accept that the war is over. Him and his band hole up in the daytime and go around at night making raids. There's a price on his head, but until now, he's managed to slip away from us."

"A worse bunch I've never seen," James replied.

The Hanks family was in better hands with the militia. First, James gave the lieutenant a full accounting of what happened the previous night. Afterward, he went inside and found Mrs. Hanks attending her husband.

"These militia troops can take better care of you than I can," James explained. "They'll see that your husband gets the proper treatment, so I'll be on my way now. I'm trying to get to Oregon, so I can find my family."

"God bless you, sir. I shudder to think what would have happened to us if you hadn't been here last night."

The oldest boy was sitting in a chair by the door. James walked over to him. "Son, that man you shot is still alive and will probably survive. The one I shot is done for."

It was a lie. Maybe there were times when a lie was justified. The boy did not have to live with the knowledge he killed a man. Even when circumstances justified it, it could weigh heavy. During the war, he had seen young men, still boys really, come face-to-face with the brutality of fighting. They soon became hardened to it all, or they became casualties. Those that survived did so at a price. They would forever be haunted by the memory of it. This young boy was not a soldier; he had no need to live with blood on his hands. With that, James took his leave of the Hanks family.

The lieutenant was waiting outside by the porch. "This is dangerous country right now. You best watch yourself."

"That I will," James answered.

The aftermath of the war had followed him. Would he ever escape its clutches?

Chapter 14

The Inheritance

The days following Uncle Lewis's death, Kate's mood alternated between anger and sadness. The grief from losing the man who had done so much for her and the children overwhelmed her. Anger toward those that took his life simmered within her. At times, her wrath was directed toward fate itself. Fate, she sometimes felt, led to the loss of her husband and now her uncle.

They were all impacted by the loss of Uncle Lewis. Olaf went to the fields each day, but there was sadness etched on his face. James Junior became more silent and withdrawn. The two younger children would often pause in their play and look toward the hill where their uncle was buried.

All that had happened left Kate with a dilemma. Did she still belong in Oregon? She was tempted to pack up and go back to Tennessee. But leaving would mean turning her back on her vow to find justice for her uncle. This conflict left her in constant torment.

*   *   *

The following week, Kate was helping Helga with the breakfast dishes. From the kitchen window, she saw a buggy drive into the yard. "Looks like we got company."

Helga looked out the window. "Yaw."

From the front porch, she watched a man get down from the buggy and pull a valise out of the back. It was Mr. Packwood, her uncle's attorney. At the bottom of the steps, he reached up and tipped his black bowler hat. "Good day, missus."

"Good day, Mr. Packwood."

"Please excuse this intrusion, Mrs. McKane, but there is the matter of your uncle's estate that I need to discuss with you if I might have a few moments of your time."

"Of course, Mr. Packwood, please come in."

She was confused. Why was he coming to see her? Her uncle's possessions had not entered into her mind. He came in and took a seat on the settee. "Coffee, Mr. Packwood?"

"No. Thank you kindly, but I'd like to get right to the point if I may."

"Certainly." Kate sat down on the other end of the settee.

Mr. Packwood opened the valise and took out some papers. "Early this spring, Mr. Harrington came to me and made out an entirely new will. Your uncle realized he was getting on in years, and he also was preoccupied about other things. He wanted to make sure that if anything happened to him, his property would be taken care of."

A sad reminder. Kate nodded.

"Mrs. McKane, your uncle never had a family of his own. I believe he came to think of you and your children as his family. With your permission, I'll read the will."

"Yes. Please."

"I'll skip over the legal introductions and get right to the point." He picked up a paper and started to read:

"I, Lewis Harrington, being of sound mind, but also being aware of the uncertainties of life, hereby bequeath that upon my death, my assets are to be divided as follows: To my loyal employee, Olaf Hanson, and his wife, Helga Hanson, I bequeath the sum of five hundred dollars. To my brother, Walter Harrington, I bequeath the sum of one hundred dollars.

"The remainder of my estate I bequeath to my niece, Katherine Harrington McKane. This includes my estate known as Harrington Farms, consisting of approximately four thousand acres in Union County, Oregon. Included are all buildings and improvements. This further includes all livestock, farming tools, and property of Harrington Farms.

"Also included is the sum of three thousand four hundred dollars, currently deposited in the Portland Bank & Trust Company, Portland, Oregon.

"This further includes 100 shares of the Northeast Oregon Agricultural Co-op.

"The rest is just some legal verbiage," Mr. Packwood said.

Kate was stunned. No, more like totally bowled over. Her head was spinning. Never in her dreams did she think her uncle would trust his possessions to her. He was family, but she had only known him for little more than a year. "I don't know what to say, Mr. Packwood. I never expected anything like this."

"That's the way your uncle wanted it. Of course, there will have to be a probate hearing at the courthouse before all this becomes final, but that's a formality. With your permission, I'll take the necessary steps to have it put on the court agenda."

"Of course."

Mr. Packwood put all the papers back in the valise. "I believe that's it. If there are any questions, I have an office in La Grande. You can find me there most of the time. I'll let you know when the probate hearing will be held. For now, it looks like you're a landowner, Mrs. McKane."

There was a whirlwind going through Kate's mind. She didn't know how she felt about all this. A huge responsibility had landed on her shoulders. "You sure you wouldn't like some coffee, Mr. Packwood."

"No. Thank you again, but I need to get back to my office."

Kate walked the attorney outside. She gave Mr. Packwood a wave then went back in the house. Just like that, her life had changed again; was it for better or worse? She had never owned any property. How could she ever cope with Harrington Farms and its many problems? It meant her plan to go back to Tennessee had to be put aside, at least for a time. And there were the settlers; they were looking to her for support. This was what her uncle wanted, but was it what she wanted? Covington and his henchmen, it was all so overwhelming she felt like crying.

Kate fretted until time to prepare the noon meal. Then, she joined Helga in the kitchen. When Olaf arrived from the fields, she called him aside and explained about the will. "I'm happy to see the farm will stay in Mr. Lewis's family," he said.

"Olaf, I don't know a thing about running a place like this. First of all, I want you to stay on as overseer. I need your help very much."

"Of course, missy. It would be my pleasure to stay. Helga and I have come to feel like this is our home, so we'd like very much to stay here. And don't worry. I think you will do well."

Olaf agreeing to stay on took away some of the burden. His farming skills were essential to their success. That would still leave the Tennessee option open. If she did go back, she could turn the farm over to him.

But while Olaf could run the farm, justice for Uncle Lewis still depended on her. The sheriff was content to call it an accident—that she would never accept. Avery Benton had to be pressured until something was done. She couldn't do that in Tennessee.

*   *   *

The lack of justice made her restless. The sheriff, he needed some prodding. He wouldn't appreciate it, but she didn't care. The next day, during breakfast, she asked Olaf to drive her to La Grande. It was a lot to ask with him busy in the fields. But she just couldn't sit around doing nothing.

"We are getting low on supplies," he replied. "We can stock up while we are there."

When Olaf drove the wagon into the yard, Kate went out, and he helped her up. He tapped the team, and the wagon lurched forward. The meadow wildflowers were still in bloom. The mountain peaks rose up toward the cloudless blue sky. Kate wished she had more appreciation for it. But today, her mind was fixed on the sheriff, leaving her unable to enjoy anything.

In La Grande, Olaf stopped the wagon in front of the courthouse and helped her down. "I'm going to look at some plow shears," he said.

"All right. I won't be long."

Kate pushed open the door of the courthouse and started down the hall between the newspaper offices. At the foot of the stairs, she was surprised to see E. G. Covington coming down. He was the last person in the world that she wanted to see. For a moment, she was tempted to turn and walk out. Standing face-to-face with the man she knew was responsible for her uncle's death was tormenting. To avoid speaking, she turned her head to one side.

Covington wasn't put off. He reached up and tipped his hat. "Good morning."

Now, aren't you the perfect gentleman, she thought to herself. "Morning," she mumbled.

She went to the second floor and opened Avery Benton's door. The sheriff was in his office taking a pot of coffee off the stove. He turned toward her; a frown spread across his face. She found some pleasure in being a source of annoyance to him.

"Mrs. McKane." What brings you here today?"

"I think you know the answer to that."

"If it's about your uncle, I don't have any new information. You care for some coffee?"

"No. Thank you. I just wanted to know what was being done about my uncle's death."

"I haven't been able to find any information that points to anything other than an accident," he said as he poured a cup of coffee.

"Mr. Benton, his body was found out in the middle of nowhere after he left the farm with a young man none of us had ever seen before. Uncle Lewis was an excellent horseman; the likelihood of him riding up into the foothills, then falling off his horse into a ravine is something I just don't believe."

"Well, I can tell you that I've seen this kind of thing happen many times. The best horsemen around have been thrown from their horses on occasion. It was an accident as far as I can tell."

Kate's anger was near out of control. She had expected nothing less, but that didn't make it any easier to swallow. His story never wavered. Feeling helpless and disgusted, she turned to leave.

"You know, miss, your uncle may have been involved in some unsavory activity himself," the sheriff said. "I think some of the settlers he lured up here were becoming suspicious of his motives. If it turns out not to have been an accident, then there're other suspects besides Mr. Covington."

The last shred of her control was slipping away. She started to speak. Her emotions choked her. All she could do was storm over to the door. She slammed it on the way out. Downstairs, her anger boiled over, bringing with it the tears.

Almost in a daze, Kate started toward Main Street then changed course. Her anger and frustrations needed venting. *Covington*, she thought. She was angry enough now to take him on. Guided by rage, she walked toward the freight yard. Once there, she walked through the wagons to the office. The freighter was sitting behind his desk. Her entrance seemed to startle him. "I wasn't expecting a visit from you."

"I didn't come into town with the intention of visiting you. It seems that nobody else in town is interested in what I have to say, so maybe I can get your attention."

E. G. Covington closed the ledger in front of him and pushed it to one side, then pointed at a chair in front of the desk. "Have a seat."

Kate sat down in the chair and looked at him.

"I don't know what this is all about," he said. "I'm sorry to hear about your uncle. After all, he and I were business partners, although it now looks like he didn't plan to live up to his end of the deal."

"Mr. Covington, my uncle was an honest and honorable man. I know that he would not break a business deal that was made in good faith."

Covington leaned back in his chair. "Mrs. McKane, how well did you really know your uncle? As I've heard, you only met him for the first time last year. I've known him for many years; maybe he wasn't the honorable man you thought he was or that I once thought he was."

"I knew my uncle well enough."

"Well, the truth is, your uncle and a man named John McDonald came to me about a business venture. They needed my help to establish an agricultural business plan they had for this area. Without a means of getting their crops to market, their plan was hopeless. I agreed to make my freight wagons available in return for a fair price for my services. That's honest business and something I never backed down from."

"Well, it seems you decided to use the agreement to your own advantage."

Red spread over his face. "That's a lie!" he roared. He reached into his desk, pulled out a sheet of paper, and handed it to her. "This is the agreement that your uncle and John McDonald helped me draw up." Kate read the contents.

NORTHEAST OREGON AGRICULTURAL CO-OP GROWERS FREIGHT AGREEMENT

The **Northeast Oregon Agricultural Co-op Growers** and **E. G. Covington Freight Company** hereby agree to the following:

E. G. Covington Freight Company will provide freight wagons and drivers for the purpose of transporting agricultural products of the co-op members to markets in all mutually agreed locations.

The co-op members agree to submit all requests for freight services at least 30 days in advance of actual shipping dates. The co-op members further agree to provide said freight company an estimate of needed wagons and drivers at least 30 days in advance of shipping.

The co-op members agree that E. G. Covington Freight Company will have the first priority for all freight requirements of co-op members. Co-op members are required to obtain a release from said Freight Company before using other freight services unless said Freight Company cannot provide the needed services.

It is further agreed that the co-op members will provide security for the freight company in the form of armed escorts to accompany wagons of said freight company on its deliveries.

After reading the first page, Kate turned to the second one and continued reading:

Clauses and exclusions

E. G. Covington Freight Company is granted just fees for freight services in accordance with the following terms: rates will be assessed by E. G. Covington Freight Company based on prevailing rates in the immediate area, hazards involved in travel, damage to wagons, and other freight company property, and other unforeseen hazards or requirements.

Each individual member is required to pay for freighting their products. In the event of nonpayment, the charged fees shall be applied to a lien against the individual member and individual member's assets, including future crops and real estate property. The schedule for payment of shipping fees will be determined by Covington Freight Company. Unpaid fees may be demanded at any time by Covington Freight Company.

At the bottom was a place for each individual settler to sign or make their mark and a place for Covington to sign. The last paragraph in fine print was most distressing. She called it to his attention.

"Your uncle insisted on having that stipulation in the agreement. He said it would help us control the settlers and protect our investment."

"I don't believe you. I know that Uncle Lewis took great pains, to be honest with the settlers. These people have just lived through some terrible times, and many have nothing left, so he would never try to trick or defraud them in any way."

"Well, Mrs. McKane, you're believing what you want about your uncle, but again, you didn't know him all that well. I'm sorry to be the one to have to tell you, but that's the way it happened. If word got out among the settlers that your uncle had misrepresented himself, they would be upset and angry. I only made the freight deal; your uncle did all the talking with these people."

"I don't believe any of this, Mr. Covington. Not only that, you are trying to take the settlers land from them by tricking them into signing loans they can't pay back. Between the loans and the freight agreements, these people don't have much of a chance."

"The loans are legal agreements between me and some of the settlers. I am only offering them an easier way of acquiring a title to their land. These agreements are strictly between me and them and nobody else."

"They didn't realize what they were signing."

Covington shrugged his shoulders.

"Another thing, Mr. Covington. What do you know about a railroad survey being done by the war department?"

"There's a party in the area doing a survey for a possible railroad through the valley. What's that got to do with this?"

"Well, I've heard the survey might run through some of the settlers' lands."

"So what?"

"It would make that land worth more money. In fact, it would probably make most of the property in the valley worth more money, wouldn't you say?"

"Perhaps. What are you getting at?"

"Mr. Covington, with the possibility of land values going up, it might just be tempting to get your hands on as much of it as you can."

"Nonsense. Now I'm rather busy here, so if there's nothing else, I'd like to get back to work."

"Just one more thing, Mr. Covington, and then I'll go. What about this man named Palmer that came out to our house making threats?"

"I don't know anyone named Palmer. If someone is threatening you, that's a job for the sheriff. As I told you, Lewis Harrington did some things that likely didn't sit so well with some people. It's not surprising that folks were gunning for him."

Nothing but lies, that's all she kept hearing. She was now more convinced than ever that the man sitting across from her was the source of her uncle's business problems and the cause of his death. She could listen to no more. The door slammed behind her as she stormed out. She reached the street, seething to the point she could hardly see.

Olaf was yelling for her. "Missy, are you ready to go?"

Rage and sorrow, she battled them both back to the wagon. Olaf helped her up into the seat. He climbed up beside her and snapped the reins. The wagon rolled down the street out of town.

The sheriff's and E. G. Covington's attempts to thwart her spurred her determination. The truth would be made known—she wouldn't stop until it was all out in the open. This thought helped relieve her anger and frustration.

Olaf sensed her mood and left her to her thoughts. There was little talk on the way home. At the house, she hurried into Uncle Lewis's room.

For more than an hour, Kate sorted through all the papers around the roll-top desk but found nothing useful. As she was about to give up the search, she found a folder in the bottom drawer of the desk. In it was a copy of the freight agreement. Her hands trembled as she read.

The first part of the agreement was the same as what Kate had read in Covington's office. The difference was a later paragraph which read:

"The co-op members agree that E. G. Covington Freight Company will have first bid on all freight requirements of co-op members. In the event said Freight Company cannot provide the needed services at competitive prices, co-op members may seek other freight services without any obligation toward Covington Freight Company."

This indicated the original agreement that Uncle Lewis and John McDonald had agreed to was much less binding than the one Covington was now using. On the next page, the contents got more interesting:

"During the term of this agreement, E. G. Covington Freight Company will provide freight services to co-op members at a fixed fee of $15.00 per wagon load for the first two years and $20.00 per load thereafter. The terms of this agreement will be five years unless terminated, reduced, or extended by mutual agreement of the parties concerned.

"In the event of nonpayment by any member, E. G. Covington Freight Company has the right to terminate its agreement with said member and shall have the option of a lien against future crops of the member until all fees are paid."

This was certainly a much different agreement than the one Covington had produced in his office, one that was much fairer toward the settlers. There was no lien against their land, just against future crops, and it did not bind the members to use Covington's services. This was proof that Uncle Lewis did not try to deceive the settlers. With this information in hand, how would she use it? Kate knew nothing about legal matters. In truth, this might not provide much relief from the problems with Mr. Covington. However, it did prove that Uncle Lewis intended to keep his word.

*   *   *

For days, Kate pondered her predicament. There was just no way to go back to Tennessee now, she concluded. There was too much at stake here.

*   *   *

On a Sunday afternoon, they were resting on the porch after Helga's delicious dinner. The two youngest children were playing in the yard. Olaf and James Junior were playing checkers, using a chair bottom as a table. Kate had dozed off. She awoke and noticed a group of riders crossing the meadow. Palmer and his henchmen, she feared. But the man in the lead didn't look like Palmer. He was riding what looked like a draft horse. It was Mr. Grigg, their neighbor, leading a group of the settlers.

The group rode into the yard, dismounted, and tied their horses to the fence. Hiram walked up to the porch; his companions stood by their horses. "Afternoon, Mrs. McKane," Hiram said.

"Good afternoon, Mr. Grigg. Tell your friends to come down and have a seat."

Hiram turned and motioned for the other five to come down. There was Amos Garrett, a tall, dark-haired man; Frederick Handley, a tall, almost bald man with a scar on his chin; Thomas French, a portly man with graying brown hair; Thomas Roddingham, a young man with a long, yellow beard and long hair; and Barton Files, a short, red-haired man who walked with a slight limp. To accommodate them, Helga went inside to get more chairs.

After everyone was seated, Hiram Grigg said, "Mrs. McKane, there's a lot of talk going around about the agreement that Mr. Harrington and Mr. Covington made about our business here in the valley.

"When Mr. Harrington came up to me in Missouri, he explained how everything was set up here in Oregon. He told me he would supply me with everything I needed until I got my farm up and going. Your uncle also said there would be freight wagons to take my crops to market. He even showed me a copy of the agreement."

"And he meant what he said," Kate replied.

"We've been hearing stories that some of the settlers have signed agreements with Covington that will put them in debt and force them to lose their land. These stories have been bothering us something awful. You know, most of us depended on Mr. Harrington to look after our rights. We're just simple farmers, and there's many among us that can't read or write at all. Mr. Harrington told us it was all right to sign the agreement with Covington, and we all trusted him."

"I realize you did," Kate said. "The trouble is, Uncle Lewis was deceived by Covington just like some of the settlers. He was trying to find a way to make it right and was in the process of getting everyone together when he lost his life. I believe that Uncle Lewis was killed for trying to stop Covington."

"You think Covington and his bunch killed Mr. Harrington?"

"I'm sure of it."

Worry crossed Hiram Grigg's face. "If that's the case, then maybe we're in danger, too."

"That's possible, Mr. Grigg, but Covington is not yet in a position to carry out his intentions. It's your land he's interested in, but he won't move against you until the time is right. You'll have to go along with him this year, but be in a position to get out from under him before he gets you too indebted to him or he has a mortgage on your claims. Just don't sign any agreements with Mr. Covington without letting someone look it over first."

"I take it you're trying to fight him," Hiram said.

"'Til the bitter end," Kate replied.

"If that's the case, you and your family may be in danger," Hiram replied.

"That may be, but we got no choice but to try and do what's right. My uncle didn't bring you all the way up here to be robbed by a greedy man."

"What can we do to help?" Hiram asked.

"I plan to go ahead with my uncle's plan to meet with all the settlers and lay everything on the table. At that time, we can decide how to deal with Covington and that bunch of cutthroats that work for him."

"That might be risky."

"Yes, it will. What happened to Uncle Lewis is a reminder of how dangerous these men are. I know it's getting toward summer, and most of you are involved with getting your crops planted. I will wait until a little later in the year, maybe after the fall harvest. We got a little time, and that will give us an opportunity to come up with some plans."

"What about our harvest this year?" Mr. Garrett asked. "It looks like Covington is the only freighter around here with the means to haul our crops. The other freighters are hauling for the mines down south."

"I think it will be all right to use him this year," she replied. "Like I said, he's not yet in a position to put you out of business because you don't yet have title to your land, nor have you acquired any debts to him. He'll have to get his hooks in a little deeper before he can do anything."

Kate's advice seemed to bring the men some relief. They talked for a time then the visitors got up to leave. Hiram said, "Mrs. McKane, I trusted your uncle, and I trust you. There're some of the settlers that are afraid about all this. I'm going to try and talk to as many as I can. Maybe I can help you out a little."

"I appreciate that, Mr. Grigg. Give my regards to your wife."

As Kate watched the men ride away, she felt a heavy burden settling on her shoulders.

Chapter 15

Missouri Traveler

Although he was a war veteran, the violence at the Hanks farm left James shaken. The war, at its bloody worst, made more sense than the cowardly but deadly nature with which these guerrilla fighters conducted themselves. The war was fought for a broader cause; at least, he had once felt so. Those ruthless men he had just encountered, what was their cause beyond that of pure meanness? The effects of the raid lingered. Now, every shadow concealed a desperado. Every tree, every bend of the road would send his hand down to the pistol. A rustling in the leaves or movement in the grass would cause him to flinch.

The next few days passed without incident. James now found himself in rolling hill country covered by a pine forest. The local people left him to his business. That suited him. Then the memory of the farm raid began to fade. The jitters faded to boredom from the long days in the saddle. At night, he camped among the pines; often, it was a cold camp. Maybe it was over-caution from the raid or exhaustion from the long day's ride. He just didn't take the time to build a fire. His meal would be hardtack and the risk of a broken tooth.

His rations were low when he crossed into Pulaski County. Like it or not, he had to ride into one of the local towns and restock. Late in the afternoon, he reached the outskirts of a settlement. It wasn't large. There was a livery stable, a dry goods store, a small newspaper office, a marshal's office and jail, and a general store. He tied the reins at a hitching rail and stepped up on the wooden sidewalk.

The general store building was built of unpainted clapboard siding with a wooden shingle roof. An overhang supported by small pine poles ran the entire width of the building and extended from the storefront over the wooden sidewalk.

A large poster on the side of the building caught his eye. On it were the

147

faded images of three men. The faces in the images were not very clear, but they looked very much like the three strangers he and his confederate companions had traveled with back in Kentucky.

WANTED BY THE STATE OF MISSOURI for Robbery and Murder

Isaac Tannahill

Dalton Tannahill

Rutherford Stevenson

By Colonel Danforth Whitfield, 14th Missouri Militia

As James had suspected all along, the three men were nothing but common outlaws. From what he saw in that tavern in Kentucky, they knew their trade very well. Now, he fully understood why they never revealed their names.

He pushed open the door and stepped into the store. It was a one-room affair with a large potbellied stove in the middle. To one side was a glass counter that ran the width of the room; all the walls supported shelves packed with merchandise. A young man wearing a white apron was behind the counter. "Afternoon."

"Afternoon," James replied. "I need a few supplies."

"Take a look around."

The store's merchandise included farming tools, shoes, and wool coats, men's and women's clothes, and an assortment of firearms and ammunition. Near the stove was a large wooden barrel filled with pickles; hanging from the ceiling were several cured hams, a large side of bacon, and salt pork. On the shelves were bags of unground coffee, sugar, flour, and tea.

James got a pickle from the barrel lime, sweet and tart, like those he grew up with. As a boy, he would slip into the big plantation cellar and stuff himself on pickles, sometimes until he had a bellyache. He selected one of the hams, sugar, and coffee. He placed his selections on top of the glass counter and waited for the clerk to tally it up.

"Anything else?"

"Can you grind that coffee for me?"

"There's a grinder over there; you can grind it yourself."

Not a very accommodating attitude for a store clerk, James concluded. He paid for his supplies and took the coffee over to the hand grinder. When he was done, he took it all out to the saddlebags. His last stop was at the livery

148

stable to buy a bag of oats.

James was tempted to spend the night in town. But he hated to waste daylight. Moreover, the people here made him uncomfortable, and he was behind schedule. He rode until dark.

James set up camp beside a small creek near the road. He had some cured ham for supper and crawled into his bedroll. Amid the sound of frogs croaking and the buzzing of night insects, he fell off to sleep.

Later, James awoke. There was something amiss. The frogs and insects had ceased their night chorus; the air was deathly still. Suddenly, there was a large streak of lightning in the west, followed by a loud rumble of thunder. A storm was forming.

His carelessness jumped out at him. He had not bothered to secure his gear before going to sleep. Cursing his lack of planning, he fumbled around in the dark until he found the oilcloth and covered his weapons and powder. Then he spread his rain slicker over his food supplies and hoped it would do.

Without warning, the wind hit with a fury, quickly ripping away the oilcloth and rain slicker, sending them hurtling into the woods next to the camp. The rain followed the wind, falling in sheets and drenching him to the skin. There was a loud crash from the nearby woods. Lightning had struck close to camp.

The only refuge available was under a large tree. Dangerous, he knew. If lightning struck the tree, he was in peril. For several minutes, the storm poured out its fury. Then the rain subsided, and the thunder grew fainter; the brunt of it had passed. Light rain continued to fall. It didn't matter much—he was already soaked to the skin.

In the darkness, it was difficult to assess the damage to his camp and supplies, but he suspected the worst. He spent the rest of the night sitting under the tree in his wet clothes.

At first light, he got a look at what remained of his gear. His supplies were soaked. Most of the food was ruined, and his weapons were questionable. His ammo was in a pouch, but it might have leaked. The Henry and shotgun had been exposed to the storm. Only the pistol, which he kept in his bedroll, had been spared. He cursed himself again.

If the state of his supplies wasn't enough, he discovered his horse was missing. He concluded the gelding must have broken its hobbles and fled, probably scared by the lightning strike. Now, the question was, how far had it wandered? Still soaked to the bone, he started north along the creek bank.

For at least an hour, he walked and saw no sign of his horse. He concluded it had gone in another direction and started back south when a rider emerged from a clump of bushes holding a rifle.

Raiders were his first thought. But it was a woman. She was wearing a baggy shirt and pants and a large, floppy hat. Her long, blonde hair was tied in the back with a white rag. "What are you doing on my property?" she asked.

With the barrel of the rifle pointed at his chest, he couldn't afford to antagonize her. "Pardon me; I didn't realize I was on your property."

"Well, you are. I would like to know what you're doing, wandering around completely soaked along my creek bank."

"Again, my apologies for trespassing. I'm looking for my horse. He ran off during the storm last night."

"What are you doing around here anyway? I don't recall seeing you before."

"I'm just passing through on my way to Independence."

"That's an interesting story, but this country is full of renegades and cut-throats. When I see strangers, I get scared."

James sized up the woman. She was attractive in a plain sort of way; however, he would have found her more appealing if he weren't looking at her over the barrel of a rifle. "I didn't mean to alarm you. I just wanted to find my horse."

She waved the rifle at him. "You lead the way back to your camp. I want to see what you've been up to."

"Do I look like a bandit?"

"You look more like a wet dog. Just start walking, and don't stop until we get to where you were camped."

With the rifle pointed at him, James had no choice but to walk back down the creek bank with the woman following behind him until they reached the remains of his camp.

The woman shook her head. "Looks like you didn't take very good care of your supplies. Don't it ever rain where you come from?"

James was irked at her criticism and embarrassed. He gave her an affirmative nod.

"I'm starting to believe you're not an outlaw, but I still don't know what you're really up to. First of all, hand me those guns you got there on the ground."

He resented her ordering him around. Not wanting to find out if she would shoot him or not, he picked up the weapons and handed them to her. "The pistol in your belt," she said. He handed her his remaining weapon.

"Now, you have a seat there on the ground until I get back. I'm going to look for your horse. Likely, he didn't get too far away. If I find him, I'll bring him back, and if I don't, I guess you'll have to walk to wherever you're going."

Filled with a mixture of anger and remorse, James sat down next to a tree. What a poor excuse for a frontiersman he was turning out to be. His horse and supplies were all ruined or missing. To top it off, he had been humiliated by a woman. He leaned back against a tree, cursed his luck, and dozed off.

The rustling of the bushes next to the creek awoke him. He started to reach for his weapons then remembered he didn't have any.

"I hope you're decent!" the woman yelled.

"That I am!" James yelled back.

She emerged from the bushes, leading his horse. "I found him down the creek a ways, just grazing."

"I'm grateful for that."

Her demeanor had changed. She pulled the floppy hat off and wiped the sweat from her brow with her sleeve. "You look like you could use some dry clothes and hot food. Saddle your horse and ride up to my place. Once you get out on the road, it's just a short distance to the north. I want to remind you to be on your best behavior when you get up there. My husband will be home soon. He's a jealous man and might not understand. I'll be expecting you shortly."

Without further word, the woman put the hat back on her head and rode back toward the road.

The idea of hot food appealed to him. He hated to waste time, but he was exhausted and drenched to the skin. Moreover, he was getting trail weary. He thought it over. Maybe the woman would have a spare room where he could spend the night. The idea of sleeping in a real bed clinched the deal. He rounded up what remained of his gear and saddled his horse. When he was on the road, he rode north and found the house.

It was a small affair made of heavy pine timbers with a lean-to at the back, also made of pine. The front of the house had a small porch; both the roof and porch were covered with wood shingles. At one side of the house, a rock chimney extended above the roofline.

The woman was sitting on the porch in a rocking chair with the floppy hat at her feet. "Get down and stay awhile. My name is Sarah Fennigan. What do they call you?"

"James McKane."

He dismounted, led his horse up to the porch, and tied the reins to one of the porch supports.

"After we eat, you can put your horse down in the corral. He can pasture with my livestock, and I've got some oats in the barn. I got some fresh coffee brewing on the stove; it should be ready by now. Come on inside."

The interior was simple. The kitchen held a small woodstove, some handmade cabinets, a table made of thick hand-hewn planks, and some wooden chairs. On the stove was a pot of coffee. On the table were a loaf of homemade bread and a platter of butter and cheese. It was the most appetizing food James had seen since leaving Tennessee.

"Have a seat, please," Sarah said. She picked up the coffee pot from the stove.

When James was seated, she placed a cup of steaming coffee in front of him. It was the tastiest meal he had enjoyed since Aunt Mary's cooking. He was so hungry he forgot his table manners. When he looked up and noticed Sarah was watching him intently, he was embarrassed.

"Looks like it's been a while since you had a good meal. Cooking is certainly more fun when you have someone to enjoy it with."

"Well, your husband is a lucky man, being fed like this all the time."

"Yes. I guess he is." Her voice was so low he had to strain to hear.

When he was finished eating, Sarah said, "You look a little worn out. There's a lean-to behind the house with a bed inside. I suggest you go and get some rest. When you get inside, you can hand me those wet clothes, and I'll dry them on the clothesline. Don't worry about your horse. I'll take care of him."

James didn't like leaving her tend to his horse; it didn't seem right, but he was too exhausted from lack of sleep to protest. He left Sarah to the task and went out to the lean-to and stepped inside. It wasn't the lap of luxury, but the bed was inviting. As he was taking off the wet clothes, there was a knock on the door. He handed the garments out and then lay down on the mattress. It was nothing more than a large bag filled with shucks but was much more comfortable than the hard ground on which he had been sleeping. He was soon snoring.

*   *   *

James awoke and wondered how long he had been asleep. He got up and poked his head out of the door. The sun was midway in the afternoon sky—he had slept for several hours. Embarrassed at sleeping away much of the day, he looked around and did not see Sarah, but his dry clothes were hanging on a peg on the door. He took them into the lean-to and dressed. He wanted to help Sarah to pay for his food. Sleeping on the shuck mattress reminded him of home with all its comforts—so much so, he felt tempted to spend a night before moving on.

He stepped out into the afternoon sun. Sarah was below the house, in a pen filled with chickens and standing in front of a makeshift structure of wooden planks nailed to posts with a wood shingle roof. She had a chicken in one hand and a bucket in the other. Feeling curious about what she was doing, James walked down the hill.

"Setting hen," Sarah explained. "I'm moving her away from the rest of the chickens. She gets cranky and pecks the others."

152

James didn't pretend to know much about chickens. What he did know was the farm was in a run-down state. The fences were in disarray, and the yard was overgrown with weeds. Next to the house was a wagon with a broken axle. He had to conclude that Sarah's husband must not be much of a farmer.

Beyond the chicken house was another building of similar description, except it, was larger and surrounded by a corral made of split logs.

Sarah stepped out of the pen with the bucket of eggs and hen and started walking toward the corral. She opened the corral gate and disappeared into the other building with the eggs and chicken. In a few minutes, she came out minus the chicken but still carrying the bucket of eggs.

"I would be interested in a night's lodging and board in return for doing some work for you," James said. He could have paid for the food and lodging, but he decided to try and save some money. Besides, from the looks of her farm, he suspected she could use some help.

Sarah studied him for a moment. "You don't look much like a farmer to me, but if you can stand the pace for one day, I'll supply you with a bed for a night or two and some food to go with it."

"That's fair enough."

"I need to get these eggs up to the house," Sarah said. "After that, I'll see about getting some supper."

James followed her back up the hill toward the house. When they were at the top, he stopped. She turned around. "Sarah, you really live here alone, I believe."

"Well, the truth is, yes; that is, I do now. I didn't know if I could trust you or not, so that story about a husband was to make sure you behaved yourself. I was married, but my husband, Frank, went off to the war and never came back. I tried to get him not to go, but he went anyway, leaving me with this pile of rocks to earn my living with."

"I guess it is tough living out here alone and dangerous as well."

"Yes. It is scary. During the war, there were raids on several farms around here. I remember hiding in the cellar one night while some Jayhawkers from Kansas rode through the countryside. Since the war ended, it's let up some, but you never know. My husband and his family were staunch Southern supporters, so that kept the Confederate gangs from bothering us, but there were always the Union folks to worry about. Anyway, I'm so poor; hopefully, they won't bother with me."

Sarah's woes moved James to pity her. How many had the war left in such a state? Husbands and fathers were gone or left maimed. Widows with children struggled to survive. Where was the justification, the reasoning behind it all?

"Come on into the house, and I'll fix us something to eat."

They went inside. James sat at the table while Sarah prepared some fried pork, greens, and fried pies. He had to remind himself not to get used to it. In a day or two, it would be salt pork and hardtack again.

Sarah served the meal hot off the stove. Even with simple rations, she was a good cook. James enjoyed every bite. While he was still eating, she got up from the table and got a towel from one of the cabinets. "Bath time," she said.

James finished eating and went out and sat on the front porch step. The sun was just setting in the west, casting a patch of red across the sky. From the creek, frogs and other night creatures were starting up their evening chorus. From the distant woods, he could hear a Whippoorwill call. How peaceful it all seemed. But his experiences had taught him peace could be an illusion.

Sarah was on the bank, getting ready for her bath. She tossed the floppy hat down on the ground, then the baggy pants and shirt. She waded into the water.

Shame came over him for watching her bathe. He got up from the step, sat down in one of the chairs, and faced the other direction. He thought about Kate. How long had it been since they had been together? Being around a woman again reminded him of how much he missed his wife. *What was she doing tonight?* He wondered. *Did she and the children arrive safely in Oregon? How were they faring in their new life?*

Out of the blue, he was struck with a chilling thought, one that scared him to the core. What if she had met someone else? After all, she believed he was dead. Kate was a young, attractive woman; thus, men would certainly be interested. The thought left him shivering, wondering what he would do if that turned out to be the case.

Sarah interrupted his thoughts. She was coming up the path, rubbing her hair with a towel. "The creek water sure feels good after a hot, sweaty day."

They sat on the porch for a time and talked. Then she yawned and got up from her seat. "If you want to earn your keep for a day, then you better get rested up good. Tomorrow will be a long day, so I suggest you turn in soon and get some sleep. Now, I bid you a good night."

James decided a bath would do him good. He had ridden for days without bathing, so he surely reeked. He went down to the creek and stripped off his clothes. He felt embarrassed standing on the bank completely naked. Before stepping in, he took a quick look around. No one was about. He waded into the water. It took his breath away. The water was so cold; all he could tolerate were a few splashes. He got out, dried himself using the sleeve of his shirt, and then walked back to the house. He could feel the shuck mattress inviting him. He crawled into the lean-to and fell asleep.

*   *   *

154

Clank, clank, clank. The sound reverberated in his head. He awoke, and the clanking was still there. He listened some more. It was the sound of a bell. He dressed and stepped outside. A pale glow was peeking over the eastern horizon. Outside, the bell sounds were louder. He listened and determined they were coming from the barn. He walked down and found a small herd of cattle inside the corral. One of the cows had a bell around its neck. *A little strange,* he thought. He looked in the barn and saw Sarah milking a cow. "Good morning, sleepy head. I can tell by the hours you keep that you're not a farmer," she said.

"I guess you're right about that. What's the purpose of all these cattle?"

"That's how I make my living out here. I sell milk and eggs in the local town. That's about all I can produce on this pile of rocks. Have you ever milked a cow?"

"Can't say that I have."

"I don't have time to teach you; grab this bucket and carry it down to the creek."

Sarah handed him a bucket of warm milk. She took the one she had just finished in hand, and they walked down to the creek. "This is the spring source that feeds the creek; the water is coolest here at the mouth."

There was a rope line running into the creek. Sarah grabbed it and pulled up a large metal can. She removed the lid and poured the two buckets of milk inside. Then she put the lid back on and lowered the can back into the water.

"I'm almost done with the milking," Sarah said. "You go and feed the chickens while I finish in the barn. After that, we'll have some breakfast before the real fun begins."

She pointed out a bag of oats in the barn. James took it to the chicken house. As he carried the bag, he thought. *So it's come to this, the son of a Southern gentleman reduced to feeding chickens. What would my family think?*

The chicken house reeked of manure, feathers, and smells he couldn't identify. He walked carefully among the squawking birds, trying to watch where he stepped. The smell was making him ill. He dumped the grain into a wooden trough and went outside. He caught his breath in the fresh air before going up to the house. Sarah was working at the wood stove, frying eggs and bacon; a pot of coffee was brewing.

When breakfast was over, they went out and started walking the split rail fence around the farm. In sections, the rails had fallen away. James helped lift them back in place. It was hot, backbreaking work. Soon, James felt his back was ready to break, but he kept his aches to himself. His manly pride would not let him admit the work was getting him down.

About midmorning, Sarah stopped, removed her hat, and wiped the sweat from her brow. When James tried to stand up straight, his sore back resisted.

Just as bad, blisters were forming on his hands. "I believe we've earned a nice drink of water from the well," she said.

It was the best news James had heard all morning. They walked back to the well behind the house. He got the bucket, lowered it, and then drew it back full of water. He was proud to note that his skill at drawing water from a well had improved. Like the creek, the well water was cool. Sarah let part of it run over her hair and face before taking a long drink. James did likewise. The cool water was refreshing, restoring some of his energy, but the pain in his back remained.

They rested a few minutes, and then Sarah picked up her hat. "Time's wasting, so let's get back to it."

They spent the rest of the day wrestling with the fence timbers, stopping only for a brief lunch of sandwiches, and then they were back at it again.

When all that remained of the day was a pale curtain of orange in the western sky, Sarah stopped and took off her hat. "I reckon you've earned your keep, so let's call it quits."

At last, James thought. He couldn't remember when he had felt so tired and sore. His hands were now raw from handling the rough logs. His back ached, so he had to stoop when he walked; his legs were weak and tired.

They started toward the house; Sarah was in the lead. Near the house, she stopped and turned around. "Mr. McKane, you do a good day's work, a lot better than those no good loafers from town that I've had to use in the past."

"I'm glad you feel that way. I feel like I've done a week's work, but I'm glad I was able to help you out."

She paused a bit longer. "James, I hope you don't think I'm too forward, but I'd like to ask you something."

"What is it, Sarah?"

"Are you a married man?"

"Yes, I am. In fact, I'm on my way to Oregon to try and find my wife and children. They moved away during the war, and now I'm trying to locate them."

"Hard to imagine a wife going off and not telling her husband about it."

"There's a reason for that. She thinks I was killed in the war."

"That's terrible, all that grief for no reason. I know what it's like to lose someone."

"That's why I have to get to Oregon, so she can start to enjoy life again."

"I hope you find her soon. Anyway, I didn't mean to be forward, but good men are hard to come by right now. Running this place by myself is almost more than I can handle."

"An attractive lady like you shouldn't have any trouble finding a good husband."

"I hope so, but I'm getting tired of looking. Come into the house, and I'll fix some supper."

They had some sliced ham, homemade bread, and an assortment of canned vegetables. To James, it seemed that Sarah could stir up a gourmet meal on a minute's notice, but maybe that was a requirement for a farm wife.

After supper, James helped her with the evening chores. Afterward, Sarah went down to the creek for her evening bath. Then, James went down and had another try at the cold spring water; this time, he was able to tolerate the cool temperature. The water relieved his tired body and aching back. When he returned to the house, Sarah was sitting on the front porch.

They visited for a time. James talked about his life in Tennessee before the war. He talked about the plantation, his family, and their way of life.

"What's it like to be wealthy?" Sarah asked.

"I guess it's good that you are free from want," James replied. "At the same time, you overlook so many other things that are really important in life. I didn't appreciate my family enough, and now they're gone, leaving me to chase halfway across the country to try and find them.

"Losing my family, along with all the pain and suffering that I experienced during the war, has made me realize that some things cannot be taken for granted. When I was growing up on the plantation, everything was handed to me, and I assumed it would always be that way. There were servants running around waiting on me hand and foot, tending to my every need."

"I never had anything like that," Sarah said.

"The war taught me how isolated my life has been," James added. "I didn't even understand the causes of the war. I just went into it because I thought it was such a noble thing to do. In my view, it was the way to preserve the style of life I had always been privileged to enjoy, but in the Army, there were poor men who didn't have anything; I had to wonder what they were fighting for. Were they fighting so I could stay a wealthy man, and they could stay poor? That's when I started to realize how shallow my understanding about life really was."

"I never understood the war, either," Sarah replied. "I never understood why my husband, Frank, went off to fight with the Confederates. We were just poor hill people trying to scratch a living from this rocky soil. Frank talked over and over about things like state's rights, but I just never understood how that benefitted us. We were poor dirt farmers when it started and would still be poor dirt farmers when it was over, regardless of the outcome. All the war did was leave me here on this pile of rocks without a husband."

"I think most of us lost something," James replied. "I can cope with the loss of my family's fortune, but the loss of my family itself is more than I can live with."

Sarah got to her feet. "James, I wish you the best in finding your family. Since you plan to be moving on tomorrow, I think you need a good night of rest for your aching bones. Besides, if I think about it long enough, I might decide to kidnap you, and that wouldn't be fair to your wife and kids. Good night. I'll see you in the morning before you go."

James got up and went around to the lean-to. As he prepared for bed, he looked around the small room. A palace, it was far from, but for these past two days, it had provided the comforts of one. He was going to miss this shuck mattress and Sarah's cooking.

*   *   *

The next morning, he was tired and sore. He dressed and went down to the barn for his horse and gear. Sarah was not around. The cows were grazing in a nearby pasture.

James saddled the gelding. The horse had benefitted more than he these past few days. Grazing with Sarah's cattle had put a few pounds on its frame and gained it some much-needed rest. He rode up to the house and tied the reins to the front porch.

Inside, Sarah was preparing breakfast. Eggs and bacon were frying on the stove next to a pot of brewing coffee. A plate of thick, buttered toast was sitting on the table. The aroma of the kitchen made his stomach growl.

"I'm going to miss your cooking, Sarah. Your next husband will sure be a lucky man."

A slight smile formed on her face, but she offered no comment.

They ate in silence. James finished, pushed back from the table, got up, and started for the door.

"Wait a minute," Sarah said. She stepped into a small side room and came out with James's weapons. "I almost forgot about these. I guess it's safe to give them back to you. Oh, I oiled them up. They should be good as new."

How could he forget his weapons? It embarrassed him. James took the pistol, Henry, and shotgun from her. Then, he walked to the door with Sarah following.

"I noticed you're rather low on traveling supplies," she said. "I packed a few things for you. Consider it part of your payment for helping me."

"Thank you. I appreciate it."

"Be careful out there, James. There's plenty of danger between here and Oregon."

"I will."

"If you ever come back this way, stop in for a visit."

"It would be my pleasure," James said.

158

Sarah stood on the porch while he secured his weapons and rations then mounted. She waved her hand as he rode out of the yard. At the road, James looked toward the house, but she had already stepped back inside and closed the door.

For a time, James kept the horse in an easy trot. Tree limbs and other debris from the storm lay in the road, some large enough he had to steer the gelding around them.

Independence—the jumping-off place to the west. He hoped to be there soon. At the onset, he figured this would be the easy portion of the journey. To the west was where he expected to have the most difficulty with the mountains, Indians, and other dangers he had not heard about. With what he had experienced to date, did that prophecy still hold? If it did, then what would the rest be like?

Chapter 16

A Heavy Burden

Summer was near at hand. Olaf spent most of this time in the fields causing Kate to wonder if the burden of running the farm might be taking a toll on him. She asked Helga. "No, dear," she replied. "Olaf knows we are all depending on the farm for our survival. He's a strong man, used to hard labor."

Kate still felt concerned for him. Without Olaf, she would be lost. To ease his burden a bit, she told him to hire some more men to help out. He found a few willing workers in La Grande. Now, she and Helga had to spend more time in the kitchen preparing food for more workers. But she didn't complain, taking a cue from Helga, who worked from dawn to dusk without muttering a word of complaint or protest.

Time slipped into mid-June. Kate was mopping the floor in the main room. When the job was done, she stepped outside to empty the bucket. Out of nowhere, a man stepped around the house. Kate froze. The cold, hard face of Palmer was staring at her. Her lips quivered. "What are you doing here?"

"I just came by to be sociable," Palmer replied. His piercing, dark eyes sent shivers through her.

"I don't believe we have anything to visit about."

"On the contrary, I believe we have considerable to talk about."

Like a cat, Palmer sprang up on the porch; his cold, dark eyes fixed on her. "I'm going to tell you a few things for your own good. I've been hearing stories about your plan to stir up trouble with the settlers, and that ain't a wise thing to do. Your uncle did the same thing, and as I've been told, he ain't around anymore. Best thing you can do is let things go on as planned. I hope that's clear to you."

The mention of Uncle Lewis pushed away some of her fear. "Did Covington send you out here to scare me?" The tremble in her voice probably masked her attempted bravado.

160

Palmer's dark eyes narrowed. His hand was on her arm, squeezing. "I didn't come here to answer any questions; I came here to give you a warning. Don't talk to the settlers anymore."

Kate recoiled. At that moment, Helga stepped out on the porch. She stopped, startled by the man holding Kate's arm. "What's happening here?"

He released Kate's arm and stepped back. "You best remember what I told you. The next time, I won't be so easy on you." He disappeared around the corner of the house.

Kate was forced to sit down on the porch to regain her composure. Tears dimmed her vision. Rage filled her.

Helga stood beside her. "What was that man doing here? Did he hurt you?"

Kate wiped at her eyes. "No, he came to scare me. It seems the word has gotten out I'm trying to help the settlers. They're trying to shut me up, just like they did Uncle Lewis. They think I'll wreck their plans, and the truth will come out about my uncle."

*   *   *

When Olaf came in from the fields, Kate told him about Palmer. He swore, a rare thing for him. "Looks like we need to keep extra guards around the house. I thought we were rid of that bunch, but I guess not. If you want, I can have more of the men stay here each day until we finish with the crops."

Kate hated to keep any of the men away from the fields. As it was, they were getting behind schedule. But her safety couldn't be ignored. She reluctantly agreed to let one of the older men remain behind each day in place of the younger ones. The two boys had been of little use in protecting them. Palmer had had no trouble getting up to the house.

"None of the men are gunmen," Olaf explained. "But maybe the sight of one of the older men will discourage that bunch from coming around."

*   *   *

Her fear subsided—Palmer's boldness raised Kate's ire. This was her home. She wasn't going to tolerate being threatened on her own porch. The next morning, after Olaf and the workers went to the fields, she went outside to see who was guarding the house. A middle-aged man with graying hair was standing by the yard fence smoking a pipe. She was quick to conclude he was little more help than the boys at protecting them. "Can you drive a buggy?" she asked.

"Yes, ma'am."

"Please go down to the barn, hitch the team to the buggy, and bring it up to the yard."

"Yessum, but Mr. Olaf said for me to stay close to the house."

"That's fine. Olaf works for me. I want you to drive me to La Grande."

"Yes, ma'am." He tapped his pipe on the fence and put it in his front pocket. Kate regretted having to overrule Olaf's orders. The men were accustomed to following him, not her. This time it couldn't be helped—there were more pressing matters at hand.

Kate went back into the house where Helga was finishing the breakfast dishes. "Let's take the children for a buggy ride."

"That's a wonderful idea, but there's so much to do around the house. I have to get the noon meal ready."

"Let it go for a little while. Leave that meat cooking on the stove; it will be done by the time we return. You baked yesterday, so there's plenty of bread already made. You need to get out, and so do the children."

The truth was, Kate didn't want to leave Helga and the children alone while she was gone. Besides, the children had seen La Grande only once; Helga rarely went anywhere. The ride would be good for all of them.

The hired man pulled the buggy into the yard. Kate shooed the children out then urged a reluctant Helga. She sat in front with Drew on her lap. Helga and the other children sat in the back. James Junior had a scowl on his face; the driver looked uncomfortable. He tapped the team; the buggy rolled forward.

It was a pleasant morning. Spring was fading into summer, but the temperature was still bearable. The meadow and surrounding countryside were still green. Drew fell asleep before they were on the road.

"There's an eagle!" James Junior called out.

The large bird circled over them.

"He's looking for a rabbit," James Junior said. "He's going to have rabbit for breakfast."

"I hope the rabbit gets away," Alice said.

Kate smiled at the children's bantering. She held her hand over Drew's sleeping face to ward off dust stirred up by the buggy wheels and horses' hooves.

"Drop us at the courthouse," Kate instructed the driver when they arrived in La Grande.

Kate woke up Drew and helped him down from the buggy. Helga and the other children climbed out. "Find a place to park the buggy, then wait for us," she told the driver.

She reached into her dress pocket and got out a bag of gold dust, the local currency. "Helga, see if you can find some candy for the children."

162

Helga took the bag and herded the children toward Main Street. Kate went into the courthouse directly to the sheriff's office. She found Avery Benton sitting behind his desk. Her entrance brought a look of torture to his face. "I have something to report."

The sheriff leaned back in his chair. "And what would that be?"

"I had another visit from that man they call Palmer. He threatened me."

"What kind of threat did he make?"

"He warned me not to talk to the settlers. What do you intend to do about it?"

"I keep hearing about this Palmer feller, but nobody except you has ever seen him. My deputies and I have searched the entire valley, but we never got a glimpse of the man. The same goes for that young fella you claim rode off with your uncle. Until these men are produced, they ain't much I can do."

"I believe Mr. Covington can tell you where they are."

His face contorted like a man encountering a sudden pain. "Now, miss, you've got to stop making accusations you can't back up."

"Let me tell you, Sheriff before this is over, I intend to prove every last bit of it."

"I'll come out to your place and have a look. That's the best I can do. I'll see if I can get a line on this man that keeps showing up out there."

"I appreciate that, Sheriff. Forgive me for bothering you."

Frustration, that's all she could get from Avery Benton. Well, getting him to come out was something of a miracle, not that it would do any good. Kate left the sheriff's office.

The buggy was parked on Main Street near the general store. Helga and the children stood nearby. The driver was sitting in the front seat, smoking his pipe.

Each of the children had rock candy and licorice. Drew's face was covered with black residue. Kate laughed. She worried about them breaking a tooth on the hard candy. But it was good to see them enjoying themselves. There had been so little to enjoy recently.

They loaded into the buggy and drove home. The children were happy. Even James Junior had opened up a little. Kate tried to do the same. *Would the sheriff keep his word and come out? Probably not*, she concluded. At that thought, her attempt at happiness faded.

It was near noon when they reached home. Hungry men would be showing up to eat. Helga's efficiency took over. She put the meat on the table and sliced up fresh vegetables from the garden. When the men arrived, the meal was ready.

"How is the work coming along?" Kate asked Olaf.

"Well, I think we should be done sowing grain by the end of the week," he replied.

Kate was pleased with the news. But in spite of it, she just couldn't relax. So much depended on their crop; the livelihood of them and the new settlers was at stake. And even in Olaf's capable hands, there was so much that could go wrong.

The men ate and returned to the fields. Shortly, Sheriff Benton arrived, accompanied by a young man, not much more than a boy. He was slender with a broad face and small mustache. The faded hat on the young man's head partially covered his bushy, brown hair. A deputy's badge was pinned to his red-flannel shirt.

Kate waited on the porch while the sheriff and his deputy dismounted. "Where did you see this man?" the sheriff asked.

Kate pointed toward the end of the porch. "He came from around that side of the house."

The sheriff walked over to the side of the house with the young deputy following. He leaned over and studied the ground. Then they walked out to the meadow and looked around. The sheriff walked around the entire perimeter of the meadow, looking down at the ground.

They came back to the house. "Someone walked from the meadow up to the house," the sheriff said. "Looks like they had a horse waiting out there, but I can't follow the tracks very far because they lead back out to the road. Once they get on the road, they are covered by all the other tracks."

"Is that all you can do?"

"For now. If this feller comes back again, get word to me in town; I'll try to find him, but I can't do anything else right now."

"Surely," Kate said sarcastically.

The sheriff left her angry and disappointed but not surprised. The local law was indifferent to her problems.

Her inheritance was taking on a new meaning. Not only did she acquire her uncle's property, but his problems as well. She was not equipped to deal with this. All her life, there had been someone to help her; first, it was her mother and father, then her husband. Now she was alone—a chilling thought it was.

The firm decision she made to remain in Oregon wavered. Olaf could take over the farm. The settlers could find their own way to deal with Covington. She thought some more. That would be unfair to Olaf. He didn't bring the settlers up here. She couldn't justify dumping her problems on him.

Kate compromised. She would put off her final decision until next spring. Then she would decide whether to stay in Oregon and take on the unpleasant task she had inherited or take the children and go back to Tennessee

Chapter 17

The Journey Continues

During the long days in the saddle, boredom was James's companion. He longed for someone to talk with, to pass the time. Most days, he rode until dark to make up for lost time. Now, he regretted the day spent helping Sarah. But time spent couldn't be undone. Usually, he made do with a cold camp at night, taking his sustenance from hardtack or cold meat left over from breakfast.

The Osage River presented him with a major obstacle. It was running high and filled with debris. Crossing here was out of the question. He rode along the bank, looking for a more suitable crossing or maybe a ferryboat.

It was quiet along the river. Birds fluttered among the willows and cottonwoods, and insects buzzed about him and his horse. He passed a family fishing along the bank. The shirtless man, dressed in muddy pants, looked up but did not speak. A young girl and boy sat under a tree playing with a small dog.

A few miles down the river, there was a trading post. He stopped and tied his horse in front of the small, log building. An elderly man and woman were inside. The man had long, white whiskers; his lower lip and chin were covered with tobacco stains. The woman's long, white hair fell down her back in a tangled mess. She was sitting in a wooden chair dipping snuff with a piece of small root.

The interior of the store was similar to many others James had found in Missouri. It was sparsely furnished with a handmade counter of red oak, a few straight-back chairs, and shelves along the walls filled with canned goods and salted meats.

"Good morning," James said.

"Yes, sir," the man replied. The woman looked at him and nodded her head.

165

"Somethin' fer ye this morning?" the man asked.

James pointed to a slab of bacon on one of the shelves. "I'll have a chunk of that bacon."

The man pulled down the slab of bacon and chopped off a portion using a large knife.

"I'm looking for a place to cross the river," James said.

"Ludbill's Ferry, 'bout two mile down the river is your best bet. That'll be fifty cents for the bacon."

James felt the bacon price was a bit high, but he didn't quibble. He gave the man a small gold coin.

The storekeeper studied the coin, then put it in his mouth and bit down. Satisfied, he put the coin in his pocket. "Much obliged."

James put the bacon in one of his saddlebags. Then, he started down the river looking for the ferry. The dense brush along the riverbank made the going tough, almost tearing his clothes away and scratching at his skin. Hordes of mosquitoes swarmed around his face and ears. Finally, the brush gave way to open country. The ferry was a short ride down the river.

The worthiness of the vessel was questionable. It was a raft of oak planks mounted on empty drums secured to a cable stretched across the river. There were ropes connected to each end of the ferry, threaded through pulleys on each side.

James had a bit of luck. The boat was moored to a small, wooden dock on this side of the river. A man wearing a sea captain's hat and a faded leather vest and pants was sitting on the dock, smoking a corncob pipe. A teenage boy dressed in a tattered cotton shirt and pants was sitting on the side, dangling his feet in the water. The boy wore an old felt hat that covered most of his ears.

"A fine day to you," the man said. "Would you be wantin' to cross the river?"

"I would."

"Twenty-five cents, and we'll take you across."

"Agreed." James tossed the man a coin.

"Lead your horse up on the boat, and we'll pull ye over."

With some urging, James got his horse up on the boat. The gelding was nervous. He held tight to the reins to keep it from jumping off into the river.

"On your feet, Oliver," the man said. "Give the rope a pull."

The boy got up and pulled on the rope while the man used a long pole to push the boat into the current. "Give it a hard pull, Oliver."

The current drove the boat downstream until it pulled the cable taut. *Would it hold?* James wondered.

"You ain't a wanted man, are ye?" the man asked as he worked at the pole.

"Not that I know about." He chose to forget about the tavern raid in Kentucky.

"That's pleasing to hear. There was a company of militia through here yesterday, looking for outlaws and holdouts from the war. Paid good money to take 'em across, they did."

Militia, they seemed to be everywhere, James thought.

Sweat formed on the man's brow. He had the pole all the way to the bottom of the river, pushing with all his might. "Give it a hard pull, Oliver. Lad's a little peculiar at times if you know what I mean, but he's a steady worker."

The boy looked at them with a toothy grin as he tugged at the rope.

"Mind ye, I ain't got no opinion one way or the other about the recent conflict," the man said. "I'm just a poor river man trying to eke out a living the only way I know how. Union men, rebels, I took 'em all across when they asked, long as they paid, that is. Pull hard, Oliver. Pull hard, lad."

Near the other side, the boat turned sideways, startling his horse. James struggled to keep it on the boat. The man righted the boat with the long pole. The boy gave a hard pull; the boat bumped into another small dock.

The man gave the boy a pat on the shoulder. "Well done, lad."

James led his horse off the dock onto the sandy beach and mounted.

"I'm obliged to ye," the man said.

"How far is Independence?" James asked.

"A four or five-day ride, I reckon."

Welcome news with him already behind schedule. It was well into summer, and he still needed a guide to take him the rest of the way. The winter snows were not far away.

*   *   *

James tried to make up some time. The Missouri days were hot. He rose early, wanting to cover as much distance as possible while it was cool. By the end of the day, both he and his horse would be exhausted.

About midmorning on a particular day, James stopped to wipe the sweat from his brow. He was startled by the sound of loud singing. He listened. It seemed to be coming from behind. He turned around. A man on a mule was coming around a bend in the road.

"Thine eyes have seen the glory of the coming of the Lord," the voice boomed.

This was a curious sight—the man and the mule. James waited as the man rode toward him, still singing at the top of his voice. He was tall. Despite the heat, the man was wearing a black frock coat and a black hat with a tall crown and large brim. He had a long, black beard. When he was closer, James noticed the man's piercing dark eyes.

"Good morning, my brother," the man boomed out. "And might I ask where you're bound for this glorious day?"

"Independence. If I may ask, mister, who are you?"

"Around these hills, they call me the Reverend Sam."

"I'm James McKane."

"It seems we're going in the same direction, so I guess we'll be sharing the road for a time," the reverend said.

"So it seems."

Some company would keep away the boredom. But the sight of the man sitting on the mule was almost comical. How out of place he looked.

"I'm a saver of lost souls for these hill people. With all that's transpired these past few years, there's many a soul that needs saving—I can tell you that."

"You got a church somewhere?"

"The countryside is my church. Wherever I'm at, that's my church. The work of the Lord goes on everywhere, not just inside the walls of a church."

James nodded. There were some peculiarities about the reverend. When the man talked, he stared straight ahead, as if he were in a trance. And his voice, how it reverberated when he spoke.

"The truth is, I once had a church; that is, my father did. He came down from Illinois and opened up a church in Montgomery County. Daddy tried to tell all the folks that God, not politics, was his interest in life, but it seems word got out that he had sheltered a particular group of people. These people supported a cause not popular with the rest of the folks in the county. One night, the church went up in flames. Those people opposed to my father's preaching burned it to the ground.

"Well, sir, my father never got over that. A year later, he passed from this world a broken man. Daddy had dreamed of serving his fellow man, but that dream went up in the flames that consumed his church. I vowed on his grave that I would take up his work of caring for the poor hill people. That's what I've been doing ever since."

"That seems like a noble cause," James said.

"I tell you this. God has brought his wrath on this land for the war and all the killin' and destroying that went on. The war was brought on by another evil: slavery. One man taking another into bondage is evil in the sight of God."

That struck a chord in James. The man was an abolitionist. Having been raised in the slave culture, he had never stopped to question the morality of the issue, but since the war, he was finding himself more skeptical about certain ideas.

168

They rode together until mid-afternoon when the reverend turned to James.

"There's a small town just over the next hill. I have some business there."

That was convenient for him. His supplies were low. "I'll ride in with you if you don't mind."

"That would be my pleasure."

They encountered no end of stares when they rode down the dusty main street. The sight of the reverend on his mule, accompanied by another stranger, fueled the curiosity of the local people.

The town was typical of what James had found in Missouri. Along the dusty main street were an assortment of businesses and a few scattered houses. A few wagons were parked in front of some of the businesses; in a small park, men were tossing horseshoes.

Reverend Sam stopped his mule in the center of town. Then, he got a bible from his saddlebag and positioned himself on the sidewalk. For a moment, he stood with his head bowed, then raised his eyes to the sky. "Repent, for the time of God draws near," he boomed.

People stopped and listened. With his loud resounding voice, the reverend had the power to captivate and hold an audience. He pounded on the bible as he spoke. "The day of reckoning is at hand, my friends. The word is your only salvation."

In a short time, the reverend had drawn a large crowd. A few tried to heckle him, but he was undaunted, drowning them out with his own words. "Doubters and sinners be gone from among us!" he yelled.

Near the end of the sermon, someone started passing a hat among the crowd. People reached into their pockets and pulled out money.

When he was finished, the reverend pulled a large, red handkerchief out of his pocket and wiped away the sweat from his brow and face. One of the men stepped out of the crowd and handed him the money they had collected.

"Bless you, my brothers and sisters!" the reverend yelled.

The reverend put the money in a leather pouch. As James started for his horse, he noticed three young men standing nearby. One was tall and lanky and had scraggy whiskers. The other two were younger and had rough appearances like their companion.

"Say Reverend; you sure got them country bumpkins going with that hellfire and brimstone talk," the tall one said. "Yes, sir, them hicks sure coughed up their coins when they heard you light into 'em like that."

"It was the work of the Lord. I'm merely the Lord's servant."

"Well now, Reverend, I reckon you're gonna share your take with your fellow men; you're gonna share it all with three of your fellow men right now."

"This money is for my work. These funds are for the people of the hills that need my help."

"You can always bilk a few more hicks. Now, hand me that collection." The man reached into his pocket and pulled out a knife. "Give me that money, or I'm gonna cut you up good."

"You'll not take from the needy," the reverend boomed.

James looked for someone in authority, but there was no one. A few people were watching but seemed to have no inclination to intervene. He hoped maybe the reverend would not risk his life for the meager sum, but it was plain to see the man was going to stand his ground. Foolish on one hand—yet admirable on the other.

That left James and his pistol. He was reaching for it when the knife wielder lunged at Reverend Sam. The reverend, surprisingly agile, stepped to the side, allowing the knife to miss him completely. The young man stumbled, caught his balance, and straightened up, then turned for another try. Too late. A fist slammed into his nose. The knife fell from his hand; he staggered and fell into the street.

"He broke my nose! The old bastard broke my nose!" the young man yelled.

One of his companions swung his fist at the reverend, landing a glancing blow on his head. The preacher barely flinched. He grabbed the man, lifted him off his feet, and heaved him toward his fallen companion.

The third man looked at his two companions sprawled in the dust, then turned and ran down the street; the spectators laughed.

The reverend was unfazed. He walked calmly over to his mule. James was embarrassed for not intervening. But it happened so quickly he had been unable to react. The remaining crowd, seeing it was over, dispersed down the dusty street.

The reverend mounted his mule, and James got back up on his horse. They rode down the street. Behind them, they could still hear the wounded attacker yelling, "He broke my nose!"

Outside of town, James turned to the reverend. The preacher was sitting on the mule staring straight ahead. "That was quite a lick you put on that man's nose."

The reverend continued to look straight ahead, and for a moment, didn't reply. James started to speak again, but the reverend said, "Defending the poor is my mission in life. The small sums I collect, I use mostly to help the poor hill people. I won't tolerate stealing from the destitute. Only sinners of the lowest intent would take from those that have so little. Besides, maybe a whack on the nose will help that man see the error of his ways."

James doubted a ruffian could be reformed by a broken nose but guessed it might be possible. He decided it best to drop the matter. After riding a short distance, the reverend looked at him. "Of course, I'll pray for the Lord's forgiveness for not turning the other cheek."

James nodded. He was a little disappointed for not being able to pick up some supplies, but maybe what he had would last until Independence.

They camped off the road in a little grove of oaks. The Reverend Sam cooked beans with salt pork and some pan bread that put James's to shame. "Reverend, you're a handy man with a skillet."

"A man must acquire many skills to survive in this world."

Afterward, the reverend sat by the fire and read from the Bible. Later, he got up and walked out from the camp. James could hear him making his prayers. The man amazed him. He could still hear the smack of the fist against the would-be robber's nose. Well, a man of the cloth had a right to defend himself, just like anyone else, but he still wondered about his traveling companion. It was late. James got out his bedroll and prepared to sleep.

*   *   *

The next morning, Reverend Sam was not in camp. James's first thought was he had gone on without him. Then, he saw the mule grazing a short distance away. He stirred the fire and got a small blaze going. He was putting some bacon into the skillet when the reverend came out of the woods; water was dripping off his hair and beard. "Thought maybe you were lost," James said.

"I was having a bath in the nearby stream. Cleanliness is a desirable trait in a person, even when accommodations are limited. I now feel like a new man, ready for this glorious day the Lord has provided."

With James's concurrence, the reverend took over the cooking. The crisp bacon and pan bread hit the spot. After eating, they caught their mounts and set out down the road.

"Son, where did you say your destination was?"

"To Independence, then on to Oregon," James said.

"A journey of considerable distance. Off to seek fortune and fame, maybe in the goldfields?"

"No. I'm off to find the family I lost during the war."

"Then I wish you Godspeed in your journey. I know the loneliness of not having a family, but I have the Lord with me, so I'm never really alone. I'll pray for you to have a safe journey."

"I appreciate that."

"I'll be leaving you shortly. There's a crossroad just a few miles up ahead. I'll be going on to Sedalia from there. The other road will take you to Independence."

When they reached the crossroad, the reverend stuck out his hand. After shaking it, James felt like his had been in a bear trap.

"God bless you, Son," the reverend said.

The reverend rode away on the mule. *He was a most interesting man*, James felt. He would miss his company.

James did not stop at noon. Instead, he chose to push on toward Independence. He pulled a bacon sandwich left from breakfast from one of his saddlebags and kept riding. For the rest of the day, his only stops were to water and rest his horse. He rode until near dark.

He chose to camp in a clearing near the road. He unsaddled and hobbled his weary horse and started setting up camp. A voice from the woods behind the camp startled him. "Evening, my friend."

James turned with his pistol drawn as a man stepped out of the darkness.

"No need for arms, my friend. I'm just a weary traveler like you."

The man was dressed in a suit, vest, and string tie. Here in the hills, he looked totally out of place. James judged him to be a drummer of some sort.

"Name's Henry Philpott," the man said. "I represent a company out of Kansas City. I got a line of household wares that any housewife would be honored to own, but try to tell these hill hicks anything. These bumpkins don't know the difference between a silk purse and a sow's ear."

James was annoyed by the man's attitude. He let it be.

"No need for a fire," the man went on. "Don't want to call unwanted attention to yourself. I got a wagon back in the woods out of sight. You just can't be too careful with all the scallywags running loose in these hills. Bloody cutthroats, they are. I got coffee and something stronger if you feel the urge."

It was late, and he was tired. He decided to accept the man's offer. "Some coffee would be appreciated."

The drummer led James back into the woods. Despite his cordiality, something about Henry Philpott planted seeds of distrust in James's mind. In the woods, behind a clump of bushes, was a small canvas-covered wagon. Nearby was a team of draft horses. Next to the wagon was a coffee pot sitting on a bed of coals.

The man reached into the wagon and handed James a large, white cup. "Help yourself to some hot coffee."

James filled the cup. He stood by the wagon and sipped on the coffee. The drummer seated himself on a fallen tree trunk near the wagon.

"I tell you, it's hell to survive out here in this wilderness," the drummer said. "Most of these dirt farmers don't have a copper cent to their name, and the few that do are too ignorant to know a good product when they see one."

"The war left many of them in need."

"I can tell you it wasn't much better before the war. I been working this territory for many years, and it's always been like this. What's a man to do?"

The drummer's complaints didn't interest James. He drank the last of the coffee and handed the cup back to the man. "I got a long day ahead of me, so I'll be turning in now."

"Friend, I didn't get your name."

"James McKane."

"Well, James, before you leave in the morning, you need to take a look at my wares. I got a fine line of products for the traveling man."

Henry's products didn't interest James either. He gave the man a quick nod and went back to his own camp. He still didn't trust the drummer; as a precaution, he put his pistol under his blanket before going to sleep.

Later in the night, James was awakened by a sound close to his bed. He opened his eyes and waited until he was able to make out a dark figure near his gear. He eased his hand under the blanket and brought out the pistol. The figure started dragging his saddlebags across the ground.

James sat up and cocked the pistol. "Leave my gear alone."

The startled drummer dropped James's saddlebags. "Please, Mr. McKane, I ain't had a sale in days. I was just looking for a little something to tide me over."

"I can appreciate hard times, but not stealin'," James said. "You're going to have to get your things and get out of here. I won't share a camp with a man that can't be trusted."

"In the middle of the night? Mister, you must be crazy. Besides, I was camped here first."

"Wasn't me who got caught stealin'," James replied. "Now, get your wagon and get on out of here."

The drummer grumbled but complied. He walked back to his own camp, with James following close behind. He retrieved his team and swore several times as he tried to harness the horses in the dark. When the team was ready, he hitched up the small wagon and drove out to the road. James walked along behind and watched until Henry Philpott and his wares disappeared into the darkness.

*   *   *

The sun was peeking over the horizon the next morning when James crawled out of his bed. After a quick breakfast, he found his horse and brought it back to camp. While saddling the gelding, he looked back to where the drummer had been camped. There was something lying on the ground. He walked back and found a Sedalia newspaper near where the wagon had been parked.

Curious as to what might be in the news, James picked up the paper and started reading. The date on the front page was June 12, 1865.

There wasn't much of interest until he reached the bottom of the front page. There, a headline about the Farley gang caught his attention. He had almost forgotten the encounter at the farm house.

MEMBER OF THE FARLEY GANG ESCAPES

Pratt Henderson, a reported member of the Elias Farley gang, escaped from the Pettis County Jail. Henderson was being held in the jail awaiting trial for a number of crimes against the people of Missouri. He had been captured in a shootout at a farmhouse in Reynolds County.

Henderson escaped by tying bed sheets together and climbing out a second-story window. The authorities are searching the immediate area.

The news report distressed James. Pratt Henderson was the only member of the gang that had seen his face. And now, this desperado was on the loose again. Something else to worry about—the last thing he needed. It seemed this bunch could pop up almost anywhere here in Missouri. He would have to be extra careful until he was out of this state. He tossed the newspaper down and went over to his horse.

By late afternoon, James could see the spire of a building rising up toward the sky. Independence—he was almost there. The first leg of his journey was coming to an end. What lay ahead?

Chapter 18

Kate's Plan

Summer came to the valley—Kate struggled with the heat and her inherited problems. Through the long, hot days, she labored to find a way to protect the settlers as well as herself. How could she save these poor people from a powerful and greedy man like Covington? Her resources were limited, her knowledge and skills likewise, so what could she do? Soon, she found her mettle wilting like the grass in the meadow. Her nerves were frayed, ready to snap. Sleep became elusive, coming only late at night, if at all.

*   *   *

In early July, Olaf planted an idea. They were seated at the table having breakfast. "Missy, now that planting has been completed, we need to find a way to get our own crops to market."

"Yes, I know. I've been worrying over that myself."

"Well, before all the problems started, your uncle had planned to use Covington, just like everyone else. With the trouble that's going on now, we can't do that."

What Olaf had just said reminded her of something. She remembered Uncle Lewis had mentioned doing their own hauling. "One thing we can do is try to haul everything ourselves."

"Yaw, but we don't have the wagons or the drivers," he replied. "Traveling in this country can be risky. We are lucky this year that we will be marketing mostly oats and barley. Grain will keep, but next year there will be fruits and vegetables that we have to market quickly."

Kate saw only one solution. They had to provide their own transportation. "We have to find our own wagons and drivers. That's the only way we can survive."

"That will take some money," Olaf said.

"How much?"

"A good wagon will cost you at least one-hundred-fifty dollars; then, there're the drivers. It'll cost you at least ten dollars a trip for a driver, and you'll need good draft horses; they'll cost you at least two hundred dollars each if you can find them."

"We've got to do it, Olaf. I should have enough money in the bank to buy some of the wagons and horses; we should be able to pay the drivers out of what we sell. I'll find a way to get the rest."

"I don't know, missy. It sounds risky to me."

"We can't leave our crops out in the fields to rot. I'm going to do it."

Olaf said no more. He was skeptical, and that troubled her. But time was short, and she knew no other way.

Kate helped Helga with the breakfast dishes then went out to the porch to escape the heat of the house. There, she sat and thought.

A freight company of our own, she kept running the idea through her mind. Euphoria would be followed by doubts. She didn't know anything about business. Well, her father was a businessman, a successful one until the war started. Maybe it was in her blood. And it would solve some of their problems. Best, it would help break the hold Covington had over them.

She carried the idea beyond just their needs. It could be the answer to the settler's problems as well. Like the settlers, their farm needed freight service. Those who signed the agreement were bound to Covington. She studied over the matter. There was a legal way around Covington's agreement. If the settlers sold their crops in the field, they would need no freight service. The agreement with Covington only specified freight hauling. That was it—a way out. Moreover, Harrington Farms had no freight agreement with Covington. They could buy the settlers' crops and take delivery in the field. Yes, that was the answer. She had a plan; happiness swept over her.

Then another beast reared its head, sweeping the euphoria away. E. G. Covington would not take this lightly. What happened to Uncle Lewis was proof aplenty as to how far he would go to protect his interests. He would not hesitate to use violence against her if he felt threatened. She had better give this some more thought. There were the children, Olaf and Helga, all who could be in danger if this situation turned violent.

Kate agonized over what to do. She came to the conclusion there was no safe, peaceful way around this dilemma. She had to proceed and, at the same time, find a way to protect all of them from Covington and Palmer. A challenge, she knew, but several poor people were depending on her, and she couldn't let them down.

That evening, she laid out her entire plan to Olaf. He listened patiently.

His silence left her to conclude he had his doubts, which troubled her. She would be stymied without his help. "Do you have any suggestions?" she asked.

He shook his head.

"Then it's settled. I want to start right away by looking for some of the things we need, like wagons and horses. We don't have a lot of time, so I want to start tomorrow."

Olaf slowly nodded his head. His hesitation left her discouraged and frustrated. If he could just show a little enthusiasm, it would lighten her burden. It would be up to him to select the horses and wagons and to hire the drivers. Her only hope was he would come to see things her way. A cautious man by nature, he would just need a little time to come to grips with her plan, so she hoped.

The next thing was to get the word out to the settlers. Planting time was over; the settlers would be free. Now was an opportune time to try and get the rest of them behind her.

Having a plan didn't take away her worries. Could she handle such a responsibility? Just the thought of it sent chills down her spine. Oh, how she missed Uncle Lewis. She needed his wisdom and determination. And James, how she missed her husband.

James and Uncle Lewis were alike in many ways. It was true they came from different backgrounds, but there was a common thread between the two men. James was also a take-charge person who would take on any obstacle to get what he wanted. Their marriage had been a testimonial to the type of man he was. His family never approved of their union. They were members of the landed aristocracy, while Kate's father was a merchant. That did not sway him in his determination to marry her. This was the kind of determination and leadership she needed now.

*   *   *

The following morning, Kate prepared to set her plan in motion. "Olaf, today I want to start looking for some wagons and horses," she reminded him during breakfast. "Do you have any ideas about where to start?"

"Croft, the livery owner in La Grande, might have some ideas. He deals in horses."

"When breakfast is over, hitch the buggy and take me there."

"Yes, missy," he said softly.

Kate left the children in Helga's care. Olaf was waiting in the yard with the buggy. He tapped the horses, and they rode across the meadow and out to the road. Although it was early morning, the heat was already oppressive. To add to that, Kate had to hold her hand in front of her face to ward off the

177

choking dust from the horses' hooves.

In La Grande, Olaf parked the buggy in front of the livery stable. Kate was nervous about going in. She knew so little about buying horses and wagons. Riding, yes, but buying horses, no. She felt like an intruder, trespassing where she had no business. When Olaf opened the stable door for her, she gagged. The interior reeked of manure and rotting hay. She had to fight the urge to go back outside. *Pull yourself together*, she told herself. If she was to be successful, then she had to show some spunk. A freight line owner couldn't be put off by the smell of manure.

In back of the stable, they found a short, stout man with a balding head and large, dark mustache shoeing a horse. "Morning," he said. "Can I help you?"

"Mr. Croft, this is my employer, Mrs. McKane."

The man dried his hands on his leather apron. "Mrs. McKane, what can I do for you?"

"Please, call me Kate. I'm interested in buying some wagons and horses."

"I don't have any draft horses right now. E. G. Covington buys most of what I get. You might find something over in Pendleton."

Kate was disappointed but still determined. She thanked Mr. Croft and then followed Olaf toward the door.

"Wait a minute!" Croft yelled. "I just remembered something that might help you."

Kate stopped. "What would that be?"

"'Bout a month ago, there was a wagon master through here. He had brought some folks up from the Midwest, Iowa, I think, and he had a bunch of teams and wagons he wanted to get rid of; said he'd sell the whole lot for a fair price. I didn't have any need at the time; besides, the horses and wagons were both in poor shape. Some good pasture would help the horses, and some repair work on the wagons might get them going again. I 'spect you might get a good deal from this fella."

Her enthusiasm surged. "Where can we find this man?"

"I seem to recall that he was headed for a place over near The Dalles, on the Columbia."

"Do you know that area, Olaf?"

"Yaw, but it's not a good place, I think. There's gold over there. Those gold towns are rough and rowdy."

"We'll have to take our chances on that. Thank you, Mr. Croft. How long does it take to get over there?"

"There's a stage that goes once a week from here every Wednesday, and it takes about four days to get over there," Croft replied.

"Thank you again. Do you know this man's name?"

Mr. Croft thought. "I believe it was Robert or Reuben. No, I got it, Rupert Berry. Ask for a man named Rupert Berry."

"Thank you again, Mr. Croft," Kate said.

Outside, Kate turned to Olaf. "Next Wednesday, I want you to be on that stage. Go over to the place Mr. Croft was talking about and see if you can make a deal with this Rupert Berry. I will give you the authority to act on my behalf. You know horses and wagons, so you can get a better deal than I ever could. I've noticed frontier men don't like the idea of dealing with a woman anyway."

He reluctantly agreed. Kate hated to send him off on a mission that he didn't have any enthusiasm for, but they had to act and act quickly if they were going to survive. Before leaving town, Olaf bought a few farm supplies. Kate bought supplies for the house and candy for the kids.

The ride home was more uncomfortable than the one to town. It was now noon, the temperature was hotter, and the dust seemed thicker. Kate felt she was going to choke.

When they were home, she tried to clean the dirt from her face and hair. Then, she took the supplies into the kitchen, helped Helga empty a sack of flour into a metal can, and did the same with a sack of sugar. They put two cans of lard on a shelf and stored the rest of the supplies in the cellar.

After the noon meal, Kate distributed the candy to the children. Then, it was back to her plan. With Olaf off next week to see about horses and wagons, she concentrated on getting the word out to the others. She poured herself a cool glass of tea and went out to the porch.

Someone on horseback would be the quickest, she reasoned. But who? She didn't know where all of them lived. Olaf would probably know, but he would be off to look at horses and wagons. Solving one problem creates another, she lamented.

She sipped on the tea and thought. An idea sprang into her head. Hiram Grigg would know where all the settlers lived. The planting was done; he would have some time. She would pay him for his trouble. No doubt, the Griggs could use some extra money. What's more, the other settlers might be more inclined to listen to him.

Her eyelids grew heavy. Kate leaned back in her chair. With the plan set in motion, she felt more relaxed. She drifted off to sleep.

*   *   *

Kate awoke. Wind was whipping across the yard. Tiny dust pellets driven in from the road pelted her face. In the western sky, clouds were forming above the mountains—a storm was approaching. She felt a sudden surge of

179

panic. Where were the children? She rushed into the house; it was empty. Next, she tried the yard; they were not there. Now, her panic was running to near hysteria. Then, Helga came out of the chicken house adjacent to the barn with Alice and Drew in tow. Helga had a basket of eggs in hand. "Have you seen James Junior?" Kate yelled above the noise of the wind.

"I think he's in the barn with Olaf. You know those two are most always together these days."

She relaxed. "Good." Her troubles were making her paranoid.

They herded the two young children into the house. Before going in, Kate stopped on the porch and looked at the dark and ominous clouds. Olaf and Helga had told her that summer storms were rare but could be severe when they did occur.

Kate helped Helga prepare the evening meal as the storm moved across the valley. It turned out to be what the locals called a typical summer storm with a lot of wind and lightning but only a small amount of rain. By the time the evening meal was ready, the storm had passed over them, and the sun was shining again.

While eating, Kate tried to strike a conversation with her children, but only Alice provided much of a response. "Helga made me some new doll clothes," she said.

"That's good. What about you, Drew?"

The young boy was tired and almost asleep in his chair. She turned her attention to James Junior.

"Well, young man, what have you been doing these days?"

"Not much," he mumbled.

"I hear that Olaf has been teaching you a lot of things."

"Yaw, the boy is a good learner and good helper," Olaf replied.

Try as she did, Kate could not get much of a conversation out of her oldest son. She regretted not spending more time with him. Her problems had kept her attention away from him. Now, his attitude concerned her. Grief, she figured, was still working on her son. He was probably still missing his father; she could only hope that time would heal his sorrow.

When the supper dishes were washed, Kate put the children to bed, and then she retired for the evening. That night, she got some much-needed rest.

*   *   *

The next morning, Kate asked Olaf to saddle a horse for her. When the breakfast dishes were done, she changed into her riding clothes. Out in the yard, the saddled mare was waiting for her.

"Be careful, missy," Olaf said as she was mounting.

"I'm only going for a short ride over to the Griggs. I should be back before noon."

The hot, dry weather had turned the meadow brown. The small amount of rain the previous day held down the heat and dust. One thing the summer weather had not stifled were the views of the mountain peaks; they still held their majestic grandeur.

When she arrived at the Grigg farm, Hiram and Nancy were in front of their makeshift cabin. Hiram was scraping rust from a plow shear, and his wife was washing clothes in a large vat she had heated with a wood fire. Their team grazed near the cabin.

"Good morning, Mrs. McKane," Hiram said.

"Good morning, folks," Kate said. She dismounted and tied the reins to a small tree.

Nancy looked up from her washing and waved.

"You're out early," Hiram said.

"Yes, Hiram. I have something I would like to discuss with you."

"Yes, ma'am."

"There's some coffee inside!" Nancy yelled.

"Thank you, but I can only stay for a short while," Kate replied. "Hiram, I've been giving a lot of thought to the problems with Covington. I have a plan in mind to deal with him, but I will need your support to get it done."

Hiram put down his file. "How can I help you, Mrs. McKane?"

"I need someone to get a message out to all the settlers about my plans. I believe you know where most of them live, so I would like for you to deliver the message about what we are doing and to warn them about making any deals. I'll pay you for your services."

"I can deliver your message. It will take me about two days to make all the rounds, but you don't have to pay me."

"I appreciate that, but I really would like to pay you for helping me."

"Well, Mrs. McKane, I think what you're doing will help me and all the other settlers, so that's enough pay for me. I know your uncle went to a lot of trouble and expense to get us up here, so I wouldn't feel right about taking any payment from you."

"All right, Mr. Grigg."

"What kind of plan you got in mind, Mrs. McKane?"

"I'm going to find a way to get your crops to market without using Covington. I will buy your crops from you and take delivery in the field. We'll do our own freighting to the markets."

"What will Covington say about that?"

"It doesn't matter. We're not breaking any of our agreements with him, but we're choosing not to use his freight service."

"That seems like a big undertaking. How will you get that much grain to market?"

"We're buying our own wagons and teams, and we'll hire some drivers. Olaf is leaving on Wednesday to look for some wagons and draft horses."

"As I said, Mrs. McKane, that's a big undertaking. You'll likely be putting yourself in danger trying to help us."

"I believe that's the way Uncle Lewis would have wanted it. I'm trying to continue on with his dream, and to do that; I need to tell everyone about our plans. I know many of them have been worried, so I want to set their minds at ease."

"I'll start tomorrow getting the word out. I think most of them will listen, but I hope it won't lead to any more trouble like what happened to Mr. Harrington."

"So do I. We've come too far to give up now."

"That's so, but this Covington ain't going to like any of this. Who knows what else him and his hired gunmen might do?"

"That's true, Mr. Grigg. We just have to be careful and try to be ready for him next time."

Kate outlined the exact message Hiram was to deliver, and then he went back to his plow. She walked over to the house and talked with Mrs. Grigg for a few minutes.

"I hope nothing happens to any of us," Nancy Grigg said.

"So do I," Kate replied.

"Hiram and I lived through so much of this back in Missouri. You know, we're just simple folks who want to farm our land and get along."

"I know, and like Uncle Lewis, I want to see the people here prosper and not have to live under intimidation and threats or have their property taken away by greedy men."

She shared their concerns but couldn't let it show. She had been thrust into the role of a leader; a scared leader could not instill confidence in her followers. Kate said goodbye to Hiram and Nancy and started back home.

While riding across the meadow up to the farm, she saw her two youngest children playing under a large poplar tree in back of the house. These children had already lost a father and an uncle; she didn't want them to suffer any more losses.

Chapter 19

Independence

The high steeple rising up above the prairie served as James's guide into Independence. He was back in civilization again with the first leg of his journey behind him. He was feeling a sense of relief. All that was required of him here was finding a guide and getting on to the Rockies.

The high steeple that he followed into Independence sat atop the courthouse on Main Street. This place was called the jumping off place to the West, or so he had heard. If that were the case, then a lot of people were getting ready to make the jump. The streets were crowded with wagons, buggies, ox carts, and horses. For a moment, the jam of people made him homesick for the prairie.

James was quick to discover why Independence was called the jumping off place to the West. Businesses catering to travelers crowded Main Street. There were dry goods stores, emporiums, wheelwrights, blacksmiths, harness-makers, and wagon-builders. One such establishment, going by the name of Anull Brothers, advertised themselves as suppliers of everything from household goods to wagons and draft animals.

With night fast approaching, James had to find a place to lodge for the evening. He tried the hotels along Main Street without any luck. He was considering just riding out onto the prairie and setting up camp when he noticed a small hotel on a narrow side street, next door to a grog house. The elderly clerk advised him they had an empty room. It wasn't luxurious, just a bed surrounded by four walls; he rented it.

He took his horse to a livery stable, collected his saddlebags, and walked toward the hotel.

The door of a grog house swung open, nearly striking him. A burly man in a sweat-stained cotton shirt and wool pants rushed out on the sidewalk, pulling a small man along by the scruff of his neck. The smaller one was wearing a bright red vest over a starched white shirt, striped gray pants, and a bowler hat. Once on the sidewalk, the larger man gave the smaller one a hard push on his neck, sending him face down into the street, where he narrowly avoided being trampled by a passing wagon.

The larger man sneered as he pointed toward the one in the street. "You're damn lucky I didn't break your scrawny neck. Cheatin' at cards will get you killed in this establishment."

Some of the bystanders laughed. The smaller man rolled over and pushed up into a sitting position, picked up his hat and dusted it off, put it back on his head, and got to his feet. He dusted off his vest and pants. The big man was still leering at him from the sidewalk. "I'll not be manhandled by an overgrown lout with the brains of a squirrel, who couldn't recognize his own name if it be written across the side of a barn."

Again, the man reached down and wiped at his pants. His hand darted down to his boot and came up holding a knife with a slender blade. "By damn, this'll cut you back down to size, I reckon."

The big man shrugged his shoulders, but James got a look into the man's eyes and saw some of the swagger had given way to apprehension. "Be on your way before I shove that pig sticker up your bloomin' ass."

"Fat chance of that," the smaller man replied. He stepped toward the sidewalk, holding the knife in front of him. He stopped in front of his adversary and swung the knife back and forth.

With his size advantage being diminished by the knife in the other man's hand, the bigger man turned toward the crowd. The bystanders seemed content to let the confrontation take its course—no one offered any support. He stepped back toward the grog house. When there was some distance between him and the knife, he said, "Card cheatin' bum, I shoulda broke your sorry neck, and next time I will." When he turned his back to go inside, the smaller man sat back on his haunches like a cat, ready to pounce. A shot rang out.

A constable on horseback was just down the street. "That'll be enough of that. I should lock up the two of you. Maybe the judge would see fit to give the both of you a few days on a work gang. That'd take the steam out of ya, I reckon."

The small man put the knife back in his boot. "I was merely exercising my right to defend myself. This lout assaulted me."

"Bum had an extra card up his sleeve," the larger man replied.

The lawman put away his pistol. "Any more trouble from either of ya and it's the jail. I hope both of you understand that."

So much for civilization, James thought. It was just as dangerous here as the country he had just crossed. He went to the hotel and up to his room on the second floor.

His immediate concern was the security of his valuables. He looked over the room. The furnishings were sparse. There was just a small bed, chair, a nightstand, a bureau with four drawers, lamp, and a washbasin. There was a door to the hallway and one small window overlooking the street.

Would the gold be safer on his person or in the room? He had seen for himself the rowdiness of Independence; perhaps the room would be safer. Now, the question was, where?

He pushed the bureau back from the wall and pried loose one of the floorboards. There was enough space underneath for the bags of gold and money. He kept out enough for his needs and stashed the rest under the floorboard. He pushed the bureau back in place and hoped his hiding place would not be found.

The next order of business was supper. He locked up the room and went out to the street. Laughter rang out from the grog house. A young lady with a heavily painted face beckoned to him from the doorway as he passed.

James pretended he did not see her and hurried on. On Main Street, he stopped in front of a shop with a window full of ladies' dresses. They reminded him of Kate and days past. Before the war, they would take a steamboat to Nashville. In the finest shops, he would watch while she shopped for dresses. He could tell from the look in her eyes when she fancied a particular one; he would urge her to buy it.

Remembering brought loneliness. It all seemed so long ago now. It felt like an eternity since he had shared time with Kate and his children. He felt an urge to just mount up and start toward Oregon tonight. But that could not be. He let out a deep sigh and walked on down the street.

Near the end of Main Street, there was an eatery. It was a small place with only a dozen tables, all covered with red tablecloths. He seated himself, and a tall, skinny man with a bushy mustache took his order. Behind the counter, a heavyset woman was cooking on a wood stove. The only other customers were an elderly man sitting in the back and a young man in a dark suit and bowler hat sitting near the door.

James ordered a steak. It was served burnt on the outside and tough as leather. As bad as it was, it still beat salt pork and hardtack. The coffee was stale and rank but hot.

He finished eating and started back toward the hotel. On the street, a team of oxen was pulling a cart loaded with hay. On one street corner, a group of young men were engaged in a game of dice. Independence was turning out to be a town of contrasts ranging from the rowdy frontier element to elegantly dressed gentlemen and their ladies. James stepped aside to let a man dressed in a flashy white suit and red vest and a young woman dressed in a blue velvet dress and large hat adorned with ostrich plume pass down the sidewalk. As he

185

reached up to tip his hat, the woman looked in his direction and smiled.

The commerce of Independence was in full motion. In front of an establishment advertising itself as trail outfitters, a man was hawking his wares. "Best trail goods this side of Saint Louis, my friends."

After giving the man and his store a quick glance, James moved on. He was tired and wanted to get back to his room for some rest. He found the narrow side street to his hotel. In front of the tavern, the same painted woman was hanging on the arm of a man dressed in buckskins. She chortled with the man trying to wrangle a glass of grog.

While her attentions were diverted elsewhere, he hurried on past. In the hotel lobby, the clerk was snoozing behind the counter. A man wearing a fancy suit and vest was sitting in a chair reading a newspaper. James guessed him to be a drummer. The man looked at him over the top of his paper, said nothing, and went back to his reading. James went up the stairs to his room. The gold, was it safe? He was feeling paranoid about his stash; so much depended on it. He closed and bolted the door, then pushed the bureau back. His stash was undisturbed. His nerves settled. Independence was making him as jumpy as the trail up had done.

What he needed was a bath. Both he and his clothes reeked of horses and sweat. *Was this little hotel equipped with bathing facilities?* he wondered. There was a quick way to find out. He went downstairs and woke up the clerk. The young man stirred to life and rubbed his eyes a few times. He had long, red hair and a face covered with freckles, and he was wearing an ill-fitting black suit. "Help you, sir?"

"Yes. I need a hot bath."

"Certainly, sir. The gentlemen's bath is located down the end of the hall on the left."

James found the bath. He stepped inside and was greeted with a face full of steam.

An elderly man with snow-white hair and slightly stooped shoulders handed him a towel and bar of soap. He pointed toward a cloud of stream. "There's an empty tub down there. I suggest, sir, that you leave your clothes and valuables here. There're a lot of thieves about."

Wise advice, James figured. He removed his dirty trail clothes and handed them to the attendant. He found the tub and waited until a boy of twelve or thirteen with shaggy brown hair came in with two buckets of steaming water. He poured the hot water in, then got a bucket of cold water and poured part of it in with the hot. "Try that, sir," he said.

He stuck his foot inside but pulled it quickly back out. "Still too hot."

The boy poured in the rest of the cold water. James tested it with his foot again. "That'll do."

There was nothing like a hot bath after long tiring days. He lay back in the tub and let the water sooth him, so much so, he caught himself dozing off. He grabbed the soap and scrubbed the dirt and odor from his body. When he felt clean, he got out of the tub and dried himself with the towel. He left coins for the attendants, collected his clothes, dressed, and went back to his room.

James lay down on the small bed. It was narrow, and the springs poked him. He made allowances; after so many nights on the hard ground, it was comfortable.

*　　*　　*

Next morning, James awoke with thoughts of a guide and some clothes that didn't smell of horses and sweat. He dressed and went downstairs. The lobby was empty.

The bright morning sun blinded him when he was outside. The doors of the grog house were open, but it looked deserted. Breakfast, then a shave and haircut, and he would be off to look for a guide. At a small haberdashery on Main Street, he bought a cotton shirt, pants, and a new pair of boots. A barber got rid of several weeks' growth of whiskers.

This morning, the little eatery was crowded. A group of teamsters had taken over the front; a large family took up three of the back tables. James seated himself at the very back. A large woman with a white apron over her faded dress took his order for ham and eggs.

The food had improved since last night. Even the coffee was better this morning. So much so, James ordered another cup. He finished his meal, paid, and went out to start his search for a guide.

How would he go about finding a guide? He knew nothing about Independence. *The hotel*, he thought. Maybe someone there could help him.

A gray-haired man with thin-rimmed glasses was behind the hotel counter. "Good morning, sir," he said.

"Morning. I'm looking for a guide to take me to the Rockies. Perhaps, you might know of someone."

"No, sir, but I suggest talking to the people at Anull's on Main Street."

"Thank you," James replied.

Two young women were standing in front of the grog house. One was tall and slender with long, brown hair, wearing a bright red knee-length dress. Her companion was shorter and heavier with dark hair and was also wearing a red dress.

The short one had sized up James as he was walking toward them. "Say, handsome, how about buying me a drink?"

"Sorry, ladies. I got business to attend to."

The other woman approached him. "How about coming upstairs with me. I can promise you a good time." Her arm rested on his shoulder.

"Sorry again."

He removed the woman's arm and started walking away. "Say, mister, I believe this belongs to you."

James turned. A man was holding up the arm of the slender woman. In her hand was the pouch that held his money.

"Damn, how did she do that?"

"These are two slick ones," the man replied. "They can pick a man's pocket without him being aware. Fortunately, they can't escape my sharp eye."

The man took the pouch from the woman and carried it over to him.

"I'm obliged," James said.

"Think nothing of it, my friend." The man looked back at the two women. They showed no remorse about the incident. "What do you suggest we do about these two?" he asked James. "Calling the constables seems appropriate."

"I suppose you're right, but I got my funds back. Maybe I'll just let it be this time."

"That's a generous gesture on your part, my friend, but I think you should at least get an apology from these two. Kit, Lucy, apologize to the gentleman."

The two women mumbled a half-hearted apology, then turned and went into the grog house.

"Thanks again, sir. My name is James McKane. I'm in your debt, it seems."

"Don't mention it. My name is Jack Riley. I'm a reporter with the Kansas City Star."

Jack Riley was about six feet in height and rather slender in build. He was dressed in a dark suit, starched white shirt, and dark leather shoes. His hair was short, his eyes dark, and he had a thin, black mustache. "Where are you off to, my friend?" he asked.

"Over to a place called Anull's for some information about where I can find a trail guide. I'm trying to get to Oregon."

"Take my advice. Anull's won't give you the time of day without making a profit in the transaction. I suggest going down to the freight yards. I know a man there that might be able to help you. If there's a guide to be found around here, he'll know about it. If you can wait a short time, I'll show you the yards."

"I'm in your debt again," James said.

"Then meet me here in about two hours, and we'll be off."

"All right."

While waiting for Jack Riley, James decided to look for provisions. He walked down Main Street past a narrow alley where a group of men were standing. At first, he paid them no attention. The face of one caused him to look closer. He stared straight into the face of Pratt Henderson—the wounded raider from the Hanks farm.

What a predicament this was. Pratt Henderson was the only member of the gang that had seen his face and could identify him to the others. Henderson gave him a cold stare. "I know you," he blurted out. "You're the bastard that shot me back in Reynolds County."

This was no place for a confrontation—he was unarmed and outnumbered. James hurried away. A short distance down the street, he looked back and saw two of the men standing on the sidewalk, looking in his direction. Then, one started down the sidewalk behind him; the other crossed the street.

Just when he had put the raiders out of his mind, they had to show up here. James walked briskly down the sidewalk. He mumbled a quick apology after colliding with a man coming out of an emporium. He glanced over his shoulder. He saw the one on the opposite side of the street, but where was the other one?

There was a grog house up ahead. Maybe he could lose them in there. He ducked through the door. There were two customers and a burly bartender inside. "You got a back door?" James asked.

The bartender pointed toward the rear. James walked to the back and stepped through the door into the alley. He looked up and down. The alley was empty. Then, he moved cautiously toward the street. Why didn't he have the sense to bring his pistol? When he reached the street, there was no sign of his pursuers.

James hurried along until he reached the side street to his hotel. It was still too early to meet Jack Riley, and he didn't want to loiter around outside with two desperados looking for him. He went into the hotel. The elderly clerk nodded at him as he crossed the lobby. At the stairway, James looked around again before starting up to the second floor.

He locked the door to his room and sat down on the bed. It was as if the war was still on. Fate had conspired to put him on a course with these violent remnants of the conflict. Riding on was out of the question until he found a guide; that meant he had to be out and about. "Damn," he swore out loud. From his window, he looked over the street below. There was no sign of Pratt Henderson and his companions. He gathered up his pistol and went outside.

There was no sign of Jack on the street. He walked over to the grog house and looked inside. There were a handful of customers inside; the newspaper man was not one of them. The two women from earlier were standing next to the bar. They looked his way, frowned, and then turned their backs to him.

Damn it, where was the man? James was impatient and apprehensive. He walked up to Main Street and looked up and down. There was no sign of Jack or the raiders. With nothing else to do, he walked back down to the grog house and leaned against the side of the building. After a half hour, he was about to give up and start for the yards on his own. "Mr. McKane, my rebel friend."

He looked toward Main Street and saw Jack walking toward him. "My apologies, but my business took longer than I anticipated. Are you ready for a look at the freight yards?"

"That I am," James replied. "How did you pick up on me being a Confederate soldier?"

"Just a hunch, my friend, just a hunch."

They walked up to Main Street and started down the sidewalk. Every few steps, James turned around and looked back over his shoulder.

"You seem a bit jumpy," Jack remarked.

"Just the crowds. I've been on the trail so long people make me jumpy. That, and memories of the war."

"I covered the whole bloody mess for my paper. I covered many of the major battles. I never saw the like of dead and wounded men. Turned my stomach at times."

"Mine likewise," James replied.

"One thing about it, you could tell what a man was made of. I saw many of them, like old Ulysses S. Grant himself. Coolest man I ever seen under fire he was. You know, during a battle, he would sit around and whittle on a piece of wood while the fighting raged all around him. He never made anything out of the wood except a big pile of shavings."

James could not muster much enthusiasm for a conversation about a man the Confederate troops had come to hate during the war. To the general's credit, he had been magnanimous by offering a number of concessions to the defeated troops, letting them keep their horses and side arms. Regrettably, Grant's subordinates had not always carried out his orders.

"You know, although I covered the war from the Union point of view, I had an opportunity to see many Confederate troops as well," Jack continued. "I never met General Lee personally, but I heard a lot about him. I don't think there's any question that, as a leader, he had few equals. As for the Confederate troops in the ranks, I seen 'em marching across the cold ground without any shoes and half starved, yet when the battle was over, the whole place would be littered with bodies. Those boys, even in their pitiful condition, could sure give an account of themselves."

This was old news. James knew the whole story. He listened patiently as Jack talked about his war experiences until they reached the end of Main Street. There, they started down a side street until reaching an open field. On the other side was a large pen built of thick, oak planks. Jack led the way across through an open gate to where several wagons were parked. At one of the wagons, a large, muscular man was working on an axle.

190

At their approach, the man stopped his work and wiped the sweat off his forehead with the back of his arm. "Jack Riley, you old scoundrel. I ain't seen you in a while."

"Business," Jack replied. "This is my friend, Mr. McKane. He's looking for a guide to get him to Oregon. You know anybody that might be interested?"

"Wilbur Gibbins," the man said. "Don't really know anybody that might be interested in taking one man up over the trail. Ain't many guides around these days? Those that are still here work for wagon trains."

Disappointment: that was all James could muster. He stood to the side while Jack and Wilbur talked. When the conversation concluded, he and Jack started to leave.

After they took a few steps, Wilbur yelled, "There's a man I forgot about! I don't know how the two of you would get along, but he used to live up in that country. I'm told he knows it like the back of his hand."

Now, this was getting somewhere. James's enthusiasm returned. "How do I find this man, and what is his name?"

"Name's Wilford Johnson. He's got a little place out on the prairie. You go up the river to Saint Jo and then go straight east about ten miles."

"Thanks," James said. "Maybe now I can get on my way to Oregon."

"I wouldn't get my hopes up too much if I were you," Jack said. "I doubt this feller will be interested in a trip all the way to Oregon."

"I'll just have to convince him," James replied. "I've noticed that money can change a man's mind about a lot of things."

The excitement of finding a guide caused James to forget about the raiders. When they reached the grog house, Jack stopped in front.

"After that walk, I need some refreshment. I'll see you later, my friend. Unless, of course, you would care to join me."

"Thanks, but I've got some other business to attend to. I'm obliged for your help, Jack."

Jack went inside the grog house. James turned and started toward his hotel. After taking a few steps, he felt something in his back. "Don't try anything foolish," a voice behind him said. "I been waitin' a long time to get my hands on you. My shoulder's still busted up from that slug you put in me back in Reynolds County."

James froze in his tracks. "What you and your bunch had in mind for that farm family wasn't so pleasant either."

"Yankee dirt farmers don't deserve anything better. Now we're gonna walk out of here nice and easy. There're some more folks here in town that would like to meet you. Now start walking, and don't forget I got a pistol in your back."

They walked a few steps then James felt the pistol being removed.

191

"That's far enough," another voice said. "Put that pistol down."

It was Jack.

James turned around. He was standing face-to-face with a young man, probably not more than sixteen years old, with long, shaggy hair and whiskers. He had a bandage on his left shoulder and a pistol in his right hand. James had just met the other man he shot at the Hanks farm. Jack was behind the young man holding a pistol to his back. "Put your pistol down," Jack said again.

The young man looked at James, then frowned and dropped his pistol. "I sent someone for the constable," Jack said. "We'll keep this one under wraps until he gets here."

"You fools are making a big mistake," the young man said. "My brother will hunt you down like a couple of dogs."

"That may be, my friend, but it won't do you much good if you're in jail," Jack said.

When two constables arrived on horseback, Jack explained the situation to them. They handcuffed the raider and waited for another constable to arrive in a wagon to haul the man to the Independence jail.

After watching the constables load up the young man, James turned to Jack. "How did you happen along when you did?"

"When we were coming back from the freight yard, I saw two men following us. I decided to duck out of sight and see if they would play their hand, and that one did. What's this all about?"

James explained about the night raid on the Hanks farm.

"The Farley gang! Damn, you sure picked a crazy bunch to mix it up with. Old Elias is like a bloodhound when he gets after someone. You can bet he'll be after you for sure. I advise you to stay out of sight until your business here is finished."

"You know about this Farley character?" James asked.

"I guess just about everybody in Missouri knows about him. He's been on a vendetta against all Union supporters since '63."

"Hell, the war's over. Can't these people accept that?"

"I don't think Elias ever will. You see, he was serving in the Confederate army down in Arkansas when he got word that Union supporters had murdered his father and burned their farm to the ground."

"That would be a tough thing to come to terms with, but how many does he plan to kill and burn out before he stops?"

"I don't think he'll ever stop until somebody stops him," Jack said. "When he found out what happened, Elias came back to Missouri and started a reign of terror that hasn't stopped yet. The Confederate surrender won't stop him."

"That one I just encountered must be Elias's brother. How did he get involved?" James asked.

"The story goes when Elias got back to Missouri, he found the boy hiding in the woods, scared to death the Union people would find him, too," Jack replied. "Elias took his brother with him when he went on his rampage."

"I can understand his rage at what happened," James said. "My own family suffered at the hands of the Yanks, but it's got to end sometime. Anyway, I may have a guide, so I'll be moving on."

Jack reached into his pocket. "In the meantime, here's something I suggest you keep with you." He handed James a small pistol.

"I already have a pistol."

"That military issue might have been all right out on the battlefield, but here you need something that you can keep out of sight."

James doubted he would ever need the small pistol. To accommodate Jack, he took it and put it in his pocket.

After leaving Jack, he went back to the hotel. His nerves were on edge. From now on, every shadow and every alley would be filled with danger.

*   *   *

That afternoon, things took a turn for the worse. James received a notice that there would be a court hearing for Lem Farley the following week, and his testimony would be required. Being already behind schedule, he certainly didn't want to spend an additional week in Independence.

That evening, James went out for an evening meal. He started to leave the small pistol in his room, but at the last minute, he put it back in his pocket and left the other in his room. Independence, he already found, was unpredictable.

James walked past the grog house and the sounds of laughter from inside to Main Street. He walked down to the same little eatery from the previous evening, where a young girl with long, blonde hair took his order.

There were only a handful of customers inside; two well-dressed men were sitting at the next table. James paid them no mind until he realized they were talking about the Farley gang. "I hear that one of Farley's men was captured right here in Independence today," one of the men said.

"Just down the street here," the other one replied. "Not only that, the one they got was Lem Farley, old Elias's brother."

"Entire state'll be better off when that whole bunch is strung up," his companion replied.

Lem Farley's capture was news all over town. Elias would have heard about it by now. James had been a thorn in his side too many times. The old raider would be out for revenge. He tried to put it out of his mind and had a supper of steak and fried potatoes with hot coffee. Tonight, the steak and coffee were better than the previous night.

After eating, James started back down the crowded sidewalk to the hotel. Laughter rang up and down the street from the crowded grog houses. Often, he had to step aside to let people pass.

The grog house next to the hotel was going strong, just like the others. He considered stopping in for a quick round but decided against it. He was tired and didn't like rubbing elbows with the rough frontier crowd.

The hotel clerk was nowhere in sight. *A little strange*, he thought. He went on up to his room. He unlocked the door and stepped inside. As he was closing the door, he felt something in his back. "Get on inside and close the door," a voice commanded.

He considered trying to escape down the hallway. The gun barrel pressed deeper into his back, spoiling that idea.

It was dark in the room. When his eyes grew accustomed to the darkness, he could make out someone sitting in a chair on the other side. A man was lighting a lamp. When the room was illuminated again, James saw two other men standing next to the one in the chair.

The seated man stood. He was tall with long, stringy, black hair and a thin, hawkish face. Despite the summer heat, he was wearing a long, black frock coat. Along one cheek was a long, jagged scar. The one at the lamp was also tall and gaunt. The other was a young man with a red beard.

The one behind gave James a push, sending him further into the room. James turned around. Pratt Henderson had a pistol in his hand and a twisted grin on his face. "Looks like we meet again."

"Look him over good and make sure he ain't got any weapons on him," the one with the scar said. James took him to be Elias Farley.

As Elias and his companions were talking, James remembered the small pistol in his pocket. He worked his hand inside and drew the pistol up into his sleeve.

"Empty out them pockets," Pratt Henderson ordered.

James pulled his pockets inside out.

"Looks like he's unarmed," Pratt said.

"We found some weapons here in the room," Elias said. "Man must be a fool to wander around unarmed."

Elias looked at James. "My men tell me you're the fella that shot us up down in Reynolds County. Cost me one of my men and wounded Pratt and my brother in the process."

"You were planning to burn out those poor farm people," James replied.

"Murderin' Yankee dogs, the whole lot of 'em," Elias said. "They don't deserve anything better."

"They were just poor farmers."

"Enough about it. Have you seen service in the war?"

"That I did. I served on the side of the South, but I don't support what you and your men are doing."

Elias glared at him. "You know, boy, you're the worst sort of all, shootin' at your own comrades."

James knew it would be futile to try and reason with Elias Farley. There was madness in the man's eyes. The only thing he could do was try to find a way to escape.

The small pistol in his sleeve would only be effective at close range, and he was outnumbered four to one. He would need surprise and considerable luck to make his escape.

"We're gonna take you out of here to a horse that's waiting out back," Elias said. "You get outta line with us, and we'll drop you in your tracks." He motioned to Pratt Henderson. "See if they's anybody out in the hall."

Pratt opened the door and looked up and down the hallway. "It's empty."

"All right, let's get him out of here," Elias said.

Pratt walked behind James and stuck his pistol in his back. "Start walking toward the door, then down the hall to the stairs. I'm gonna have this pistol in your back, so don't get any ideas. I've still got a score to settle with you as it is."

They walked to the door with two of Elias's men in front, followed by James, then Pratt Henderson, and Elias. They went down the stairs then across the lobby to the back door. James still had the pistol up his sleeve, but he had to wait for a better chance to use it. One of the men pushed open the back door and looked up and down the alley. "Looks empty." Pratt pushed James toward the door.

In the alley behind the hotel were five horses. Pratt pointed to a black one tied near the door. "Get up on that one." He had to turn his attention away for a moment to untie the reins of his own horse. This was James's chance. He shoved the small pistol into Pratt's stomach.

"Damn, he's got a gun in my belly!" Pratt yelled.

Elias swore. "I'll be damned if I shouldn't let the bastard shoot you for being so careless."

Elias turned toward James. "Mister, with that little pea shooter, you can't get more than one of us, so you ain't getting out of here."

A commotion broke out at both ends of the alley. "Drop your weapons!" somebody yelled.

Constables and sheriff's deputies with guns drawn and carrying lanterns swarmed into the alley from both ends. "Throw down your weapons!" one of them yelled again.

Elias raised his pistol. "Stand and fight!" he yelled

The raiders were thrown into confusion. One raised his pistol, but before he could get off a shot, there was a flash from the top of a building on the other side of the alley; the man dropped to the ground. The lawmen's lanterns were making the raiders easy targets.

"You fellas better give it up!" a constable yelled.

When James saw Elias look in his direction, he could see pure hatred in the raider's eyes. "Not until the death sentence is carried out for this traitor." There was a shot from across the alley. Elias stood up straight for a moment, a surprised look on his face, and then dropped to the ground. Seeing their leader fall, Pratt and the other man dropped their weapons and raised their hands.

"You okay, reb?" someone yelled.

Jack Riley stepped out of the crowd and walked toward him.

"Jack, what are you doing here?"

"Since our altercation with Lem Farley earlier today, I knew it would only be a matter of time until Elias came around after you. I've had someone watching the hotel since this morning. As it turned out, we didn't have to wait long."

James was angry. Jack had used him as bait to get at the Farley gang and a good story for his newspaper. "I don't like being put out on a limb like that; I could have been killed. Besides, how did you know they wouldn't kill me there in the hotel?"

"To start with, there were only four of them, but they brought five horses," Jack replied. "They were intending to bring you out and try to bargain Elias's brother out of jail."

"The least you could have done was let me know," James fumed. "Besides, why would the law be willing to bargain over somebody like me? Nobody here even knows who I am."

"I guess old Elias was getting desperate."

"You still should have let me know."

"There wasn't much time," Jack replied. "When I got the word they were at the hotel, I didn't have time to get word to you, but I had the situation covered. As you saw, there was a crack shot up on the roof across the alley. All bets were covered."

Jack's explanation didn't totally mitigate James's anger. His life had been put on the line just as a means of getting a good story. He stood aside to let the lawmen carry out their duties, seething at the newspaper man.

When he reasoned it over in his mind, the anger eased. He was alive, and a dangerous man and his henchmen could no longer prey on the people of Missouri. Maybe it was worth the risk. He let his rage pass.

"Look at it this way, my friend," Jack said. "You're a hero for helping put away one of Missouri's best-known renegades. By tomorrow, every newspaper in the area will want your story. Before long, everyone in the state will want to know about you."

James wasn't interested in fame; he just wanted to get on the trail and get to Oregon. Although feeling tired and frustrated, he had to spend some time in the lobby telling his story to the authorities. When the lawmen were satisfied, they departed. James went up to his room.

There, the weight of his encounter came down on him. Death had been close by this night. During the war, it had never been far away; he had come to accept it. It was more personal this time. The look in Elias Farley's eyes haunted him. If the rifleman's aim had been off or had been slow, his wife might now be a widow. His night was a restless one.

*   *   *

James awoke, feeling tired but ready to get on with his journey. Downstairs, the lobby was full of people. Jack was sitting in the corner, talking to a group of men. He saw James standing on the stairs and motioned with his arm. "Come on down and meet some people. These gentlemen are newspapermen from around Kansas City. They want to hear your story about Elias Farley."

This was the last thing James wanted or needed. He was behind schedule and could ill afford more delays.

They descended over him like a swarm of bees. They asked him about the encounter in Reynolds County and the gang's attempt to kidnap him the night before. The questions rolled at him like an avalanche. He wanted to throw up his hands in protest. As the morning waned, they collected their notes and departed. Only Jack remained.

"Well, my rebel friend. I told you this would make you a hero."

"I don't want to be a hero, Jack. I just want to be on my way. I've got to find that guide and get to the Rockies."

"And I wish you the best of luck on your journey. If I can be of further service, please let me know. Now I've got a story to write, so I'll be on my way."

The two men shook hands, and Jack walked out of the lobby. James had no doubt Jack's final account would differ significantly from the facts. He would embellish it with exploits of pure fiction. Well, maybe that's what sold newspapers.

Outside the hotel, some young boys were rolling a large metal hoop along the street. One looked over as James stepped out. "That's him! That's the one that got old Elias Farley!" the boy shouted to his companions.

The other boys stopped and looked at James.

"I didn't really get Elias or anybody else," James replied. "Besides, somebody getting killed is nothing to be celebrating about."

The boys gave James a strange look and then ran down the street. He continued past the grog house and up to Main. With the guide issue hopefully put to rest, he had to find a horse. The gelding was trail weary and might not last until the Rockies. Also, he needed a packhorse. In the sparsely populated country to the west, he would need to carry more supplies.

The outfitters along Main Street drove hard bargains. Their prices were high. Finally, feeling the need to get on his way, James struck a deal with one of them. He bought a roan saddle horse and a steady draft animal. Out of the deal, he also acquired a sheepskin coat, oil cloth, ammo for his pistol and the shotgun, bacon, salt pork, dried beef, and, although he hated the stuff, some hardtack. He stored it all in the stable.

Now, all that stood in the way of getting out of Independence was testifying against the Farley gang. He entertained a notion of just riding out and leaving the matter behind. Elias Farley was wanted around much of Missouri; surely, they didn't need his testimony. Besides, Elias himself was gone. The remaining members could be convicted without his presence. Tempting as it was, his conscience wouldn't permit him to ride on. Those that remained were cruel, ruthless men; there had to be assurances they would not be set loose to raid and plunder again.

On the way back to the hotel, James thought about his valuables. Did Elias and his men find the stash? He picked up his stride and was nearly in a run when he reached his room. He pushed the bureau aside and felt the worry disappear. His gold and money were still in place.

The excitement of the previous night had robbed him of much of his sleep. James lay down on the bed and soon drifted off. He was awakened after a short time by a knock on the door. When he opened it, a heavyset man with a large mustache and dark, bushy hair was standing in the hall.

"Mr. McKane, I'm Sheriff Deaton. I need to talk to you about the Farleys. I came to remind you about the hearing for Lem Farley next week. I also want to talk to you some more about last night."

"Sheriff, I'm on my way to Oregon, and I'm already behind schedule," James said. "Can I give you a written statement about all this?"

"That would be up to the prosecutor. You can talk to him over at the courthouse."

The sheriff finished his interview with James then accompanied him to the prosecutor's office on the second floor of the courthouse. He was a short, wiry man with gray hair and an ill-fitting suit.

The attorney listened intently as James explained his situation. At first, he insisted on having him available at the trial. James held his ground. He pointed out that Jack Riley was available, and there was the Hanks family in Reynolds County. In the end, the prosecutor agreed to take a written statement about the entire matter. A clerk was summoned, and James gave him a detailed account. He signed the document and left the courthouse. At last, he could get on his way.

On the sidewalk, he encountered a small boy selling newspapers. The headline caught his eye.

ELIAS FARLEY KILLED IN SHOOTOUT

Elias Farley, the leader of a band of Confederate guerrillas that has plagued Missouri since 1863, was killed in a shootout with local authorities yesterday. Ironically, James McKane, an ex-Confederate cavalry officer, was instrumental in the demise of the rebel gang leader. Mr. McKane's first encounter with the Farleys was at a farmhouse in Reynolds County, where one of the gang was killed and two more wounded, including Lem Farley, the brother of Elias.

Lem Farley was arrested yesterday morning after accosting Mr. McKane on an Independence street. Later in the day, Elias and some of the gang tried to kidnap Mr. McKane from his hotel room, but he was able to outwit them. In the resulting shootout, Elias and one of his henchmen were killed. Two others were captured.

It is hoped that yesterday's action will rid the state of the violence that has plagued it for the past few years.

Well, Jack Riley would have a more colorful account, but he wasn't going to wait around for it. He had a journey to complete.

Chapter 20

The Neighbor

Just as Kate had found the winters of northeast Oregon to be unbearable, she was finding summer to be more of the same. But it was more than just the heat. The summers in Tennessee were hot—she was accustomed to that. It was the dust. Clouds of it stirred up by passing horses, wagons, and buggies drifted over the meadow and settled over the house. She was forced to choose between sweating indoors or sitting on the porch and choking on the dust.

More bad news came. Olaf returned from his horse hunting expedition to The Dalles empty handed. "The man had already sold the entire lot," he explained to Kate.

"We'll just have to keep looking," she replied.

*   *   *

Early the next morning, Kate was helping Helga with the breakfast dishes when she heard footsteps across the front porch followed by a knock on the door.

It's a bit early for visitors, she thought. Feeling apprehensive, she went to the door. On the porch was a tall man wearing a large white hat and buckskin clothes with graying hair hanging below the hat. He had a small mustache and deep blue eyes. And their visitor wasn't alone. Several mounted men were waiting near the gate. The large contingent raised her caution higher; she wished Olaf was here. She studied the man. He looked peaceful enough. When she opened the door, he took off his hat. "Good morning, miss. I understand you own this farm now."

"Morning. And yes, I do own this farm."

"I'm sorry to trouble you, miss, but my name is Lawrence Granville. I own a cattle operation over near the creek; it seems some of my stock may have strayed onto your land. I and my men would like permission to ride out and take a look. I'll pay for any damages my cattle may have done."

"Of course, Mr. Granville. Do whatever you need to do, but please let my overseer know. I think you'll find him down at the barn."

"Thank you. And please call me Lawrence. 'Mister' is a title for a rich man, and I assure you I'm not a member of that class."

The man's informality added to Kate's uneasiness, but she tried not to let it show. "All right."

"I heard the unfortunate news about Mr. Harrington. I wasn't well acquainted with him, but we talked on a few occasions. I had some reservations about all the settlers he was bringing up here, but there's room for all of us, I guess. Please accept my condolences."

"Thank you. And yes, I believe there is room for all of us."

He put his hat back on. "I'll be going now. Thank you for your cooperation."

"All right. Just stop by the barn and tell Olaf. Make whatever arrangements you need with him."

Lawrence Granville joined the other riders. He talked to them for a moment, and then they all rode down toward the barn.

"Was that Mr. Granville at the door?" Helga asked when Kate closed the front door.

"Why yes, do you know him?"

"Oh yes. Well, not personally, but he's well known throughout the valley."

When the dishes were done, Kate got out her sewing basket and seated herself on the settee. The heat would soon force her out, but she wanted to get some work done before having to endure the dusty porch.

While she worked on a pair of pants for Drew, a thought came to her out of the blue. It was courtesy of her uncle. Occasionally, it would slip into her mind. *Kate, you are a young and attractive woman; you need to think about finding you a good man*, he had advised.

Now, why did I suddenly remember that? she asked herself.

She heard horses leaving the yard. Kate put her sewing down and looked out the window. Lawrence Granville and his men were riding back toward the road. She hoped everything had worked out with Olaf. They had enough problems dealing with E. G. Covington; problems with neighbors they could do without.

Then out of nowhere, the image of Lawrence Granville took center stage in her mind. *My gosh! Is he the reason I suddenly remembered Uncle Lewis's advice?*

Lawrence Granville was a distinguished-looking man. Even in his working clothes, he carried himself as a gentleman. She tried to dismiss the thought. How could she entertain such notions? For a start, the man was likely married. Not only that, James McKane had been the only man in her life. Kate had never gotten over him, and she didn't know if she ever would.

Her interest in sewing had been swept away. Kate put it aside, leaned back against the settee, and closed her eyes. Memories of her husband, James, came to mind. She remembered the first time she met James McKane. She was working in her father's store in Clarksville when he strolled in the front door looking wild and carefree. He was a handsome man with brown hair and blue eyes. There was an air of confidence about him, yet, he did not come across as arrogant.

On this day, James had been dressed in common clothes, like a laborer, but his mannerism suggested he was from the well-to-do class. He looked around the store then asked her about some gloves. Kate helped him sort through the entire stock until he found a pair that suited his fancy.

During the search, their eyes met several times. Each time, Kate quickly looked away. She felt out of place exchanging glances with a rich, young customer. After he made his purchase and left the store, she asked her father about the young man.

"Oh, that's Albert McKane's only son, James. The McKanes have a large plantation to the north of town. They are one of the richest families in Montgomery County."

Kate put James out of her mind, but not for long. He showed up again a few days later. She was busy with a customer when he came in. He bided his time, pretending to look at merchandise until she was free. He then had her show him their entire line of men's shirts. She could tell by the way he kept looking at her out of the corner of his eye there was more than shirts on his mind. He finally selected an expensive silk import.

He paid for the shirt and started to leave. At the door, he paused. "I don't believe you told me your name."

"I didn't. It's Kate. Kate Harrington."

"Kate Harrington, I'm pleased to meet you. My name is James McKane."

"Yes. I know."

"Well, since you've already heard of me, I hope you haven't heard anything bad," he said.

"Oh, do people usually say bad things about you?"

"Not that I'm aware of, but who knows? I guess it depends on who's doing the talking."

After a few minutes of small talk, he said, "There's a bakery next door that has the best sweet rolls in Tennessee. Would you care to join me for one?"

Kate tried to put him off, but he was persistent. Finally, she went with him just to get him out of her hair. They nibbled on sweet rolls and sipped hot coffee. The entire time, James kept his eyes on her, making her nervous. In the end, she made an excuse about her father needing her in the store to get away from him.

She hoped that would be the end of it, but a few days later, he was back again. She saw him approaching the front door, prompting her to hide in the stock room. She sat among the bolts of cloth and racks of clothes until he left.

"Young Mr. McKane was asking about you," her mother said.

"Well, I'm glad he's gone."

That was not to be the end of the matter. Kate found out just how persistent James McKane could be. He made repeated visits to the store. If she was busy, he would bide his time until she was free, then talk to her on some pretense of buying merchandise. Once, he came into the store just as it was opening.

"You know, Kate, we're wasting these fine spring days," he said. "Such weather is meant for riding. I would like for you to go riding with me this coming Sunday afternoon."

A request to go riding with James McKane would have thrilled many of the Clarksville ladies, but not her. She declined, but he persisted. "Just this one time," she finally told him.

The following Sunday afternoon, James arrived at her house riding a frisky black stallion and leading a roan mare. They rode around Clarksville then out into the countryside. It was early April, and the wild flowers were in bloom, covering Montgomery County like a many-colored blanket. They found themselves on McKane Plantation and rode across the vast estate until stopping to let the horses rest under the shade of a large oak tree. "Kate, I've known many girls, but none of them can hold a candle to you."

His directness shocked her. "James, this has been a pleasant afternoon, but I think it's time we stopped and looked at this situation. You and I are from two different worlds."

"We may be from two different worlds, Kate, but there's no one in my world that makes me feel the way you do."

"That may be, but you better keep looking. I've got to get back now. Thank you for a lovely afternoon."

She wheeled her horse around and started back across the plantation. James followed along behind her. They rode in silence to her home. Kate got down from the mare, waved good-bye, and went into the house, hoping that would be the last of his visits.

Her hopes did not materialize. One week later, James showed up at the store. "Kate, I've got some tickets to an Italian Opera that's touring the country. It will be here in Clarksville next week. I would like you to be my guest."

Again, Kate was caught in an uncomfortable situation. She tried to argue out of going, but being ever so determined, James persisted until she agreed. The next week, a coach driven by a team of white horses pulled up to her house. James escorted her to the coach, where a servant held the door open. Kate felt so out of place. People on Main Street stared, making her self-conscious and nervous.

The opera was beyond her. She tried to enjoy it; James would explain each scene, but she just knew too little about it. Because it was all in Italian, she didn't understand a word of it. But if the opera itself wasn't enough, things came to a head as they were leaving.

A woman was waiting in front of the opera house. James introduced her as his Aunt Mary. From her perfect brown coiffure to the hem of her velvet dress, the woman beamed of wealth and snobbery. After the introduction, she gave Kate a condescending look. "Oh, yes, you're that storekeeper's daughter. James, I do hope your mother is not aware of these little liaisons."

Kate was stunned. She stood for a moment, not knowing what to say. Then tears flooded her eyes, prompting her to run down the street feeling humiliated and angry. When she stopped to catch her breath, James rushed up to her. "Kate, please, Aunt Mary treats everyone that way. It wasn't you."

The tears continued. "James, you know this will never work. Your family will never accept me, and you know it. We must end this here and now."

She left him standing on the sidewalk. From that moment on, misery became her constant companion. He came back to the store the next day, but she hid until he was gone. The next day, he was back again; she made another retreat to the back. Her mother made excuses for her: "Kate is not feeling well today," or "She's visiting relatives."

When he came up the sidewalk again, she started for the store room. "Kate, I've run out of excuses," her mother said. "You have to deal with this young man yourself."

Her mother was right. She reluctantly stayed to face him.

When James walked inside, Kate hardly recognized him. There was a sad, downtrodden look on his face, and his eyes were bloodshot. "Kate, I can't apologize enough for Aunt Mary's remarks. The truth is, I can't live without you. My family will come around when they get to know you."

Something in the pleading look on his face got to her. She could not deny he had aroused feelings in her as well—something no other man had ever done. She had hardly smiled since the night she left him standing on the sidewalk. "This will not be easy, you know."

"I know, Kate, but I'll do everything in my power to make my family understand."

In addition to the McKanes, Kate's own family had little enthusiasm for their plans. "You'll have trouble fitting in out there," her father said.

Early that summer, James and Kate started life together by taking a steamboat to Nashville, where they were married in a small, private ceremony. They enjoyed a week of honeymooning in Nashville before returning to the plantation. Upon their return, the McKanes were visibly upset and made little attempt to hide their feelings.

"I'm simply shocked, James," Martha McKane said.

James tried to make Kate's transition to plantation life as smooth as possible, but his family stood in the way. Kate's mother-in-law, Martha McKane, avoided her most of the time. James's father, Albert McKane, seemed to hardly be aware of her existence. Even worse, James's Aunt Mary never ceased with her criticism.

When the children started arriving, Martha softened a bit. She enjoyed having grandchildren around, but there was always some distance between the two of them.

Kate resumed her sewing, but as she thought about James, a smile played on her face. It was still visible when her daughter, Alice, walked into the room. "Mama, why are you smiling?"

"Oh, I was just thinking about something from long ago. Besides, can't I be happy once in a while?"

"Yes, Mama. I wish you were happy all the time."

Kate grabbed her daughter and gave her a big hug.

*   *   *

That evening, as she was helping Helga with the dishes, Kate saw a rider come into the yard. It was Lawrence Granville. This worried her. *There must be some more trouble with his cattle*, she thought.

She dried her hands on a towel and went out to the porch. What caught her immediate attention was that Lawrence had changed from the buckskin clothes to a starched white shirt and pressed pants. He stopped his horse just short of the porch.

"Mrs. McKane, me and my men, found a few strays over in one of your grain fields. Have your foreman go out and take a look, and we'll settle the damages. Something spooked those critters to drive them all the way over here, but like I told you and your foreman this morning, I'll pay for all damages."

"That'll be fine, Mr. Granville."

"Lawrence, please," he reminded her.

"All right, Lawrence. And to be fair, please call me Kate."

"All right, Kate, it is."

She thought that was the end of it, but to her surprise, he dismounted, walked down to the porch, and removed his hat. He stood, fumbling with his hat, looking like a nervous boy. "Was there something else, Lawrence?"

"Kate, I hope you won't think I'm being too forward, but I was wondering if you would like to come and have a meal with me at my house sometime. You see, I lost my Matilda two years ago. That house is rather lonesome now."

Kate was floored, caught off guard, left to struggle for an answer. He seemed like a gentleman; she didn't want to hurt his feelings. But the thought of going to his house, well, that was different; she didn't feel comfortable with the idea. "You see, Lawrence, I have three children to look after, so it's hard for me to get away."

"Bring 'em along. It's been a long time since the laughter of children has been heard around my house. My oldest son is living in Portland; the next oldest is in California, so it's just my youngest, Ben, and me at home now. A lady and some young folks would sure make us feel happy again."

With the children invited, Kate felt better; she agreed to come for dinner the following Sunday.

"I'll send Ben over with the buggy. I got one of the best cooks in Oregon. I'll see he goes all out for you."

"All right."

After watching him ride away, Kate started to regret her decision to have dinner with Lawrence. He seemed to be a very lonely man. She understood loneliness, but her loneliness was for her husband. He, on the other hand, was looking for a wife. Kate wasn't ready to marry again. She would never be ready until she got over James.

That evening, Kate talked to Olaf about Lawrence's cattle. "Please go out and have a look. Mr. Granville promised to pay for any damages."

"Yaw, he told me the same thing earlier. All right, missy. I'll go out in the morning. You think this stockman's word is good?"

"I believe he'll do what he says."

*   *   *

After Olaf rode off the next morning to check the grain field; Kate took up her sewing. She sat on the settee, trying to concentrate on her work, but Lawrence Granville kept invading her thoughts. Had she been too hasty accepting his invitation to Sunday dinner? What would come of it? Would it take her to a place she didn't want to go?

Was she being too self-centered about this? James had been gone for a year and a half. Maybe it was time to get on with her life—put the past behind and move on. There were the children to consider. They—especially James

Junior—needed a father. Her oldest son had become a source of worry for her, one that she didn't know how to deal with. He was off in some distant world of his own most of the time, talking little to anyone, even Olaf.

She put it aside. There were too many other problems to deal with that left no time for Lawrence or any other man. She had to set him straight right off so he wouldn't get his hopes up.

*   *   *

E arly Sunday morning, a young man arrived in a surrey pulled by a team of white horses. *He's early*, Kate thought. She had just finished getting the two youngest children ready and still had yet to prepare herself. "Helga, please invite the young man in while I get ready!" she yelled.

Kate looked through all the dresses in her closet. Since many of them were presents from James, she felt guilty about wearing them. She had to settle for a light blue dress she had bought before she and James were married.

She dressed and went downstairs. The young boy was sitting on the settee, sipping a glass of tea. He had blue eyes, a sharp face, and long, neatly-trimmed brown hair, and he wore a pressed white shirt and wool pants. Kate guessed him to be fourteen or fifteen. "You must be Ben," she said.

The boy stood up, held his hands at his side, and gave her a nervous look. "Yes, ma'am."

James Junior started down the stairs, followed by Alice and Drew. The younger children bounded down enthusiastically, but her oldest son shuffled down slowly with a withdrawn look on his face. He did not want to come, but Kate had insisted.

"Ben, these are my children. That's James Junior, Alice, and Drew."

The children nodded at Ben, and he did likewise. They all seemed a little ill at ease in each other's presence.

"Ma'am, I 'spect we need to get going," Ben said.

"All right. James, take your brother and sister out to the buggy and help them up."

While the children were getting settled in the buggy, Kate went into the kitchen where Helga was preparing the Sunday meal for her and Olaf. "You look lovely," Helga said.

"Thank you. We'll be home before dark."

"Go and enjoy yourself. You're a young woman. You deserve to get away from the house and have a good time."

"It's just a social visit with a neighbor, that's all," Kate replied.

"Of course, dear," Helga said.

Kate was surprised she was being so defensive about spending the day with Lawrence Granville. Even worse, she dreaded going.

They drove through the parched meadow out onto the road. Kate covered her face with her hand as a shield against the dust raised by the horses' hooves.

None of them showed much enthusiasm. Ben stared straight ahead at the horses and did not speak. Kate's children were in a silent mood as well. She wanted to start a conversation but couldn't think of anything appropriate to say. *What a way to start a Sunday outing*, she said to herself.

Ben drove north to a fork in the road, then turned northeast. "I guess you spend most of your time helping your father," Kate said.

"Yes, ma'am."

"I guess your father has a lot of land."

"Yes, ma'am. Runs along the creek for nearly five miles."

Young Ben just wasn't much for talking, so Kate made no further attempt. She had to wonder how Lawrence Granville had acquired so much land. It was her understanding that much of the land here was public land, available for homesteading only. Of course, Uncle Lewis and John McDonald had acquired large tracts, so it could be done.

The northeast bound road was less travelled, therefore less dusty, allowing them to breathe easier. After a short drive, Ben pointed ahead. "That's our house."

"It looks nice," Kate replied.

Ben drove the surrey through a wide gate made from pine timbers into a large yard that surrounded a two-story white house. Across the front of the house was a porch supported by small white columns. In the front was a picture window that looked out across the porch to the front yard. On the second floor above the porch were two more large windows.

Ben parked the buggy near the front and helped Kate down. Then, she helped her children out of the back. Drew had drifted off to sleep and raised a cranky protest at being disturbed.

Lawrence Granville stepped out on the porch. He was wearing another starched white shirt and wool pants with blue suspenders. Today, he had combed his hair straight back. "Kate, I'm so glad you could come."

"Thank you. This is my family. This is my oldest, James Junior, his sister, Alice, and brother, Drew."

Lawrence extended his hand to James Junior. "How are you, son?"

"Fine," the boy mumbled as he gave Lawrence's hand a half-hearted shake. Kate looked on with embarrassment, vowing to have a word with her son when they were home.

"Please come into the house," Lawrence said. He walked with them to the front door and held it open until they were all inside. The large front room contained a rock fireplace. The wood floor was covered with a large blue carpet; a large settee and matching chairs sat the center of the room. On the walls, there were a number of portraits, including one of a young woman with long, blonde hair.

Lawrence noticed Kate looking at the portrait of the woman. "That's my Matilda."

"She was a lovely woman," Kate replied.

"Yes. She was."

In one corner of the room was a piano. "Did your wife play?" Kate asked.

"Yes. She played very well. I can still picture her sitting and playing something soft, humming to herself as she played."

On one side of the room was an ornate staircase. The handrails were made of polished brass, and the stairs were covered with thick red carpet. Another doorway opened into a dining room and kitchen.

"It's a beautiful house, Lawrence."

"Thank you. Cost me a fortune to have all this stuff shipped up here, but I wanted Matilda to be happy. She had a hard time adjusting to such a life, so I did my best to make it easier for her. In spite of all I did, I lost her."

"I'm sorry," Kate said softly. The house and fancy trappings seemed out of place here on the Oregon frontier, but Lawrence Granville must have cared very much for his wife

"The meal will be ready soon," Lawrence said. "In the meantime, let's enjoy ourselves. Ben, take the kids out back and show them a good time."

The children followed Ben outside; Kate and Lawrence seated themselves on the settee. "Kate, how do you like living here in Oregon?" he asked.

"I admit I'm having trouble getting used to it. The winter was really bad."

"The climate can be harsh at times."

"There's more than just the climate. There are other things here that I find hard to accept."

"And what are those?"

"The system of justice, for one thing. My uncle met with foul play last spring, and I can't get anything done about it."

"I didn't know that. I was told that his horse threw him."

"That's what certain people would have everyone believe."

"Well, I know Avery Benton doesn't get in a big hurry about things, but I've been told he's basically a fair man," Lawrence said. "Course, I never had many dealings with the sheriff."

"My uncle was involved in a business deal with a man in La Grande named E. G. Covington. I know that Covington was behind what happened to my uncle; he was probably killed by a bunch of hard-noses that work for him."

"I've known Covington for some time now," Lawrence said. "I've had him haul for me. If you don't watch him, he'll rob you blind. He runs a first-class freight operation, but you've got to be careful dealing with him. Trouble is, most of the time, he's the only one in this area you can rely on. The other little lines stay busy working the gold fields in the south."

Kate hadn't meant to get off on her problems. She just wanted to have a polite meal with Lawrence and then be on her way.

"Life can be hard up here," Lawrence said. "I first came up here before Oregon was a state. We packed up and left Texas back in the '50s. In spite of the hardships, I've come to like the place very much. I spent several years on the coast and did well as a stockman. I came over here when the place started settling in the early '60s, and I've been here ever since. I filed a claim for 160 acres, bought out two claims next to mine, and I've got a grazing permit for a large tract of land along the creek. There's a good market for beef here, especially in the mining areas to the south. My only sorrow was losing Matilda two years ago. Since that time, life has been hard for me."

Kate understood loss. Your life was just never the same again when you lost someone close to you. It left a void in you that could not be filled.

An elderly man appeared in the doorway. He had a tanned, wrinkled face and was slightly stooped at the shoulders. "Dinner."

"You're in for a treat," Lawrence said. "Henri here is one of the best cooks in Oregon. I stole him from one of the mining camps, which left me under the threat of being lynched by some of the miners. My wife, God bless her, tried her best, but she just could never cook like Henri. Fact is, I've never found many that could."

The kitchen and dining area was one large room with a large cook stove at one end. On the wall were a number of mahogany cabinets with glass doors. Near the cook stove was a small oak table, and in the center was a large mahogany table and a set of straight-backed chairs.

They called the children inside. Henri served them roast duck and dressing, new potatoes, English peas, and plum pie. "You were right, Lawrence; your cook is certainly an excellent chef," Kate said.

If it came to a contest between Lawrence's cook and Helga, it would be a tossup as to who was the best, in Kate's opinion.

After eating, they sat on the porch. A light breeze drifted in from the mountains, keeping the temperature comfortable. The younger children played a game of tag in the front yard. Ben and James Junior went out to the corral to look at some horses.

Lawrence leaned back in his chair. "Kate, I hope you won't take offense in what I'm about to say. I'm a lonely man living here in this big house out in the middle of nowhere. I really need a woman to help me with the place and to take some of the loneliness away."

Kate again was taken aback by his directness. He was, in every indication, a gentleman, but he was offering something she could not accept.

"My son, Ben, he's a good boy, but he needs a mother's touch," Lawrence continued. "He's growing up rather wild and untamed, lacking in the social graces, if you know what I mean. I'm just an old stockman myself, so I can't help much in that area. He needs a woman's touch to hone his skills before he sets off into the world."

"Lawrence, I know how you feel. I was recently widowed myself, but I just don't think I'm ready for anything like this yet. You've certainly been a gentleman and a good neighbor in every respect, and I appreciate that. I appreciate the excellent meal and the opportunity to spend the day here."

"It's been my pleasure, and all I ask is that you keep it in mind," Lawrence said. "Remember, you got three fine children that need a father to help them get through the troubles that this life can bring. I've had some experience in that area. Good women are hard to find out here. I sensed the first time I met you that you were a good woman, and I had better make my pitch while I could."

Kate smiled at his remarks and put aside her affront at his directness. They talked some more; then Kate reminded him they needed to get home. Lawrence looked a little disappointed, but he yelled for Ben to bring the surrey. While Ben was getting the buggy ready, Kate rounded up the children.

Lawrence stood in the yard and waited until Kate and the children were seated for the trip home. "Kate, I hope you didn't think I was too bold with what I said earlier."

"No, Lawrence, you were being honest and direct, and that's a good thing. I'm flattered, but like I told you, it's just too soon for me."

The disappointment lingered on Lawrence's face, but he remained cordial. He waved to them as they drove out the gate onto the road. Kate had to admit he had raised a good point about the children needing a father, again causing her to wonder if she was putting her feelings above the children's welfare. But her late husband James stood in the way. Anytime she tried to picture life with another man, she would think of him—any other man paled in comparison to the man she loved and lost.

When they were home, Ben helped her down, and then she got the children out of the buggy. "Tell your father we enjoyed our visit very much."

"Yes, ma'am."

Ben tapped the horses on the flank. Kate and the children stood in the yard and watched him drive away. As they were walking into the house, Alice looked up at her.

"Mama, is Mr. Granville going to be our new father?"

Kate reached down and gave Alice a hug. "Not anytime soon. It's too early to be thinking about anyone except the father you had in Tennessee."

Chapter 21

The Guide

James rose early, ready to bid farewell to Independence and all the problems he had encountered here. He retrieved his gold and money from under the bureau, went downstairs and woke up the clerk, settled his account, and stepped out into the street.

The grog house door was open, but there were no sounds coming from within. Main Street was deserted aside from a handful of merchants setting up their displays. Breakfast tempted him, but he decided against it. He had to get used to dried beef and hardtack again anyway. At the livery stable, he saddled his horses and loaded his gear.

The street was empty save for an occasional cart or wagon. The sun was peeping over the eastern horizon as he rode out of Independence. After riding north a few miles, he turned west and rode until he struck the banks of a river. Chunks of driftwood swirled around in the muddy current. Along the bank were thick stands of willow and cottonwood trees. With the river came unwanted company; hordes of mosquitoes swarmed around his face and neck.

Ahead of him, the prairie spread out to the horizon; he felt intimidated by the sight. It would be so easy for one not accustomed to this country to become lost. And the worst of it, his instructions for finding Wilford Johnson were brief; he might ride around out here for days and never find the man.

Under a few patches of white clouds floating in the bright blue sky, he followed the river until midmorning. The hot sun glared down on him. He munched on a strip of dried beef and continued on, fighting the heat and mosquitoes. Near St. Joseph, he left the river and rode due east. There was no way of knowing if the route he was following would lead him to his prospective guide; he was relying on guesswork. The man was supposed to live ten miles to the east; that's all he knew.

Two hours later, he came up on several wagons parked alongside a creek

213

bank. Some women were cooking over a campfire. Nearby, a group of men were seated under the shade of a cottonwood. A man dressed in homespun garb with a short, gray beard got up and approached James. "Afternoon."

"Afternoon," James replied.

"We just came back from Nebraska," the man said. "We started west last month, but they got Indian troubles up there, so we turned around and came back. We're going down to Kansas and try again next year. We hope the Army will have the Sioux under control by that time."

That was discouraging news, James thought. He had to cross Sioux country himself. Maybe this Wilford Johnson would know a safer route to follow.

"You're welcome to sit a spell and eat with us," the man said.

"I appreciate your offer," James replied. "I'm behind schedule, so I need to get going."

"Be careful out there; it's a dangerous place."

James took his leave and rode on. He rode until late afternoon without locating the elusive Mr. Johnson. The empty prairie seemed endless—there was no sign of human habitation in any direction. He started feeling dejected. Then, up ahead was a small rise. That would give him a better vantage point, so he rode over. From the top, he looked around but saw only flat, empty land. Desperation took hold of him. He needed to be heading west but required the services of a guide. He climbed down and rode on east until he reached another creek.

He got down, filled his canteen, and let his horses drink. The heat had drained him of much of his energy. To refresh himself, he bent down and splashed water over his face and hair. When he stood, something poked into his back, calling to mind recent events. Acting on instinct, he moved his hand toward the pistol. "Don't try it, mister," a soft voice said.

James moved his hand away from the pistol. "Look, I'm just passing through and needed some water for me and the horses."

"I been watching you tramping around my place for the last hour," the voice said. "What's you doin' out here anyway?"

"Looking for somebody. Maybe you know him."

"Maybe. Who you lookin' for?"

"A man named Wilford Johnson."

There was a soft chuckle. "Yes sir, mister, I know that man quite well."

What was funny about the matter? James wondered. Still, he felt relieved. "Then maybe you can tell me where to find him."

"No need. You done found him. Well, that is to say, he found you."

"Then...that means you are Wilford Johnson."

"I've been him for a long time."

This was his lucky day. "Say, how about taking that gun barrel out of my back?"

"Yeah, I guess you're harmless enough."

James felt the gun barrel being removed and the sound of a pistol being uncocked. He turned around, and his jaw dropped. Standing in front of him was a tall, clean-shaven black man wearing a floppy hat with a large brim, a shirt of coarse brown material, and buckskin pants.

What kind of deceit was this? he fumed silently. The freighter in Independence never said anything about Wilford Johnson being a black man. If he had the time, he would go back and pummel the man. Now, what was he going to do? He was short on time and needed a guide. But he had never hired (or even considered hiring) a black person to work for wages. This arrangement was completely out of the question. Damn—fate had it in for him.

Wilford studied him for a moment. "What's your business with me anyway?"

James didn't feel like discussing his situation with this man. "Well, I guess it don't matter much now."

Wilford laughed. "Didn't find what you came looking for, I take it?"

"You might say that."

"Somebody didn't give you all the facts, I 'spect."

"That they didn't. I came out here in need of a guide to Oregon." As soon as the words were out, James regretted revealing his reason for being here.

Wilford laughed again. "Hell, mister, I ain't been up in that country in some years now. Best chance you got is to go back to Independence and catch a wagon train going that way."

"No time. I got a wife and kids up there who think I'm dead. I got to find them as soon as possible."

"First of all, you getting a late start. You'll be lucky to get to the mountains before the snows set in, and mister, you ain't seen snow like they get up in them mountains."

"I'm aware of the risks. I'm prepared to pay well for a guide."

"That so! How much you planning on paying?"

He started not to answer. Wilford Johnson was drawing him in. But, what did it matter now? "Five hundred in gold for a down payment at the start, and another five hundred when I find my family in Oregon."

There was a spark of interest in Wilford's eyes. He studied James a moment before speaking. "Ride down to my place. It's just down the creek a ways."

Desperate as he was, James didn't want to pursue this any further. And this man had a take-charge attitude that was annoying. It was something he wasn't used to, being the son of a Southern planter. He started to tell Wilford

Johnson that was the end of the matter, but he hesitated. He was down to his last option. Reluctantly, he mounted up and followed him.

Down the creek, there was a copse of willows. On the other side were a sod cabin and a corral made of willow poles.

The weight of James's dilemma crushed down on him. How could he ever accept an arrangement with Wilford Johnson? He was very different than the slaves back at McKane Plantation. He had a commanding air about him that was bothersome to no end; it would be impossible to deal with such an attitude all the way to Oregon.

The plain truth: James was dealing with a black man in a way he had never thought about. That was what really troubled him. He had never harbored any ill will toward the slaves, but at the same time, he had felt their place in life was different than whites. But things had changed. The slaves in the South were free now, and he supposed those in the rest of the country would soon be free also. The Union couldn't justify freeing slaves in the South while allowing the practice on their own soil.

While James wrestled with his thoughts, Wilford had been studying him. "Maybe now you got some doubt about this."

James tried to steer around answering him directly. "How much you really know about the country up there?"

"Considerable amount, I guess. I was raised in the mountains up there."

"And you've been over the Oregon Trail before?"

"Hell, mister, I used to lead wagon trains over the trail."

James thought some more. The man did have experience, probably more than anyone else he could find at this late date. Pushing his prejudices aside and thinking about the welfare of his family, James decided to explore the possibility of using Wilford Johnson as a guide. "You have any interest in making a trip up to Oregon?"

"It sounds to me like you don't know where your family is at up there," Wilford replied. "What are you gonna do about the rest of the money if you can't find them?"

The insolence of the man knew no bounds. James was angry now—truly angry. Wilford Johnson had the nerve to question him about the money. On the other hand, he had already committed to paying another five hundred. "Once we get there, we'll search around, and if they can't be found, I'll still deliver the other five-hundred, that is, if I agree to this arrangement."

"This arrangement bothers you, does it? Maybe you particular about who you travelin' with. I 'spect you from the South somewhere. I 'spect your family had a bunch of slaves. That right?"

"Yes."

"They tell me the war is over, and that issue has been settled," Wilford said. "You got a strong need to be in Oregon, and I doubt you could get there on your own. I lived up there in the mountains a good portion of my early years. I speak the Crow, Blackfoot, Shoshone, and Sioux tongue. I also know some of the tongues of the smaller tribes as well. Mister, I don't think you gonna find anybody better qualified on short notice."

More arrogance on Wilford's part, but James had to admit the man had a good argument. He had to weigh how he felt about Wilford as a guide against his pressing need to get to Oregon. He thought. Finding Kate and the children was more important, even more, important than the ideals he had been raised with. "I suppose we could give it a try."

"Wait a minute. I ain't said nothin' about agreeing to take you there. I was just pointing out the flaws in your thinking. You see, I don't know if I want to be traveling with you. I'm a particular person myself."

Seething rage boiled up in James. He was tempted to just mount up and ride away. Wilford Johnson's insolence seemed to know no bounds. Never in his life had a black man spoken to him in such a manner. That was the last straw. There had to be a better way to get to Oregon.

"You can sleep here tonight," Wilford said. "You got everything you need. I'll sleep on your offer, and we'll talk about it again tomorrow." Without further word, Wilford turned and walked toward the cabin.

James let his anger settle a bit. It was late in the afternoon, and this was an excellent campsite. He needed a night's sleep to decide what to do and didn't feel like looking around for another location. He set about making camp while pondering what he was going to do. The thought of riding all the way to Oregon with Wilford Johnson ate at him, but every time he considered packing up and riding on, the faces of Kate and the children came to mind.

*   *   *

James stirred in his bedroll. A faint orange glow spread across the eastern sky. Light from a lamp illuminated one of the cabin windows. He got up, walked to the creek, and splashed some water on his face to drive away the sleep. For most of the night, he struggled with his feelings and reached a conclusion: getting to Oregon overrode all else. He had risked his life to reach this point, and there could be no turning back now.

Wilford Johnson emerged from the cabin. He rubbed his hands through his graying hair. When he saw James was awake, he walked over. "I been thinking about you needin' to get to Oregon. I make my living here selling horses to the Army and anybody else that comes along. It takes a bunch of years to make the kind of money you talking about. I ain't been up that way for a spell, but I can break away from here for a time."

That settled the matter. "How soon can we leave?" he asked Wilford.

"I got a little business to attend to before we start. I 'spect we can be on our way in a day or two."

"Agreed."

"I'm gonna be gone for most of the day," Wilford said. "I got some horses to round up and sell. You can camp here until I get back."

Wilford saddled his horse and rode away. James spent the day going over his gear, thinking all the while about being reunited with his family again. At last, the final leg of the journey was set to begin.

*   *   *

Late that afternoon, James looked out across the prairie. A herd of horses was approaching. He watched. Soon, he could see Wilford driving the herd.

They were wild-looking range ponies with shaggy manes. James helped drive them toward the corral. When all the horses were inside, he closed the gate.

Wilford rode in and dismounted, then tied the reins of his horse to a corral post. "Gonna be a man here early in the morning to buy these horses," he said. "After that, we can be on our way."

Welcome news to James. That night, he had a peaceful sleep, dreaming about his family.

*   *   *

The next morning, James was packing his gear on the packhorse. When he looked out across the prairie, he saw riders near the house. They rode up to the cabin, and a heavyset man with a short beard dismounted. Wilford stepped out of the cabin and greeted the men. "They in the corral."

The one who had dismounted went around to the corral. He studied the horses. "I'll give you three hundred for the lot," the man said to Wilford.

"You robbin' a poor man," Wilford said.

"It's me that's gettin' robbed. These horses are wild. They'll need breakin' before I can sell 'em."

Wilford haggled with the man until a price of three hundred twenty-five dollars was reached. The man pulled out a wallet and counted out the money. Wilford counted it again then signed a piece of paper. With the transaction completed, the man yelled to his companions.

They opened the corral gate and urged the wild horses out on the prairie. Wilford and James stood and watched as the horses and riders made their way across the broad, flat land.

When the herd was out of sight, Wilford turned to James. "We can be on our way now."

James finished getting his gear ready. Visions of a great reunion with his family flashed through his mind.

Chapter 22

The Prairie

Wilford looked at the cabin and corral that comprised his home. "When a man lives in luxury such as this, it's hard to leave it behind," he said with a grin.

James offered no comment on Wilford's attempt at humor. They rode out onto the prairie with Wilford in the lead and James following on his own mount and leading the pack horse. They followed a northwest route that took them into Iowa late in the afternoon. Near nightfall, they struck the Missouri river and made camp. Fuel was limited, but Wilford got a fire going using some dried grass and limbs from a cottonwood tree.

The day's ride had been mostly in silence, with few words passing between the two men. It was much the same when they camped. Wilford cooked a pan of beans and brewed a pot of coffee. James, still uncomfortable with his guide, did have some appreciation for the man's culinary skills. This meal sure did beat salt pork and hardtack. They sat across the campfire from each other, keeping to their own thoughts. Wilford finished eating, rinsed out the cooking utensils in the muddy river, picked up his rifle, and walked out into the darkening prairie. James found it a bit peculiar but was too tired to give it much thought. He got out his bedroll and was soon snoring beside the dying fire.

*　　*　　*

Darkness was yielding to the early light of dawn when James stirred from his bed. Wilford was frying bacon over the campfire, and a pot of coffee was brewing in the coals. He glanced in James's direction, but neither man spoke. They ate in silence. After eating, they caught and saddled the horses, started across the prairie. This day was much like the previous one. The only

220

sounds were the crunching of the horses' hooves on the soft earth and the occasional cry of a hawk or the lonesome cooing of doves.

At noon, they stopped at a small stream to water the horses. Their noon meal was leftover bacon from breakfast. At mid-afternoon, Wilford stopped and wiped the sweat from his face. "There's a ferry crossing just ahead," he said. Another thirty minutes of riding brought them to the crossing. The boat, a small craft with a single smokestack, was on their side of the river. James's anxiety arose at the sight of a contingent of Union soldiers on the other side. Keeping a wary eye on the troops, he helped Wilford get the skittish horses up on deck. James paid the captain, a crusty Irishman with a short, gray beard, twenty cents.

When the boat docked on the Nebraska Territory side, the Union troops lined up to take it back across. To James, this was comforting. Better to have the river between him and the blue-clad soldiers.

The troops stood aside as they led their horses off the boat. A tall non-com glanced at James but did not speak. He and Wilford mounted up and rode away. They struck the south bank of the Platte River and followed it until nightfall. After a supper of beans and salt pork, like the previous night, Wilford took his rifle and disappeared. James's curiosity and concerns were aroused. What was the man up to? Was he checking the campsite, or did he have more sinister motives for these excursions?

*   *   *

The next day was more of the same. They followed the course of the Platte River across the Nebraska prairie. The land lay before them like a large tabletop covered with tall prairie grass mixed with colorful primrose and daisies that stretched all the way to the horizon. It was a clear summer day with a blue sky dotted only by a few fleecy white clouds. They had the country to themselves, except for an occasional rabbit or prairie dog and numerous assortments of birds.

Wilford broke his silence. "There's a road that connects to the Old Fort Kearney Road, but there's usually too many folks on it. Best we stay away from the main roads for now."

By the second day in Nebraska, Wilford took up another annoying habit. He started riding off for long periods of time, leaving James to himself. "Just stay close to the river," was all he would say before galloping off.

On two occasions over the next few days, Wilford rode out early and did not return until almost dark. When James asked him for an explanation, he replied, "I'm checking the country ahead of us."

James's distrust rose. His imagination conjured up disturbing theories.

221

Perhaps Wilford planned to lie in wait and rob him. After all, why make an arduous journey to Oregon when he could take the money now? All of it, not just what he had been promised. James vowed to keep his eyes open and be prepared.

* * *

There was evidence of settlement and commerce in this part of Nebraska Territory, but Wilford steered them away from most of it. On the sixth day out, a group of riders appeared in front of them. James, alarmed, watched them closely. Wilford gave them only a casual glance. When he realized they were Indian, James reached down for his pistol. "No need for concern," Wilford said. "They're Pawnee."

The Indians stopped a short distance in front of them and watched. After a time, one of them rode out from the group a short distance. Wilford rode out to meet him.

The remaining Indians sat on their ponies and watched with expressionless faces. A few of them carried ancient-looking muzzle-loading rifles; the rest carried bows and arrows. One had a small deer slung over the back of his horse.

Pawnee apparently wasn't one of the Indian languages his guide spoke. He and the Indian communicated with sign language. The Pawnee turned and made a sweeping motion across the prairie with his hand. There were a few more exchanges, then Wilford rode back to him, and the Indian joined his companions.

"We got to be careful from now on," Wilford said. "The Pawnee have seen signs of a band of Sioux nearby. I thought there would be less chance of finding them on this side of the river, but they out there."

James didn't know much about Indians, but the news distressed him. He remembered his grandfather's stories about the early days in Tennessee when they had battled the Indians there. More so, he had heard that the Plains tribes, like the Sioux, were fierce fighters. That night, he dreamed of the Sioux riding in and taking their scalps.

* * *

The next day, they were vigilant. Wilford was silent, but James could see the usually expressionless face carried hints of concern. Since his guide reported to know Indians, his concern amplified James's own worries.

Just before noon, Wilford turned around and looked toward James. "I'm going to ride on ahead a ways and look around. Stay close to the river. If I'm not back by dark, go ahead and set up camp."

Before James could protest, Wilford rode off across the prairie. Anger consumed him as he watched his guide disappear into the distance. He was paying a high price for his services. Therefore, he expected the man to stay close at hand in case there was trouble. He vowed to speak to Wilford that evening and get the matter settled.

James did not stop for a meal at noon. Instead, he munched on dried beef and kept on riding.

Taking Wilford's advice, he followed the winding course of the river for the entire afternoon. The few scattered cottonwoods and scrub bushes along the bank would provide some cover, whereas out on the open prairie, he would be a sitting duck. With growing anxiety, he watched the prairie for his guide's return but saw nothing but empty space stretching as far as the eye could see. The sun faded into an orange glow, and Wilford still had not returned. James worried. Had the man encountered the Sioux? Or had he run out and left him to fend for himself? A pretty fix that would be: alone out here on the prairie with hostile Indians nearby.

Both he and the horses were weary. Next to the river was a clump of willow trees: a good place to camp. After staking out the horses, James gathered up some dead limbs and built a small fire. He fried some salt pork and brewed a pot of coffee. The greasy meat was tasteless, in part because worry over Wilford's long absence had taken his appetite. What would he do if his guide did not return? Maybe he could backtrack and reach a settlement somewhere. That is if he could avoid the hostile Indians.

In the fading light, James washed the frying pan in the river. In the distance, a coyote set up a mournful cry, followed by several others. Or were they coyotes? Indians, he had read, used animal sounds to communicate. He was letting his imagination rule his reason. A nearby sound sent him reaching for the Henry; it was the horses grazing. He placed the Henry nearby and lay down to sleep.

He was awakened by the sound of an approaching horse. He grabbed the Henry and stared out into the darkness. "Easy inside the camp," he heard someone say. It was Wilford.

Wilford rushed into camp, dismounted, and started kicking sand over what remained of the campfire. James was outraged. He resented him riding into camp and taking over without saying a word. He started to speak up, but Wilford spoke first.

"There's a band of Sioux camped about three miles ahead of us. We got to keep the fires out tonight, and at first light, we got to find a place to cross the river. I'll feel better with the river and some distance between us and them."

Now that he understood Wilford's reasons, James's anger abated somewhat. At that, he was still unhappy that the man took things into his own hands without telling him first. After all, he was the one in charge. But with the Sioux nearby, he felt this wasn't the time to press the point.

"We better keep a watch out tonight," Wilford said. "I'll take the first one and then wake you when it's your turn."

James crawled back into his bedroll and tried to sleep, but it didn't come easy.

*   *   *

He awoke and looked around. There was faint light in the eastern sky. Morning. What happened to his watch? Why hadn't Wilford called him? The camp was deserted, bringing back the fears and doubts. Perhaps, the thought of encountering the Sioux had prompted his guide to abandon him. He was cursing his fate when Wilford walked into camp, carrying his rifle. "Why didn't you wake me last night?" James asked.

"I couldn't sleep, so I took the whole night."

Was it that Wilford didn't trust him to stand watch? He exploded into anger again. He was a war veteran; that certainly qualified him for sentry duty. With the prospects of a Sioux encounter, he would have to let it ride for now, but afterward, he and Wilford had to come to an understanding.

With the Sioux close by, they couldn't risk a fire. Their breakfast was hardtack. Wilford retrieved the horses, and they saddled up and followed the banks of the Platte. "This river can be a bear to cross at times," Wilford said.

They searched for a safe place to ford the Platte. Beyond a small bend, Wilford stopped his horse and studied the river. "The channel is a little wider here," he said. "This is the best we're gonna find. Tie your stuff down good and try to keep it dry when you cross."

James wrapped his ammunition and some of their food in the oil cloth he had bought in Independence.

"Give me the packhorse; then you cross first," Wilford said.

There. Wilford was giving orders again. Well, he did hire him for his knowledge of the frontier. At the moment, he didn't have a better plan. James handed over the reins of the packhorse then urged his mount into the stream.

The water was shallow near the bank, but further out, the channel deepened. As the river rose, his horse became nervous and started thrashing around. James tried to calm the roan; while doing so, some of his gear floated into the river.

James reached to retrieve his gear. The horse jerked, sending him out of the saddle into the water. He tried to hold onto the reins, but the roan fought until they were pulled out of his hands.

224

The last James saw of his horse; it was being carried down the river by the current. He had to let go of the supplies he was holding and try to reach the bank. The current was swift, pulling him under. When his feet struck the river bottom, he lunged toward the surface and swam the remaining distance to the bank. By that time, his horse had disappeared around a bend in the river. Damn the luck—he was stranded out on the Nebraska prairie with no horse.

While James was struggling in the river, Wilford used a small bush to cover up their tracks. Then he plunged off into the river, pulling the pack-horse behind him.

Wilford kept his own horse under control, but when they were in the middle of the stream, the packhorse started pulling away from him, forcing him to release the reins. Like the roan James was riding, the packhorse thrashed around in the water as the river current carried it downstream. Wilford urged his horse up out of the water onto the sandy bank, then got off and dropped down on the sand. "I didn't expect the water to be that swift or that deep." After catching his breath, he got back to his feet. "I'm going to ride down the river and try to catch up with the other horses."

Much of James's gear was lost. He still had the pistol, but it was wet. The rest of his weapons were on his saddle floating down the river. Bad luck had become his companion these days. And it wasn't done with him yet.

He heard voices on the other side of the river; faint at first, then louder, and they were of a language he didn't understand. Through a small opening in the bushes, he looked across the Platte. There were Indians approaching. The Sioux party, he assumed. He counted a dozen riding in a straight line toward the river bank.

What a desperate situation he faced. Here he was, alone, horseless, and outnumbered with only a wet pistol to defend himself. He had to credit Wilford for taking the time to wipe out their tracks on the other side. But did it matter? There were plenty on this side that could easily be seen from across the river.

The Sioux stopped their horses a short distance from the bank and dismounted. One of them was holding something in his hand that seemed to have captured the interest of the others. James strained to see what it was. He wasn't sure, but it looked like a pistol belt, probably taken from a soldier. Whatever it was, it was keeping their attention diverted from him.

His immediate dilemma was getting away undetected. About ten feet down the bank, there were bushes and tall grass that would conceal him. That is, provided he could just get there undetected.

Summoning his courage, he started crawling across the open space, staying as close to the ground as possible. The ten-foot space now looked a mile across. At any moment, he expected the Sioux to come charging across the river and run him down.

When he was across the open space, James paused to calm his nerves and let his heart settle down. He peered around at the Indians and was relieved to see their attentions were elsewhere; in fact, they now seemed to be quarreling among themselves.

James moved down the river, using the bushes and grass as cover. He listened for the sound of pursuing horses, but none came. When he traveled for what he figured to be a half mile, he spotted Wilford in the distance, leading the other two horses. He hurried down and explained about the Sioux.

"We got to get some distance between them and us and hope they don't have friends out here somewhere," Wilford said. "We lost most of the food, so we gonna be livin' off the land for a time. One good bit of luck is we are on the other side of the Loup and won't have to worry about crossing it. Since we're on the North side of the river, we won't have to worry about crossing the South Platte, which is a lot worse than what we just encountered. But we'll still have to cross the North Platte and Laramie Rivers to get to Fort Laramie."

They rode straight west until they were out of sight of the river and then followed a course that paralleled the Platte for the rest of the day. At sundown, they kept riding and didn't stop until well into the night. Riding across the prairie at night was risky. In the darkness, a horse could step into a hole, but this night, they had to take that chance. They didn't stop until both themselves, and the horses were exhausted.

They spent the rest of the night in a small ravine, trying to get some much-needed rest. James would drift off for a time, then wake up and stare out into the dark night, imagining Indians everywhere. In the morning, he felt exhausted but appreciated the daylight since he could see what was around them.

James found some hardtack in his saddlebags. It was the only food that survived the river crossing.

"Too risky to start a fire anyway," Wilford said.

They saddled their horses and started across the prairie. This morning it was quiet—too quiet for James's liking. There was something ominous about the silence. The horses needed water, leaving them no choice but to ride back over to the river. The Platte was deserted. They watered the animals, filled their canteens, and rode away. After a couple of miles, the ground began to shake. In the distance, there was a rumble like thunder. "What's that?" James asked.

Wilford listened for a moment. "Buffalo stampede. Head back for the ravine."

They turned and rode at a full gallop for the ravine. When they reached the gully, they urged the horses down inside. James looked over the top and saw a sea of brown coming in their direction. "I hope they turn before they reach us," Wilford said.

It turned out to be close. The leaders of the herd turned when they were only a hundred yards or so from the ravine. The shaggy animals thundered past them, their thundering hooves pounding the ground as they went; a few of the shaggy beasts almost tumbled into the ravine on top of them.

When the last buffalo had passed, they scrambled out and watched the herd racing across the prairie.

"That's a sight you don't see as often as you used to," Wilford remarked. "White men keep killing off the buffalo. Soon you won't be able to find herds like that. We need some meat. I'm gonna trail after them and see if I can pick up some rations. You best wait here until I get back."

This time, James didn't even mind that Wilford was giving orders. After the tiring night, he felt content to sit and wait, at least for a time.

In time, the wait began to play on James's nerves. He sat in the ravine for what seemed like an eternity. What had happened to Wilford? Had he run into the Sioux? Maybe he was not coming back. He stared out across the prairie until he spotted his guide riding toward the ravine with something slung across the back of his horse.

Wilford rode up with a hindquarter of buffalo meat. "That's all I could carry. I had to leave the rest for the buzzards and the other varmints, but this'll feed us for a few days."

"How are you going to cook it? There's no wood out here away from the river."

"There's other fuel out here. While we're traveling today, I'll pick up enough for a cook fire when we stop tonight."

James couldn't imagine what Wilford was talking about, but he was the frontiersman. He guessed the man knew what he was doing.

They traveled, keeping a wary eye out as they went. At one point, Wilford stopped, got down from his horse, and walked over to a pile of what appeared to be dried buffalo dung. James was puzzled by this sudden interest in manure. He watched as Wilford got a sack from one of his saddlebags and scooped up the entire pile. "I take it you've got a need for that," James said.

"That's the fuel I was talking about."

"Well, I find it hard to hunger for anything cooked over manure."

"Suit yourself," Wilford replied. "Out here, folks have been using dried shit for fuel for some time. I never heard about it harming anybody."

During the day, Wilford found several more piles of manure that he retrieved and put in his sack. "I've got enough now to cook a meal," he said. "When it's dark, I'll get a fire going and cook up this meat. Less chance of the smoke being seen then."

The day passed uneventful. At sundown, they stopped beside a small bluff that rose up some twenty feet above the prairie floor. "We can build a fire up against this bluff. That will help keep the flames from being seen, and the darkness will help hide the smoke. It's risky, but we got to eat."

Wilford got out his knife and sliced the buffalo meat up into small strips. When darkness had settled over the prairie, he got a few clumps of dried prairie grass and started a fire with the dried manure. James was still repulsed by the idea of eating meat cooked over burning dung, but after a time, the smell of the frying meat and his hunger started swaying his opinion. By the time the meat was done, James had totally forgotten about the manure and picked up one of the cooked strips.

"Don't taste bad after all," Wilford said with a grin. "Out here, you got to make do with whatever the land provides you. Here the land doesn't provide you with wood, but the buffalo provides something that works just as well."

James was too hungry and tired to disagree. He ate some more. He might not like the way Wilford Johnson conducted himself at times, but the man was a superb hunter and a good cook—both skills he lacked. He had hunted for sport when he was a young man and had achieved some success. But here on the prairie, where your survival was at stake, it was a different matter.

The trials of the last several days led James to rethink some of his ideals. He was starting to realize that some of his dislike for Wilford and his ways was the result of prejudices he had harbored all his life. These prejudices were the result of his upbringing and the social climate where he had spent most of his life. He was in a different world now and a different social order.

They filled themselves on buffalo meat. Then, Wilford cooked the rest and packed it away. "We got enough for another day."

That night, James had a peaceful sleep.

*   *   *

The next morning, they had cold buffalo meat for breakfast. The sun was rising in the east, promising another hot day, when they saddled up and started across the prairie. "We're low on water again," Wilford said. "We've got to ride over to the river, water the horses, and fill up the canteens."

James dreaded riding over to the river; it seemed to be a magnet for trouble, but it was a risk they had to take.

It turned out to be quiet along the river bank. They watered the horses, filled their canteens, and set out. The sun arose to a pale blue sky. As they had always done since entering Nebraska, they continued a course parallel to the Platte. In early afternoon, the river turned northwest. Mid-afternoon, they encountered an Army patrol. James, ever apprehensive toward blue-clad soldiers, watched nervously as the troops approached. The leader, a captain with a red beard and a wad of tobacco in one cheek, held up his hand for them to stop. "You gents are taking a bit of a risk traveling through here alone," the captain said.

"We're in a hurry," James replied.

"The Sioux are up in arms," the captain said. "Thought we had 'em tamed down a bit after all that ruckus last year. But they're at it again. They attacked some travelers just to the west of here yesterday. Better keep a wary eye out."

After a few minutes of talk, the captain gave the order, and the column of haggard soldiers moved on. As he watched the bluecoats ride away, James had a disturbing thought. Kate and her uncle had traveled through here sometime last year. Had they escaped the Indian problems the captain mentioned? He was left tormented, not knowing the fate of his family.

"The Platte splits up here," Wilford said. "We'll be following the North Platte now. The river will lead us to Fort Laramie. With a few more days of riding, we should be there. There are a few trading posts along the way. We can pick up supplies at one of them."

*   *   *

A Few miles up the North Platte, they reached a small way station. The proprietor was a crusty Irishman with a deeply tanned face, a turned-up nose, and a short, red beard. "Where ye bound for, gents?" he asked.

"Oregon," Wilford replied.

The trading post was stocked with strips of dried buffalo meat, barrels of sugar, flour, bacon, coffee, and beans, and several jugs of Irish whiskey. "Ye fellas be travelin' alone, I take it. Been some Sioux trouble, you know. Best keep an eye on ye scalp."

James had no appreciation for that comment. They bought some beans, coffee, dried buffalo meat, and bacon and got on their way.

*   *   *

The next two days passed peacefully. Keeping with the pattern he had established since entering Nebraska, Wilford led them around most of the settlements. The days were long and boring. Worse, the hot sun showed them no mercy. Their canteens would soon be empty, and they would ride over to the river to refill and water the horses. With no recent sign of the Sioux, James hoped their Indian troubles were over. He found out the next day how futile his hope was.

*   *   *

The day started peacefully. A light breeze held down the heat. A hawk soared above them, riding the thermal currents while watching the prairie below. A few insects buzzed among the brown grass. The prairie seemed peaceful enough. But by mid-morning, they could see a column of smoke spiraling up into the blue sky. "What do you make of that?" James asked.

"Hard to tell. Might just be someone's campfire."

The look in Wilford's eyes said otherwise. James could tell he was expecting more than just a campfire. They rode toward the smoke and reached its source around noon. It turned out to be coming from behind a small rise. They stopped at the base of the hill. "You wait for me while I go and check on that fire," Wilford said. "If I ain't back shortly, light out straight for Fort Laramie. Keep following the river, and you'll find it."

Wilford's words carried an ominous implication. James got out the Henry and waited at the base of the knoll. He raised the rifle when he heard a rider coming down but lowered it when he saw Wilford. "What did you find?"

"Ain't a pretty sight. We best be getting on out of here."

"What did you find over there?" James asked.

"Just some folks we can't help."

"I'm going over to take a look."

Before Wilford could protest, James urged his horse up to the top of the short knoll. Below, he could see the burned-out hull of a wagon. Two bodies were lying next to the wagon and another out a short distance.

With a sickening feeling, he rode down. Next to the wagon were the remains of two men who had probably been shot then mutilated and scalped. The other body was a woman. Her head was covered with blood, and in her hand was a small pistol. James figured she had shot herself rather than be captured.

For four years, James had been part of a bloody war. In it, men died by the thousands. In time, soldiers became hardened to it all. But there was something different here. This wasn't war. This was just wanton cruelty; that's all he could make of it. He felt the nausea rising as Wilford came down with the packhorse. "They probably tried to hide behind this hill, but the Indians found them," he said.

James could offer no comment. Without speaking, he got down from his horse, feeling sick to the point he could hardly stand. "I told you we can't help these poor folks," Wilford said. "If we hang around here, we might be in the same fix."

"I'm not leaving until we give these people a decent burial."

In the burned-out wagon, James found a shovel with part of the handle burned away. He dug relentlessly in the prairie soil until he had three graves started. The sweat poured off his back, but he kept at it until Wilford took the shovel from his hand. He dug for a time, then James took over again. When they were finished, they buried the three victims. James felt inadequate at not having any words to say over the graves, but there was nothing left inside of him.

Wilford led the horses over and handed him the reins of his mount. "We best be puttin' some distance between us and this place."

"We just buried these folks and don't even know their names," James said. "We can't even tell the world who they were."

Wilford nodded.

"What do you figure these folks were doing out here?" James asked when they were on the other side of the hill.

"Probably some folks that didn't have the money to join a wagon train or were just in a hurry to get somewhere and didn't want to wait."

"That was the work of savages," James said.

"It might seem that way to a white man," Wilford replied. "The Sioux have seen the same and worse done to their own people, so they fightin' back the only way they know how. Violence begetting violence—that's what we got here."

That didn't satisfy James. He couldn't get the massacre out of his mind. For the rest of the day, he kept picturing the burned wagon and mutilated bodies in his mind. The inhumanity of it angered him; the brutality frightened him. That night, they made a cold camp and ate dried meat and leftover beans.

"We need to keep a watch out tonight," Wilford said. "I'll take the first one."

Wilford picked up his rifle and walked out into the dark night. James got out his bedroll and tried to sleep. The murdered travelers wouldn't let him have any peace. He tossed and turned until his time to stand watch.

James took the Henry and stationed himself a short distance from camp. There was little moon that night, leaving the prairie in near pitch darkness. The night air was silent except for the distant howling of coyotes, the occasional scurrying of night creatures among the grass, and the horses grazing nearby.

Sleepiness overcame James, so he got up and walked around for a time. As his eyes grew accustomed to the night, he looked out across the dark landscape. The prairie had a calm and peaceful look. With the violence they had seen earlier that day, it seemed out of place: a deception, he knew. For most of the night, he alternated between sitting on the ground and walking around to stay awake.

When the first faint light appeared in the eastern sky, James walked in to wake up Wilford, but he was already awake. "See anything out there?" Wilford asked.

231

"No. It was a quiet night."

After breakfast of dried meat, they rode over the river to water the horses and fill their canteens. Then they set out, following the course of the North Platte River. Faint clouds early promised rain, but by mid-morning, they had dissipated, leaving a clear sky and a merciless sun to beat down on them.

Noon fare was more dried buffalo. In the afternoon, Wilford stopped his horse and studied the ground. "What are you looking at?" James asked.

"Horse tracks. Looks like Indian ponies."

"How can you tell?"

"These horses are unshod. Indians usually ride unshod ponies."

"You think this could be the bunch that attacked those people back there?"

"Could be. They goin' the same way we're goin'."

"What are we going to do?" James asked. "We stand a good chance of running into them if we keep going in this direction."

"We got to find a way around them," Wilford said. "We're getting close to Fort Laramie. If we can get around this bunch, we can soon be there." He studied the tracks some more. "I think we'll follow them for a ways."

James didn't care for that idea. "Why?"

"If we follow them, we'll know where they're at and can get by them when the time comes."

The idea didn't catch on with James, but he decided to rely on Wilford's judgment. Down the trail, they found an empty whiskey bottle. "Looks like they got hold of some liquor," Wilford said. "They're getting drunk and careless now. They don't expect anybody to be following them, so they've got their guard down."

That didn't do much to alleviate James's concerns about following the tracks of a Sioux raiding party. If they followed them long enough, they were bound to catch up with them. Then what?

They followed the tracks until late afternoon. "We're getting close now," Wilford said. After another half hour of tracking, Wilford turned around and said, "They just ahead of us. I 'spect they pretty liquored up by now."

"This is our chance to get around them and get away," James said.

"Yeah. But I'd like to make the odds a little more in our favor."

"How do you plan to do that?" James asked.

"Since they're liquored up, I can get in to their horses. We'll scatter 'em out across the prairie. By the time they realize what's happened and get their horses rounded up, we'll be in Fort Laramie."

James didn't have any enthusiasm for this plan either. He felt it made more sense to just ride around the Indian camp. If the Sioux were drunk, they would be gone before the Indians were sober enough to follow them.

"You wait here," Wilford said. "I'm going to find their camp. I think they'll be over close to the river."

Before James could protest, Wilford rode off. Danger was nothing new to James. For four long years, it had been his constant companion. But out here on the prairie, it was a different kind of danger—one that left him nervous and jittery. He had heard the stories about Indians, about how they could conceal themselves. He sat on his horse with a nervous hand on the Henry and waited.

When a rider appeared, James breathed a sigh of relief when he saw it was Wilford. "I spotted their camp just a short ride from here. Most of them are staggering drunk now. We can easily get them horses out of camp."

It still sounded like a fool idea to James. He was tempted to tell Wilford to call it off. But again, he decided to trust his guide's judgment.

In the twilight, they made their way toward the Indian camp. The Sioux were camped inside a small depression with one side sloping down toward the river. Scattered around the camp were a dozen warriors. Two were sitting beside a small fire, passing a bottle back and forth. The rest, it seemed, had succumbed to the effects of the whisky.

To one side of the camp, the Indian's ponies were tethered to a rope line.

"Wait here," Wilford said. "I'm going over to cut that line and turn the horses loose. Then we can start driving them across the prairie. Time they sober up and find them missing; we'll be long gone."

James got out the Henry and watched Wilford make his way down the side of the depression toward the horses. When he was at the bottom, Wilford crawled slowly over to the rope line and got out a knife.

Unknown to Wilford, one of the Sioux was sitting back behind the horses, out of sight. Moreover, he appeared to be sober. Horrified, in the fading light, James saw the Indian sentry start creeping toward Wilford with a knife in his hands.

The Sioux was poised to thrust the knife into Wilford's back. Lacking any way to warn his guide, James raised the Henry to fire. It wasn't a good shot— the man was barely visible to him—but he squeezed off a round from the rifle.

The Indian dropped the knife and grabbed at his side. Startled, Wilford turned and saw the Indian drop to the ground. By this time, he had the rope line cut. He started slapping the ponies on the flanks, sending them up the bank toward the prairie.

The two Sioux sitting beside the campfire heard the gunfire and staggered to their feet. Whisky and surprise muddled them; they could not determine the direction of the shots. One grabbed a rifle but had not spotted Wilford.

James used this opportunity to grab the reins of their horses and ride down the bank. When he reached the bottom, Wilford jumped up in the saddle. "Let's get out of here!" he yelled.

The Indian with the rifle turned and fired toward them. The whiskey spoiled his aim, and the round sailed over their heads. More shots were fired from the camp as they were scrambling up the bank. They all missed, but one was too close for comfort; James heard the zing of the round as it passed.

As they cleared the top of the depression, yelling erupted from the camp. The Indians fired a few more shots, all well off the mark. Wilford urged the Sioux ponies into a run. "That'll keep them afoot for a while!" he yelled. Some of the Sioux came up from the depression and fired at them, but they were out of range. The rounds landed behind them.

"Now, let's put some distance between them and us!" Wilford yelled. They rode until exhaustion overcame them and their horses then made camp. The horseless Indians would not be able to catch up with them. They hobbled the horses, got their bedrolls out, and slept until the sun was well up into the sky.

*   *   *

Wilford threw off his blanket, picked up his rifle, and had a quick look around. James stirred out of his sleep. For breakfast, they had dried buffalo to eat, and then they rounded up the horses. "We should be in Fort Laramie soon," Wilford said.

*   *   *

That afternoon, they could see a series of bluffs on the other side of the river. "Scott's Bluffs," Wilford explained. "I been told there's now a fort on the other side of the Platte, but it's too dangerous to cross here. We'll have to stay on this side and hope them Sioux don't find their horses too soon."

After a short ride, Wilford said, "We're out of Nebraska. They used to call this Idaho Territory, but I don't know what it is now. We've got to cross the river."

The North Platte channel was wide at this point, but the swirling water didn't look all that inviting to James. Their last crossing was still firmly etched in his mind. "Probably the best we gonna find," Wilford said.

James started across the river, leading the packhorse behind him. The water came up above his stirrups, but he held on and made it across. As it turned out, the river crossing was the least of their worries.

When he looked to check Wilford's progress, James saw movement out on the prairie. He watched. Indians—and they were riding straight for them. Wilford, his back to them, had not seen the approaching danger.

The Indians raised their rifles in the air and let out a series of loud yells.

James yelled and pointed to the charging party coming toward them. Wilford glanced over his shoulder then urged his horse across the stream. The water slowed his progress, and the Indians were now close enough to get off a few shots. James reached for the Henry. Before he could fire, one of the Indians got in close and fired. Wilford grabbed his shoulder.

The Henry roared in James's hand; one of the charging riders fell. The rifle was effective, but he didn't have many rounds. He counted at least a dozen in the approaching party. Either the Sioux had recovered their horses more quickly than expected, or this was a different band. But it didn't really matter. Whoever they were, they meant business.

James's shot with the Henry gained some respect from the Indians. They dropped back a bit, giving him time to ride over to where Wilford was struggling out of the river; blood was running down his guide's arm and the front of his shirt.

"Let the packhorse go," Wilford said. "He'll slow us down."

James dropped the reins of the pack animal. As they rode away from the river, they could hear the splashes of the Indian's horses plunging into the water. Both he and Wilford urged their horses to the limit. Shots from the Indian's rifles were now hitting the ground behind them. They were out of range, but for how long?

When the horses could go no further, they took refuge in a small gully lined with tall grass. From inside, James peered through the grass and watched. The Indians had stopped their mounts a short distance away. After watching the gully for a minute, the Indians split up. Five of them started down the gully to cross and come up behind them, James figured.

It didn't even require James's experience as a cavalry officer to realize they were in a predicament. The Indians would soon have them surrounded. He looked at Wilford, who was now slumped over in the saddle; his face looked drained of strength. It was on James's shoulders to find a way for them to survive. His dream of being reunited with his family would end here in this small gully unless he came up with something fast.

James reminded himself he was a soldier who survived four long years of war. Often, the Confederate forces had found themselves outnumbered. More than once, he had seen well-planned cavalry charges rout larger forces. However, he had to also consider the Sioux were excellent horsemen as well. After analyzing the situation, he concluded their only chance was to surprise their attackers and catch them off guard.

He looked at Wilford. "Can you ride and use your rifle?"

Wilford raised his head. "I reckon. What you got in mind?"

"We're gonna charge that bunch that's coming up behind us," James said.

"That sounds like a way to get killed," Wilford replied.

"I'm open to other suggestions."

"All right. Tell me what you plan to do."

"We're gonna spread out and charge that group on this side. I counted five, so we got to make every shot count."

James peered through the grass and saw the five Sioux had crossed the gully and were coming up behind their position. They were riding close in, leaving them in range of he and Wilford's rifles.

His other concern was the shape of their horses. Had they rested enough to take them up the bank and charge the Indians? All he could do was hope. He motioned to Wilford, then took a deep breath and urged his mount up out of the ravine, startling the Sioux.

The Indians were about one hundred feet in front of them. James let out a loud rebel yell. Before they could react, he got off a round with the Henry, dropping one of the Indians. The remaining Sioux on this side of the gully were thrown into confusion.

One of the Indians turned to fire at Wilford, but James got off another round from the Henry. The Sioux dropped his rifle and tried to stay on his horse. Another tried to get a shot at James; a round from Wilford sent him tumbling to the ground.

Another Sioux charged toward James, holding out the butt of his rifle to knock him off his horse. A round from Wilford's rifle caused him to turn his horse around.

They pushed their tired horses past the remaining Indians. James expected a chase. But the Sioux rifles were silent. He looked over his shoulder and was in for a surprise. The remaining Sioux had crossed the gully but were not giving pursuit. They were just sitting on their horses, watching. Wilford turned and looked. "They givin' it up!" he yelled.

When they were safely away from the Sioux, James turned his attention to Wilford. His guide was bent over in the saddle, barely hanging on. James reached out and grabbed the reins of his horse, bringing it to a halt. Wilford sat for a moment, then slid out of the saddle and sat down on the ground. "I've lost too much blood."

James took another look to ensure the Indians had not followed them then inspected Wilford's wound. It was in the shoulder area; luckily, no bones appeared broken. That wouldn't matter if the bleeding wasn't brought under control. He knew all too well from his war experiences such a wound could be fatal if not treated.

In his saddlebags, James found some rags to press on the wound to slow the bleeding. Wilford remained slumped on the ground, his breathing now labored.

Wilford looked at him. "Fort Laramie is just a short ride to the northwest.

You best ride on ahead and try to get some help out here. Whatever happens, don't stop until you reach the fort."

James ignored the advice. Wilford was in no shape to be left out here alone. The man was now too weak to defend himself, leaving him easy prey for the Sioux or anything else that might happen along.

"It's the only chance," Wilford mumbled.

Despite Wilford's urging, James refused to leave him out here alone. If he could get the bleeding stopped, maybe he could get him mounted, and they could ride to Fort Laramie. When he got up to get some more rags, he noticed a group of riders to the Southeast.

Luck was unfriendly to them. Had the Sioux taken up the chase again? James reached over and picked up the Henry. There would be little he could do. Both he and Wilford were trapped. The only thing he might manage would be to take maybe one or two out before they got to them. The only advantages he would have were the Henry's accuracy and speed. And that was tempered by the fact he only had a few rounds left.

James waited. The riders came closer. Were his eyes deceiving him, or were they wearing blue? He watched a little longer. They were wearing blue. How could he ever have imagined the sight of men in blue uniforms being such a welcome sight? "Looks like we got company. A bunch of bluecoats riding up from the southeast."

Wilford managed to raise himself up for a quick look. "That's why those Sioux gave up the chase. They knew they were soldiers nearby."

The army contingent consisted of a column of twenty haggard-looking soldiers led by a young lieutenant. After halting the column, the officer, a skinny young man with stringy brown hair and a small mustache, looked over James and Wilford. "Looks like you men been in a scrap. Sioux?"

"They jumped us coming across the Platte," James said. "Wilford took a hit in the shoulder and has lost a lot of blood."

The Lieutenant looked at Wilford. "The doc at Fort Laramie might be able to patch him up if he can make it that far."

The lieutenant ordered two enlisted men to tend to Wilford. After bandaging the wound, they got him back on his horse.

The lieutenant gave the order, and the troop resumed its march. James rode beside Wilford, helping him stay in the saddle. In a few miles, they could see Fort Laramie in the distance. It might be a Union post, but now it looked ever so inviting.

Chapter 23

The New Plan

K ate sat on the porch enjoying an early morning reprieve in the weather. A shower during the night had dropped the temperature, and this morning, the air was dust-free. Drops of moisture left from the rain glistened from the grass in the meadow. The early morning air was cool and refreshing: a pleasant time that would be made more so if it weren't for the woes she faced.

Olaf emerged from the barn carrying a pail of milk. "Missy, we need to start thinking about the fall harvest," he said.

"Yes, I know. What do we need?"

"We need to find a threshing crew. With all the settlers' crops to harvest, we'll be working most of the fall getting everyone's grain in."

"And we have to find a way to get ours to market," she said.

"Due the problems with Covington, that's a problem for us," Olaf said. "He's the only freighter here who has enough wagons and the drivers to get a big crop to market."

"I've already put out the word to the settlers to go ahead with Covington this year," she said. "Covington is mean and greedy, but he's not dumb. He's not yet in a position to try and put the settlers out of business, so I expect him to be reasonable for now."

"That still leaves us in a tight spot," Olaf said. "We got a large crop of grain to market, and we can't expect Covington to help us. He had problems with Mr. Lewis, and I expect he feels the same way toward us."

"I know. And that's why I still plan to buy our own wagons and teams. Like I told you before, that's how I plan to defeat this man. Next year, we'll buy the settlers' crops at the farm and do all the hauling ourselves."

"Yaw. The problem is, we haven't found enough wagons and teams."

"I know, but we'll keep looking," she replied.

"It's a big risk, missy."

"It's a chance we have to take. The settlers know about this plan, and Covington has got to learn he can't ride over us anytime he wants to. He has to learn we mean business."

Olaf shook his head and went into the house. At times, his caution tried her patience. But he was a good, dependable man. Without him, she couldn't manage this place. All else aside, they had to stand firm or risk losing everything. Pride, stubbornness, a thirst for justice—she wasn't going to be driven out. They would get their crops to market, and there would be justice for Uncle Lewis. She wouldn't rest until both were accomplished.

This year, they had to assume a dual role. Part of Uncle Lewis's plan was to supply the settlers with free seed stock until they were able to buy their own. At that time, Harrington Farms would assume its role as a seed stock supplier. Until that happened, they had to support themselves by selling a portion of their crop. The rest they would hold back for seed.

*   *   *

The weight of Kate's problems was making her restless. It was time to act. She could hold off no longer. "Today, I want to start looking for some wagons and teams again," Kate said to Olaf as they were eating breakfast.

"Well, you know, we didn't have much luck around here the last time," he replied. "I don't expect it'll be any better this time."

"Nonetheless, we have to try. Please get the buggy ready. We'll go to La Grande and start again. First, I need to talk to be bank about a loan."

The summer weather had chased away the effects of yesterday's rain. The hot sun glared from a bright blue sky. Clouds of dust drifted from the horses' hooves. This time, Kate didn't pay it much mind. Her thoughts were elsewhere.

A rider came down the road toward them. It was Lawrence Granville riding a sorrel horse. When he was even with the buggy, he stopped.

"Morning, Kate, Olaf."

"Morning, Lawrence," she replied as Olaf stopped the buggy.

"You folks are out and about early this morning."

"Yes. We're on our way to La Grande to look for some wagons and teams," Kate replied.

"Oh."

"Yes. We're starting our own freight business."

"That's an ambitious undertaking," Lawrence said. "I thought you were farmers."

"That we are. The problem is, we don't have a reliable way to market our crops. My uncle tried to set up a deal with E. G. Covington, but that didn't work out."

"I see. Well, you better keep an eye on that old buzzard. He's got most of the long-haul business in this area. He leaves the mining freight to the small concerns, but he doesn't like competition for his line. He can be a nasty man when he wants or needs to be."

"I know," she said. "We'd better get going."

"Of course. I'd like to have all of you over again."

"Thank you. We'll try to remember," Kate replied. "Right now, we're rushed for time."

"I understand." He reached up and tipped his hat. "Good day, Kate, Olaf."

He was a subtle but persistent man, Kate concluded. But that would be as far as it went. Lawrence was a gentleman and good neighbor; let it stay at that.

"He's right about Covington," Olaf said. "He will be mad when he finds out what you're doing."

"That's his worry. This is a free country. I have the right to start a freight business if I want to. He'll just have to get used to the idea, that's all. Not only that, I still think he's behind the murder of Uncle Lewis; he stands a chance of hanging if I can prove it."

"I don't want to see anything happen to you, missy."

"I appreciate your concern, but I'm tougher than some people might think."

Olaf nodded.

"Take me to the bank," Kate said when they reached La Grande.

Olaf parked the buggy in front of La Grande's one and only bank and helped Kate down. She walked across the wooden sidewalk and pushed open the door.

Going into the bank made her nervous. She had rarely visited a bank, let alone been involved in bank transactions of any kind. In Clarksville, she had, on occasion, taken money from the store to be deposited in the bank; that was the extent of her involvement.

The banker was a small, gray-haired man wearing thin, wire-rimmed glasses, a starched white shirt with a red band around the upper portion of his right sleeve, twill pants, and dark blue suspenders. He gave her a look of surprise that suggested he didn't get many women customers. "Good morning, madam."

"Good morning."

"Can I be of some assistance to you?"

Kate wasn't sure about how to proceed. "Maybe. I'm going to start a business. I wanted to talk to you about some of the things I will need."

"Are you talking about a loan of some sort?" the banker asked.

"Yes. Maybe."

"And what kind of business are you talking about?"

"A freight company."

"Miss, I didn't get your name."

"McKane. Kate McKane."

"Miss McKane, are you alone in this proposed venture?"

"Yes. That is, I'll be the only owner. My overseer, Olaf, will be helping me."

A slight smile formed on his lips. "Surely, Mrs. McKane, you don't plan on operating a freight line by yourself. Even if you have help, managing a freight company is a daunting task."

"Why? And by the way, I didn't get your name either."

"Gordon. Benjamin Gordon. Now really, Mrs. McKane, you don't think a young lady like yourself could operate a freight line in a place like this, do you?"

"Yes, I can. And I resent the implication I can't."

"I'm sorry, but I just couldn't invest any of the bank's money on such a venture. Maybe if you could decide on a more suitable business, like a dress shop, then we could look more favorably on your proposal."

Her voice started to rise. "I don't need a dress shop."

"As you should know, there are already a number of freight lines in this area. I don't think there is enough business for another one," the banker said.

"Yes. I've already met the owner of one of them."

"If you're talking about E. G. Covington, he's already a bank customer. I wouldn't want to hurt him by helping a potential competitor."

There was no doubt how the banker felt, so it would be pointless to continue. "Good day, Mr. Gordon, and thank you for your time." She slammed the door and stepped out on the sidewalk. The banker's attitude was indicative of E. G. Covington's influence in La Grande.

That would make her job more difficult, but she would find a way to stop Covington's scheming and make him pay for his crimes. There was nothing else to be done here, so she went back to the buggy where Olaf was waiting.

"Well, I take it the banker wasn't much help," he said.

"None at all."

"Yaw. He's much like Covington," Olaf said. "He came here just over a year ago. He likes to take advantage of poor people by charging high interest rates so high that people have a hard time paying him back. He won't hesitate to foreclose on you if you don't make your payments on time."

"Greedy and ruthless, both of them," she said.

"What now, missy?"

"Take me back home. I have to think about this some more. I'm not going to be stopped by these people."

Helga had a noon meal waiting. Kate ate in silence. How was she going to finance her business? There weren't many options; she had to use what money she had or find another source of financing. The money she had in the bank might set everything up, but there was the matter of operating capital. Being a woman was another strike against her. The next banker would probably be like the one in La Grande; women were not meant to operate freight lines. The thought made her seethe with anger.

Kate spent most of the afternoon sitting on the porch brooding about her problems. She was getting up to help Helga with the evening meal when she saw a rider coming across the meadow. It was Lawrence Granville.

It annoyed her that he was calling so late in the day. She was in no mood for conversation, especially about his search for a wife. Not wishing to be rude, she waited on the porch as he rode into the yard and dismounted.

"Kate. I'm glad you're here."

"What can I do for you, Lawrence?"

"I thought of something that might interest you. I don't know why I didn't think about it this morning," he said.

"What's that?"

"I know a man in Baker County who runs a freight line. He's getting on in years and has been talking about quitting. I think you might be able to buy him out. He raises his own stock and has several freight wagons."

"That sounds interesting, but now I'm having trouble raising all the capital I need," she said.

"Sounds like you've been talking to the banker in La Grande."

"He infuriated me."

"Yes, he's famous for that. I do my banking in Portland. It's inconvenient, but I don't have to deal with the likes of Banker Gordon."

"Do you have any idea how much this man would ask for his wagons and stock?" Kate asked.

"Hard to say. I would guess somewhere between three and four thousand dollars or the equivalent in gold dust."

That might require more money than she had in the bank. Without a source of funds for the rest, she couldn't take advantage of what Lawrence proposed.

"Kate, why do you want to take on such a responsibility?" Lawrence asked. "You've got a nice place here that will make you a good living."

"I'm trying to honor an obligation for my uncle. That's the only way I can do it."

"That's commendable. Are you prepared for all the risks that go with a venture like this, especially out here on the frontier?"

"I'll do whatever it takes," Kate replied.

"You may have to consider putting up your land here as collateral. You could borrow a tidy sum on this place."

"I may have to do that. I don't want to risk losing what Uncle Lewis spent so many years building, but I know he would want the welfare of the settlers to come first."

"There is another possibility."

"What's that?" she asked.

"I could lend you the money you need."

His offer stunned her. "That's a generous offer, Lawrence, but I couldn't borrow from you."

The hurt look on his face made her regret what she had just said. Some tact would have been better. "What I mean is, I wouldn't feel right borrowing from you since we just recently met, and you don't know very much about me," she explained. "I really do appreciate your offer. It was a very neighborly thing to do."

"I have some other motivation as well," Lawrence explained. "I've been forced to pay Covington's high prices for some time. I would like to see him with more competition. Help drive his prices down."

"I don't know. I'll certainly keep your offer in mind, and again, I thank you for everything. You've made my day a little brighter."

"I'm glad, Kate. I'm always here to help if you need it."

"That's comforting to know," she said. "Would you care to stay and have supper with us?"

"I appreciate the offer. I hear your cook is very handy in the kitchen, but I have to be getting home. I do hope you will have dinner with us again soon."

"We'll try to come over again when things settle down a little."

As she watched Lawrence ride away, Kate wondered if he was using the current situation for his own benefit: finding a wife. Her doubts about his true intentions made it difficult for her to get involved with him.

$$*\qquad*\qquad*$$

At breakfast the next morning, she asked Olaf to saddle a horse for her. He left one of the mares saddled and waiting in the yard.

Kate mounted and rode toward the Grigg farm. On the main road, the familiar heat and dust were her companions.

The side road to the Grigg farm was less traveled, which kept down the dust. When she reached the Grigg farm, it looked deserted. *What had happened to them?* she wondered. Alarming thoughts raced through her mind—Palmer and his henchmen, Indians, so many misfortunes could occur out here.

Kate tied the reins to a small tree and walked nervously toward the open door. "Come in, Mrs. McKane," she heard a weak voice call out.

Inside the cabin, Nancy Grigg was lying on the bed. "I'm sorry I didn't get up. I'm feeling poorly this morning. Hiram is out in the fields."

"It's all right," Kate said.

Kate got a chair from the table and sat down next to the bed. "What's wrong, Nancy?"

"Oh, I'm just a little run down, that's all. I'll be all right with some rest."

"Can I get you anything?"

"No. Thank you."

"Nancy, has E. G. Covington been around to see you recently?"

"Yes. I think that was the man that was here about a week ago. He was telling Hiram about a freight agreement he had to haul our crops. While they were talking, he showed Hiram a piece of paper."

"Did he talk about lending you money to buy your land?" Kate asked.

"I don't know. I think it might have come up, but your uncle and you had already talked to him about that. I think Hiram turned him down. The man was mad Hiram wouldn't accept his offer."

"I'm glad your husband turned him down," Kate said. "I hope the others do the same."

"Poor Hiram," Nancy said. "He doesn't know much about such things. You know he can barely read and write at all. When people come around asking him to sign papers, it just confuses him. He's a good farmer, but he just doesn't have any book learnin' to speak of. That makes it hard."

"Don't worry about that. We're going to get to the bottom of this thing with Covington. He's not going to cheat people out of their land and livelihood."

"I hope so, Mrs. McKane. We're just poor hill people trying to make a living."

"I know," Kate said. When she looked at Nancy Grigg lying on the bed, weak and exhausted, she couldn't help but feel pity for these people. They were trying to survive in a new and harsh land, an effort that could sap their strength and take away their willpower. "Nancy, do you need a doctor?"

"Oh no, I'll be all right with some rest."

"Are you sure? I can have the one from La Grande out here."

"Thank you, Mrs. McKane, but that won't be necessary."

"Well, if you do, you have Hiram let me know, and I'll send for him."

"That's kind of you, but I'll be all right."

Kate knew Nancy was worried about paying for a doctor. That might cause her to wait until it was too late. "Remember, you let me know if you need the doctor. And don't worry about the cost."

Kate thought about her poor neighbors all the way home. They were resilient people, but the harsh climate, the difficulties of farming, and these new problems would take a toll on the strongest of people.

And there was Covington out and about pressing his scheme. Hiram getting out the word might not be enough to thwart his greedy plans. Some had gotten the word too late, and there were others who still might be tempted. She felt the weight of the world settling on her shoulders.

Time was now her enemy. Harvest time was near, and that would leave little time for anything else. For now, all she could do was hope for the best. When the crops were in, she would sit down with all of the settlers and lay the cards on the table.

The approaching harvest meant time was running out for implementing her new plan. Crops were worthless if they couldn't reach the market. They needed reliable freight, but all she had going at the moment was an idea. Horses, wagons, and drivers: all those things needed to turn it into a reality she did not have. And getting them might well take more time and resources than she could ever muster. What was she going to do?

When Kate was home, she sat on the porch and went over her options. She was down to her last one, it seemed. Lawrence Granville's offer was still on the table, but the idea filled her with remorse. But was there any choice? She would have to find a way to put aside her personal concerns and do what was best for all of them. She let out a deep sigh; life just never came easy.

Chapter 24

Fort Laramie

James and Wilford accompanied the column of soldiers across the Laramie River to the fort. A large two-story building stood out from the rest of the post. To the right, set among several tents, was a series of small buildings. Beyond the perimeter of the post, a cliff rose up from the prairie floor. Soldiers stood and watched as they approached the fort through a group of tents.

It was a mixed experience for James. These soldiers wore the same uniforms as those he fought for four, long bloody years. On the other hand, they had saved he and Wilford from the Sioux. This being a western post probably meant these soldiers had not been involved with the recent war. At the same time, trust wasn't won overnight.

To the left of the tents, several wagons were parked. A wagon train on the way west, James assumed. When the column stopped, he asked the lieutenant about the wagons. "That's a group of people bound for California. The problems with the Sioux have got them holed up here until the trouble eases."

The lieutenant ordered two enlisted men to see Wilford to the infirmary.

While his guide was being tended to, James looked around the fort. Several Indians were lounging around a large adobe building. After the troubles he and Wilford had just experienced on the prairie, he found them unsettling. Were they Sioux? Looking at them reminded him of the three mutilated bodies out on the prairie and their encounter today at the river. Why would the army permit these people to hang around a military post? The Indians gave him a blank stare as he walked past them into the building.

Inside was a well-stocked store carrying everything from tools to foodstuffs to saddles and harnesses to clothes. A good thing. Before setting off the Rockies, they would need to restock.

Two young men in blue tunics and dark blue pants were looking through men's clothes. One had a lone stripe on his uniform sleeves, but the other had none. Probably getting ready to be mustered out, James surmised. When the young buck private spoke, James was taken aback by the Southern accent.

Galvanized Yankees. He had heard stories about Confederate prisoners being converted into Yankee soldiers for service in the west. The idea that Southern men would turn their backs on their own land and serve the Union had angered him once. Today, it didn't pain him so much. The war was over.

In the back of the store, a short man with a receding hairline and a large mustache was stocking shelves. He paused when James approached. "Help you, mister?"

"Just checking your wares."

James took stock of what the store had to offer. He needed winter supplies, more ammunition, and food rations. Today he settled for a slab of bacon, salt pork, sugar, and some coffee, then set out to see about Wilford. He walked out past the Indians again, still perplexed as to why they were allowed to hang around. The soldiers were fighting them out on the prairie and being forced to tolerate them here. Where was the reason in that?

A soldier provided James directions to the infirmary. It was in a small, white building beyond a group of long buildings housing the enlisted men. As he was walking up the steps, Wilford emerged with a bandage around his shoulder.

"Doc says I can't ride for a while. Says I should stay in the infirmary for a few days. I told him I would mend faster out on my own."

Some of Wilford's strength had returned. But his shoulder was out of action; bad news for James. Lament as he might, it would do no good. They were stuck here for now.

They retrieved their horses and looked for a camp site. About fifty feet beyond the wagons was a small willow tree, the only one in the near vicinity. They stowed their gear underneath, then unsaddled the horses and hobbled them. James took stock of the land around the fort and noticed there was no vegetation. Since they were stuck here, it was to their advantage to put some flesh on the horses. How they were going to do that, he didn't know.

James found a few dry limbs between their camp and the river and started building a campfire. As he went about the fire, he noticed a man standing beside one of the wagons, looking in their direction. After watching James get a fire going, the man walked over. He was of medium height and had a stocky build. His hair was dark and unkempt like his beard.

"Something I can do for you?" James asked.

The man looked in Wilford's direction. "I came over here to give you some advice, mister. I got a wife, two daughters, and all my worldly goods in that wagon over there. I get uneasy when strangers come around. And I get real nervous when one of his kind is around."

"Sir, I can assure you that neither Wilford nor I have any designs on your possessions," James replied.

"You best heed what I'm telling you. You best keep him away from our wagon."

"Look, mister. We're going to be on our way as soon as Wilford's shoulder mends to the point where he can travel again. In the meantime, you leave us alone, and you have my assurances we won't bother you."

The man glared at James. "I'm holding you responsible if anything happens."

Without further word, he started back toward his own camp where a small group of men had gathered. The man spoke briefly to them then climbed inside one of the wagons.

Wilford's face teemed with anger. This presented James with a serious dilemma. Since leaving Missouri, it had been just the two of them for most of the trip. Their encounters with others had been brief. It had been tense between the two of them at the onset; occasionally, it still was. But time and the dangers of the trail had broken down some of the barriers. In part, James was dependent on Wilford's skills, but there was more, something deeper.

Reality had confronted him. James had come to realize he was no longer the swaggering young master, cocky and full of confidence. Four years of death, suffering and the destruction of his way of life had humbled him a great deal. His birthright was back in Tennessee, trampled under by the hooves of Union horses. More so, the past four years, he had ridden into battle with the sons of farmers and laborers and found death and suffering had no prejudices. The sons of aristocrats could be struck down just as quickly as those poor souls fighting beside them.

There had been a time when someone berating a black man would have hardly caused him to raise an eyebrow. Now, when the man from the wagons had raised the issue, he had been taken aback by it. James McKane, the son of a planter and slave owner, had not only undertaken a journey across the miles; he had undertaken a journey in his heart as well.

Wilford was on his feet, the anger still visible on his face. "I got to walk a ways."

The rifle in his hands concerned James. Was his guide going to exact revenge from the man who berated him? He breathed more easily when Wilford walked out onto the prairie away from the wagons.

After a supper of salt pork and some coffee, James got out his bedroll to sleep. Wilford still had not returned; with his wounded shoulder, that was cause for worry. But the man was a product of the frontier quite capable of taking care of himself. He put the matter aside and went to sleep.

*   *   *

James stirred in his bed. From the nearby wagons, there was a commotion going on. Men were talking, more like yelling at times. *What had aroused them so?* he wondered. He got up. Wilford was also awake and was getting out of his bedroll.

At the edge of the wagons, a group of men were talking and looking toward James and Wilford. They continued to talk, still loudly at times, then started toward the camp with the irate man from yesterday in the lead. "I told that white feller with him he was responsible for anything that happened," the man said to his companions.

James waited until the group reached the edge of the camp, then he held up his hand. "That's far enough. What's troubling you men?"

"I warned you yesterday," the leader said. "I told you that you were responsible for anything that happened. Now some of our harnesses and food supplies are missing."

"We don't know anything about that," James replied. "We've been here all night."

"That ain't so," another man said as he pointed toward Wilford. "I saw him walking back toward your camp after midnight."

"That doesn't mean he was over around your wagons," James replied. "We don't have any of your belongings over here."

"Search their camp," another yelled. "If they got any of our stuff, let's hang both of 'em."

Wilford stepped in front of the crowd with his hand on his pistol. That put James in a spot. Such defiance would only antagonize these men. He had to find a way to calm the situation before violence erupted. He stepped between Wilford and their accusers. A shot came from the direction of the post. A group of mounted soldiers was approaching.

The leader of the troops was a dark-haired man with a neatly trimmed, dark beard, wearing the twin bars of a captain. Behind him were four enlisted men. "What's all this ruckus about?" the captain asked.

The leader of the group pointed toward James and Wilford. "Those two stole some of our harnesses and supplies last night."

"We didn't take anything," James said.

The captain reached into his pocket, pulled out a plug of tobacco, bit off a hunk, and put the rest back inside. "You say these men took some stuff from you?"

"That they did, Captain," the leader replied.

The captain spit on the ground. "How come I don't see any harnesses in their camp? I don't see any draft horses around here either, so what need would they have for harnesses?"

"I suppose they hid it around here somewhere and planned to sell it later."

The captain spit again. "What else you got missin'?"

"Some food, coffee, stuff like that," the leader replied.

The captain looked at James. "You take these people's food?"

"No. We bought our own. The man in Suttler's store will tell you that."

"Well, that may be the case, all right, but we're gonna have to take a look in your camp."

Wilford was still standing with his hand on his pistol, showing no inclination to do otherwise. The captain looked at James. "Tell him to get his hand away from that pistol unless he wants to get shot."

Wilford removed his hand from his pistol, but defiance remained on his face.

The captain ordered two of the enlisted men to search their camp.

While the rest watched, a corporal and a private looked through all their gear. "Just a slab of bacon, salt pork, and a little coffee and sugar," the corporal reported. "No harness or anything like that."

The captain spit more tobacco juice on the ground then looked at the men from the wagon. "Mr. Gates, I believe you and your men made a mistake. There was a bunch through here last night, and I 'spect they took your stuff. I'm telling all of you the colonel ain't got no patience for this kind of foolishness. You're camped on army property; if this happens again, you might find yourself brought up on charges. Now, good day, gentlemen."

The captain turned his horse and started back toward the fort with the enlisted men following behind. The other men started back toward the wagons. "Gates, you're always jumpin' to conclusions," one of them said.

"I tell you, I still believe they're the ones that done it," Gates replied. "I'm gonna keep my eyes on them two, and when I catch 'em, there'll be hell to pay."

Wilford waited until the men were back in their own camp. He then walked toward his horse. "I got to ride out on the prairie and get this out of my system."

James hated to see his guide risk hurting his injured shoulder again. He also understood Wilford's feelings. He helped get the horse saddled and watched him ride out of camp.

A woman was now standing near one of the wagons, looking in his direction. She looked familiar. Then James remembered. She had been standing beside one of the wagons during the confrontation. She started toward him, not more trouble, he hoped.

She was a small, brown-haired woman wearing a plain cotton dress. There were a few freckles around her nose, and her face was tanned. James judged her to still be a young woman, though the wrinkles on her face portrayed a difficult life. "Hello, I'm Edna Todd," she said.

"I'm James McKane. Did you get the soldiers?"

"Yes. I heard Gates talking to the other men early this morning. I knew he was stirring up trouble. He's always doing something like that. He's a married man, but when his wife is not around, he stands and leers at me. Gives me the willies, the way he acts."

"I do appreciate you alerting the soldiers. We were in a tough situation."

Edna leaned up against the willow tree and watched James get his breakfast. He didn't want to appear ungrateful for her help earlier, but now she was annoying him. The confrontation left him agitated with no inclination for conversation.

"We've been stuck here for so long," she said. "I came out from Cincinnati with my husband, Joshua. He was a store clerk back home, but he heard all those stories about the opportunities out west. We sold everything we had and bought passage on a wagon train. Out on the Nebraska prairie, he got sick and died. Poor man had dreams, but he never realized any of them."

"I'm sorry to hear about that, Edna."

Edna tried to get a conversation going, but James's unenthusiastic responses made her realize he wasn't in the best of moods. "If you ever get lonesome and need some company, come on over," she said before leaving.

He figured that was a suggestive remark. He politely bid her goodbye and finished fixing his breakfast. When it was done, he leaned back against the tree to enjoy it.

They needed some more rations. After breakfast, he went back to Suttler's store. The Indians were loitering again this morning. *Guess the army don't consider them a threat*, he thought.

Some men from the wagon train were inside the store. In good fortune, the agitator, Gates, was not with them. They left James to his business.

Seeing the travelers gave James an idea. Ever since he had heard about Kate and the children leaving for Oregon, he had hungered for news about them.

An elderly man with white hair and sparse white whiskers was behind the counter. "You been here a long time?" James asked after buying some salt pork.

"Over three years," the man replied.

"You probably remember a lot of the people that pass through here."

"Some, but I can't keep up with all of them."

"Over a year ago, a young, dark-haired woman with three children came through here with an older man. You remember them?"

"Folks of all ages pass through here. Plenty of women and children among

251

them."

The man thought for a moment. "Dark-haired, you say." He thought some more. "Come to think of it; I seem to remember a young lady with dark hair traveling with an older man. This older feller seemed to be the one in charge of a party of folks headed toward Oregon. Seems like they spent a day or two here then went on."

This was welcome news for James. He realized the people the man remembered might not have been Kate and her uncle, but he felt it was his family. They had made it this far, giving him hope they had reached Oregon safely.

*   *   *

Wilford returned late in the morning, still in foul mood. He said very little while James helped him unsaddle his horse. Well, that had been his nature for most of the trip, but James could sense the man's anger. "I hope we can be getting out of here soon," Wilford said after seating himself under the tree. "I don't like being around these people."

"I'm ready to go right now," James replied. "We have to wait until your shoulder is mended; the best we can hope for is you having a speedy recovery."

"Damn speedy, I hope." Wilford leaned back against the tree and said nothing else.

*   *   *

The next day, James was stirring the cook fire. He looked up and saw a column of soldiers riding behind a group of Indians. Strange, he thought. He pointed it out to Wilford. "Indians leading soldiers," he remarked.

"Pawnee scouts," Wilford replied. "Looks like that bunch has been roughed up a little bit."

Several of the soldiers were bandaged up; some could hardly stay in the saddle. "Things are heating up," Wilford said. "Hope we can get to the Rockies without any more trouble."

*   *   *

The days at Fort Laramie settled into a monotonous routine. In spite of his injured shoulder, Wilford spent much of his time out on the prairie away from camp. There was no recurrence of the problems with the men from the wagon train, but Edna Todd became a frequent visitor.

The boredom was now taking a toll on James. He was itching to get started again. With a hopeful eye, he watched Wilford very close, trying to determine how much use he was getting out of his arm and shoulder. He appeared to be getting better but still had not totally mended.

James noticed that during the day, the people from the wagon train herded their stock away from the fort to where there was some grazing. He learned that travelers camped close to the post, so the women and children were safer. This resulted in the grass in the near vicinity being grazed away, so they herded their livestock out where the grass was better. He decided to do the same with their horses.

During the end of their second week at the fort, Wilford cooked breakfast over a small fire. Afterward, he saddled his horse without any help from James. Moreover, he was now up to tending the horses. With the horses in tow, he rode out toward the prairie. James looked up and swore under his breath as Edna came out of her wagon and walked toward him. The woman meant no harm, he knew, but he found her endless chatter so boring. And that wasn't all of it. The woman was trying to lead up to something but couldn't find a way to get it out. "Morning, James."

"Morning," he replied as he cleaned up the iron skillet.

She stood near the tree and watched. "You know, you could use a woman's help."

"I suppose. I've been cooking and cleaning for myself ever since I left Tennessee this past spring. I just can't seem to get very good at it."

"There's a touch to it. Why don't you come over to my wagon some time, and I'll cook you a delicious meal that you won't ever forget?"

A good home-cooked meal was a temptation hard to turn down, but he kept silent about it. A bit rude, he knew, but the woman had some ulterior motive, he was sure. She fell silent, stared down at the ground for a moment, then looked back up at him. "James, you ever consider taking a wife?"

Well, now it was out. Thoughts of Sarah back in Missouri came to mind. Were men that hard to find these days? "I already have one," he replied. "I'm on my way to Oregon to find her and my children. They left while I was away in the war."

She sighed. "I expected as much. Good men are hard to find out here."

"I'm sure you'll find one."

"I hope so. That invite still stands. Before you leave, come and have a good meal. Now, I'll leave you to your business."

*   *   *

It was near sundown when Wilford returned with the horses. "My arm and shoulder are getting better," he said as he dismounted. "I hope we can get out of here soon."

"That is my greatest wish," James replied. "We've got to make sure you're ready."

*   *   *

Edna's visits became less frequent and shorter in duration. James assumed it was because he was no longer husband material.

*   *   *

In another week, Wilford was mended to the point he wanted to ride out on a hunting expedition. James welcomed the idea. A hunt would be a good way to test whether his guide was at full strength again. If he proved able, they could get out of here.

They rode northwest from Fort Laramie up a large embankment and out onto the prairie. In front of them, a peak rose up from the ground. In the distance, they could see the Laramie Mountains. "I been keepin' my eye on a herd of elk," Wilford said. "Some good elk meat would be mighty tasty right now."

James agreed. How sick he was of salt pork. They struck a small stream and followed it a short distance. "Try to stay downwind from them," Wilford said.

They spotted the elk herd just beyond the stream, grazing on the sparse prairie grass. They slowly worked their way toward the herd, trying to avoid being spotted. Before they were in range, one of the elk looked up and broke out across the prairie with the rest of the herd following. "I'm going to try and get a shot," Wilford said.

Wilford and the fleeing elk disappeared over a small rise. James heard a shot. He waited. What was keeping him? Indians, maybe he had run into the Sioux. As his worry was peaking, a horse and rider came over the rise. An elk was draped over the horses' back. "We can have a good meal tonight!" Wilford yelled.

Beyond a welcome change in diet, the good news for James was Wilford seemed to have gained the full use of his arm and shoulder. At last, they were ready to move on.

"I think we can leave here in a day or so," James said when they were back in camp. "I need to get some supplies tomorrow. The following day we can get on our way, that is, if you feel ready."

"I been ready ever since I got here."

Wilford slow-roasted one of the hindquarters over a small fire. The odor of cooking meat made James's mouth water. "Nothing like good elk meat," Wilford commented.

Feeling neighborly, James took a portion of the elk over to Edna's wagon. After giving her the meat, they had a short conversation. While there, he passed on the news of their pending departure.

"Thank you for the meat," she said. "I hate to see you go, but I promised you a meal before you left, so tomorrow night, you show up here for a going away supper."

He promised her they would come for supper the following evening. Then he took his leave and went back to camp. The elk was ready. James ate his fill, savoring every bite. Salt pork would be back on the menu soon enough; he appreciated the brief chance for something more tasty.

After eating, Wilford, keeping with his custom, picked up his rifle and walked out toward the prairie. Being a quiet man by nature, he kept most of his feelings to himself. The confrontation with the men from the wagon train was also eating at him—that James understood. His nocturnal wanderings gave him a chance to be away from camp and the wagon train.

*   *   *

James stirred from his bedroll. Faint rays of dawn were peaking over the eastern horizon. He noticed Wilford was already gone with the horses. He got up, had some cold elk meat, and made a list of supplies for the trail. The clerk greeted him when he walked into Suttler's store. "I figured you'd be halfway to Oregon by now."

"My guide was wounded, so we had to hole up here until he mended."

He bought ammunition for his pistol and shotgun, some bacon, beans, salt pork, coffee, sugar, and flour. "Any of the troops here have Henry rifles?"

"That's not regular issue. Why do you ask?"

"I got a Henry I bought off a Union soldier back in Tennessee. Trouble is, I only got a few rounds for it."

"I've been told a couple of troops in C Company have Henrys. You might work out a deal with them. Don't stock Henry rifles or ammo myself."

"Where would I find these troops?"

"Part of 'em are out on campaign. The ones in camp are on duty right now. After hours, a few of them usually stop in looking for whisky. Come back about six."

James finished his business and went back to camp. He hated approaching Union troops about anything, but he needed ammo for the Henry. Money, as was usually the case, would be the key to striking a deal. Being stuck out here in the middle of nowhere, these soldiers might jump at a chance to supplement their pay.

Late in the afternoon, James went back to the store. When he walked inside, the clerk nodded and pointed toward two soldiers in back. They were both privates. One had a mustache and blonde hair; the other was dark-headed.

"Either of you fellas know anybody with a Henry rifle?" James asked.

The privates looked him over before answering. "Yeah, I do," the dark-haired one said. "Why?"

"Well, I got one I bought from a Union soldier back in Tennessee, but I can't find any ammunition for it."

"There's a fella in our company with one. How much you willing to pay?" the dark-haired one asked.

"How much you think he could spare?"

"Hard to say. You'd have to ask him."

"I'll pay in gold," James said.

"You wait here. I'll go over to the barracks and fetch him. If he's interested, I'll bring him back over here."

The private went back to his barracks while James waited in the store. When the soldier returned, a young, slightly built soldier with long, stringy red hair was following him. The dark-haired one pointed to James. "There he is."

"You looking for some Henry ammo?" the other asked.

"That I am," James replied.

"My brother in the Wisconsin Militia was issued a Henry during the war. When he was mustered out, he sent the rifle to me along with a couple boxes of ammo. I could spare maybe thirty rounds, but the price has to be right."

"Ten dollars in gold," James offered.

The private demanded twenty, which James reluctantly paid. To keep it secure, he took the ammo and put it inside a saddlebag he had brought from camp. "I'm obliged, gentlemen."

It was late when James returned to camp with his ammunition. Edna was expecting them, and he wanted to be on time. He asked Wilford to come with him, but he was hesitant. "We were invited," James said.

After considerable prodding, Wilford walked over with him. He took a seat on the ground behind Edna's wagon while James joined their host. She was cooking stew over a small fire. Near the wagon, there was a pitcher of tea, and pies were frying over another small fire.

When the supper was ready, Wilford came around and filled a plate, and returned to his seat behind the wagon. Edna lived up to her promise. The meal was delicious. With this being their last good meal until Oregon, James savored every bite. "That was certainly a fantastic meal, Edna."

"Thank you for the compliment, James." Edna took his bowl and silverware, then walked around where Wilford was now seated on the wagon tongue. Someone yelled as he was handing his bowl to her. "What the hell are you doing hanging around this woman's wagon?"

Wilford and Edna looked up to see Gates coming toward them.

"Boy, what are you doing hanging around here?" Gates demanded.

James heard the commotion. He walked around the wagon just in time to see Gates berating both Edna and Wilford.

"Mr. Gates, these men are here at my invitation," Edna said.

"Woman, have you taken leave of your senses, letting the likes of these two hang around our camp?" Gates fumed.

"We were just having supper," James said.

Gates grabbed Edna by the shoulder. "You been warned about this!" he yelled. She struggled to free herself, but Gates kept his grip.

A fist slammed into the side of Gates's head. His eyes rolled then he slumped to the ground. Wilford stood over him.

For a moment, James was stunned. How were they going to get out of this? The man deserved it, but his companions would not see it that way. The other members of the wagon train heard the commotion and were gathering around. Before anyone could do anything, an elderly man with short whiskers pushed his way to the front. "I'm the wagon master. What happened here?"

James pointed to Gates. "That man grabbed the lady, and Wilford was just trying to protect her."

Gates was lying on the ground, out cold.

"Some of you men carry Gates over to his wagon," the wagon master said.

Two men stepped forward, picked up Gates, and carried him toward one of the wagons.

"We're leaving in the morning," James said.

"All right. I'll keep Gates under control tonight, but both of you best be gone tomorrow. Trouble is, I don't know what to do about you, Edna. Gates ain't likely to forget this."

Edna looked away and did not answer.

James and Wilford took their leave and walked back to camp. This latest confrontation was the final straw. They were left with no choice but to get out of here—the sooner the better. Violence was sure to happen if they remained here much longer.

When they were in their camp, James could see Edna and the wagon master talking. For her sake, he hoped they could find a peaceful solution.

Chapter 25

The New Business

*W*as this the right thing to do? Kate kept asking herself. The thought of entering into a business agreement with Lawrence Granville worried her, even scared her a bit. Would he try to use this as a way of influencing her feelings toward him? She was on the verge of calling it off, then she thought of all the settlers that were depending on her. These poor people were desperate—that she couldn't overlook. She took a deep breath, called on her courage, and vowed to go through with it.

Lawrence was waiting for them on the porch. "Good afternoon," he said. He walked out to the buggy and helped Kate down. "One of the men will take care of the buggy," he said to Olaf.

They went inside and had a seat on the settee. "Lawrence, I've decided to take you up on your offer," Kate said. "If it still stands."

"Of course," he said.

"You have to understand; it's strictly a business deal," she said. Once the words were out, she felt a little foolish.

Lawrence seemed to take no offense from it. "Of course, Kate. Have you decided how much you need?"

"I think two thousand dollars will cover everything." She shuddered at the thought of asking for so much money.

"That can be arranged," he said.

His quick willingness to accept her request kicked up her concerns. Well, there was no turning back now. The dice were cast.

"I'll have all the paperwork done up tomorrow," Lawrence said. "As soon as everything is in order, I'll ride down to Baker County and have a look at those horses and wagons."

"I appreciate that," she replied.

After their discussion concluded, Kate and Olaf started home. "Olaf, what

258

do you know about Lawrence Granville?"

"I've never heard anything bad about him. He was concerned about Mr. Harrington bringing a bunch of farmers up here, but he remained neighborly."

"Did you ever know his wife?"

"I only saw her in town a few times. She was a dainty little thing, not cut out for life up here. He built her that fancy house just to make her happy."

That was certainly in Lawrence's favor. It was hard to find fault with a man who went to such lengths to make his wife happy.

After supper, Kate got the children off to bed then took a seat on the porch. The business deal with Lawrence would not leave her in peace. She kept reminding herself a business deal gone sour had started this current state of affairs. Not that Lawrence was in any way like E. G. Covington, but still, she fretted. She had never been in debt to anyone in her life, at least not in a financial way. That in itself was enough to keep her awake at night. *Just hope for the best*, she finally advised herself. With that thought, she went to bed.

*   *   *

The next morning, Lawrence arrived with the loan papers. "You can have an attorney look it over if you like," he said.

Kate looked over the papers. Her limited knowledge left her feeling embarrassed and totally inadequate, knowing if all was in order. "I think I will have someone take a look at it. Please don't be offended. I just don't know much about such matters. I trust you, but I just want to understand everything."

"That's quite all right, Kate. I would do the same thing."

After a few minutes of small talk, Lawrence got up to leave. "Kate, I want to invite you and the children over again. That house is so lonesome. You and the children give it life."

"That's kind of you, Lawrence. I'll let you know."

Lawrence had just helped make her burdens a little lighter; her coldness toward him made her a little ashamed. She just hoped he wouldn't take offense from it—maybe even call off the deal. He gave no indication that he was upset by her put-off. Perhaps, in time, she might have a better state of mind toward Lawrence.

*   *   *

That afternoon, Kate had Olaf drive her to La Grande so Mr. Packwood could take a look at the loan agreement. She found him in a small office near the Union County Courthouse. It was a little wood-frame building with two small windows in front. After knocking on the door a couple of times, she

259

heard a voice invite her inside.

Mr. Packwood was sitting behind a small desk in the middle of the room. Behind him was a wooden shelf filled law books and a copy of Oregon statutes. On the north side of the room was a pot-bellied stove, and in front of the desk were some wooden chairs.

"Mrs. McKane," he said. "To what do I owe the pleasure of this visit?"

"Business," she replied as she handed him the loan papers. "This is a loan agreement I'm preparing to sign. I need you to look it over."

"Please, have a seat." He looked over the papers while she waited. "Looks like a standard loan agreement," he said. "Lawrence Granville is agreeing to lend you the sum of two thousand dollars. You are agreeing to pay him four hundred dollars a year for five years plus five percent interest."

"I just wanted to be sure."

"Mrs. McKane, forgive me for being nosy, but your uncle left you rather well off."

"This is a business loan."

"Really!"

"Yes. We're starting a freight company to haul farm products."

"That's interesting," he said. "Do you know anything about that kind of business?"

"Very little, I'm afraid."

"Then are you sure you want to take a gamble like this?"

"Yes. I have to do this to help the settlers Uncle Lewis brought up here."

"Well, it's a tough job running a freight line here."

"I've been in tough situations before, Mr. Packwood."

"There's another thing," Packwood said.

"What's that?"

"You know E. G. Covington has most of the long haul freight business around here. He's not going to like the idea of competition, especially business he feels is his."

"I have the freedom to enter into a business," she said. "I'm not violating any of the agreements he had with Uncle Lewis like he's trying to do."

"All that may be, but I'm still worried about what happened to your uncle," the lawyer said.

"You know anything about what happened to Uncle Lewis?" she asked.

"Only suspicions. I know about the business arrangements he had with Covington. It didn't work out very well."

"Well, Covington will not stop me. I'll tell you something else. I'm going to get at the truth about Uncle Lewis's death before I'm done."

"You better be careful," he said.

Kate finished her business with Mr. Packwood and started back to the buggy. To her unpleasant surprise, she met E. G. Covington coming down the sidewalk in the other direction. Of all the people to meet, why did it have to be him?

"Mrs. McKane," he said in a dry voice.

Kate nodded her head but did not speak. She started to walk on past, then had a thought. "Mr. Covington, I have some news for you."

He stopped and looked at her. "What would that be?"

"I just wanted to tell you you're going to have some competition."

"From whom?" he asked.

"From me. Harrington Farms is starting its own freight line."

Covington laughed. "Do you have any idea of how to run a freight line?"

"I'm going to learn," Kate replied.

"You won't last a month. Running freight wagons in this country is risky business. There are Indians to deal with, rivers to cross, and other dangers you can't even imagine."

"That may be, Mr. Covington, but we're going to give it a try."

He grinned at her. "Let me point out something to you. I have an agreement with several of those dirt farmers your uncle hauled up here. They agreed to let me have their freight business. I got their business already sewed up."

"That doesn't matter," Kate replied. "You don't have an agreement with us. After this year, we're going to buy their products and haul them to market in our wagons. It's all legal."

The grin melted from his face. He walked up close and stared directly into her eyes. "Let me tell you something, Mrs. McKane. I'm not going to be thwarted by you or anyone else. Your uncle was a foolish man and wouldn't listen to reason. We had an agreement, but he didn't want to live up to it. Don't you make the mistake of getting in my way? You understand?"

She cringed from the cold, hard look in Covington's eyes. The seriousness of what she was undertaking was being driven home. Here in front of her was a ruthless man who would fight any attempt to thwart his ambitions. A chill ran down her back; she swallowed. *But I'm not going to be deterred either*, she thought. She tried to summon up her courage, to stand toe-to-toe with him.

"Missy!" she heard someone yell. She turned and saw Olaf standing next to the buggy. Kate left E. G. Covington standing on the sidewalk and started down the street, feeling his cold stare on her back.

"Was he bothering you?" Olaf asked.

"No, we were just discussing business," she replied.

E. G. Covington was in her thoughts all the way home. Between him and his henchman Palmer, she had made some dangerous enemies just like Uncle Lewis had done. A chill ran down her spine. She had to look toward the side of the road so Olaf would not see her tears.

That night, Kate tossed and turned. The fat was in the fire—she couldn't turn back now. But how would it all end? Would her family have to suffer?

*   *   *

The next morning, Olaf told her they had to start getting their threshing crews together. When the crew was in place, they would go from farm to farm, harvesting the grain crops.

"In that case, we need to get our wagons and teams ready," she said.

"I hope you find everything soon. We don't have much time. Fall will be here before you know it, and we got to get the harvest over before winter hits."

"I'm taking the loan papers over to Lawrence today," Kate said. "He may be able to get us the wagons and horses very soon. He knows someone who may have wagons and teams to sell."

"You want me to drive you over there?" Olaf asked.

"No, Olaf. I know you have other work to do, so I'll ride over by myself."

"That's a long ride alone."

"It's okay. I know the way."

After breakfast, Olaf saddled one of the horses and left it in the yard. With the loan papers in hand, Kate went out and climbed up into the saddle.

Cooler weather had moved into the valley, breaking the hot spell that had baked them for most of the summer. Kate enjoyed the feel of the cool air through her hair as she rode. She was in no big hurry. She let the horse jog along while she enjoyed the late summer scenery. The meadow was brown, but clouds were building over the mountains, promising much-needed rain. *I hope I don't get wet,* she thought.

When Kate found the road that led northeast toward Lawrence's ranch, she turned her horse and was startled by a group of riders next to the road. They were Indians.

Kate sat on her horse, frozen with fear. The Indians looked at her with expressionless faces. One of them was an older man with his hair hanging in long braids down the front of his cotton shirt. Behind him were two younger men and two boys. One of the young men had long hair similar to the older man, but the others had shorter hair. They all carried rifles; one had a few rabbits tied to his saddle.

Kate didn't know what to do. She was here alone confronting Indians with unknown intentions. She looked up and down the road. There was no one in sight. *Be brave*; she counseled herself. She urged the horse forward. As she passed, the older man held up his arm with his hand spread out flat. It seemed like a friendly gesture, but Kate didn't know these people's customs. Maybe it was a form of greeting. "Good morning," the man said.

The man's English surprised Kate. "Good morning," she replied.

There was no further conversation with the Indians. She moved on past them without incident. Kate took their actions to be friendly, but the encounter left her so nervous she could barely hold onto the reins.

As she was riding away, she looked back over her shoulder. They were now moving on to the north.

When Kate reached Lawrence's, house she was still shaken. He was standing on the porch, watching her as she rode into the yard. "Kate, you're white as a ghost."

"I just ran into some Indians back there."

"Did they bother you?"

"No. It was just coming up on them so suddenly, I guess. Scared me out of my mind."

"Probably just some Umatillas out hunting. They're usually friendly. Bannocks are a different story, but they don't usually get down here in the valley."

"That's gratifying to know."

She gathered her composure. "I got the loan papers all signed and ready to go," she said.

"Good. I'll take a few of my men and ride down to Baker County and see about those wagons and teams. I expect harvest time to be upon you soon. You'll need to be ready."

"Yes. I've got to get word out to the settlers again. We're going to have to change our plans. I had planned to let the settlers go ahead with Covington this year, but now I don't think that's a good idea. I've got to let them know we'll buy their crops outright. I had an encounter with Covington yesterday, and now the die is cast with him. He wasn't pleased to hear what I had to say."

"Like I told you, Kate, he's a dangerous man, so don't provoke him too much."

"I wasn't trying to provoke him. I just wanted him to know he can't get away with what he's trying to do. Someday I'm going to see him brought to justice for what he did to my uncle."

"Just be careful," Lawrence said.

"I will. I need to get back now," she said.

"I'll have one of the men ride back with you."

"It's all right. I saw the Indians ride on. I've got to get use to this country anyway. I don't think they meant me any harm."

"I'm sure they didn't, but just the same, I don't feel good about you riding back alone."

Kate reluctantly agreed. She rode back home with one of Lawrence's hired men. He was a tall, slim young man with shaggy brown hair and a mustache, wearing a bright red flannel shirt. He was a quiet man, so most of the ride was in silence.

There was no sign of the Indians. When they reached the turn-off to her house, Kate thanked the young man then rode across the meadow to the yard. She explained about the Indians to Olaf. "That's why it's not a good idea for you to ride out alone," he said.

"They never tried to harm me," Kate said.

"Just the same, those people are dangerous. You can never trust them."

Kate didn't want to debate the point as they had more pressing matters. She explained that Lawrence was leaving to look for wagons and horses. "I need to get new word out to the settlers. We've got to change our plans from what I told them earlier. There is no chance of us doing business with Covington at all now. I want the settlers to know that we'll buy their crops at the farm and do all the hauling ourselves. That way, they can bypass Covington entirely."

"Yaw. It's getting very busy for me now. As you found out today, it's not safe for you to be out alone. We may have to hire somebody."

"I think it's better if we talk to them personally," Kate said. "Maybe we can hire someone to work here for a few days while we are gone. Are those young men Uncle Lewis hired last spring still around?"

"I suppose."

"See if you can hire them for a few days."

Olaf shook his head. It pained Kate to go against her overseer's wishes, but this time it was necessary.

*   *   *

The next morning, Olaf set about hiring some temporary workers. While he was gone, Kate thought about what to tell the settlers and how to get word to them. They were scattered around the valley. She figured it would take at least two days, maybe more, to locate all of them.

Lord, please give me the strength to do what must be done, she prayed.

Chapter 26

The Rockies

The faint rays of dawn were spreading across the eastern sky as James and Wilford prepared for their departure from Fort Laramie. James had managed to do a little bargaining with one of the wagon train members for a pack horse. After the business with Gates, he had been hesitant about approaching any members of the wagon train. But these people were poor. A good price for a horse turned out to carry more weight than Gates' ranting. They had just finished packing their gear when Edna walked into camp. "I just came to say goodbye and to wish you a safe journey," she said.

"Thank you," James replied. "I hope everything has been settled since the trouble last night."

"Yes. I'm going to stay here and wait for another wagon train. I don't want any more problems with that lunatic, Gates. The wagon master will talk to the people at the fort about me staying until another train comes through."

"I'm happy to hear that," James said. "Thank you again for the delicious meal last night."

"You are welcome."

They mounted and rode out of camp. After a short distance, they turned and waved to Edna, who was still standing in their now abandoned camp. She watched until they were just specs riding to the northwest.

"We'll be leavin' the North Platte soon," Wilford said. "After that, water will get scarcer."

Wilford was showing no lingering effects from his shoulder wound. James found that reassuring, but now there was another worry. The delays in Independence and Fort Laramie had cut into their schedule. Now, it was a race against time to reach the Rockies before snow closed up the passes.

*   *   *

The first few days passed without incident. They saw no signs of the Sioux. Their biggest challenge was dealing with long, boring days in the saddle.

Early one morning, James decided to see if he could get a conversation out of Wilford. "How did you come to know so much about the frontier?" he asked.

Wilford's initial reaction was to stare straight ahead and remain silent. Then, a look that James took for remorse flickered briefly on his face. "When I was a boy, maybe nine or ten years old, my family was living in a small settlement in Illinois, just across the line from Missouri. My father was a freedman who gained his freedom when his master set him free in his will.

"Daddy worked for a number of years, saving his money until he was able to buy my mama from her master. My mama had learned to read and write and do some figuring. It used to annoy white folks something awful that she had more education than many of them.

"We lived in a little settlement made up of free blacks and was doin' well until one day some slave hunters came by and claimed we were hiding runaway slaves. They even claimed some of us were runaways."

Wilford paused before continuing. "My father and some of the other men put up a fight 'cause they didn't want to go back to slavery. My father was shot during the fight along with some of the others, and they burned our house. I don't know what happened to my mama or my younger brother. I never saw any of them again. The slave hunters grabbed me and took off across the prairie.

"The second night, they were drinkin' heavy and forgot to tie me up good. I was able to get out of the ropes and take off. By the time they woke up, I was miles from that place. They came after me, but I managed to hide, so they finally gave up and went on. I wandered around out there for days without food or water. When anyone came close, I would hide. I finally got so weak from thirst and hunger; I passed out."

"What happened to you?" James asked.

"It was during this time an old trapper named Noah Anderson came along. He was on his way back to the mountains after a visit to St Louis. He found me there nearly dead and gave me some food and water. When he had me back around, he took me to the mountains with him.

"Old Noah was well known in the mountains. He knew all the other mountain men like Jim Bridger and Vasquez and was well known by most of the Indian tribes up there. He had spent most of his life in the mountains, and the tribes let him hunt and trap on their lands. He knew the tongue of the Crow, Snake, Shoshone, and several of the smaller tribes."

"Sounds like a true mountain man," James remarked.

266

"He was. We trapped and hunted all over the mountains, living alongside the other mountain men and the Indians. The Indians took me in and taught me their ways and how to speak their tongue.

"I used to go with Noah and the other trappers to the big rendezvous they had each year. It was a big get-together attended by trappers, Indians, and fur buyers from places as far away as St. Louis, who came up to buy beaver pelts. Everybody had a high old time, and the thing sometimes lasted for weeks."

This was the most that Wilford had said since leaving Missouri.

They rode for a couple of minutes in silence, and then Wilford gave out a hearty laugh. "Old Noah was a crafty old character."

"How?"

"I remember one year the beaver was scarce, so we had to move to new territory. The Hudson's Bay Company had most of the territory on the other side of the mountains, so we made a risky venture into Blackfoot country. Now, that was scary business, given the Blackfeet's dislike of outsiders. They didn't allow anyone to hunt or trap on their lands."

"That does sound risky," James said.

"Well, we had a piece of luck along the way. When we were in the mountains, we ran across a young Blackfoot warrior who had shot a deer and was trying to find it when he had the misfortune to get between a grizzly sow and her cub. That old grizzly had already charged his horse and knocked the boy to the ground. The bear was getting ready to finish him off when we happened along. We rescued the Blackfoot boy from that bear.

"As luck would have it, the boy was the son of a chief. The young man was so grateful, he took us back to camp with him and told his father about us saving his life. Turned out the old chief knew some English. He put aside his dislike of outsiders and offered us the hospitality of his camp." Wilford laughed again.

"You find amusement in that story?" James asked.

"You see, it was while we were in the Blackfoot camp that old Noah took a liking to the chief's daughter. She was a comely young woman, probably not more than sixteen years old, and pretty as a mountain flower. It was the first time I ever saw Noah show much notice in a woman. He had been a bachelor all his life, but there was something about that little gal that got him all heated up. And I think she took a liking to him too, although he was getting along in years by that time.

"Old Noah actually went and talked to the chief about the woman. The trouble was, the chief wanted horses for her, lots of horses. We didn't have any horses, except for the ones we were riding and one old packhorse. That didn't stop Noah. He knew there was a Crow village to the south, and the Crows had several horses. Noah made a promise to the chief we'd be back. We left the Blackfoot camp and rode south. When we found the Crows, we waited until dark, then went in and drove off over thirty head. We made it back to the Blackfoot camp with twenty."

"What happened?" James asked.

"The Crow and Blackfeet are bitter enemies. When the Blackfoot chief found out they were Crow horses, he was very impressed. Horse stealin' is a big thing with those people, so he gave Noah, his daughter for the horses. By this time, we were a big hit with the entire village.

"The only trouble with all this was Noah was also a friend of the Crows. He started feeling guilty about running off horses that belonged to his friends. A few nights later, we sneaked back to the Blackfoot camp and drove off ten of the horses and took them back to the Crows."

"And neither side got suspicious?"

"Naw. The Crows and Blackfeet were always stealin' horses from each other, so they blamed each other for their losses. We were heroes to both tribes, and Noah got a bride out of the deal to boot. From her, Noah and I learned the Blackfoot Tongue."

"How come you left the mountains?" James asked.

"I stayed there until Noah died in his sleep one night. By that time, he had a son, but after he died, his wife and child went back to her people. With Noah gone and the beaver supply playing out, I decided to leave the mountains and see what I could find elsewhere.

"On the way out of the mountains, I ran across a wagon train that was having trouble crossing a stream. I stopped and helped them. The wagon master gave me a job, so I spent a few years guiding wagons over the Oregon Trail.

"After one of the trips to Oregon, the wagon master didn't have the money to pay me, so he gave me that strip of land where I was living when you found me. I been spending my time since raising and selling horses."

For the first time since leaving Missouri, Wilford had opened up. In his doing so, James felt that some of the remaining tension between them had eased away. A good thing—given the dangers of traveling out here, to cope, there had to be some trust between them. Danger had no prejudices out in this country.

*   *   *

The next morning, there was a chill in the air. The sun was rising to a sky filled with low clouds. "We should reach the Platte Bridge Station today," Wilford said. "The last time I passed through, there was only a small army garrison and a trading post."

This morning they rode in silence. After a couple of hours, James pointed out a sod house with some wagons parked around. "What do you make of that?" he asked.

"Looks like somebody put in a trading post of some sort," Wilford replied.

The building turned out to be sold in front with a back made of pine logs. Over the door was a crudely written sign:

Eli's Way Station

It was a combination trading post and grog house. As they rode up, two young men staggered out the door. One was tall and had a short, dark beard; his companion was shorter and had long, brown hair.

"The horses need watering," Wilford said as he dismounted.

James dismounted and handed the reins to Wilford. He started toward the door, but a commotion caught his ear. He turned and saw the two young men stopped in front of one of the wagons.

A young woman was sitting in the front seat of the wagon, staring straight ahead. She was wearing a bonnet with strands of blonde hair hanging out and a plain cotton dress.

"What do we have here?" one of the men said.

"Dirt farmer's woman," his companion replied.

The young woman tried to remain passively indifferent to the men by continuing to stare straight ahead.

"Hell, miss, why don't you get down off that wagon and come with me and leave those sod busters behind," the tall man said. "I can show you what a good time with a man is really like."

The girl blushed slightly but said nothing.

The man's companion urged him on. "Hell, I don't think she even likes you. She likes sod busters all covered with dirt better than you."

"She don't know what she's missing. One night with me, and she'll shoot the next dirt farmer she sees."

Two men emerged from the trading post. One was an elderly man wearing a black coat and hat. The other was a younger man wearing similar clothes.

They saw the two men taunting the woman in the wagon. "Kindly refrain from insulting my wife," the older man said.

"Wife! How could a sweet thing like her be married to a dried-up old geezer like you?" one of them replied.

The girl was now openly embarrassed. Her face was red; she stared down at her lap.

Before anymore was said, an older woman emerged from the back of the wagon and took the younger woman by the shoulder. "Cecilia, come on back

269

now."

"Looks like she's got her mother along to take care of her," one of the drunks said. "Maybe you can get her mother to go with you."

The older man spoke again. "I'll tell you again not to bother my wives."

The two drunks looked at each other. "What did that old man say?" one asked.

"These are my wives," the older man said. "I will thank you not to bother them any further. We just want to be on our way."

"How come you got more than one wife?" one of the young drunks asked. "It ain't natural for a man to have more than one wife."

"For us, it is," the older man said.

One of the drunks reached for his pistol. "It just ain't right. Maybe we should make 'em both widows so they can ride off with some real men."

The older man stood his ground. "We are not violent people. We just want to be on our way."

James figured the liquor was talking for the two young men.

One of the drunks stepped in front of the older man and put his hand on the man's chest. "You ain't going anywhere, old man, until I'm finished with you."

"Please, mister. We're men of God, and we don't believe in violence against our fellow men," the older man said.

The drunk gave the older man a push, sending him back into the younger man behind him.

The older man recovered his balance. Then, he and the younger man tried to push their way toward the wagon, but the two drunks blocked their way.

Now, James had seen enough. A few other people had come out of the building and were watching; it was apparent none of them intended to intervene. "These people don't seem to be bothering you, so why don't you just go on and mind your own business," he said.

The taller drunk sized up James. "What are you, another sod buster?" The man reached for an old Colt in his belt. "You got a gun on you. Why don't you try to back up your words?"

How was he going to get out of this? James was not a gunman. He didn't want a fight with the two men.

The man looked at his companion. "I think we need to string this one up along with those two sod busters." He walked up to James. "Pull that pistol, or I'm gonna string you up. Or maybe I'll just shoot you and be done with it."

The man reached for his pistol. Before it was halfway out of his belt, a blow to the head sent him reeling to the ground.

The man's companion reached for his pistol. Too late! Wilford grabbed him by the front of his shirt and hurled him into the side of the sod building.

The pistol dropped to the ground.

The elderly man and his younger companion used the confrontation to make their way into the wagon and drive away, leaving James and Wilford to deal with the drunken men.

Seeing it was over, the crowd broke up and went back inside the trading post and back to their grog. James was afraid the sight of a black man striking two white men might provoke the crowd. As it turned out, they were more concerned with the liquor.

James and Wilford gathered up the drunken men's pistols. They emptied the chambers and flung them out onto the prairie.

"Trouble seems to have a way of finding you," Wilford remarked as they rode away.

Wilford was right. Ever since leaving Tennessee, trouble always seemed to be close to him.

They crossed over the Platte Bridge, leaving the North Platte River, and struck the Sweetwater. The prairie country was giving way to higher ground. The green of the prairie was replaced with a landscape stark and brown, dotted with rock outcroppings.

The Sweetwater turned out to be nothing more than a trickle of muddy water. In the distance, James could see a strange rock formation that resembled a large whale.

"That'll be Independence Rock," Wilford explained. "It's one of the landmarks of the Oregon Trail."

That afternoon, they rode into a valley that ran alongside the river. The rock formation lay alongside. Mountains were visible in the distance.

Wilford dismounted and starting climbing up the side of the rock formation. James hated to waste time. In short order, his curiosity overruled his haste; he dismounted and started making his way up the formation.

The surface was covered with inscriptions of names and dates: "Elsa Bronfield 1843 and Hiram French passed here 1856."

"Most of the wagon trains stop here," Wilford explained. "Many of the people left a record of their passing."

From the top of the large rock, they could see out across the prairie from where they just came and the mountains ahead. James's spirits arose. The mountains meant they were getting closer to his destination.

"We got some rough country to pass," Wilford said when they were back down. "I hope the horses don't throw a shoe."

They had to ride single file beside a narrow channel with deep water that cut through a rocky gorge. The going was slow and treacherous; it was a place where a horse could lose its footing on the rocky surface. "This place is called Devil's Gate," Wilford said.

Progress was slow that afternoon. The channel opened up a bit, but the going remained treacherous. The footing didn't improve until late in the afternoon.

They camped that night beside the river. James hobbled the horses so they could graze on the sparse vegetation while Wilford cooked beans and salt pork. "Gonna be hard on the horses from now on," Wilford said as they were eating. "Water is harder to find further west, and there ain't much for them to eat."

*   *   *

The next morning, a red cloud rolled up in the west. "Looks like a storm," James said.

"Maybe," Wilford replied.

Wilford studied the sky. "That ain't no rain cloud; that's a dust storm."

The sky became blocked out by a wall of red. The air soon filled with choking red dust.

They covered their faces and rode into the swirling red dirt. The dust particles stung their faces like tiny pellets and blocked their vision until it was impossible to tell where they were going. The dust was so thick James could hardly make out Wilford riding next to him. He tried to pull his hat down over his eyes for protection against the red particles, but it seemed the entire earth was being picked up by the wind and hurled at them.

To avoid getting lost, they tried to stay close to the river bank; in the thick dust, even the streambed was not visible at times.

The dust came on unabated the entire afternoon. For relief, James would get out his canteen. He began to worry his water would run out. All that was available was the muddy river, hardly even fit for the horses.

When darkness fell, the dust storm began to subside. The entire country was left covered with a layer of fine, red powder. The slightest disturbance would raise clouds of the red menace.

That night, they soaked rags in the muddy water and tried to wash away some of the accumulated dust from their faces. They gave it up as a waste of time. There was no wood in the area, so they had to make do with leftover salt pork. Sleeping was a chore. There were no places free of dust to put down their bedrolls.

*   *   *

The next day, they endured dust from the horses' hooves. The only relief they could find was to ride in the shallow waters of the river. "Gonna be like this until it rains," Wilford said.

Two drier, dusty days passed. They pleaded with the sky for rain, but none came.

*   *   *

As hope was fading; nature relented with a promise of relief. Storm clouds were building in the early morning sky. "Looks like rain at last," Wilford said.

That day, it only threatened. The following day, they awoke to a sky filled with low, overhanging clouds. By mid-morning, a slow drizzle was falling. They got out their raincoats and rode hunched over in the saddle. With the rain came cooler temperatures. By evening, the temperature had dropped further, leaving them cold and tired.

Wilford found some brush along the river to build a fire. James had his doubts the wet wood would burn, but he underestimated his guide's persistence. It smoldered and smoked; then a few red flames sprung up. Supper was beans and bacon. As night settled in, they huddled around the little fire. Throughout the evening, there would be periods of drizzle. The best they could do was cover themselves under their rain slickers and try to sleep. "I hope I don't come down with a bout of pneumonia," Wilford said.

*   *   *

Rain stayed with them the next few days. There would be drizzle followed by periods where it would let up. The sun would peek though breaks in the clouds then retreat. "It's a sign fall is approaching," Wilford said.

Fall: the very thought worried James. It meant winter was close behind. With that came snow and mountains that could not be crossed until spring. Every day, he thought of his wife and kids and yearned so to see them again. The idea of being delayed until spring left him in a state of depression. So much of himself was invested in this trip. He had said what would likely be his final goodbye to his father and aunt to come up here; the thought of being long delayed was intolerable.

Then the gray skies gave way to the sun. With that, warm weather returned. That evening, Wilford hung a line between two scrub trees with some rope so they could dry their clothes. Hot coffee chased away the remaining effects of the chilling rain.

The weather cycle changed. The days were still warm, but now the nights were chilly, forcing them to sleep close to the campfire.

For several days, James had watched the mountains to the west. They never seemed to get any closer. He could swear the tall peaks were moving

273

away from them, always keeping their distance. Then, after several more days of riding, the white peaks became clearly visible. Snow had fallen in the higher elevations. Winter in the Rockies was near at hand.

On a particular afternoon, they stopped on top of a small knoll to rest the horses. James looked up and spotted a large eagle circling high above them. "That eagle has an interest in something here on the ground," he said.

"That eagle keeps circling until he finds a meal down here," Wilford replied. "He'll keep circling and keeping a sharp eye out until he sees something that looks like good eating, and then he'll swoop down and get it."

"Kinda like what I'm doing," James said. "I'm scouring this country to find my family; the trouble is I have to do it from here on the ground. If I was like that eagle, I would just circle around until I found them, then swoop down for a big reunion."

*   *   *

The next morning, they were forced to dig out their coats for protection against the cold north wind that blew in during the night. Two hours of riding took them into the edge of a pine forest. The tall trees blocked most of the wind but also shaded out the sun, leaving them to shiver.

By afternoon, the weather warmed. Ahead of them, the peaks of the Wind River Range stood clear. Their white peaks were a constant reminder of the approaching winter. Then, the land turned into a gentle incline up toward the mountains. "I think we'll reach South Pass by this afternoon," Wilford said.

Before reaching South Pass, there was a small settlement with a trading post, livery stable, and a few houses. Being low on supplies, they stopped at the trading post. It was stocked with tack and harnesses, canned goods, and dried meat. A tall, thin man with a dark mustache clerked the establishment. There was a contingent of men dressed in buckskins sitting around a stove. "Trappers," Wilford told James.

James tended to their supplies while Wilford talked to the trappers. "By chance, did you men come down from the mountains?" Wilford asked.

"We came down from Fort Hall," one of them replied.

"How's the trail?" Wilford asked.

"The trail was clear when we came down, but snow's beginning to fall higher up. Won't be long before the passes will start fillin' up, and it won't be safe up there."

The trapper's news disturbed Wilford. His experiences had taught him well about the treachery of these mountains in winter. He expressed his concerns to James as they were leaving the trading post. "We're getting here late. It's going to be difficult to reach the passes before the heavy snow sets in."

These were words James didn't want to hear. He didn't question the validity of Wilford's assessment, but he fretted at the idea of being stuck here for the winter. His heart ached for his family and would do so until he was reunited with them again.

Beyond the settlement, the land continued to rise until they reached a saddleback that led into the Rockies. "This is South Pass," Wilford said. "We're in the Rockies now."

They made camp that evening on the banks of the Big Sandy River. Wilford, the camp cook gourmet, stirred up a supper of beans, pork, and hot coffee. The hot liquid helped relieve the chill of the night air. After eating, they spread out their blankets close to the fire. Since they left Fort Laramie, James had worried about the effects of riding for days in the rain and now the cold temperatures. There was no medical help of any sort for who knew how many miles. Well, it had been like that in the war; he found a way to survive then, and he could do the same again—so he hoped.

*   *   *

The next morning, they forded the river, getting wet in the process. They rode the rest of the morning damp and cold. By noon, their fortunes improved; the weather turned warm.

This day they followed a river valley that took them deeper into the mountains. James found the mountains awe-inspiring, even more so than the mountains of Tennessee. The snow-covered peaks seemed to reach all the way into the cloudless blue sky. "This is the Bear River Valley," Wilford said.

The land continued to rise up into an evergreen forest that blocked out much of the sunlight. In a clearing, they encountered a band of Indians. Startled, James reached for his rifle. Wilford stopped him. "These are Shoshone. They been following us for some time," Wilford said.

James was annoyed Wilford hadn't pointed out the Indians. "Why did they wait so long to show themselves?"

"They were looking us over first."

The leader of the group was an older man with a broad face, wearing a necklace around his neck and a cotton shirt and pants. He and Wilford met in the clearing and talked in the Indian's tongue. After a short conversation, they dismounted. The remaining Indians did the same.

James was reluctant. He didn't feel comfortable being in a clearing surrounded by Indians. With their Sioux experiences still fresh in his mind, trust was hard to come by. He remained on his horse until Wilford motioned for him to dismount. He set his faith in the man—after all, he knew these people, so he got down from his horse.

Wilford and the Indians sat down in the middle of the clearing. One of them produced a pipe. They lit it and passed it around to each one in the group. When it came to James, he took a quick puff and nearly choked. Some of the Indians laughed at his difficulty with the pipe.

"This is a peace offering," Wilford said. "It's a custom to smoke with your friends when you meet."

Wilford and the Indian leader appeared to be old friends. After talking with Wilford, the Indian leader looked over at James. "You are going to the Oregon country?" he said in English.

"Yes. I'm trying to find my family."

"It is a dangerous trail. You must be careful as you travel."

James understood that.

One of the Shoshone retrieved a deer from his horse and hung it up in a tree. One of the Indians started a fire while some of the others gutted and skinned the carcass. They cooked the venison. While they were eating, one of the Indians took a fancy to the Henry rifle. "Fine gun," he said in broken English.

James shook his head.

The Shoshone got up, walked over to his horse, and brought back a bundle of furs. "Good pelts. Beaver pelts. We trade."

"Sorry, I don't need any beaver pelts," James replied.

The Indian then went over, led his horse out into the clearing, and handed the reins to James. "You take for gun."

"I don't need another horse," James said. "I need the rifle to protect me during my travels."

The Indian's face held no expression. *Does he understand what I'm saying?* James wondered. To clear the air, he walked over and pulled the Henry out of his saddle, and held it up in the air. "No trade."

Wilford looked over at him. "Better be a little more diplomatic about it."

What other way was there to address the issue? The Indian wanted his rifle, but he couldn't afford to part with it. In his mind, that was the end of the matter.

Out away from the others, Wilford explained, "These people can be touchy about such things. The Shoshone are usually friendly. I've been a friend of theirs for years, but you've still got to be careful around them."

"I can't afford to give up this rifle," James said.

"Then try to find a diplomatic way to deal with it." Wilford pointed to the one he had been talking to. "That man over there is known as a great man among his own people and among all the settlers that have come up this way. He's helped many a traveler across rivers and other obstacles. His name is

Washakie. When I was leading folks over the Oregon Trail, him and his people would come out and help us if we were having trouble crossing a stream or running low on food."

"I'll try to convince the man in a polite way that I have to keep this rifle," James said.

The Indian was still eyeing the Henry. James decided to try another approach. He walked over and got the sheepskin coat from his gear and showed it to the Shoshone. "For you."

The Indian looked at the coat then at the rifle. "I need gun, not garment. A garment will not protect me from my enemies or kill game."

"Rifle no good," James said. He got out the Henry and some ammunition from his saddlebags. When the weapon was loaded, he pointed it in the air and pulled the trigger. It only clicked. He repeated the procedure again with the same results. "No good. You take this coat. It will protect you from the cold wind and snow."

The Shoshone took the coat, looked at it for a moment, and then put it on. The garment was a good fit. The man seemed pleased. James hoped he would not find out the round he loaded the weapon with was a dud. It was in with the rounds he had taken from the sleeping Union sentry in Nashville. He was now glad he had not thrown it away.

Wilford swapped stories with the Shoshone until well into the evening. Finally, most of the camp grew weary, and they started lying down next to the fire to sleep. James was apprehensive, but Wilford seemed at ease with the Shoshone, so he got out his own bedroll and settled in for the night.

*   *   *

The next morning, James awoke and found the Indians were gone. Wilford was busy getting the horses ready for the day's travel. "The Shoshone left some meat behind," he said.

After a breakfast of cold venison, they started down the cold, damp trail through the tall, silent pines. "You seem to get along well with those Indians," James remarked.

"Me and Noah used to spend a lot of time with the Shoshone. We used to spend some of our winters in their camp along the Snake River. They treated us well."

"Any idea where we are?" James asked.

"We're pushing into the Gros Ventre."

On both sides of them were mountain slopes covered with forests of pines mixed with maple and oak. The leaves of the hardwoods were aglow with bright colors; fall had made its appearance. Late in the day, the forest gave way to open country. They camped that evening next to the river.

The night air was cold. They wrapped themselves in blankets and sat next to the fire. When weariness overcame him, James lay down and managed to drift off to a short sleep. He awoke, feeling stiff and sore from sleeping on the cold ground.

James stayed in his blankets while Wilford poked at the fire. When a blaze was going, he got up, stretched to get rid of the soreness, then got a pot of water and placed it on the fire. They sipped on hot coffee until dawn.

That morning, there was some smoke in the distance. "There's something up ahead," James said.

"That'll be the cabin of a mountain man friend of mine," Wilford replied. "He used to run traps with me and Noah back in the old days."

$$* \qquad * \qquad *$$

Early that afternoon, they left the river valley and started up an incline that leveled out into a forest of pines mixed with a few hardwoods. Late in the afternoon, they reached a log cabin sitting in a clearing. A large man with a long, dark beard and thick, bushy hair emerged from the cabin, followed by an Indian woman and some children.

"Wilford, my friend," the man boomed out in a voice so loud it could have been heard throughout the Rockies. "Get down and come in the cabin."

Wilford and James dismounted. The man motioned to a young boy who was standing beside the cabin. "Take care of their horses."

They followed the man and the rest of his family into the cabin through an opening covered by a blanket. There were two rooms portioned off by another blanket. Along the back wall was a fireplace made of rock. In the middle was a large table made of hand-hewn pine planks and a few homemade chairs. On the side was a small cabinet.

"This is Linus Hutching," Wilford said. "He's one of the toughest old mountain men ever to run a trap line."

Linus let out a big laugh. "Those were the days, eh, my friend?"

"Yeah," Wilford replied. "Those were the days."

"I'm James McKane."

Linus extended his hand. Afterward, James felt like every bone in his had been crushed.

"Lilli put on some more stew for our visitors," Linus said.

The woman picked up a knife and disappeared through the blanket door.

"Linus, I didn't know you was a family man," Wilford said.

"Cost me a bunch of fine horses," Linus replied. "Her daddy was a Crow Chief. Gave me a passel of youngins, but she's a fine woman. Helps me enjoy my old age."

The woman reemerged through the door with some strips of meat in her hand. She gave them to a teenage girl. The woman had long, black hair that hung down the back of her deerskin shift. The teenage girl was dressed in a bright red cotton dress. She had long, dark hair like her mother but was lighter in complexion. The rest of the family consisted of a young boy and girl playing behind the blanket that divided the room and the older boy tending their horses.

Wilford and Linus talked about old times until the woman motioned to them.

"Elk stew, lads," Linus said. "It'll put the fat on your ribs."

They seated themselves at the table. "What brings you lads up the trail so late in the year?" Linus asked as they were waiting to be served.

"I'm on my way to Oregon. I hired Wilford as a guide," James replied.

"Well, lads, it's a bit risky to be travelin' in these mountains so late in the year. Won't be long until the snow will be blowin' so thick, you can't see the horse you're sittin' on."

"We had some delays getting up here," James said.

"For now, let's eat some stew," Linus said.

The woman and girl set wooden bowls of steaming stew in front of each of them then lay wooden spoons down on the table.

The stew was hot, and to James's surprise, it was rather tasty. Wild game such as deer and elk was new to him. He was finding that in the hands of a skilled cook, it could be delicious.

"It's been a long time since we ran trap lines here in the mountains," Linus said as they were eating. "Lads, I miss the days when Bridger and all the mountain men were up here. We'd run our lines. We'd sneak over into the Hudson's Bay Company territory and even up in Blackfeet country. Damn, those were the days."

"That was a great time," Wilford said.

"They're tearin' it all down now," Linus said. "Settlers are comin' in, building towns and plowing up the ground. It just ain't like it used to be. These settlers are making trouble with the Indians, too. Many of the tribes I used to trap and hunt with won't even let me on their land now. They say all white men are bad."

Wilford nodded his agreement.

When the meal was over, the woman and her daughter cleared the table. Linus got out a foul-smelling jug of liquor and passed it around. James took a quick sip and passed it on to Wilford. It burned his lips and had a foul taste that he couldn't get out of his mouth. Wilford turned up the jug and had a long drink before passing it back to Linus.

Not being in a festive mood, James decided to leave the drinking to

Wilford and Linus. He got up from the table and started for the door.

"Have another drink, lad," Linus said.

"No thanks! Tomorrow will be a long day."

James left Wilford and Linus to their jug, stepped outside, and got his saddle and saddlebags. He checked to ensure his valuables were still in place before building a small fire out away from the cabin. Then, he got out his blankets and went to sleep. In spite of the cold night air, he enjoyed a good night's sleep and didn't wake up until the sun was rising over the mountains to the east.

The empty jug was sitting in the middle of the table. Wilford and Linus were slumped over in their chairs, their faces down on the table surface, snoring. A night of reminiscing about old times and a jug of liquor had overtaken them.

At the fireplace, the woman and her daughter were stirring a pot. The woman motioned to James to have a seat at the table. The girl carried over a cup of steaming coffee. It was just the thing. The hot, steaming liquid drove the chill from his bones.

Next to the table, the two young children were playing with a set of horses carved out of wood. The young boy let out a loud shriek, prompting a warning from his mother about disturbing the sleeping men.

The older girl brought over a bowl of gruel. It didn't have much taste, but it was hot.

As James was finishing his breakfast, Wilford and Linus began to stir. They sat up, shook their heads, then got to their feet. Their wobbly attempts at walking indicated the liquor still had a hold on them. Linus stumbled outside, with Wilford following.

Linus shook his head for a moment. "Head for the creek. The cold water will put the life back in you."

A small stream ran through the woods behind the cabin. The two of them rushed out to the bank. Linus waded into the icy creek until the water was up to his waist. He splashed water over his head, shook like a dog, and then repeated the process. Wilford plunged in and had a go. They stumbled back out, soaking wet. Watching this ritual made James appreciate even more that he had declined to drink with them.

Back inside, the woman set cups of coffee and two bowls of gruel on the table. Linus and Wilford declined the gruel and gulped down the coffee. Linus gulped down another cup, then got up and walked over to James and slapped him on the back. "You missed a roaring good time last night, lad. There's nothing like a few belts of good liquor to get you going."

It might have been fun last night, but today in the saddle, there was no place for a hangover.

Wilford had another cup of hot coffee. James was saddling the horses when he emerged from the cabin, still wet, looking worse for wear. It was going to be a long day for him. James sympathized, but time was precious. The best he could hope for was that Wilford would not go to sleep and fall off his horse.

"Better keep an eye on the sky, lads," Linus said. "The mountain trails are tricky this time of year, and we are due for a blizzard soon. If anyone can get you through these mountains, Wilford can. Good luck to the both of you."

After bone-crushing handshakes with Linus, James and Wilford mounted and rode slowly away from the cabin, pausing to wave at the mountain man and his family.

As they rode back down into the valley, James was worried and a little annoyed that Wilford would not be at his best today. He thought it over and came to realize that he and his old friend were reminiscing about life in the mountains. A man couldn't be faulted too much for that.

By noon, Wilford seemed to have recovered from his hangover. "We have a big decision to make when we reach Fort Hall," he said.

James knew what that decision was—the very thought overwhelmed him. Stuck here in the mountains for the entire winter, wondering and worrying about his family—he just couldn't accept it.

Chapter 27

The Harvest

K ate and Olaf returned from their visits with the settlers feeling a bit of despair. Covington had convinced ten of them to sign loan agreements with him. And as expected, these agreements stipulated repayment terms that would be difficult to meet. And to go along with that, these same ten had signed the new freight agreements as well. Kate, for a moment, was frustrated with the gullibility of these people. But she held her tongue. She realized they were just poor, uneducated people trying to survive.

On the bright side, all was not lost. Most of the settlers agreed to sell their grain to Kate with delivery to be taken at their farms. That would keep the freight deal from getting out of hand, but Kate had no idea how to deal with the loan agreements. For the time being, she felt she had done all she could.

Fall settled into the valley, bringing cooler nights. With the harvest staring them in the face, there was little time to enjoy it. Kate, feeling the weight of her burdens, seated herself on the porch for a short rest. She looked toward the meadow; a cloud of dust coming from the road caught her attention. Palmer and his henchmen, she feared. But the dust cloud was moving too slow for riders on horseback. It was either wagons or buggies. She walked to the edge of the yard and waited. A group of wagons turned off the road toward the house with Lawrence Granville in the lead. "Good day, Kate!" he yelled. "Here are your wagons!"

Kate was speechless and overwhelmed. She counted the wagons as they drove in: twenty in all.

"Some of them need work," Lawrence said as he dismounted.

"Will they last through the harvest?" Kate asked.

"With some repair, they should."

"Are the horses part of the deal?"

"You own the whole works. I got my friend to sell the entire lot for twelve hundred dollars. He wanted to quit and move back east."

Amazed—that's how she felt; Lawrence had accomplished it all so quickly. From her perspective, it was really more like a dream come true. E. G. Covington had a fight on his hands now. That is if she could come up with some drivers.

"Who are those men driving the wagons?" she asked.

"Some of them work for me. The rest have been working for my friend."

"You think those who worked for your friend might stay on and work for me?" she asked.

"They might. Mule skinnin' is all most of them know, and there's not many places they can get a job right now."

"Tell them to get down and eat with us. They must be tired and hungry after their trip."

Now, the trick for them would be to get a big meal ready on short notice. Helga, seldom daunted by a challenge, took over. She got a ham from the cellar and several jars of canned vegetables. Helga fried the ham while Kate heated the vegetables.

There were far too many to sit at the kitchen table. Most of the men filled their plates and sat down on the porch or out in the yard. With all the men fed, Kate used the opportunity to look for Lawrence. She found him sitting on the porch step. "How much does a wagon driver earn?" she asked.

"Probably ten dollars a load on up, depending on how far you plan to go," Lawrence replied.

When the meal was over, Kate assembled the men in the front yard. "When the fall harvest starts, I need drivers to haul grain to places as far away as Portland; also to La Grande and south to the mining camps. If anyone of you wants a job, there'll be one for you."

Most of the drivers not working for Lawrence Granville indicated they would be interested. Olaf had looked over the wagons and suggested to Kate that she hire some of the men to help with the wagon repairs. She hired three for that purpose. She hired two more to help care for the draft horses and reiterated her promise to the rest that they would have work shortly.

After the meeting, Kate saw Lawrence walking toward his horse. She went over to him. "I want to thank you," she said. "Your help has gone far beyond what was in our agreement. You've taken a big load off my shoulders."

He pushed back his hat and looked at her. "Kate, you know I want to see you succeed. Also, you better start keeping an eye out for Covington. He will soon get wind of all this, and he won't be happy. Don't underestimate that old buzzard; he'll fight for his interests."

"I know, but he's got a battle on his hands now."

Lawrence mounted. "When are you coming over for another visit?"

"The harvest is going to keep us busy for most of the fall, but the first chance we get, we'll come over," Kate replied. "I'll let you know."

There was disappointment in his eyes. Kate realized she had been somewhat evasive with Lawrence. After all, he had done for her, she felt a little guilty. She still felt his real intentions went beyond business, but all that aside, he had been a lifesaver. She only hoped he understood her reluctance to let their relationship go beyond business.

Lawrence's men had their saddle horses tied to the back of the wagons. They retrieved them and rode up next to their boss. As Kate watched, Lawrence and his hands rode away.

*   *   *

They were very busy the next few days getting the wagons ready for the harvest. Having the extra hired men required more cooking. Helga spent most of her time in the kitchen. Kate divided her time between helping with the household chores and checking with Olaf to see how the work on the wagons was progressing.

For two weeks, they prepared for the harvest. The next day after finishing with the wagons, Olaf told Kate the grain was ready. After breakfast, he left for La Grande to round up a threshing crew and the rest of the drivers. Their plan was to have the crew and wagons go from farm to farm until the crops were harvested.

While Olaf was in La Grande, Kate and the children worked in the barn, clearing away storage space to hold the new crop. The trips to market would take time, so temporary storage would be needed, and there was seed for next year that would have to be stored.

James Junior helped move old harnesses and assorted junk items out of the barn. Kate found her son was a willing helper; if only his attitude would improve. The younger children were thrilled to be doing what they thought of as adult work.

Olaf returned in the early afternoon and announced he had found a threshing crew. A group of newly-arrived Norwegian immigrants had set up camp on the outskirts of La Grande and were in dire need of work. The group included several strong men and older boys. They spoke only a little broken English, but Olaf said he found a way to communicate using what English they did know and the similarity between Norwegian and Swedish.

"We need to take one of the wagons to town," Olaf said. "We need all the sacks we can get our hands on and some tarps. The barn won't store everything, so the rest we'll have to store outside until we can get it to market."

The next morning, Kate accompanied Olaf to La Grande in one of the wagons. The wagon, although rough riding, was a little more comfortable since it sat up higher above the dust.

When they arrived in La Grande, Olaf parked the wagon in front of the emporium. After selecting the supplies they needed, a young boy wearing a dingy flannel shirt helped Olaf load the wagon. Kate helped with some of the lighter items. After handing up a pile of sacks to Olaf, she stood back away from the wagon. A voice startled her. "So you're really going through with your fool plan." Kate turned and was dismayed to see E. G. Covington.

"That's right. You won't get any business from the settlers."

"I have that business under written contract. Your uncle and I made a deal which the settlers agreed to. You can't legally take my business."

"I'm reminding you again that your agreement was to provide freight services to the farmers, as needed. That's part of the deal. The trouble is, Mr. Covington, you've tricked yourself. We are buying the settlers' grain from them at the farm, so they don't need any freight services. You don't have a freight agreement with us, so we're providing our own. It's all legal and doesn't violate any agreements you made."

His eyes narrowed into small slits. "And I told you when this freight line business of yours came up that I'm not a man to be taken lightly, woman. I've outdone men far better than any of that bunch your uncle brought up here. Shipping anything in this country is dangerous business and is best left to those who know how to get it done. Anything can happen between those farms and the markets. I'm telling you for the last time for your own good to forget this foolishness."

The freight owner had a twisted, mean look on his face that was intimidating. She was determined to put up a brave front and show him she wouldn't be swayed by his threats. She glared back at him. They stood locked in eye contact. Sweat formed on her brow; she hoped her skirts would hide the shaking in her knees.

"Heed what I'm telling you," he said before turning and walking away.

Olaf finished with the supplies, and they started home. Fear was Kate's companion. This was a cruel and greedy man she was dealing with. That put her and her family in danger, but there was no turning back now. "Olaf, I think we need to keep a watch posted at night," Kate said when they reached home.

"Does this have anything to do with your talk with Covington?"

"Yes. He is not happy with what we are doing."

Kate had the men start taking turns watching the house at night. For the first two nights, everything was peaceful. On the third night, Kate was awakened by the sound of a shot. She jumped out of bed, grabbed a robe, ran downstairs, and cautiously opened the front door. She looked toward Olaf's quarters and saw him step out with a shotgun in his hand. Kate stepped out on the porch.

"You better stay in the house, missy," he said.

"What happened?"

"There were shots coming from the barn," he replied.

"I only heard one."

"There were several."

She put aside his warning and walked to the barn with him. One of the hired hands was sitting on the ground by the corral, holding his shoulder. Kate knelt down next to the man to get a better look. "What happened?"

"Some riders came through the meadow," the man said. "They were carrying torches. I think they intended to set fire to something, maybe the house or barn. Maybe both."

"Maybe the wagons," Olaf said. "How many were they?"

"Hard to tell in the dark. Maybe five or six."

The other hired men had awakened to the commotion and were standing next to the corral.

Kate tried to look at the wounded man's shoulder but couldn't tell much about it in the dark. "Help him into the house," she said to a couple of the others.

They helped the man into the house and sat him on the bed in Uncle Lewis's room. With Helga's help, they got his shirt off so they could get a better look. Fortunately, it was only a flesh wound.

"Who started the shooting?" Kate asked.

"I called out to the riders," the man said. "One of them fired a shot at me, and I shot back with that old rifle of mine. I ain't much of a shot, but I guess it scared them a little. They fired a few rounds toward the barn, and one got me in the shoulder. After that, I saw them riding back across the meadow."

"Tomorrow somebody will drive you to the doctor in town," Kate said.

"Ain't no need, ma'am," he said.

"I insist," she replied. "You're working for me. I want to be sure you'll be okay."

Kate and Helga bandaged the man's wound. He got to his feet and stepped out the door just as Olaf came in and set his lantern down.

"I tried to track them, but in the dark, I couldn't find much."

"This was compliments of Mr. Covington," Kate said.

"You sure?" Olaf asked.

"Yes. I think it was meant to be a warning to us. The next time it'll be more serious."

"The men are worried about it," Olaf said. "They are laborers, not gunmen. This thing tonight has left them a little scared."

"I can understand that," Kate replied. "I hope they won't quit."

"I'll try to talk to them," Olaf said. "The threshing crew is ready to start, so we need drivers. We've got to stay on schedule to get the grain out before winter sets in."

"Maybe Covington and his bunch were surprised we had a guard out," she said. "Maybe they'll think twice before coming out here again."

"Maybe," Olaf said. Wishful thinking, they both knew.

Realistically, Kate knew E. G. Covington would not be scared so easily. She expected him to try again and to be more careful the next time. After Olaf left, she went back to her room. For the rest of the night, she tossed and turned, worrying about what might happen next.

*   *   *

The next morning, one of the other men drove the wounded man to La Grande in the buggy with instructions to report the incident to the sheriff after the doctor treated the man's wound. Kate knew Sheriff Benton would take no action, but at least he would know what was going on out here.

There was a bit of good news that morning. The other men agreed to stay on and help with the harvest.

*   *   *

The Norwegian threshing crew was gathered in the yard before daybreak, ready to start harvesting grain. The leader of the group was a tall, elderly man with graying hair dressed in a colorful red sweater and stocking cap.

Olaf got the men organized into working crews. A few were used as additional wagon drivers. Then, they started off toward the fields in the wagons. Kate and Helga remained behind to cook for the men. To save time, they decided to cook the food at the house and haul it to the workers. Olaf left a team hitched to the buggy.

During the harvest, the house would be unguarded; that worried Kate, but it had to be. There just wasn't anyone to spare; every man was needed in the fields. Her only hope was Covington wouldn't try to attack them in broad daylight.

They spent most of the morning cooking. When it was done, they loaded it into the buggy. Helga drove the team while Kate and the children went along to help serve.

Kate mused to herself that this was the first time she had ever been across her own property. They followed a road that led from the back of the barn through a pine and hardwood thicket. The ride was pleasant. From the hardwoods hung leaves of bright red and orange, announcing fall had arrived.

287

Squirrels scrambled among the tree tops, and rabbits dashed across the trail in front of the buggy.

The forest gave way to an open meadow of dry, brown grass that fronted the field where the men were working. Some of the men were cutting oats with large scythes. Others were using wagons to haul the cut stalks to a hand-operated thresher that removed the grain. The large number of full sacks indicated a productive morning.

Olaf looked up from the thresher and saw the buggy approaching. He yelled to the men. They all stopped working and walked toward the end of the field where Helga and Kate were now waiting. They served the hungry men baked ham with thick slices of bread and cherry pie. Helga also brought along a large pitcher of tea that the thirsty men gulped down.

Kate found Olaf sitting on the back of one of the wagons, eating his meal. "You men are getting a lot done, but do you think we can get all the settlers' crops harvested before winter?" she asked. "It seems like a large task to me."

"Yaw, it is, but while we are working here, the settlers are also starting on their own crops. Some have families that can help. They have to do everything by hand, but they'll have at least part of it done before the crews get to their farms. It'll be close, but I think we can make it."

*   *   *

The harvest routine continued for several days. It put a strain on all of them. Kate and Helga had to spend long hours working over the hot stove to feed the men. The men, in turn, worked from early in the morning until dark harvesting the grain. At night, they would haul in the day's results and store it in the barn.

One day while Kate was helping Helga cook, she saw Olaf returning to the house. Alarmed, she rushed outside. "Is there something wrong?"

"No, it is going well," he replied. "We've got more grain than we can keep in the barn, so we are going to start hauling some of it out. There is a mill in La Grande that will take some, and we can take a few loads to the mining camps in the south. The drivers are waiting at the barn to start loading."

Kate liked the sound of it. After all, they had suffered this past year; it was a relief to see things going the right way. She wept for a moment. If only Uncle Lewis could be here now to share in what he had started.

Of course, the current situation had to be tempered with reality. They were getting into the more dangerous aspects of the harvest. When the wagons were out on the road, they would be easy targets if Covington decided to move against them.

Olaf left to go help load grain. From the porch, Kate saw a rider coming across the meadow. It was Lawrence Granville. Surprised, she waited for him in the yard. "Good day, Kate," he said.

"Good day, Lawrence. What brings you over here?"

"I heard you were getting ready to start moving some of your grain to market. I also heard about somebody shooting at you the other night."

"Yes. I know who was behind it."

"So do I. I think they're waiting for another chance at you. There's a good possibility they'll hit your wagons once you get out on the road."

"I'm worried about that, but I guess it's a chance we'll have to take."

"Maybe not. My men will escort you to La Grande and the other local places. They won't attack you on the main road with us along. If you decide to go south or west, I know some routes that will be safer. Covington will probably expect you to take the main roads and will have people waiting to ambush you."

"I appreciate your offer, Lawrence, but I can't take you away from your own work. Besides, you've already done so much for me."

He looked at her and grinned. "I'm just protecting my investment."

Kate was too tired and overburdened to protest. And deep down, it was a relief to her. She was getting deeper in debt to Lawrence. But at the same time, she recognized the dangers they were facing, and the protection of their crops and the safety of her crews came first.

Lawrence went down to where Olaf was helping load the wagons while Kate went to help Helga with the cooking.

*   *   *

By the time the wagons were loaded, Lawrence Granville's men had arrived. After the noon meal, Olaf, the wagons, and the escort set off on their deliveries in La Grande. As they drove away, Kate said a silent prayer they would complete their deliveries safely. Then she and Helga took food to the remaining workers.

It was after dark when the wagons returned, all empty. "The mill wants another load," Olaf announced proudly.

"Did you have any trouble?" Kate asked.

"No. We didn't see anybody along the road, but with Mr. Granville and his men with us, they probably thought twice about trying anything."

Today, good fortune had been with them. But the worst was yet to come, she feared. Realistically, Lawrence could not protect them all the time. Soon they would be out on the road by themselves, and that would be the big test.

*   *   *

E arly the following week, they finished the last of the grain at Harrington Farm. Olaf had already left for Baker County with several wagon loads of grain. Again, Lawrence had gone with them to guide them over the back roads.

With Olaf gone, one of the Norwegians was running the crews. He seemed to handle the men very well, which was fortunate. Kate again felt lucky to have another capable man who could step in and take over. Hiram Grigg was also working with them now, as his farm was the next stop for the harvesters.

The workers stored the last of the grain in the barn then left for the Grigg farm. As she watched them leave, Kate hoped that Olaf would be back soon with the wagons. They would probably have to start taking grain west to Portland and maybe on to Salem before it was all sold. In addition to the problems they already faced, the weather would soon turn. The morning air was getting cooler, indicating that winter was not far away.

With Nancy Grigg not feeling well, Kate and Helga loaded the buggy with two cured hams and flour and went over to help with the cooking. "It takes a lot of food for working men, and I know some of these people don't have very much," Kate told Helga.

*   *   *

I t was late when they returned from the Grigg farm. There was no sign of Olaf and the wagons. In front of the barn, there was a load from the Grigg farm to be stored. Kate pitched in and helped the driver unload the wagon while Helga went in to start the evening meal.

By the time supper was over, Kate felt she was ready to collapse. After getting the children tucked in, she went to bed. Her rest was short. She woke up to someone beating on the front door. She ran down the stairs and found Helga on the front porch. "There's a fire in the barn," Helga yelled.

Kate looked and saw flames coming from one side of the log building. In a panic, she drew her robe around her and raced across the yard with Helga following. Two of the drivers and a young Norwegian boy were dragging sacks of grain out of the burning building.

"The grain on the other side is on fire," one of the drivers shouted.

Pushing aside Helga's protests, Kate ran inside. Smoke stung her eyes and lungs, but she grabbed a sack of grain and pulled it outside. She took a few gulps of fresh air and went back in again.

They managed to get all the sacks that were not burning out of the barn. Gasping to breathe, they had little time to rest. The flames had spread to the floor and walls of the structure. In their favor, the thick logs burned slowly.

"Get some buckets and form a fire brigade!" Kate yelled. "There's a well on the other side of the barn."

James Junior and the young Norwegian boy pumped water while the adults formed a line to pass the buckets to the burning barn. They worked feverishly to control the fire and save as much of the barn as possible. By the time they got the flames under control, it was dawn. The early morning light revealed one wall of the barn was totally destroyed, along with most of the floor, and the other three walls were damaged. But all was not lost; their efforts had saved over half of the grain.

Emotions ranging from despair to anger flooded Kate as she got her first good look at the smoldering mess. She was exhausted from fatigue and lack of sleep; her clothes were covered with soot and ashes. Tears were near when she felt a hand on her shoulder. She turned to see Helga, who was also covered with grime.

"Come into the house and clean up, then we'll have some breakfast," Helga said.

"They're not going to beat me," Kate said.

"I know."

*　　　*　　　*

Olaf returned that morning with the wagons. As he looked over the ruins of the barn, Kate explained what happened.

"It's a loss, missy, but one we can recover from. The barn can be rebuilt. The grain that was lost was mostly for seed stock next year. We'll be short of seed in the spring unless we can save some of the grain from the other farms. Otherwise, we might have to find some more seed grain next spring."

"We're going to go on," she said. "There's the rest of the harvest to get done. We're going to finish it."

*　　　*　　　*

They went on, undaunted by the fire. When the crew finished with Hiram Grigg, they moved on to the next farm. By that time, most of the local markets had been filled, so they started shipping to markets further west. Lawrence Granville showed them a little-known trail through the mountains to keep Covington and his gunmen from striking them along the way. On some of the trips, Lawrence still sent some of his men along to act as guards.

For a temporary repair, they used tarps to cover the burned-out wall of the barn. There, they stored grain until they could ship it to market. The longer trips to the western markets required more storage. The hours were exhausting, but the harvest went on.

After returning from Portland, Olaf said, "We're getting better prices on the coast. In spite of the losses from the fire and some we lost along the way, we're still having a rather good year."

For Kate and the struggling settlers, that was good news. The better prices would lighten their loads.

They never let down their guard. The wagons continued to use different routes for their trips; Lawrence still provided guards for some of the journeys. Kate now kept armed guards around the house and barn at all times, hoping to discourage Covington from attacking their farm again. In a way, it was like living in a prison, but she accepted it as being necessary.

Although they had thwarted Covington for now, Kate realized the battle was not over. He would strike again.

Chapter 28

Winter in the Rockies

The little settlement at Fort Hall they found to be all but deserted. The army post had been closed; all that remained were a few buildings and a store. The few inhabitants that were left were congregated in a store. James and Wilford stopped and went inside.

The little establishment was stocked with blankets, harnesses, saddles, bridles, tools, and assorted food items. In the middle was a big potbellied stove around which a few men were gathered. Behind a makeshift counter of pine boards was a man with a short beard, broad face, and bulging eyes.

The men around the stove were dressed in buckskin clothes. Two of them were engaged in a lively game of checkers while the rest were swapping yarns.

"You gents in need of something?" the man behind the counter asked.

"Information," Wilford replied. "How's the trail to the west?"

The man pointed to the men around the stove. "You might ask those gents."

"Thanks!" Wilford turned and walked over to the stove. "I understand you men been over the trail to the west."

One looked up at him. "Yep. And I wouldn't plan on going back that way until spring."

The others were quick to agree. "You'll get buried alive out there," one said.

"I reckon that settles it," Wilford said. "It's just too risky to go on now. We can hole up here until spring, then ride on to Oregon."

James's heart dropped. His worst fear had been realized. Wilford might be right, but he just couldn't force himself to stay here until spring. That he could not accept. When he tried, Kate and his children would come to mind. He had to go on, whatever the risks.

"I've been thinking," James said. "You told me if I followed the Snake

River, it would take me to Oregon. If that's the case, I think I can make it the rest of the way without a guide. I'll pay you the full price we agreed on. Tomorrow, I'll start on to Oregon."

"You better think about that," Wilford replied. "You could get in a lot of trouble out there. You ain't ever seen snow like what comes in these mountains."

"I know the risks, and I'm prepared to face them."

Wilford looked at James for a moment, turned, and walked out to the horses. James followed behind him.

"We need a place to bed down tonight," Wilford said.

They found a small place behind the store that had a fireplace and a supply of wood. Wilford remained silent, his face expressionless, as if he was in deep thought. *He's fretting about my decision to push on,* James thought. After building a fire, they had a meal of dried meat then made their beds on the cabin's dirt floor.

*   *   *

The next morning, Wilford was gone. James was perplexed. There was the matter of the money he still owed him. He got up and walked around Fort Hall, but there was no sign of his guide. He felt bad about the money. He would never have gotten this far without Wilford. But what else could he do? He was out of time. He gathered his gear and prepared to ride on.

He bought a coat in the small store along with more food supplies and oats for his horses.

Fort Hall was nearly deserted as James rode down the street toward the trail. There were a couple of horses in front of the store; smoke came from the chimneys of the houses, but no one was out and about. It seemed the little berg had bedded down for the winter.

He rode toward the west to strike the banks of the Snake River. Except for an occasional rabbit scurrying among the bushes, the country was deserted. There was a vast loneliness about the land ahead; the mountains, partially hidden by gray clouds, were bleak and foreboding. *Was this a wise decision?* he began to wonder.

A cold, raw wind swept in from the north, biting at his face and driving home the hazards he was about to face. James began to think. He was a newcomer here, ignoring the advice of those familiar with the perils of this land. He considered turning around and going back to Fort Hall, but then he thought of Kate and the children.

Still determined, James pushed on. The longing for family continued to overrule his caution. For meager protection against the cold wind, he rode with his head down. In late afternoon, feeling cold and exhausted, he stopped and made camp.

To survive this night, he would need a good fire. He fed the horses some oats and set out to find some firewood. He was picking up pine limbs when he heard someone coming up the trail. Alarmed, he rushed back to camp for his rifle. "Hello in camp!" he heard a familiar voice call out. Wilford was back.

Wilford rode in and dismounted. "I guess if I've come this far, I need to see you the rest of the way. I want to earn the rest of that money; if you get trapped out here somewhere and freeze to death, then your ghost will come back to haunt me. I don't want no spirits bothering me, so I better come along and see you through."

He didn't want to let it show, but James was elated that Wilford decided to rejoin him. "I'm glad you're back; now help me get a fire going."

They built a large fire, cooked bacon, and brewed a pot of coffee. Afterward, they bundled up next to the flames and tried to sleep, but it didn't come easy. They had to get up at regular intervals and add wood to the fire to keep from freezing.

*   *   *

The next morning, the north wind had increased. For a couple of hours, they followed the Snake River, and then James noticed that Wilford was striking a trail back toward the northeast. "We seemed to be changing our course," he remarked to Wilford. "We're going back the way we came from."

"With winter coming on, I want to find the safest route," Wilford replied. "Better to take a longer route and be safe."

James didn't argue the point. He just wanted to make Oregon before the weather got worse. They skirted around Fort Hall and followed a small stream for a couple of days, then spent two more days traveling due north. It was cold, but the snow held off until the third day. That morning, dark clouds spread across the northern sky. Wilford watched the clouds with worry etched on his face. They bundled up against the cold and set forth. The first snow fell in the afternoon. By evening, snow was blowing across the trail, covering everything in a sea of white.

That evening, they camped near a river. The blowing snow made it difficult to find firewood. Fortunately, Wilford managed to get a few limbs from a nearby pine tree and build a small fire. They huddled in their blankets for most of the night. By morning, snow had drifted in around them. They ate some dried meat and saddled the horses. They started down the trail, but deep snow impeded their progress. "We got to get to shelter," Wilford said.

"Where?"

"There should be a Blackfoot village to the north," Wilford replied. "Maybe we can reach it. It's closer than Fort Hall."

A hollow feeling came over James. Guilt, stupidity, ignorance—he felt them all. The impact of his ill-fated decision was coming home to roost. Now, due to his shortsightedness, they were in peril.

The snow was blowing directly into their faces, blinding them and the horses as they struggled through the deep, white expanse. After a few hours, both horses and riders were exhausted. "We got to keep going," Wilford said.

The temperature was dropping. James's hands, feet, and ears were starting to feel numb. His eyes were half-closed; he could barely make out Wilford struggling in front of him. When they stopped under a pine tree to let the horses rest, James felt he was near the end of his endurance.

"I'm not sure we're going the right way," Wilford said. "Been a long time since I was up here, and the snow makes it difficult to tell where we are."

They started out again, struggling through the biting cold and the deep snow. The horses struggled. Finally, James stopped. "I can't go any further."

Wilford looked back at him. "I'll be back as soon as I can."

James sat on his horse and watched Wilford struggle off through the deep snow into the darkening countryside. He got down from his horse and lay in a deep drift. "I failed, Kate, I failed," he mumbled to himself. "I tried to find you and let you know I wasn't dead, but now I soon will be. I'm so sorry."

The blizzard whipped around James as he lay in the snow. He drifted off to sleep and dreamed about Kate. In the dream, she smiled radiantly as she floated across the snow toward him, holding out her hand. She continued to smile as they embraced.

After a time, both Kate and his father appeared to him. He was now content to lie there in the softness of the snow and dream about his family as the blizzard took his life.

Someone was shaking him violently. James stirred back to life. He struggled several times before he got his eyelids partially open, and he could see Wilford standing above him. With great effort, he struggled to a sitting position. There was a group of Indians behind them. A tall one came forward.

The Indian spoke to Wilford in English. "Looks like he's nearly finished."

"I made it to Running Elk's village," Wilford said to James. "We're lucky it ain't that far away."

With Wilford's help, James got to his feet. The first thing that caught his attention was the ragged breathing of his horse. It was lying a few feet away, almost covered in snow. Wilford got out his pistol. "He's done for. The best we can do for it is to put an end to its suffering." He fired a shot into the animal then put the gun away.

They removed the gear from the pack animal and James' horse and placed it on one of the Indian ponies. Then they loaded James on a travois Wilford had made from a blanket.

James's hands and face were numb, void of feeling. Now he was burning with fever and barely conscious. Before setting off, they rubbed some snow on his extremities to get some feeling back again.

The travois bumped and twisted through the deep snow. James would drift off and then wake for a few minutes. The fever raged. His mind was losing contact with his surroundings.

He came to in time to see teepees nearly covered with snow—the Indian camp. Next to the village was a small river. Some men came out to watch the retuning party enter the village.

The fever took over again, leaving him weak and dizzy. He was barely cognizant of being lifted from the travois, carried inside one of the teepees, and laid on a bed of furs.

Chills and shakes began to wrack his body. Then, he would be on fire. James alternated between bouts of sweating and shaking until he drifted off to sleep.

In his slumber, images floated before him. At one point, he was hovering over a beautiful lake. As he looked at the other side, he saw Kate beckon. He tried to reach her, but she disappeared into a large cloud.

Later in the dream, his father was leading him by the hand down a large hallway. At the end was an open door emitting a bright, white light. When they reached the doorway, his father disappeared inside. When James tried to follow, he was driven back by the blinding light. He repeatedly tried to enter the room, but each time the light forced him back.

There was no time reference for James to know how long he alternated between periods of partial consciousness and slumber. When he was in his partial waking state, he could vaguely make out shadows dancing on the walls. At times, he heard chanting and tasted strange concoctions.

Often, James felt he was lying in a pool of water. At times, he sensed the presence of another being close to him, but he could never make out who it was. At times, the fire returned, leaving him with the feeling he was being consumed by flames.

When he was in the sleep state, scenes of his family would appear. In one of these dreams, his mother led him across the plantation, pointing out fields and activities as they floated over the vast estate. Kate would often appear, coming at times out of a large, white cloud. Each time, he would call out to her, but she would ignore his calls.

Then, there would be scenes from the war. Once, he saw a column of soldiers marching toward him. When they were near, they beckoned for him to join them. Each time he tried to get into the line, a hand would reach out and pull him back. Other times, there would be a jumble of faces floating in front of him, some crying, others laughing.

During one of his partial conscious periods, James heard voices outside the teepee. "Looks like the fever got him."

Someone else would speak, but James could not understand the words. In the background, there was a low, rhythmic chant that seemed to build in intensity. This was usually followed by a sudden stream of cold water running down his face, followed by the chills.

Time had now lost all meaning. His spells of partial awareness were too brief and confusing to allow him to get his bearing. When he was awake, he could not tell if it was day or night.

A few times, he was able to make out a shadowy figure sitting beside his bed, mumbling strange incantations. The dwelling would fill with foul-smelling smoke that burned his eyes and nose.

One of the dreams had a terrifying twist. In this dream, he was looking down a road where he could see Kate and the children. She was holding the smallest child while the other two walked beside her. At least, he thought it was Kate and the children. All he could see were their backs. James called out to them, but they continued to walk away without answering. He called out several times, but they continued on. Seeing them moving further away, he tried to run after them, but his legs would not respond. He stood paralyzed as he watched his family walk down the road until they were almost out of sight.

James screamed at his family, but they went on until a large coach stopped, and they got inside. The door on the coach closed, and it disappeared, taking his family away. When the coach was out of sight, he fell to his knees and cried, the tears flowing down his face as he called out their names.

Then, he was fully conscious again. The sun was shining through the open flap of the teepee. His eyes cleared, and he got his first full look at his surroundings. He was lying on a sweat-drenched bed of bearskins. In the center was a small fire. Next to his bed was a pretty young Indian woman wearing a doeskin dress. Her long, black hair hung straight down her back; the sunlight illuminated an oval face with large brown eyes and light brown skin. In her hands, she held a wooden bowl filled with water.

His eyes cleared further; his mind became more focused. The finer details of his surroundings became clear. The walls of the teepee were decorated with colored linings that reached high up on the walls. The teepee was made of hides, probably buffalo. The colorful linings insulated the inside against drafts, and the dwelling was amazingly cozy. On the walls, there were drawings of riders on horseback and animals such as buffalo and elk.

The woman dipped a cloth into the bowl and let the water drip down on his face. Embarrassment rushed over him when he looked down and saw he

298

was stark naked.

The woman realized he was awake; she smiled at his modesty. James pulled a loose fur over and covered himself. The woman's smile widened.

Drum beats came from the front of the teepee, followed by chants he couldn't understand.

When he tried to speak, all that came from his lips was a weak whisper. The woman put a finger over her mouth as if to shush him. James took her hint and gave up trying to talk. He tried to rise up on his elbows; the effort made him weak and dizzy. He sank back down into the fur, feeling helpless.

The woman got to her feet, walked over to the opening, and shouted. Soon, a young boy poked his head in and called to her. The woman talked to the boy for a moment, and then he disappeared.

An older woman with graying hair wearing a calico dress came inside. She spoke briefly with the younger woman before placing a bowl next to the bearskin rug. The younger woman picked up a wooden ladle and dipped liquid out of the bowl. She raised his head and put the ladle next to his lips. He tried to swallow the liquid, which appeared to be some type of broth, but the smell alone made him sick. Seeing his reaction, the woman put the ladle back in the bowl and laid his head on the bed.

James lay on the bed feeling weak, exhausted, and sick to his stomach. There was the sound of voices outside, and then Wilford stepped through the opening, followed by a tall Indian with a light complexion. "Seems now like you might survive," Wilford said. "For a time, we didn't know if you was gonna make it or not."

"How long have I been here?" James whispered.

"Over a week," Wilford said. "The time you spent lying in the snow gave you a bad case of the fever. It's a good thing Running Elk and his band were wintering nearby, or you'd have been a goner for sure—both of us would. By the time we got you here, you were burning up. Little Deer has been here ever since, running cold water over you to cool you down. The medicine man has also been pouring all sorts of stuff into you."

"Must have done some good," James said in a weak voice.

"A lot of the credit for saving you goes to Little Deer, but we've got to give proper credit to the medicine man," Wilford said. "He's a man of great stature in the tribe, so he'll want his due."

To James, it didn't matter who got the credit. He was just happy to still be alive. As his mind cleared, he remembered his hasty departure from Fort Hall: a foolish act that almost cost he and Wilford their lives. His determination to see his family had clouded his judgment. *No more foolishness*, he told himself. He didn't want Kate to really become a widow.

*   *   *

The next day, James tried the broth again and managed to get down a few swallows. He was still too weak to get up from his bed, but he was awake and aware of what was going on around him. One of the first things he noticed was that Little Deer rarely left the teepee, even staying there at night. She was an excellent nurse; he figured he owed his life to her.

*   *   *

Over the next few days, James was able to swallow more of the broth. Soon, he could feel his strength returning. He tried sitting up. The first time it made him dizzy, and he had to lie back down. He tried again the next day and was able to sit up for a short time. After a week, he tried to stand.

Wilford and Little Deer helped him to his feet. Within a few seconds, he was dizzy; they helped him back down on the bed. The next day he did better and was able to stand for a few minutes. Thank goodness—he was making progress, getting stronger every day.

A few more days of the broth diet, and James could stand on his own for a longer time. He ate some elk meat and gained enough strength to take a few steps. With his regained strength came encouragement. The close confinement of the teepee was giving him claustrophobia. He wanted to get out and walk around. A few more days of meat and broth allowed him to do just that. He stepped out of the teepee for the first time since being carried inside.

A cold, raw wind was blowing from the north; snow covered most of the Blackfoot camp. Columns of smoke rose from the tops of the teepees. A few women were tending large pots over campfires in front of the teepees.

Indian children ran between the drifts of snow, paying little attention to the cold. They said something to him that he didn't understand then rushed off toward the river.

The sky was becoming dark and overcast, blocking out the sun and threatening more snow. It gave James a greater appreciation for their rescue and the safety of this camp.

When James stepped around one of the teepees, he noticed Wilford talking to the tall Indian with the light complexion. They looked his way, and Wilford nodded before resuming their conversation. James didn't feel like talking. His walk had taken most of his strength, so he returned to the teepee and lay down on the bed to rest. Soon, Wilford stepped inside.

"Who is that Indian you were talking to?" James asked.

"He's the chief of this band," Wilford replied. "Running Elk is the reason we are allowed to stay here."

"Why is that?"

"The Blackfeet don't care much for strangers and don't usually let them stay on their land. For many years, they would have killed anyone who trespassed on their lands. Running Elk is Noah Anderson's son. I told you a little about Noah and the Blackfoot woman he married. Running Elk grew up with these people and became their chief.

"We were lucky that I was able to find their winter camp. I remembered they usually wintered around this location. I can't tell you how happy I was to find Running Elk's village. The other bands might not have extended us their hospitality."

Thinking about their near-fatal ordeal, James's remorse deepened concerning his ill-fated decision to push on in the face of winter. "What was I thinking?" he mumbled out loud.

* * *

By the next morning, it was snowing again. The wind whipped at the teepee, causing James to fear it might be ripped up and blown away. He under-estimated the sturdiness of the dwelling; it remained intact.

The coziness of the small teepee continued to amaze him. The drop cloths did an amazing job of keeping out the drafts, and the small fire in the center kept the temperature comfortable.

Since his recovery, James had wondered about the drawings on the walls. He asked Wilford about them.

"They can represent different things," Wilford replied. "They are often pictures that tell stories of medicine dreams, battles, and buffalo hunts." Wilford pointed at one of the drawings. "That one there is about a very successful buffalo hunt. Over there is one about a successful battle against the Crows. The Blackfoot and the Crow have been enemies for a long time."

He changed the subject to Little Deer. "You can tell her I appreciate all she did for me, but I don't need nursing anymore," he said to Wilford.

Wilford grinned. "I think she's takin' a liking to you."

James didn't find the matter so amusing. "I got a wife. I don't think she would want me to have another one."

"That may be, but you see, the Indians have different views about that. They don't care how many wives a man has."

"I think it would be better if she didn't sleep in here at night. I don't want to seem ungrateful for her nursing me back to health, but I don't like the current arrangements so much."

"I wouldn't push that issue too much," Wilford said. "We're in their camp, so we have to go along with their ways for now. Best thing to do is just let it be."

Reluctantly, James took Wilford's advice.

*   *   *

The storm went on for two days before letting up. The snow had drifted up around the teepee, opening to the point Wilford had to shovel out a path by hand before they could go outside. By afternoon, the sun was out, and the snow was thawing. The warm sun made James want to get on the trail again. A quick rebuke from Wilford put that idea to rest.

"I reckon it's time for me to come clean with you," Wilford said. "It wasn't all luck that we were so near to Running Elk's camp. I knew we could never get through the mountains in this weather, and I knew you wouldn't go back to Fort Hall. I started leading us back around Fort Hall to where I remembered the Blackfeet wintered. It was still lucky we were nearby when the storm hit. Now, you have to face the fact we're stuck here until spring. If we strike out again, your wife in Oregon will be a real widow."

Under other circumstances, James would have been outraged that Wilford took it on his own to lead him away from the trail, but he knew the man was right. He would have to find some way to pass the winter here with the Blackfeet and be grateful for still being alive.

One thing James soon discovered was that while most of the adults in camp except for Running Elk and Little Deer kept their distance from him, among the children, he was a celebrity of sorts. They would run up to him shouting words he didn't understand. Other times, they would grab his hand, trying to pull him into their games.

"The Blackfeet have had bad experiences with the white men," Wilford explained. "They ain't very comfortable around you. Don't worry about it. As long as we stay on the good side of Running Elk, we'll be all right."

With the return of better weather, Wilford and the Indians went hunting. James wanted to go; he was tired of being confined to the camp. Wilford advised he was not healthy enough for a long ride. James felt up to the ride but suspected he was excluded because some of the Blackfeet might object.

Left with nothing to do, James wandered around camp. The thing that caught his attention was the poverty. The people were poor. They had meager possessions in their lodges, the horses were in bad shape, and many of the people appeared malnourished. That set him to wondering: why would they take him and Wilford in when they had so little for themselves?

Life on the frontier was whittling away at his old system of values. He had believed or at least tried to convince himself that birthright controlled a person's destiny. Where was his birthright now? His birthright had not spared

302

him the loss of his family. Neither had it spared him from the blizzard that nearly cost him his life. No, he owed his life to Wilford and a band of poor Indians, people who knew nothing of wealth and privilege.

James had heard stories from his grandfather about life in early Tennessee and battles with the Indians. Many of these stories portrayed Indians as savages who murdered and scalped white people. Here he was in a village of poor Indians who were sharing their meager rations with him and who had saved his life.

In a way, James figured the Indians were in much the same shape as he had been, fighting a war that could not be won, trying to save their way of life. There was no real doubt about the eventual outcome of their battles, just as there had been with his war. The Indians might win some battles, but they could not defeat the whites; there were too many of them. Their way of life would be changed forever, just as his had been.

*   *   *

There was a commotion in the village. James stepped out of the teepee and saw the hunting party returning with an elk. The women took over preparing the carcass for cooking. He turned to go back into the lodge and saw Wilford approaching. "We got an invite to Running Elk's lodge," Wilford said.

"What's it all about?"

"I don't know, but we best attend," Wilford said. "He's the one that's letting us stay here."

The camp was filled with the aroma of cooking meat. When it was done, the village gathered around. James and Wilford stayed in the back until the rest of the camp had been served. An older woman, one of Running Elks's wives, Wilford pointed out, brought them a serving. James found the meat tasty but somewhat tough. He and Wilford ate their fill then proceeded to Running Elk's lodge for their meeting. While they were walking, Wilford explained the protocol.

"When you reach the lodge, turn to your right around the lodge fire. Running Elk will be seated at the head of the lodge. His 'sits beside him' wife will be on his right, and his other wives will be on the right of her. They will give us a place to sit, then pass the pipe."

If the Blackfoot pipe was like the pipe they had smoked with the Shoshone, James didn't much look forward to it.

They walked to a large teepee in the center of the camp. Wilford opened the flap, and they stepped inside. The lodge was brightly decorated with a colorful drop curtain and walls depicting buffalo hunts and battles.

Running Elk was seated on a bearskin fur next to a woman dressed in a deerskin dress: the one that served them the elk. On her right were two younger women in deerskin dresses, one hardly more than a teenager. On the right of these women was Little Deer. Wilford turned right around the lodge fire, and James followed. Running Elk motioned for them to have a seat on his left.

When James and Wilford were seated, Running Elk picked up a stone pipe. After lighting the pipe, he offered it first with the stem up then down. "He's making an offering to the sun and the earth," Wilford whispered.

Running Elk took several puffs before offering it to Wilford. Wilford took a few puffs then handed it to James, who took a few puffs. The smoke burned his tongue, but he tried not to let it show. After his last puff, he handed the pipe back to Wilford, who passed it to Running Elk.

Laying the pipe down, Running Elk sat in silence, searching for words, it seemed. At last, he spoke. "The time of the Blackfeet grows short. We are losing our hunting grounds to the whites. My father was white, but he lived much the same way that our people have lived, by letting the land provide for him. The white man's diseases have taken many of us; we are not a strong people any longer."

James was moved by the speech. The man was making an eloquent discourse about the plight of his people. Running Elk's face displayed little emotion, but there was weariness in his voice that reflected the heart-felt sadness of a long, painful struggle. Running Elk, like James, had witnessed the destruction of a way of life. He felt the man's sorrow.

"Little Deer, like me, has white blood, but she knows nothing of their ways. It is my desire that when you leave in the spring, you will take her to the white world and help her learn the ways of the white people."

This request stunned James. He did not want Little Deer traveling with them. She would slow them down, and how would he explain her to Kate? His wife was not a jealous woman, but she had never had reason to be. The sight of him riding in with a pretty young woman might be more than she could tolerate.

"We can't do that," he whispered to Wilford.

"We really ain't got no choice in the matter," Wilford whispered. "We'll do as you ask," Wilford said to Running Elk.

Running Elk then spoke to Little Deer. She looked at the woman at her father's side, who James assumed was her mother. The woman, instead of returning Little Deer's gaze, looked down at the ground and did not speak. Running Elk had made his decision. The rest had resigned themselves to it.

"I don't feel right about taking Little Deer with us," James said on the way back. "I appreciate all she's done for me, but this is too much."

"We're not in a position to disagree," Wilford reminded him. "The

Blackfeet saved both our lives. The last thing we want to do is insult Running Elk. He's not too popular with some of his people over this, so we got to go along with him. If it doesn't work out, I'll bring her back on my way home to Missouri. That's the best we can do."

Wilford's directness still annoyed James, but he supposed the man was right. The Blackfeet had been their salvation. To refuse a request from their leader might put them in danger. But alas, how would Kate react?

*   *   *

Later that evening, Little Deer moved all her things into their teepee. James had no appreciation for the arrangement.

"Nothing to worry about," Wilford said. "She feels like she belongs to you."

"You need to explain the situation to her."

Wilford laughed as he spoke to Little Deer. Soon, she was laughing, causing James to wonder what they were saying. Perhaps he was better off not knowing.

*   *   *

James gradually came to accept their winter entrapment and tried to make the best of it. He longed to be on the trail, but he realized they were lucky to be alive. It would not be wise to tempt fate again.

Chapter 29

George and Young Eagle

The harvest concluded as the first days of winter settled over the valley. The remainder of the grain was stored in the makeshift barn. Most of it would be used for seed next year; the rest they would ship to market. Most importantly, they had gained knowledge and experience that would aid them in the future.

Considering all the obstacles, Kate felt pleased about the harvest. They lost a wagon load crossing a stream, thieves stole part of another load, and there were the losses from the fire. Most of all, she was happy for the settlers. The money from their grain would see them through the coming winter. At last, there was some hope for those who had lost so much.

Kate was sitting at her uncle's desk, going over their first year figures as the first winds of winter hit. She determined they would just about break even this year on the freight operation, and they had gained valuable experience. She felt at peace.

Since the fire, Covington had left them alone. But she knew he was just biding his time, waiting for an opportune time to strike. After the fire, they had been on their guard. Now, with winter settling in, they might be safe until spring. But no doubt, sooner or later, they would be dealing with the old freighter again.

Olaf now spent most of his time cutting firewood for them and for the settlers. They were taking teams of horses to the nearby forests, cutting down trees, and dragging them back to be cut up with crosscut saws.

With the outside activities at a halt, Kate decided this was a good time for the children to catch up on their education. The closest school was in La Grande: too far for them to attend. The best she could provide was home schooling. For that purpose, she had brought a box of schoolbooks from Tennessee. The front room became a school house. The children gathered reluctantly and sat on the settee, looking downcast. "Don't be so gloomy," Kate said. "A little learning never hurt anyone."

After Alice and James Junior started on their lessons, little Drew wandered from one to the other, trying to find out what they were doing. Finding little of interest, he got a toy horse and sat in the corner, entertaining himself.

James Junior protested his forced education. "Olaf is teaching me about farming," the boy said. "That's all I need to know."

"I'm very happy Olaf is helping you, but there're other things you need to know, such as reading, writing, and using figures."

He grumbled, took the books, and pretended to study the pages his mother pointed out to him.

*   *   *

By late November, winter ruled the valley. The cold wind whistled through the forest and across the meadow. The mountain peaks were white; snow would soon follow in the lowlands.

The first blizzard struck at the end of the month. As night fell, Kate stood on the front porch. Snow, carried by the wind, swirled across the yard and drifted around the steps. Remembering last winter, she dreaded the coming months stuck in the house. Well, what could she do but wait until spring? As she was turning to go inside, her eyes detected something at the edge of the meadow. She stopped and watched. Had Covington's henchmen decided to attack using the blizzard as cover? The snow made it difficult to see, but it looked like a single horse and rider. She watched a little longer. The horse was dragging something. "Olaf!"

He stepped out on the porch. "Yaw, missy?"

She pointed out toward the meadow. "There's something out there."

"Probably a wild animal."

"I don't think so," she said. "It looks like a horse and rider. They must be nearly frozen."

They watched until the horse and rider were near the yard. "It is a horse and rider, and they're pulling something," Kate said.

Olaf stared through the driving snow for a moment and said, "It looks like an Indian. They use a thing they call a travois they pull behind their horses. I better get my rifle."

"They must be near frozen," Kate said. "I don't see how they could be a threat."

"Those people can't be trusted. It may be a trick of some kind."

The horse and rider stopped at the edge of the yard. The rider was bundled up in blankets. The horse was dragging a sled made of animal skin stretched between two poles that were attached to the horse's saddle. On the sled was a small figure, also wrapped in blankets.

Kate stepped off the porch. "Missy, wait!" Olaf yelled.

She ignored Olaf and walked through the accumulated snow to the horse. The rider pulled the blanket down. A man looked at her. "Greetings," he said. "I come looking for the man called Lewis Harrington."

"I'm sorry," Kate said. "My uncle was killed last spring."

"My heart is heavy to hear this. Lewis Harrington was a friend to my people. My son is very ill. I came to seek his help in getting one of the white medicine men to cure him. Our medicine man cannot drive the sickness from my son."

"Let me take a look," Kate said. She walked to the sled, pulled back the thick blanket, and saw a young Indian boy. He had his hand over his abdomen and was moaning with pain. Kate reached down and touched the boy's forehead; it was burning with fever. She knew little about medicine but was afraid the boy might have appendicitis. A young cousin of hers in Tennessee had similar symptoms when she came down with the same affliction.

She turned to the man on the horse. "Let's get him into the house," she said. Her oldest son was now out on the porch. "Olaf, you and James Junior come and give a hand."

James Junior started toward them, but Olaf stayed on the porch.

"Olaf, please, we need some help here."

He hesitated. Kate prodded until he stepped down and walked over to them. "Missy, these people can be dangerous."

"We got a small, very sick boy and a man nearly frozen," Kate replied. "I hardly think they can be a threat to us."

"Well, you don't know these people like I do. You can never trust them."

Kate was irritated at Olaf's stubbornness but didn't have time to argue. She turned to her son. "Help me get him in the house. Be careful when you lift him."

Olaf watched them struggle to get the boy out of the sled. He relented and came over to help lift the boy up. He grumbled under his breath as they carried him across the yard and into the house. "Put him in Uncle Lewis's room," Kate said.

The boy's father dismounted and followed them inside. Olaf gave him a hard stare but said nothing. They laid the boy on the bed. Kate touched his head again. The skin was hot to the touch. She stood up to go in the kitchen but saw Helga standing in the doorway. "We need some cold water," Kate said.

Helga went into the kitchen and returned with a basin filled with water and a large rag. Kate wet the rag and placed it against the boy's burning face.

"We're going to need the doctor from La Grande," she told Helga. "Keep trying to cool him down. Maybe we can break the fever."

Helga took the rag and sat down on the edge of the bed.

"Olaf, please saddle me a horse."

"Why, missy? You can't go out in this weather."

"We've got to get the doctor out here quickly. Please get me a horse saddled."

"No, missy, I'll go," he said.

"I can't ask you to do that."

"Please let him go," Helga said. "He's more familiar with the country. He'll be less likely to get lost. In the snow, it's easy to lose your way."

Kate put up an argument before giving in and letting Olaf make the trip. He got out a heavy sheepskin coat and a large cap with earmuffs. He wrapped a scarf around his neck then went to saddle one of the horses.

It was a burden, asking Olaf to go out in such weather. But he and Helga were right about his chances being better than hers. "What will I tell the doctor?" he asked when he returned to the house. "He won't likely come out here if I tell him it's for a sick Indian."

"Just tell him there's a member of the family who needs medical attention," Kate said.

Of course, it was a lie, but there were times when it couldn't be helped. This was one of those times; the boy might not last the night without medical treatment.

From the front door, Kate watched Olaf ride into the dark night and disappear into the storm. When she was closing the door, she felt a hand on her shoulder.

"I'm sorry about Olaf, dear," Helga said. "You see, he had a bad experience with Indians when he first came here from Sweden as a young man. The Cayuse murdered his employer and burned the man's house to the ground. Olaf escaped by hiding in the woods. To this day, he still doesn't feel good when Indians are around."

"I understand."

"These two are probably Umatillas," Helga said. "Your uncle had a friendship with them. The first winter he was up here, he found a band of them nearly starved. He cut out some of his livestock and gave them to the Indians, so they could get through the winter. The government took much of their land in 1855 and was supposed to provide for them in return. Sometimes they didn't provide the promised support, and the Indians suffered."

That sounded so much like Uncle Lewis. He would lend a helping hand to anyone who needed it. She missed him so much.

While waiting for the doctor, Kate and Helga took turns bathing the boy in cold water. During the time, the boy's father took a seat outside the door. He was a tall man with long, black hair hanging down his shirt and deep lines across his dark, expressionless face. He made an imposing figure, sitting on the floor in his bright red flannel shirt and deerskin pants.

*   *   *

Olaf stumbled through the door just after midnight, accompanied by an elderly man. "I'm Doctor McBrighton," the man said as he removed a heavy coat. Then, he noticed the Indian sitting on the floor next to the bedroom door. "What's he doing here?"

"I'll explain later," Kate said. "We have a sick child in the next room."

"One of your children?"

"No, actually, it's his child," Kate said as she pointed to the Indian.

"Madam, have you lost your mind? You hauled me through a blizzard to treat an Indian."

"The boy may die if something isn't done soon."

"Are you aware that if anything went wrong, this might start an Indian war? You don't know what you're tampering with here."

"Doctor, are you a Christian man?" Kate asked.

"I try to be, but it's hard sometimes."

"Well, doctor, there is a sick child in there who's near death and needs your help. Can you live with yourself if you stand by and do nothing?"

The doctor sighed. Then, he pointed to the boy's father. "Does he realize the risks?"

"I'll talk to him," Kate said. She walked over and stood before the man. "Do you understand the doctor might not be able to save your son?"

"I ask the medicine man to use all his power," the man said. "I can ask for no more."

Did the man understand what she had asked? Kate wasn't sure. She believed he did. That would have to suffice. She walked back over to the doctor, who was now seated on the settee. "He understands."

"All right. Since I've come all this way in a blizzard, I'll take a look at the boy."

Kate showed the doctor to the bedroom, closed the door, and waited outside. The Indian man started a low chant. Drew and Alice came down and stared at the man.

"What's he doing, Mama?" Alice asked.

"He's doing what I would be doing if one of you were in there on that bed," Kate replied. "He's praying for his son in his own way."

Kate put the children back to bed. When she was coming back down the

310

stairs, the doctor emerged from the room.

"The boy has appendicitis. The only chance is to operate."

"Then go ahead."

"I'll need some hot water and bandages."

Kate got a couple of sheets and tore them up into bandages while Helga started heating water. When all was ready, they carried the water and bandages into the bedroom.

"I'll need someone to assist me," the doctor said.

"Just tell me what to do," Kate replied.

*   *   *

After an exhausting hour, they emerged from the bedroom. Helga was asleep on the settee, and Olaf had gone to their quarters. The boy's father was still sitting next to the door, chanting.

"It's in the hands of a higher power now," the doctor said.

Kate made a pot of coffee for them. Afterward, she let the doctor use her room to sleep. She woke up Helga and told her to go on to her quarters and get some rest. Then, Kate fell down on the settee and drifted off to an exhausted slumber.

*   *   *

When Kate woke up the next morning; she saw the doctor emerging from the bedroom. "How is he?"

"He survived the night. These people are resilient as long as they stay away from white people's diseases. I showed the other woman how to change the bandages. I've done all I can here."

"Well, please stay for some breakfast."

The boy's father was still sitting on the floor next to the door, chanting. *How can he go on for so long?* Kate wondered. He rode in nearly frozen and had been sitting there on the floor ever since.

Helga stepped out of the room. "I changed the bandages, and he's sleeping," she said.

They prepared a breakfast of fried bacon and eggs with big slices of toast. Olaf came in with the milk, set it down next to the table. Without a word, he turned and started toward the door.

"Have some breakfast, Olaf," Kate said.

Olaf grumbled and looked toward the door. But the smell of bacon and eggs changed his mind. He took a seat at the table.

When Kate got the children up for breakfast, they stared at the man sitting

311

next to the door. "Is he still praying?" Alice asked.

"Yes."

Kate filled a plate and took it to the boy's father. "You must be starved," she said. "There's plenty more in the kitchen."

He seemed not to hear her. Instead, he stared straight ahead as if in a trance. Kate put the plate down beside him. He would eat in his own good time, she guessed.

After eating, the doctor gathered his medical supplies. When all was ready, he took another look at the boy. "He's doing as well as expected. Now, I must be getting back to town. You never know who might need me."

"You want someone to ride back with you?" Kate asked.

"No, thank you. I've ridden this area in all sorts of weather; it's a medical man's fate, you know. I know this place like the back of my hand. Besides, I need to visit another man who lives over east of here. Stockman named Lawrence Granville."

"Lawrence Granville!"

"Yes, you know him?"

"Yes, we're business partners of sorts. I do hope he's okay."

"He's been having a few pains here and there."

The doctor bundled up and started for the door.

"Thank you, Doctor," Kate said as he handed him some gold dust.

"Yes, madam. I hope you won't drag me out again in another blizzard to attend to some sick Indian." Kate did not respond to what she felt were unnecessarily insensitive remarks.

Olaf brought the doctor's horse up to the house. Doctor McBrighton waded through the deep snow, deposited his medical tools inside a saddlebag, and mounted. The snow had stopped falling, but the sky was overcast and dark, casting a gloomy shadow over the countryside. The doctor rode through the snow-packed yard toward the meadow.

*　　*　　*

The boy opened his eyes about mid-morning. He was very thin and had long black hair. As he looked around at his surroundings, his eyes fell on Kate and Helga. His eyes opened wide with fear; he cried out with words neither of them understood.

Kate ran to the door and almost collided with the father coming in. He had heard his son's cries. He brushed on past Kate and sat down on the bed. Kate and Helga slipped quietly out of the room.

In a few minutes, the man came out. "The doctor's medicine is good. My son will live."

312

They were surprised when the man resumed his seat near the door. His face remained expressionless, but when Kate looked at his eyes, she detected a look of relief. She knew the feeling of a parent for a child went beyond all cultural barriers.

Helga came in with a pair of blankets and placed them at the foot of the boy's bed. Kate pointed them out to the father. He got up, came inside, and spread the blankets on the floor. In a few minutes, he was asleep. *Poor man,* Kate thought. *He had to be exhausted.*

*   *   *

When the days passed into mid-December, the Indian boy had regained much of his strength. He could now get out of bed and move around the house.

Over time, Kate learned that the man was called George White Horse. His son was called Young Eagle Who Soars. They were from a band of Umatillas that were camped to the north at the edge of the mountains.

"I understand you knew Uncle Lewis?" Kate said.

"Yes, one year the time was very bad for us," George replied. "We had little food for the coming winter, and the game was scarce. The white government did not provide the support it promised. They took most of our land and didn't keep their promise to provide for us. Lewis Harrington brought us some cattle and grain that helped us through the bad times. From that time on, he was always welcome in our camp. He said we were neighbors, and neighbors should help each other. We considered him a man of great honor."

Kate detected the sadness and bitterness in George's voice. But her uncle truly understood this land and its people. She missed him more than ever.

*   *   *

By the third week of December, Young Eagle was strong enough to play with the other children. Drew took an instant liking to the Indian boy. At times, even James Junior would join in their play. Kate was amazed the boys got along so well even though they did not understand each other's language. There would be a laugh or a hand gesture of some sort that seemed to let each know what the other was thinking. *Adults could learn a lot from children,* Kate thought.

George also would sit and watch the boys playing together. "Boys do not know the hatreds of their fathers," he said.

Kate found that George had learned some English from the missionaries who had been in their land. "We listened to them at first, but the other whites did not follow the words of the missionaries, so we did not listen to them anymore."

George told her he lost his wife and two other sons during an outbreak of cholera the previous year. Young Eagle was the only family he had left.

*   *   *

Christmas was approaching, so it looked like the Indians might be with them during the holidays. That left Kate with a dilemma. She had presents for everyone except for George and his son. The weather ruled out a trip to La Grande. She thought. James Junior had some clothes that were too small. Her intention was to save them for Drew, but the holidays were a special time. She searched through the clothes and found a nearly new red flannel shirt. She set it aside with a pair of pants. Now, if Uncle Lewis's clothes would fit George, all would be ready.

*   *   *

Two days before Christmas, there was a break in the weather. Olaf took his shotgun and headed for the nearby forest, hoping to get a turkey for Christmas dinner.

In Uncle Lewis's closet, Kate found a shirt and pants that might fit George. Knowing little of their customs, she was a little apprehensive about giving the Indians presents. She saw George sitting on the porch, looking out across the snow-covered landscape. She noticed that despite the cold, he would often sit outside. An idea came to her. She put on her own coat and went outdoors. "We have a holiday called Christmas that will be here in two days."

"Yes. I have heard of your Christmas."

"There is something I would like to ask of you," Kate said.

"I am in your debt. What do you wish of me?"

"I would like for you to sit at the head of our table on Christmas day. My Uncle Lewis would be at the head of the table if he was here. Since he has been taken from us, I would like for you to wear his clothes and sit in his place this year. I think it would honor my uncle's memory."

He seemed to be moved by her request. "I would be honored as well."

*   *   *

Olaf returned late that afternoon with two turkeys. He deposited the birds in the kitchen and took his leave. Since George and his son had arrived, he spent very little time in the house. Kate understood why and respected his feelings. But with Christmas just around the corner, she was worried. Would Olaf come to the table with the Indians? It wouldn't be Christmas without him present. Kate owed Olaf and Helga so much; she considered them family. The next morning, she spoke to Helga. "Like I told you, he's never gotten over that attack and the death of his benefactor," Helga said. "His employer was a man who befriended him when he first arrived from Sweden. The memory has been with him ever since. Just the same, he's a good man and will do what is right when the time comes."

*   *   *

On the night before Christmas, Olaf brought in a pine tree from the nearby forest and set it up in the main room of the house. They spent the evening putting homemade decorations on the tree and around the room. Kate popped a bowl of popcorn, and they strung it on sewing thread and hung it on the tree and over the doorway. Alice colored pictures to use as decorations. Young Eagle was a little hesitant; then, he joined the other children. It was not part of his customs, but he enjoyed himself nonetheless.

They finished their Christmas preparations with Helga's homemade taffy. Kate smiled as she watched the children pulling at the sticky treat and stuffing themselves. In the spirit of the season, she felt truly at peace.

*   *   *

On Christmas day, Helga prepared a meal of roast turkey, dressing, candied yams, canned vegetables, and large cherry pies. George kept his word and dressed in Uncle Lewis's white shirt and striped pants. He took his place at the head of the table. Olaf, maybe out of the spirit of the day, put aside his feelings and joined them. The children, under pressure from Kate, put on their best clothes.

When the meal was over, Kate passed out presents. First, there was a bonus for Olaf and Helga—they had earned every penny and much more. Then, she gave Drew a shiny red top, Alice a new doll, and James Junior a jackknife. She gave the red flannel shirt to Young Eagle and some more of her uncle's clothes to George. The Indians seemed pleased with their gifts. All the holiday lacked was having Uncle Lewis here to celebrate it with them. It was his dream that had made all this possible.

*   *   *

The break in the weather held. The day after Christmas, George and his son prepared to leave. Olaf brought George's horse into the yard but didn't stay around to say goodbye. Kate knew he was happy the Indians were leaving. That saddened her, but she understood long-held feelings didn't change overnight. The Indians had given her a new perspective on life: a deeper understanding of human nature, of the common threads that ran among all people.

George mounted his horse, then looked down at Kate. "You have brought happiness to my heart by saving the life of my son. You shared your lodge and your food with us. For this, we will always remember you. Like your uncle, you are a person of great honor."

"And we will always remember you for sharing Christmas with us," Kate replied.

Drew, saddened that his friend was leaving, and stood on the porch with tears running down his cheeks.

"Son, Young Eagle, and his father must return to their own people," Kate said.

Young Eagle was sitting behind his father. When he saw Drew's tears, he whispered in his father's ears. George answered with a nod of his head. The Indian boy dismounted and walked over to the porch. He removed an ornament from around his neck made of bear claws and small feathers and handed it to Drew.

"My son gives this to your son as a sign of friendship," George said. "They now have a friendship that will last forever."

Young Eagle ran back and got up behind his father. They rode off across the meadow and turned toward the north.

As she watched them ride away, Kate wondered if they would ever see the Indians again. True friendship always seemed so fleeting.

*   *   *

As the holidays faded into memory, Kate and her family spent most of their time in the house by the fire. The long days indoors gave Kate time to think about what lay ahead. In the spring, she would have to get together with all the settlers and push on with her plans for dealing with Covington. The freight owner was not through with them. There would be more trouble down the road—of that, she was sure.

Chapter 30

Blackfoot Hospitality

Over time, James grew acclimated to his confinement in the Blackfoot camp. When there were breaks in the weather, he would wander around the village. Most of the adults avoided him; a few would acknowledge him with a slight nod, but they rarely tried to speak to him.

James found the Blackfeet had ways to entertain themselves. Story tellers would spend the winter evenings telling those gathered around about the early days of battles, hunting expeditions, and horse-stealing raids far to the south.

Wilford took James to some of the storytelling sessions. On a particular evening, they gathered in back of one of the lodges. An elderly man, his hair long and white, was telling a story to the men sitting before him. Wilford served as an interpreter.

"That's old Talking Wolf," Wilford said. "He's telling a story about a time when he was on a hunting trip and was attacked by a band of Crows. He fled into a canyon. Once inside, he found there was no way out except through the Crows. While he was pondering his fate, the spirit of a great white wolf appeared and showed him another way out of the canyon. Since that time, the wolf spirit has appeared to him many times and helped him perform great feats in battle."

During the winter nights, James heard many stories about the Blackfeet. During the early days, the tribe's only domestic animals were dogs. They used dogs for hunting and for moving from place to place. The dog days, as this period in their history was called, were difficult, especially for the elders. Often, they were forced to leave the older ones behind since they had no way for them to travel.

With the arrival of the horse, things changed for them. With this newfound mobility, they had a better way to move their possessions. The old ones could ride on a travois pulled by a horse. Moreover, their ability to hunt and make war improved.

*   *   *

S ome of his host's customs were strange to James. He stepped out of the
teepee one morning and heard wailing from nearby. A woman appeared
with most of the hair cut from the side of her head. Soon, other women
gathered around her. The wailing woman raised her arms upward and wailed
so loudly it resonated throughout the camp.

Wilford came outside. James asked him for an explanation.

"Her husband went to the Sand Hills last night."

"What?"

"The Sand Hills is like the Blackfoot version of Heaven. When a man
dies, his wife cuts off a portion of her hair and wails. This will probably go on
for some time. They'll kill some of the man's horses so he'll have
transportation for his journey."

*   *   *

D uring the winter, James encountered other customs of his hosts, some he
found disturbing. As he was walking past a woman bent over a cooking
pot, she rose and looked at him. To his shocked surprise, part of her nose was
missing. When he was back at the teepee, he asked Wilford if she had been
injured in some accident.

"No, it wasn't an accident," Wilford said. "She got caught sharing her
favors with a man that wasn't her husband. One thing the Blackfeet don't
tolerate is an untrue woman. When a woman gets caught doing such a thing,
the punishment is having part of her nose cut off."

"Seems like a cruel thing," James said.

"To us, it is. It's the Blackfoot way, and they accept it."

As the winter started giving way to spring, James's thoughts again turned
to the trail and the quest to find his wife and children.

Chapter 31

Spring's Arrival

The Blackfoot camp remained buried under snow until spring. James grumbled. "Be patient," Wilford reminded him. "There's nothing we can do until warm weather." James tried to heed his advice but was just about to the end of his endurance when the snows began thawing.

With the first sign of warm weather, James wanted to mount up and be on the way. Wilford had to caution him again. "We've still got some business with Running Elk before we go. We can't leave until he's ready."

James cursed at yet one more unfortunate circumstance. Wilford explained it was the way things had to be. James sat, brooded, and accepted they were trapped until Running Elk gave the word.

Little Deer was the hold up. This was a fact that aggravated him, but again, the Blackfeet had been their salvation. When his feelings were under control, James noticed there was new activity in the village. A carnival atmosphere had taken hold. "What's got them so excited?" he asked Wilford.

"Sundance," Wilford replied. "It's a big event for the Plains Indians."

*　　*　　*

The next day, while James was going through his gear, he saw a hunting party returning, carrying some deer and elk. The women took over. They skinned and gutted the carcasses. The party was in full swing.

James and Wilford stayed close to their teepee away from the celebration. When the meat was ready, Little Deer brought them a generous portion. After the feast, drummers started setting up drums made of buffalo hides. Men assembled on one side of the drummers, women on the other. Soon, each group was moving in time to the beat. On into the night, the dancing continued until the dancers began to collapse from exhaustion.

James understood this was a big event for the Blackfeet but saw no need for it to delay them. He mentioned his frustration to Wilford again. "We have to wait for Running Elk to let Little Deer go," Wilford said with a hint of irritation.

Little Deer again. James didn't want to seem ungrateful for what she had done for him. But why did they have to take this girl with them? She was delaying them now and would again out on the trail. "No use frettin' about it," Wilford said. "For now, just enjoy the show. Ain't many outsiders ever witnessed a Sundance celebration? Think of yourself as a man who has been privileged to witness what not many other men from your world have seen."

*   *   *

The celebration went on. The next morning, several men built a lodge, using limbs from the willow trees growing along the river. "That's a sweat house," Wilford explained. "The Blackfeet use it as a place for purification. There is a woman they call the medicine woman who's the center of all this. Her husband has to go into the sweat lodge and be purified."

"Who is this medicine woman?" James asked.

"They choose one every Sundance. It's usually for some special or outstanding feat during the year."

The Blackfeet started the ritual by fasting. During this time, the husband of the chosen medicine woman went into the sweat lodge for the purification rite. This regimen was repeated for the next four days, except each day they moved to a different location. James and Wilford followed along reluctantly behind the rest of the village, James's impatience mounting by the day.

"This will be their final location," Wilford said on the fourth day.

The men cut down a cottonwood tree. Once the tree was down, they started engaging in a ritual that James did not understand. The men would run up to the tree and strike it with a resounding blow. His curiosity overcame him. "What's that all about?"

"They call it countin' coup," Wilford replied.

"Counting what?"

"Counting coup is hard to understand unless you're Indian," Wilford explained. "In battle, a warrior counts coup by striking an enemy with his hand or club. What they are doing with the tree represents the same thing."

Following the coup ritual, a woman transferred a bundle to another woman. Wilford explained they were transferring last year's medicine bundle from the previous medicine woman to the one selected for this year. This looked to be the highlight of the ceremony. At the center of it was a statuesque woman with long, coal-black hair, the new medicine woman, Wilford pointed

320

out. Members of the camp lined up in front of her to receive gifts. With that, James and Wilford left the festivities behind and returned to camp. Running Elk was waiting for them. Wilford talked to the chief for a few minutes then announced to James, "We can be on our way now. We'll start in the morning."

It was the best news James had heard in some time. He was so filled with apprehension; he could hardly sleep that night. From what Wilford had told him, they were not far from Oregon. Images of being united with his family danced in his head—he could think of nothing else.

* * *

As the first rays of dawn rose over the mountains, they prepared to depart. First, they had a problem to resolve. They were short a horse. To add to that, the rest of their horses were in poor shape. It was doubtful any of them would survive until Oregon. For now, they had to make do by packing their gear on Wilford's horse, the pack horse, and a pony that Little Deer was bringing. James would have to ride the pack animal. "What are we going to do about these poor horses?" James asked.

"We might pick up some in Fort Hall, or there's an outpost near the Snake that might have horses that are in better shape," Wilford said. "We'll have to make do with these until we get there. If we don't push 'em too hard, maybe they'll get us to some in better shape."

* * *

Little Deer was filled with remorse. Her father had talked to her about why he was sending her away with the two men. His father had hunted with Wilford Johnson. Wilford was one of few men outside the Blackfoot people her father trusted. He told Little Deer that she was also of the white culture. She would have a better chance of surviving in the white world. Her father told her the Blackfoot way of life was being threatened by the whites who were taking away their land. In time, their people might be no more. She didn't understand her father and was saddened to leave her people. But he had made his decision; there was nothing else for her but to abide by his wishes.

Since Wilford Johnson understood the Blackfoot tongue, she asked him how the white men took a wife. He told her the white man with him had a wife and was going to Oregon to find her. "The white men only have one wife," he explained to her. Little Deer was surprised at this strange custom of a man having only one wife. *The whites have strange ways*, she concluded.

* * *

They rode south, reaching Fort Hall in a few days. There were no horses available. They picked up a few supplies and rode on, following the banks of the Snake River. Their progress was slow, but with poor horses, it was the best they could do.

"Good thing the trading post is on this side of the river," Wilford said. "Be tough trying to ford it this time of the year."

James agreed. The water was almost bank high and filled with debris.

They didn't have to ford the Snake, but a stream emptying into it stood in their path. The channel was narrow and the current swift. "We got to cross," Wilford said.

Streams had been the bane of James's trip. As they secured their gear, he remembered their difficult time crossing the Platte back in Nebraska. Better luck this time, he hoped. They plunged off into the cold water. The horses struggled against the current, but they made it across. The only drawback was getting soaked by the river water.

His wet, cold clothes caused James to fear for his health. He could ill afford another bout with his recent illness. As if reading his thoughts, Wilford said, "We best build a fire and dry off." They stopped and built a large fire. Then, they stripped off all their clothes and lay them next to the flames to dry.

Little Deer seemed undaunted by being in the company of two men. She stripped off her deerskin dress and placed it beside the fire. James felt awkward and wanted to protest, but Wilford only laughed.

When the clothes were dry, they dressed and followed the banks of the river through the mountains of Idaho Territory. Everywhere, spring announced its presence. Wildflowers were growing in the clearings; the hardwood trees were budding out, adding their own colors to the stands of pine and fir. The mountain peaks were still cloaked in white, a reminder of the recent winter.

That night, they camped in a clearing near the river. Wilford killed a small deer, which Little Deer skinned and dressed. Then, she cooked it over the fire. James found the venison tasty. He appreciated the fact there were two good cooks with him. It saved him from starving by his own hand.

*   *   *

The next day, they rode through a stand of young pines with patches of snow where the trees blocked the sun. In places, the snow was still deep, impeding their travel. In early afternoon the forest gave way to open country.

In front of them were towering peaks that seemed to almost reach the sky. Spring had brought a renewal to the mountains. In the clearings, they encountered herds of elk and an occasional moose, some with calves by their sides.

By late afternoon, they were traveling beside a ridge that ran parallel to the river. When James looked up, he was surprised to see a group of Indians above them. He started to reach for his rifle, but Wilford stopped him.

"They been following us for most of the afternoon. If they were hostile, we would know it by now. They look like Flatheads, so they won't bother us if we don't act crazy. They can be dangerous if you provoke 'em too much. It's a little far south for them, but they're probably on a hunting trip."

They rode on, the Indians paralleling them. When it was almost dark, the Indians rode off the ridge. Wilford went out to meet them. He exchanged greetings with the leader in broken English. When the greetings were finished, they rode back to James and Little Deer.

"Is this Blackfoot woman your wife?" the Flathead asked Wilford.

Wilford grinned and pointed at James. "She his wife."

From the pointing and looks in her direction, Little Deer sensed she was the center of attention. Apprehension filled her face. The Flathead continued. "I am in need of a wife," he said. "Maybe I buy the Blackfoot woman from you."

James was at a loss as to how to deal with this situation. "She no good," Wilford said. "She very lazy, no cook, no make babies, no good for nothing."

"Maybe I take the Blackfoot woman from you," the Indian said. "I will take the no-good woman from you. The Blackfeet have killed many of my people, so maybe I take this one for myself."

The Indian's talk made James nervous. He took no offense with Wilford's degrading of Little Deer, realizing it was to sway the Flathead's interest. But would it work?

"A great warrior don't need a useless woman," Wilford said. "He needs a good rifle."

Wilford pulled his rifle from its sheath and handed it to the Indian. The Flathead took the Winchester and looked it over, then put the stock against his shoulder and looked down the barrel. "It is a good rifle, but I have nothing worthy to give in trade."

"It's a gift," Wilford said.

Does Wilford know what he's doing? James wondered. He looked over the band of poorly armed Flatheads. Most of the Indians were carrying old muzzle loaders. A couple more were carrying bows and arrows. A moot point maybe; even being poorly armed, they still had them outnumbered.

The Indian seemed pleased with his acquisition. "I thank you for the rifle."

Wilford motioned for James and Little Deer to ride on while he finished his business with the Flatheads. James was reluctant to leave him to face the Indians alone. Relying on his guide's advice, he and Little Deer urged their horses down the trail. After riding a short distance, they heard a rider coming up behind them. It was Wilford.

"They probably won't bother us, but let's not give them an opportunity," Wilford said.

They rode until dark, then camped next to the river. Their supper was cold venison. After eating, they sat huddled in some blankets that Little Deer had brought. They were heavier than those James and Wilford had been using.

*   *   *

The next two days passed uneventfully. They were now riding in a forest of dense evergreen that was damp and cold. At the end of the second day, they camped beside another small stream that emptied into the Snake. They gathered up several pine limbs and soon had a roaring blaze going. With the fire, they cooked a meal of venison and coffee. It was Little Deer's first experience with coffee. After taking a swallow, she spit it out.

Having the girl along still worried James. He was afraid of what Kate might think about him traveling around in the company of a young woman. Beyond that, he didn't know what they would do with her once they reached his family. Little Deer was ill-prepared to live in a white world. But they were stuck with her. Maybe it would work out for the best was all he could hope and let it go for now.

They had just settled into their blankets when there was a commotion from the horses. James and Wilford jumped up and found them trying to break free from their hobbles. They were trying to calm the spooked animals when there was a crashing sound in the bushes, followed by a loud roar. "Grizzly!" Wilford yelled.

The bear burst through the undergrowth into the camp. As the huge beast lumbered up close to the fire, Little Deer jumped up and scrambled toward the trees, tripping over a log at the edge of the camp.

The girl was an easy target for the bear, but the beast had turned its attention on their food supply. It tore into their gear with its huge paws, scattering their supplies all over the camp.

As the bear ravaged their supplies, Little Deer lay paralyzed. "She's hurt. We got to get her away from there!" Wilford yelled.

With all their weapons in camp, James didn't see how they would be able to do much against the bear.

"I'll try to get his attention. You see if you can get her to safety," Wilford said.

"Better be careful; that bear looks mean and hungry."

"You can count on that."

Wilford picked up a tree limb and started toward the bear, which was now tearing into a saddlebag filled with hardtack. He yelled and lunged at the bear with the limb, giving it a hard push on the rump.

The bear ignored Wilford's first attempt. He plunged the limb into the grizzly's flank again. The massive beast stood on its hind legs and let out a roar that could be heard throughout the Rockies. The fire illuminated the glaring eyes and long claws. James was amazed at the sight. The black bears in Tennessee were puny compared to this grizzly.

Wilford now had the grizzly's attention. He backed away toward the trees, the bear still on its hind legs advancing toward him. With the bear's attention diverted, James ran over to Little Deer. When he reached her, he motioned for her to stand. She tried, but her ankle gave way. As she was falling, he caught her around the waist and hoisted the girl up over his shoulder. When she was safely secured in a small clearing, he rushed back to help Wilford.

The bear had chased Wilford back into the trees. James looked around desperately for the Henry but could not find it. The grizzly had scattered all his weapons. The bear was on its hind legs again, roaring loudly, silhouetted against the campfire light. Then, a bit of luck. He found the Henry. He raised it to fire, pulled the trigger, and swore in disgust. It was not loaded.

James didn't have time to curse his stupidity. He hadn't used the rifle since his encounter with the Shoshone and had forgotten to reload it afterward. To add to his predicament, his thrashing around had caught the bear's attention. It dropped down on all fours and lumbered toward him.

His hand scrabbled wildly for the ammo pouch. The bear was almost in striking distance when his hand fell on something familiar, his pistol. He didn't know what he could do with such a puny weapon against the big grizzly, but as the animal stood on its hind legs again and let out a roar, James picked up the Colt and fired. Then he scrambled backward as fast as he could go.

The bullet cut a crease in the fur on the bear's head. The grizzly let out another loud roar that shook the trees. Then, it dropped down on all fours and crashed into the bushes beside the camp.

James could hear the bear howling as it raced through the woods. His hand was shaking so hard he couldn't hold it in one place, and the sweat was pouring off his brow down into his eyes. He got to his feet and tried to steady himself, then went back to see if Little Deer was okay.

She was sitting up at the edge of the clearing. Her ankle appeared to have a sprain. He helped her back to camp, where Wilford was sorting through what remained of their supplies. "Looks like we're going to be living off the land for a time," Wilford said.

They did what they could in the dark then tried to get some sleep.

* * *

The next morning, they got a better look at their supplies. Most of their gear was intact; it was their food supply that had been wiped out. What the bear had not eaten during its rampage was now scattered from one side of the camp to the other. They set out without breakfast.

"It's a day's ride, at least before we can find a place to pick up any supplies," Wilford said. "If we plan to eat today, we best do some hunting."

With Wilford being the best hunter, James gave him the Henry and some rounds. He took the rifle and rode off into the mountains. While Wilford looked for meat, James decided to try his hand at fishing. He found some wire in his saddlebags and fashioned a crude hook. Down the trail, a short distance was a small creek that fed the Snake. Using some string and the wire hook, he made a fishing line. Now, what would he use for bait?

Little Deer had hobbled up behind him. She motioned for him to wait. She removed her moccasins and waded into the clear water with her skirt raised almost to the waist. She stationed herself like a statue and waited. A fish came close. When it was within striking distance, her hand moved like a flash and came up with the wiggling fish. James wadded out and took it from her. She took up her station again and soon had another fish in her hands. Within an hour, they had enough perch for a meal.

Little Deer emerged from the stream and dried herself with a cloth she had in a bag. She could now walk with only a slight limp. Then they went back to camp and built a fire to cook their catch. When Wilford returned later in the morning with a deer, they were frying fish. "Looks like we're gonna eat after all," Wilford said. "That's one of the great things about life up here in the mountains. The land will provide for you."

They ate the fish, then cooked the deer Wilford had killed and saved it for later use.

Before starting out, Wilford handed the Henry back to James. "That's a mighty fine rifle," he said.

They packed the rest of their food and resumed their journey. They rode for the rest of the day, stopping only long enough to munch on some venison. They rode slowly to spare the horses as much as possible. Late in the day, they reached a trading post located along the riverbank. It was nothing more than a log cabin and a corral behind, filled with horses.

The place was deserted except for a large, balding man and an Indian woman. The man had a grumpy disposition. The woman sat in a chair next to the fireplace. She did not speak or acknowledge their presence. James bought some bacon, salt pork, coffee, flour, salt, and sugar to supplement what they lost to the grizzly bear. When the man saw James was carrying gold, his disposition softened somewhat.

James and Wilford inspected the horses in the corral. They were not in the best of shape but had fared a little better than the ones they were riding. They made a deal for a large, black gelding and a spotted mare; the owner took Wilford's horse, and James paid the difference in gold.

They camped a short distance down the river. "We're getting close to Oregon," Wilford said. "We should be there in another day if we don't have any delays," James mumbled a silent prayer. At last, his journey was nearing an end.

With the news that Oregon was close at hand, James thought sadly of his father and aunt back in Tennessee. Would he ever see them again? How long it seemed since he set out on this journey. He could hardly remember leaving Tennessee.

While staring into the flames, James reflected on himself and the man he had become. The war had humbled him, and life since that time had re-defined his character and his beliefs. The value of life and its uncertainty were clearer to him now. He had seen so many lives taken during the war. Fate was uncertain that he now understood. As a young man, he felt his comfort had been guaranteed by his station in life. But fate had turned on him and taken it all away.

His attitude toward people had changed. He owed his life to Wilford and too Little Deer and her people. He was indebted beyond his ability to repay them. There was no longer a place for arrogance in his life, but there was room for humility.

*   *   *

Little Deer became more talkative with Wilford. "What is it like in the lodges of the whites?" she asked.

"It is not so much different than the lodges of the Blackfeet," Wilford replied.

"I have a great fear of living in a strange world. I do not know their tongue or their ways. I fear they will have a great hatred of me."

"Not all the whites will feel that way," Wilford replied. "There are those with much kindness in their hearts. You will have to learn to recognize the ones with good intentions."

Wilford was trying to calm her fears, but he, too, had felt the sting of the white man's prejudices. He knew life would be difficult for the young woman.

*   *   *

The next morning, James rode beside Wilford while Little Deer rode behind, next to the packhorse. "How much time did you spend in Oregon?" James asked.

"Well, Noah and I used to spend time up there, but we had to be careful."

"Why was that?"

"They made a law up there that a Negro, even a free Negro, could not live in Oregon. For the most part, they didn't bother me since I was usually with Noah, but we had to be careful. Of course, when I was guiding wagon trains, I came through here several times. Since I was just passing through, folks didn't pay me any mind."

"You know anything about the Blue Mountains?" James asked.

"I rode through there with Noah, and the trail passed through there as well. There weren't many settlers living there at that time. Most of them went on over to the coast. I remember there was some nice country around the river that flowed between the Blues and the Wallowas."

"I believe my wife and children are somewhere around the Blue Mountains," James said.

"There are probably a few towns there now. If they're around there, we'll find 'em."

The river they followed wound through a large canyon. Beyond, there were high mountain peaks. Wilford kept a close eye on the rim of the canyon. "Good place to get trapped if there's trouble," he said.

Early in the afternoon, they emerged from the canyon and turned west. An hour later, Wilford stopped his horse. James and Little Deer stopped behind him. He took off his hat and looked around. "We're in Oregon now," he announced.

James said another silent prayer. His feelings alternated between joy and apprehension. There was joy in his heart from knowing Kate and the children were near. There was also apprehension about what state he might find them in. His homecoming in Tennessee had been heartbreaking. There was no guarantee this one would bring any better news. But he hoped with all his heart.

They spent the night camped beside a small stream. After eating, Wilford walked out into the early darkness, as was his usual routine. Little Deer had spread out her blanket and was already asleep. James sat beside the fire and continued his reflections. To the north were high mountains. He wished he could climb to the top of the tallest one and scan the countryside until he located his wife and children. He was still sitting by the fire with his contemplations when Wilford walked back into camp.

"A man never forgets country like this," Wilford said. "I've been gone for many years, but I never forget the look of a mountain or a clear stream or a big eagle circling overhead.

"Even that big grizzly that tried to claw us up the other night; it's all a part of this place, and you never forget it."

*   *   *

The next morning, they traveled north. "We better not get too far from the river 'cause the country along here is pretty dry," Wilford said. "The river is about the only source of water."

They reached the first settlement in Oregon that afternoon. It was just a small store, a stable, a blacksmith shop, and a few cabins. "We best have the horses reshod," Wilford said. "We don't want to risk them losing a shoe this close to where we're going."

While Little Deer went with Wilford to tend to the horses, James wandered into the small store. It was just a little place with an assortment of goods and a large stove in the middle. Next to the stove, two men with long beards and bushy hair wearing buckskin clothes were sitting in wooden chairs. They looked up at James and nodded as he entered.

Behind a wooden counter was a large man with long, dark hair wearing a patch over one eye? "You need something, mister?" he asked James.

"I could use some information."

"Don't sell much of that. What kind of information you lookin' for?"

"I'm looking for some people that moved up to the Blue Mountains over a year ago."

"Don't get up that way much myself." He pointed toward the men by the stove. "Those gents might be able to help you. They're trappers and have been up in that country. You know anything about that country up around the Blues, Jesse?"

One of the trappers looked over at James. "Few places up that way. Some minin' going on to the south. They's a place called Brown's Tavern over there close to the Blues. Weren't much else the last time I passed through?"

"You're behind," the other one said. "They call the place La Grande now. Got a courthouse and bunch of other businesses over there."

James bought a few supplies then went to find Wilford and Little Deer. He found the girl sitting on her horse in front of the blacksmith. Inside, Wilford was watching as a sweaty man put new shoes on his horse.

"Why doesn't she get down from her horse and rest for a time?" James asked.

"White folks make her nervous," Wilford replied.

Wilford went out and talked to her. She finally dismounted so they could shoe her horse. While the shoeing was going on, she stood in front, looking nervous.

"That squaw belong to you?" the sweaty blacksmith asked.

"The woman is traveling with us," James replied.

"She Shoshone?"

"Blackfoot," Wilford said.

"Blackfoot! You damn lucky she ain't lifted your hair by now. Those people are cold-blooded killers."

"Not this one," Wilford said.

They stood silently and watched until the horses were ready to travel. Then, they rode north out of the little settlement. After going only a couple of miles, Wilford stopped. "We may have some company."

"Who?" James asked.

"Some folks from town. I didn't like the looks of things."

James didn't understand what had raised Wilford's cautions, but he had come to respect the man's hunches. At times, Wilford seemed to have a sixth sense about things. "What are we going to do?"

"The best thing for us to do is try and draw them in before they get the jump on us."

"All right," James replied.

That evening, they stopped on a small rise that overlooked the river. "Let's build a big fire down at the base of the hill," Wilford said.

They went down to the river, found some cottonwoods, carried several limbs back, and built a large fire at the bottom of the hill. It was near dark when they got the fire going.

"That fire can be seen for a long distance at night," Wilford said.

They took up positions on the hill, wrapped themselves in blankets against the cool night air, and waited. Occasionally, Wilford would sneak back down the hill and throw more wood on the fire. James started to wonder if it was worth the effort when he heard voices in the darkness.

"This must be their camp." It sounded like the blacksmith.

"The squaw is mine," another voice said.

"Get that big black first," one of them yelled.

Five men rode into their camp with weapons drawn. It was the blacksmith, the storekeeper, the two trappers, and a young man they hadn't seen before.

"I see the fire, but I don't see anyone," the storekeeper said.

"You ain't looking in the right place!" Wilford yelled down.

One of them looked up. "They set a trap for us."

The blacksmith raised his rifle, but a warning round from Wilford's pistol caused him to drop his weapon. One of the trappers tried the same thing, but James got off a shot from the Henry that struck the ground near his horse. In the glow of the fire, the mounted men were easy targets.

"That's the last warning," Wilford said. "The next time, we'll shoot you off your horses."

The others dropped their weapons and put their hands in the air. "Hell, we didn't mean any harm," the young one said.

"Shut up, Orville!" the storekeeper yelled.

"Pa, they can shoot us down."

"The young man is talking sense," Wilford said. "It's like shooting fish in a rain barrel from up here."

James and Wilford eased down the hill with their weapons ready. James had the Henry, and Wilford now had James's shotgun.

"Get down off them horses," Wilford said. "It's going to be a long time before you gentlemen try to ambush anybody else."

The rest dismounted, but the storekeeper stayed in the saddle. "You best get down off that horse," Wilford warned. "If you don't, this shotgun will take you off in pieces."

The storekeeper glared at them then looked at the barrel of the shotgun. Deciding that a blast of shot from a close range wasn't worth the risk, he dismounted.

"You fellas take off your boots," Wilford commanded.

"The hell I will," the storekeeper said defiantly.

Wilford pushed the barrel of the shotgun up in the man's face. He looked at Wilford's eyes, again at the gun, and pulled off his boots. The rest of the group followed suit. "You gentlemen are going to have to hoof it back to where you came from," Wilford said. "We'll take your horses out a ways, then turn 'em loose. You ambushing bastards are gonna have to walk barefooted."

"I'll see you hung for this," the storekeeper said.

"Not likely," Wilford said. "You came out here to rob us and no tellin' what else. Next time you vermin will be more careful 'bout who you choose to mess with."

"Some of us can't walk that far," one of them complained.

"Then you'll have to stay here in camp until the rest of you catch up with your horses," Wilford replied. "We can't take a chance on leaving you any horses to come riding after us."

After taking the men's horses, weapons, and boots, they rode off under a barrage of swearing. For several miles, they rode before unsaddling the men's horses and turning them loose. "Take 'em some time to find these horses," Wilford said.

The sun was rising in the east when they stopped. "We should be far enough away so we can rest now," Wilford said.

They camped beside a dry creek bed. Wilford fried a skillet of bacon and brewed a pot of coffee. Little Deer was acquiring a taste for coffee, but she liked it cold. Before drinking, she set the cup down to cool. They slept until noon, then had a quick meal of salt pork before starting out again.

"Today, we should run into those mining camps we heard about," Wilford said. "I expect by late today or tomorrow we'll be close to the Grande Ronde. If your family is up in this area, we should find them soon."

His family—how comforting those words were to him. All the obstacles he had to overcome to get up here—now how worthwhile it seemed. *Lord, just let them be safe and sound.* That's all he could ask.

Chapter 32

Losing a Neighbor

Spring came to the valley and, with it, Kate's concerns about Covington. The old freighter had all winter to fume about the business he lost last fall. He would be worked up into a lather by now and seething with rage, she figured. Not only did he lose money, he had lost one of his holds over the settlers; he wasn't the only freighter around anymore. But one thing had not changed—the man was still just as dangerous; her meeting with the settlers took on a new urgency.

*   *   *

Early on a spring morning, Kate had Olaf hitch the buggy and drive her to La Grande. It was a beautiful day. A light breeze rustled the wild daisies and other flowers in the meadow and the leaves of the birch and pine trees. The surrounding mountain peaks were still crowned with white, a reminder of the winter just past.

Newborn colts were frolicking in the pasture while the mares grazed nearby. The earth had come to life and was renewing itself. "Spring is a beautiful time up here," Kate said as the buggy crossed the meadow.

"Yaw," Olaf said. "Every new spring, I'm reminded of it."

The melting winter snow left the road filled with mud puddles. Olaf avoided as many as possible, but there were too many. The horses' hooves splashed water and bits of mud on them. But Kate had become used to it; the paved roads of Tennessee were just a distant memory now.

Near the turnoff to Lawrence Granville's ranch, they saw a rider coming toward the main road. "Looks like someone is in a hurry," Olaf said.

Kate watched. "That's Ben Granville," she said. The young man gave them a quick wave and continued on down the main road toward La Grande.

"There must be some trouble out there, him being in such a hurry," Kate said.

"Yaw. Could be," Olaf replied.

On the outskirts of town, they met Doctor McBrighton on his horse, followed by Ben Granville. The two of them passed Kate and Olaf without taking notice. "Somebody is hurt or ill out there," Kate said. "We need to stop on the way back and see if we can be of any help."

Olaf nodded.

Kate had Olaf Park the buggy near the courthouse. He helped her down then she went into the Blue Mountain Times office and found Howard Klaspell at his desk. He stood up when she entered. "Mrs. McKane, so nice to see you again." He went around and pulled a wooden chair up next to the desk. "Please, have a seat."

"Thank you."

"What can I do for you?" he asked.

"Well, I need some help putting together a meeting of all the settlers. I don't know if any of them read your paper, but I would like to take out a notice describing what we plan to do. We started our own freight line last fall, and several of the settlers sold their grain directly to us. In that way, we legally avoided Covington."

"Yes, I heard about that. I also heard that Mr. Covington was very upset about the whole thing. I advise you to be very careful."

"Yes. I knew he would not be pleased, but at the same time, what we did was justified after seeing what he was trying to do."

"Oh, I agree. I'm on your side. It's just that I know Mr. Covington can be a very difficult man when he doesn't get what he wants."

"That's just something I will have to deal with."

"Just tell me what you want printed, and I can get it in next week's edition," Howard said.

"It's mainly for legal purposes," Kate said. "Many of the settlers can't even read or write, so they aren't likely to see anything that's printed in the paper. Some live so far out them rarely ever come to town."

Kate wrote out what she wanted to say in the article then gave it to Howard to look over. After getting his approval, she paid him and went back to where Olaf was waiting.

"Let's get over to the Granville ranch," she said.

They drove out of La Grande to the cutoff then turned toward Lawrence's ranch. When they were within sight of the house, they could see several horses and buggies in the front yard. "That doesn't look good," Kate said.

"Yaw," Olaf replied.

Olaf parked the buggy near the others. Kate jumped down and ran up to the house. Ben Granville was sitting on the end of the porch. "What happened?" Kate asked.

"It's my pa," he said. "The doc's in there with him, but it don't look so good. Doc said it was his heart."

Kate rushed into the house and encountered the doctor coming down the stairs. "How is Mr. Granville?" she asked.

The doctor shook his head. "His heart has been weak for some time. I tried to get him to slow down a little, but he never did. There was nothing I could do for him. Excuse me; I have to go and tell his son."

Kate's heart sank—a deep sadness fell over her. She had to push back the tears. It just didn't seem possible. Lawrence had seemed like such a vibrant man; although lonesome, he always seemed full of life. More than that, Lawrence Granville had been a good neighbor and a good friend. Without his help, they probably would never have gotten the freight business going. At times, she had been cold and distant to him, which now came back to haunt her. Tears again pushed into her eyes. Fighting back grief and guilt, Kate went outside and found the doctor and Ben Granville on the porch.

"I'm sorry, son," the doctor was saying. "His heart has been in bad shape for some time. It finally just played out. I wish I could have done more, but there was just nothing else I could do."

"Okay, Doc, thanks," the young man said before turning and walking away.

The doctor started toward his horse when he saw Kate standing on the porch. He looked at her for a minute. "Aren't you the lady who dragged me out in a storm last winter to tend a sick Indian boy?"

"Yes. The boy recovered and went home."

"Is that so?" The doctor left it at that and walked over to his horse. Feeling sad and hollow inside and struggling hard to accept what had happened, Kate walked around to the back of the house where several people were gathered. The news about Lawrence Granville had spread quickly. Ben was standing under the shade of a birch tree, talking to a large woman wearing a bright red dress.

"We're all going to miss him," the woman said. "Men like your father made this land a better place to live. He was a true gentleman and a good friend and neighbor."

Ben nodded. The tears were flowing down his cheeks.

Kate talked briefly with some of the people. A few were neighbors, and several were from La Grande. Later, she saw Ben still standing under the tree, now alone. She walked over to offer her condolences. "I'm so sorry. Your father was a good neighbor and business partner—a good man in all respects. He helped me out during a very difficult time, and I'm very grateful for that. If you need anything, please let me know."

With a voice choked with emotion, he replied, "Thank you, ma'am."

Kate's heart filled with pity. She reached out and gave the boy a big hug before walking back toward the buggy where Olaf was waiting. Another good man gone, so many in recent years, why did it have to be?

*   *   *

The following day, Kate attended Lawrence Granville's funeral. After the service, they buried him behind the ranch house next to the grave of his wife. Through it all, Kate was plagued by the thought she had not treated Lawrence as well as she might have, even after he helped her with the wagons and the harvest. He was a lonely man, looking to fill a void in his life. Now he was gone. *I guess at times; we just don't realize how fleeting life is*, she thought.

Chapter 33

La Grande

The day passed peacefully. There was no sign of the men who tried to ambush them or any other trouble. The land rose to a higher altitude. Wilford rode up to James's side. "As I recall, there is a plateau between the Blue and the Wallowa mountains," he said.

"I just hope Kate is up here somewhere," James replied.

That afternoon, they reached a river flowing high from the spring thaws. "This is the Powder River," Wilford said. "The trouble is, we're gonna have to find a place to cross; it ain't gonna be easy with all the water that's coming down."

They decided to camp for the night and try to cross in the morning. As he lay in his blankets, James found it hard to sleep. The realization that his journey was nearly over was overwhelming him, filling him with anticipation and worry. He realized he had been on the trail for almost a year. Now, at last, the fruits of his efforts were near at hand.

*   *   *

The next morning, they set out again to find a suitable place to cross the river. It didn't look promising. The high water created an almost insurmountable barrier. "No chance to cross here," Wilford said. "Let's ride on up and see if there's a town on this side. If there is, there might be a bridge."

They never found a bridge, but late that afternoon, they found a place to ford the river. The channel at this point was wide and not too deep, but the horses were skittish in the muddy water. "The Oregon trail crossed this river at the same point," Wilford pointed out.

They camped that night beside the river. James's anticipation continued to rise.

*   *   *

The following morning, they broke camp and started out early, swinging around the mining camps and continuing on north, following a well-marked road. "This may lead to a town," Wilford said.

They followed the road for a few miles until it merged into another well-used road marked with horse and wagon tracks. "Seems like a lot of folks been using this road, so it should take us somewhere," Wilford said.

The road took them to a town with a group of tents on the outskirts. The people stood and stared at them as they passed. Not a very friendly place, James concluded. The town itself wasn't any better. There, they caught the attention of those on the street and sidewalks.

There was a two-story building just off the main street. Being the largest building in town, James figured it might be a place of importance where he could get some information. "You and Little Deer wait for me," he said. "I'm going over to that building to see what I can find out."

James tied his horse in front of the building. On the front door was a sign that read:

UNION COUNTY COURTHOUSE - Dedicated 1864

No better place than this, he concluded. He pushed open the door and stepped into a narrow hallway that divided the bottom floor. He started down the hallway as a door opened, and a frail young man wearing a striped suit and horn-rimmed glass stepped out. "Can I help you, sir?" the man asked.

"I hope so," James replied. "I'm looking for a man named Lewis Harrington. I was told he might live in this area."

"I'm sorry, but I'm afraid you're a little late. Mr. Harrington was killed last year under some rather unusual circumstances."

James's heart filled with fear. "Killed!" Another heartbreaking homecoming he now expected. "Was there a young lady and three children with him?"

"Yes, sir. His property now belongs to a young lady who moved up here from somewhere down south. Tennessee, I think."

"Dark-haired lady?"

"Yes. That's Mrs. McKane, Mr. Harrington's niece. By the way, my name is Howard Klaspell."

Some hope arose. James offered his hand. "Hello, my name is James McKane."

"McKane. Are you a relative of Kate's?"

"That I am. I am her husband."

The young man looked confused. "I was led to believe her husband was killed in the war."

"A false report, my friend. I didn't get back to Tennessee in time to set things straight. When I got back, Kate and the children were already gone. I've been trying to get here ever since."

"Wow! Kate will be in for a surprise."

"Can you tell me where to find her?"

"Yes, sir. Come into my office, and I'll draw you a map out to her farm."

As James left the courthouse to find Wilford and Little Deer, he was hardly cognizant of anything around him. The moment was at hand, and he didn't even know what he would say to his family. Would they remember him? Kate would; how could she not? Well, five years is a long time; maybe they all had forgotten him. Maybe they didn't even want him around anymore. He admonished himself for such thoughts; he had risked everything for this moment, so no need to throw it away on foolish notions.

Chapter 34

The Reunion

With spring at hand, Kate set about arranging a meeting with the settlers. Buoyed by the success of their freight line, she felt she could convince more of them to throw in with her. They had been up to the task last fall, giving her the needed confidence to move forward. Those from last year would surely be on board, and maybe now more would join in, giving them needed leverage against Covington. During breakfast, she discussed it with Olaf.

"That will take us some time, and we have to be getting ready for spring planting," he said.

"I know it's a busy time," Kate replied. "On the other hand, our future may depend on this meeting."

"All right, missy. I've got some hired hands coming out from La Grande to help with the planting. I'll tell them what needs to be done."

"Thanks!"

"You know, missy, it would be faster if we had some riders on horseback that could spread out across the valley."

"Who could we get?" Kate asked.

"I'll go and talk to some of the neighbors, like Mr. Grigg. That'll get the job done quicker."

Last year, Hiram had been of tremendous help talking to the settlers. He knew them, came from the same background as them, and they would be inclined to trust him. The problem was he had a crop to get in the ground just like the rest of them. But it was worth a try. "Yes, that would be a good idea," she said. "If Hiram or any of them have the time, that is."

*   *   *

The next day, Olaf, with the help of Hiram Grigg and some other neighbors, started out for the homesteads. As they rode off, Kate said a prayer for their safe return. The wheels had been set in motion; they were going forward. *If only Uncle Lewis could share in this*, she thought.

*   *   *

Olaf returned at the end of the week. "The word is out," he said. "They will all meet at the Worth farm ten days from today."

He explained they had chosen the Worth farm because it was in a central location. That would cut down on travel time, and the settlers would lose less time from their work.

What a relief, Kate said to herself. Maybe now she could get a permanent agreement with enough of the settlers to further break Covington's hold over them. But there would be doubters among them—that worried her. Would her powers of persuasion be enough to swing the skeptics over to her side? Alas, nothing ever seemed to come easy.

She put the meeting aside to enjoy the spring day. White clouds floated in the sky against the backdrop of the mountains. Wild-flowers were sprinkled about the meadow. A group of riders turned in off the road. Palmer! She watched. There were three in the group. "Olaf, can you come out, please?"

When Olaf stepped out on the porch, Kate pointed out the riders to him. "Probably just somebody lost or maybe wanting some water for their horses."

The three rode slowly up to the gate. As they approached, the one in the lead drew her attention. Her eyes fixed on him. There was something eerily familiar about him. Who was he? What were these people doing here? She took her eyes off the lead rider long enough to take a quick look at the other two. One was a woman. Her gaze went back to the leader. *Who are you?* she wondered.

The riders looked apprehensive. They stopped just inside the gate and stared at the house.

Now that they were close, Kate studied them. The one in front had a scraggly beard that covered much of his face. There was such a familiarity about him: the way he rode, the way he sat in the saddle. The one in the middle was a Negro, the first she had seen since Tennessee. The woman was an Indian.

The Negro leaned forward and said something to the one in the lead, urging him to ride up to the house. The man looked her way, then urged his horse slowly forward until he was only a few feet from the porch. Kate fixed her eyes on the man's face. The beard covered so much of it, but there was something about him…but what?

Her knees went weak. Buried emotions were surfacing. The man was now reminding her of her late husband, James. Fate had decided to play a cruel trick on her; that's what this was.

The man looked at her. "Is that you, Kate?"

Kate's head started to spin. The man not only looked like James, but he sounded like him as well.

He paused for her answer. None came forth, so he dismounted and walked up to the porch steps. "Kate, don't you recognize me?"

The porch was spinning. Or was it her? This man looked like James, sounded like James. What kind of cruel joke was this? Hadn't she suffered enough? He was coming up the steps now with his hand extended. "Kate, it's me, James."

Everything went out of control. The walls of the house, the blue spring sky, and the distant mountain peaks were all spinning. Then she slowly collapsed on the porch.

Olaf rushed forward. "What's going on here, mister?" He reached down to pick her up. Helga had heard the commotion and was standing in the doorway when Kate fell. She joined Olaf to help get Kate on her feet.

The stranger tried to reach Kate, but Olaf blocked his way. "I'm her husband," the man said.

"Her husband is dead, killed in the war," Helga said.

"That was a mistake," he replied. "By the time I got back to Tennessee, Kate was gone. I've been trying to get here ever since."

But Olaf wasn't convinced. He turned his back to the stranger and helped Helga get Kate into the house. "Put her on the settee," Helga said.

They laid Kate down on the settee. This time, the man would not be denied. Olaf relented and stepped back but kept his eyes on this stranger claiming to be Kate's husband. Helga came out from the kitchen with a jar in her hand. "This will bring her back out of it," she said as she opened the jar and held it under Kate's nose.

Kate opened her eyes. When she looked up and saw the man standing next to her, she started to lapse into unconsciousness again. Maybe she was dead and was meeting her husband again. Another whiff from the jar woke her. The man was now kneeling beside her.

"Kate, it's really me. That was a terrible mistake about me being killed. By the time I got back to the plantation, you and the children were gone. I've been making my way across the country ever since, trying to find you."

James. Could it be possible he really was here in the flesh? She took a close look. He was thin, even gaunt, but it looked so much like him. She touched his face. "Is it really you?"

"Yes, darling it is," he said as he reached down and embraced her.

It was a day she never expected to come. Her head was light; perhaps this was all just a dream. No, she didn't think it was. It all looked to be real; the gaunt man beside her was really her husband back from the dead. Well, no, he had explained that. He had never been dead. She gathered up her strength and sat up on the settee. "Helga, can you please call the children inside? They need to meet their father."

Helga disappeared out the front door and soon reappeared with the three children following her. They stood back and looked curiously at the man in the room.

Kate stood up and called them over to her. "This is your father."

Drew looked up at James. "Are you really my daddy?"

"Yes, Son, I am." James reached down, picked up the young boy, and held him in his arms, taking his first look as his youngest child. While he was holding Drew, Alice walked up to him.

"Daughter, you're the image of your mother." James reached down and embraced his daughter with his other arm.

While James was being reunited with his youngest children, James Junior stood by the door, watching and not saying a word.

Kate looked over at him. "Son, this is your father. I know you remember him. Come on over and greet him." James Junior walked slowly over and stuck out his hand.

"This calls for more than a handshake," James said as he put down Drew, then reached out and grabbed his oldest son.

*   *   *

James was so carried away with his family reunion; he temporarily forgot Wilford and Little Deer. "Kate, there are two people waiting out in the yard who we owe a debt of gratitude. If it had not been for them, you really would be a widow now."

With Kate following behind, James stepped out on the porch and motioned for Wilford and Little Deer to come into the house. They did not respond. Instead, they continued to sit on their horses.

James realized they probably felt uncomfortable, but he motioned again. "Come on in the house!" he yelled.

Wilford and Little Deer reluctantly got down and walked toward the house. When they were up on the porch, Kate held the door open. "Please, come in," she said.

When they were inside, Wilford took off his hat and stood by the door. Little Deer stood next to him, looking bewildered by the strange surroundings.

"From what my husband has told me, I owe a great deal to both of you," Kate said. "All I can say is, thank you from the bottom of my heart."

343

Wilford nodded, then translated to Little Deer what Kate had said. She listened but remained passively silent.

*　　*　　*

Little Deer was unaware of what was going on in the strange dwelling of the whites. Wilford explained that the young woman with the dark hair was James's wife, who he had not seen in a long time. She nodded at Wilford's explanation. *So sad*, she thought. *It must be a lonely life for these white men. They have only one wife to take care of them.*

*　　*　　*

Helga appeared in the room. "Come to the table, everyone. This is a joyous time for all of us; let's eat and celebrate."

James had to urge Wilford and Little Deer to join in. He prodded them until they relented and followed them to the large table. When they were all seated, Helga looked at Olaf. "I think a special blessing is in order for this occasion."

"I don't know if I'm up to it or not, but I will try." He raised his arms upward. "Almighty God, we thank you for reuniting this man and this woman and for returning the children's father. Amen."

Throughout the meal, Kate kept looking at James. Was it really him and not some illusion? She never expected this day to come. Well, fate moved in mysterious ways, she knew. The grief she had felt at the news of his death, the long hours shut away from everything coming to terms with her loss it now seemed so unfair. The tears came, and she wiped them away. He was back; only tears of joy would be allowed today.

After eating, Kate and James walked around the farmstead. She explained through tear-filled eyes about the death of Uncle Lewis and her attempts to get justice. She explained in great detail the problems they were having with E. G. Covington and her upcoming meeting with the settlers.

In turn, James explained about the situation in Clarksville, the death of his mother, and the health of his father.

Kate was saddened to hear about the problems of James's family. She had never gotten along with them, but she was sad for James, for the loss and sorrow he felt. He also told her about his meeting with her father in Palmyra and the death of her brother in the war. Kate knew about her brother's death, but rehearing the news made her heartsick.

Now that she knew her father was living in Palmyra, Kate vowed to write him. The letters she had mailed to Clarksville went unanswered, but now she could renew family ties.

At the house, Kate found a razor that had belonged to Uncle Lewis. She also got out some of her uncle's clothes. They were not a very good fit but were an improvement over James's trail clothes.

*   *   *

That evening, Wilford got out his bedroll and was preparing to sleep on the ground. "We'll make room for you in the house," James said.

Wilford resisted the idea. White people's houses made him uncomfortable; he preferred to sleep outside, anyway. The weather was warm, and he felt at home sleeping under the stars. James continued to insist. They settled the issue by arranging for him to use a spare room in Olaf's and Helga's quarters that had a private door allowing him to come and go without disturbing the others.

*   *   *

After listening to James explain how the Blackfeet had saved he and Wilford during the winter, Helga took in Little Deer. The big woman's reassurances didn't lift Little Deer's feeling of despair. The customs of the whites confused her, left her feeling lonely and out of place. She thought of her white grandfather but took no comfort from it.

The big white woman took her gently by the arm. "Don't worry, child; I'll take care of you and help you learn English. I did not know a word when I arrived here, but you can learn just as I did."

Little Deer did not understand the white woman's words but sensed she had a kind heart. But in the husband of the white woman, she sensed a deep hatred.

*   *   *

That night, as James and Kate lay in each other's arms, they talked again about the problems she had been having and her plan for dealing with them.

"I've been filled with fear ever since I found out about the situation Uncle Lewis was in," she said.

"It sounds like you're a real fighter. Starting a freight business up here on the frontier took real strength and courage."

Kate often felt her strength and courage slipping away, but with James back in her life, things would be better.

*   *   *

The next morning at breakfast, they talked about the upcoming settler's meeting. "From what I'm hearing about this Covington fella, I doubt he's going to take very kindly to what you are doing," James said. "Taking away his freight business and blocking his attempts to take away the settler's land is not going to make you very popular with him."

"You can count on that," Kate replied. "You should meet some of his associates who have already been around trying to make life miserable for us."

After breakfast, James and Wilford walked out to the front yard. "I guess I'll be collecting the rest of my money so I can get started back through the Rockies before the snows hit again," Wilford said. "Summers are short up here. I don't want to spend another winter holed up in the mountains somewhere."

"I have the rest of the gold to pay for your services. If you're agreeable, I'd like to ask one more thing from you before you go."

"What would that be?"

"It looks like there's going to be some trouble up here with this Covington I keep hearing about. If that happens, we're going to need some help."

Wilford looked down as if in thought. "I reckon I'm not really a gunman. I can guide you through the mountains or run a trap line and most of the other things a mountain man knows, but I'm just not a gunman."

"I saw you in some pretty serious situations out there, and you always seemed to know what to do."

"I guess I can think on it a day or two."

*   *   *

Afterward, Wilford sat on the porch and thought about what James was asking. He enjoyed being back in the mountains again, and spending a little time here would be pleasant, but at the same time, he didn't like getting mixed up in white people's disagreements. He had kept his end of the agreement by getting James to Oregon and finding his family. It was best that he get on his way back home.

Wilford sat there for a time, looking toward the peaks of the Blue Mountains and the green forests, remembering the good life he had enjoyed as a mountain man, a way of life that he now missed. It compelled him and reached out to him.

*   *   *

O laf continued to keep his distance from Little Deer. He never acknowledged her presence in any manner. Helga, although she talked in a strange tongue, radiated kindness and understanding. She tried to teach her some of the white words. Often, she would point at the fire box where they cooked their food and say "stove." She did this with other things in and around the lodge.

Helga gave Little Deer a bed she found uncomfortable. It was too soft for her liking. She missed the teepee and the large bearskins she was accustomed to sleeping on. She removed the quilts from the bed and spread them on the floor, more to her pleasure.

*   *   *

W hen Helga noticed Little Deer was sleeping on the floor, she mentioned it to Olaf. His reply was something to the effect that these people didn't have the knack for civilized living; his remarks earned him a sharp rebuke. "Give the girl some time," Helga said.

To help her teach Little Deer English, Helga had Wilford teach her a few Blackfoot words so the two of them could better communicate. It worked out well, and in a week, the girl knew a few words. It was a start toward learning the ways of the whites, but it would not be an easy road.

Chapter 35

The Meeting

Kate asked James to come with her to the settler's meeting. She needed him for strength and moral support. They decided to bring Helga along to help cook for the expected crowd. Olaf declined, pointing out he was needed for spring planting. This year, they were planting both potatoes and grain, requiring more work.

Wilford took a heavy burden off James by agreeing to stay around until they were back from the meeting.

They packed the buggy and set out with Helga and the children for the Worth farm. The trip gave James his first real chance to explore the valley. He liked what he saw. The land lying between the mountains looked fertile. He understood why Lewis Harrington had chosen to live up here.

Hiram and Nancy Grigg were waiting at their farm. Hiram had made enough money from his grain crop to buy a small wagon. They trailed along behind the buggy. In an hour, they reached the Worth farm. The yard was filled with wagons, buggies, saddle horses, and some people that probably came on foot. Children were chasing each other around the yard. On one side of the cabin, a group of men were engaged in a game of horseshoes. On the other side, several women were cooking over a campfire.

The children joined in the play while James, Kate, and Helga made their way through the crowd, stopping to chat briefly with some of the people. Most remembered Kate from the trip up from Missouri but were confused about James. "I thought you were a widow," one woman said.

Kate smiled. "So did I."

James helped Kate and Helga carry the food they brought over to a large table, and then he joined a group of men under the shade of a small birch tree. Kate and Helga joined the women cooking the meal. Just before noon, Kate was informed that all the settlers were present.

With James's help, she climbed up on the bed of a wagon parked near the cabin. The crowd made her nervous. Her knees trembled. She had never spoken to a large group before, and it scared her. The assembled settlers were looking at her with anticipation on their faces. Hope, they were looking to her for some hope. Could she deliver? James smiled at her; her concerns abated a notch. She cleared her throat and started speaking.

"I know that most of you are aware of the problems we are having with E. G. Covington and his freight agreement. That is why we started our own freight company last fall so we could get around what he was trying to do to all of us. It was also why we bought crops from some of you in the field and shipped them to market in our own wagons. Those who went along with us know that, for the most part, it went well. We plan to continue doing what we did last fall. It is a legal way to keep Covington from driving you out of business with ridiculous freight rates and taking over your land."

Some of the people were stirring nervously. Kate felt a lump form in her throat, and her knees shook—some of them were not convinced. They had come up here with nothing; they were far from their roots and scared.

"The problems with Covington are not over," she continued. "I know he's obtained a lien against some of you. You will lose your land if you can't meet the terms of the loan. The interest on the notes he persuaded you to sign is very high."

This caused some mumbling from the crowd.

"My uncle was not aware of Covington's plan. When he found out what Covington was doing, he tried to stop him. I think he was killed for that very reason."

"Was this Covington's idea, or were both of them in on it?" a voice yelled.

"It was not Uncle Lewis's idea," Kate said. "He didn't know Covington changed the wording in the freight agreements. He didn't know Covington was going to try and cheat you out of your land with trickily worded loan proposals."

"If Covington's got a lien we can't pay, what we can do?" a man asked.

"That's a hard choice, I'm afraid. The only thing to do is try to avoid getting into his debt. For those of you who didn't take any loans, you just have to worry about the high freight rates for hauling your crops to market. I just explained we have a way to deal with that. For those who have made notes with him, we're trying to find some way to fight back. That's all I can promise right now."

"Looks like he's got some of us over a barrel!" someone yelled.

"Not necessarily," Kate replied. "We're looking into all this and trying to find a legal way to stop what he's doing. We've all known hard times, so don't give up without a fight."

"That's a pretty fix," a man said. "I've been breaking my back trying to get this farm going. Now I stand to be swindled out of it by this shyster."

"I understand your feelings," Kate replied. "We're attacking this thing from every possible way to get around Covington and his scheme."

"I don't see what good it's going to do!" a settler yelled.

"I don't like it," another said. "I didn't come all the way up here from Missouri to be faced with something like this."

Hiram Grigg stood up before the crowd. "I'd like to say something. I believe Mrs. McKane, and I believed her uncle. Mr. Harrington went to a great deal of trouble and spent a lot of money to set all this up. I lost everything in the war. Mr. Harrington gave me hope of a new life up here. I stand behind Mrs. McKane and what she wants to do. She is my neighbor, and so was her uncle. I know they're good people."

A few people in the crowd echoed Hiram Grigg's sentiments. "She's the best hope we got," someone said.

"I hope she don't try to cheat us, too," a young man said.

"We've got a good chance to beat him," Kate said. "Our freight line will take away much of the leverage he had against us."

"How in the hell can you be so sure?" a voice yelled from the crowd.

"Because it worked well last year," Kate replied. "We will continue to buy your crops in the field. That will allow you to bypass the freight agreement with Covington and get your crops to market. Even those of you who took loans from him will have a better chance now. One of the ways he planned to drive you from your land was to get you indebted to him with high freight rates. By not using his services, you're preventing him from doing that. There's still the matter of the high interest on the loans. We're still working on that issue. If you stick with us, let us buy your crops, and stay with the plan that Uncle Lewis had in mind, you've all got a chance."

A little optimism was coming Kate's way. The crowd settled down a bit. She felt she was winning most of them over. Hiram Grigg had helped sway a number of the doubters. She restated her promise that Harrington Farms would continue to provide the support Uncle Lewis had promised. When all but two or three agreed to give it a try, she felt her mission was accomplished.

James helped her down from the wagon. "You handled that very well. You'd make a great politician."

"If women ever get the right to vote, I might take it up. Anyway, I'm exhausted."

"I have to hand it to you, dear; you won over most of them. I think even the ones who didn't go along for now will eventually come over."

The women served a meal of pot roast and stew topped off with pies and other pastries.

By the time the meal was over, and everything cleaned, James and Kate decided it was too late to drive back home that evening. They camped at the Worth farm. The two of them slept in back of the buggy while Helga and the children spent the night in the cabin with the Worth family.

"The worst is yet to come," Kate said as they prepared to settle down. "We've still got Covington to deal with and the matter of keeping the freight line going."

"I'm going to help you with that," James replied.

Those were the most comforting words Kate had ever heard. With James back in her life, things would be different.

Chapter 36

The Retaliation

Wilford had no appreciation for the farm. It was, after all, farms and farmers that had helped bring his old life to an end. They plowed up the ground and built towns. But that was the way of things, he guessed. After the rest of them left for the settler's meeting, he decided to ride up into the mountains. "I want to see some of the country I used to know. I'll be back by tomorrow," he explained to Little Deer.

Little Deer watched him ride across the meadow and turn toward the mountains.

*   *   *

Olaf spent his days in the fields with the hired men from La Grande. He was annoyed at his wife for spending so much time with the Indian girl. What was it with these Indians anyway? Of late, they had been overrun with them. This past winter, Indians had been in the house over a month. Worse, he had to risk his life out in a blizzard getting the doctor for a sick Indian boy.

It wasn't his usual nature to carry grudges, but the very sight of an Indian reminded him of the charred body of the man who had taken him in when he arrived from Sweden. He could never get it out of his mind.

*   *   *

Little Deer enjoyed a chance to be alone. She was having a hard time getting used to the whites. The white woman they called Helga was patiently trying to help her learn her new life, but she missed her own people. Life with the Blackfeet was hard, especially for the women. It was the lot of a Blackfoot woman to spend her life waiting on a man hand and foot. Worse, some of the

Blackfeet men were mean to their wives, even beating them. Despite the hardships, she still longed for her people.

By now, she was familiar with the white people's routines. When the white man came back in the evening, he expected to be fed. With the white woman gone, it was up to her to prepare his food. Before leaving, Helga had cooked some meat. But it was cold. As she had observed, the white man would want it warm. What would she do? Little Deer had trouble with the fire box they called a stove. Helga had tried to explain it to her, but she had trouble understanding the big woman's tongue.

Still, she was resourceful. She had her Indian ways. In the backyard was a birch tree with several dead limbs. Using the limbs, she built a fire. Then, she filled a large pot with water and heated it over the flames. A few minutes submerged in the hot water, and the meat was ready. The man would want bread with the meat, and there was a loaf in the kitchen. She wrapped the bread in cloth, then buried it next to the fire and covered it with hot coals. In a few minutes, it was warm.

*   *   *

It was dark when Olaf arrived from the fields, surprised to see a warm meal waiting for him. Little Deer had placed the food on the table then gone into another room to wait while he ate.

After eating, he walked into the room and mumbled a soft "thank you." It was the first time he ever attempted to speak to her. She didn't understand the words, but this time they carried no hatred.

*   *   *

The riders waited across the meadow until darkness then rode up to the house. "I see some lights in the big house, but I don't see any down at the smaller place," one of them said.

"Never mind about that," the leader replied. "We'll burn both places to the ground. If anybody comes out of either house, shoot 'em down."

Two of the riders held up torches. Another struck some matches and lit the torches. The flames illuminated their faces. One was a young man with bushy blond hair, not much more than a boy, the other an older man with a ruddy face and stringy dark hair. When they were ready, the dark-haired one motioned for them to get to their business.

One of the men rode up to the main house and tossed a torch through a window. "Get one in that other house," the dark-haired man said.

The other rider took his torch, rode down to the other house, and tossed it through a window. "Take up positions around both houses. Don't let anyone out alive!" the leader yelled.

*   *   *

Olaf had got up to go to his own quarters when the torch came through the window. Enraged, he grabbed his shotgun and started toward the door. By golly, they wouldn't get away with this, he swore to himself. He pushed the front door open; a rifle flashed from across the yard, knocking him back into the house.

*   *   *

The shot had come from outside, Little Deer thought. There was a moan from the big room. She hurried through the door of the little side room into a cloud of smoke that left her struggling to breathe. Through eyes burning from the smoke, she saw the white man in front of the open door. She got down on her hands and knees and crawled over to him. Blood covered the front of his shirt, but he was alive.

Little Deer grabbed his arms and started pulling him toward the door. He opened his eyes and moaned, "No, no, they'll shoot you, too."

The only word she understood was "no." It seemed he didn't want her to take him outside. There was danger there. But they couldn't stay in here. She thought. The white woman had showed her a room below ground a cellar; she called it where they stored food. There was a door in the room where they cooked that led down into it. First, she had to get the man past the flames.

Fortunately, the flames were away from the door into the other room. Little Deer stayed low and pulled the big man across the floor. It took much of her strength to get him into the kitchen and over to the cellar. The door was heavy. She strained and was about to give up when it started to move. Using all the strength she could muster, Little Deer pushed the heavy door upward until there was enough opening to crawl inside.

Little Deer got the man around the waist and pulled him down the stairs, then went back, pulled down the heavy door, and latched it from the inside.

Could they breathe in the cellar? Little Deer remembered around the campfires of her people that smoke rose. Maybe that would keep it out of the cellar.

Some smoke did make its way into the cellar. But the ventilation shaft at the other end let in enough fresh air for them to breathe.

She turned her attention to the white man. The front of his shirt was covered with blood; he was still bleeding heavily. Her only chance to keep him alive was to stop the blood flow. There was nothing in the cellar to put on the wound. She tore off a portion of her skirt, placed it over the wound, and pressed it down with her hand. He moaned and groaned.

For most of the night Little Deer pressed rags against the wound. When the bleeding finally stopped, she drifted off into an exhausted sleep.

*   *   *

The next morning, Little Deer was awakened by someone pounding on the cellar door, calling out in her tongue. At first, she was too scared to open the latch. Her mind cleared, and she realized it must be Wilford. She unlatched the door. It swung open, and Wilford was standing in what had been the kitchen. "What happened here?" he asked.

Little Deer quickly explained. Wilford came down into the cellar and carried the white man out into the yard, and laid him on the ground. When he tore open the man's shirt, there was a large wound in his chest very near his heart. Another inch over, and the man would have been killed.

"He's still alive," Wilford said. "We've got to get him out of here. I'm going to get one of the wagons hitched while you keep an eye on him."

While waiting, Little Deer looked over what had been the white people's home. Both of the houses had been reduced to smoldering ruins. All that remained intact were the fireplaces, standing as lonely survivors over the ashes and debris. Looking at the remains of the houses brought painful memories. While just a small child, she had experienced her village being burned by the Crows.

Wilford drove up in one of the wagons. They loaded Olaf into the back. "Looks like you saved his life," Wilford said. "He would have bled to death if you hadn't stayed with him and tended the wound."

Knowing the white man's hatred of her, Little Deer wondered how he would feel, knowing she had saved his life. Her people believed that when someone saved your life, you were indebted to that person until you saved their life in return. She feared this man would not be happy, knowing that he was indebted to her. On the other hand, whites had different beliefs. Maybe he would not worry about such a thing.

Wilford found some rags in his saddlebags to bandage Olaf's wound. "We got to get him to a doctor," he said. He drove the wagon, and Little Deer stayed in the back, watching in case the wound started bleeding again. With each bump, a low moan would come from Olaf's throat.

People on the sidewalks stared at them as they drove into town. "There's a man in back who needs a doctor!" Wilford shouted.

"Behind the courthouse!" a man on the sidewalk yelled.

The doctor's office was located in a small, wood frame building behind the courthouse. Wilford parked the wagon by the door, jumped down, and got Olaf up. With Little Deer following, he carried him to the office and pounded on the door. It opened. Wilford carried Olaf inside and laid him on a large table in the middle of the room. Aside from the table, the doctor's office consisted of a bed covered with a blue bedspread next to the south window. Along the north wall were a series of cabinets with glass doors, most filled with jars. On the wall behind the doctor's cluttered desk was a large chart with a detailed outline of the human body. "Man's been shot," Wilford said.

The doctor took up a position next to the table. "You two wait outside while I look him over," he said.

Wilford was annoyed by the doctor's attitude, but it was to be expected. He went back outside with Little Deer following. They both took a seat in the wagon bed and waited. A few of the townspeople had gathered nearby, curious about what had happened. Wilford gave them no explanation and no attention at all.

A half-hour later, the doctor came out. "That man is very lucky to be alive. Somebody did a good job by stopping the flow of blood, or he would have died."

Wilford pointed at Little Deer. "The credit goes to her."

The doctor gave her a slight frown. "You best leave him here for a time. He'll need constant tending until he gets his strength back. I believe this man and his wife work for that McKane woman Lewis Harrington brought up here."

"That's him," Wilford said.

"Who are you two?" the doctor asked. "Did one of you shoot him?"

"No," Wilford said with anger in his voice. "Somebody attacked the farm last night and burned both houses to the ground."

"They've been having trouble out there for some time," the doctor said. "You two can go on now. After I finish tending to him, I'll get word to the sheriff about what happened."

The doctor's callous treatment of him and Little Deer ate at Wilford. He fumed until they were out of town, and he could get his mind clear. Enough about it; there were more pressing matters to worry about. Olaf would live; that was the most important thing. Now, he had to get word to the others.

Wilford helped Little Deer fashion a temporary shelter in what remained of the barn. Then, he got his horse from the corral. James, Kate, the kids, and Helga would be returning today. He wanted to ride out and get them prepared for what had happened to ease the shock a bit.

After a two-hour ride, Wilford spotted the buggy in the distance.

*   *   *

James saw Wilford riding toward them. Something was amiss. He tapped the horse on the flank. When they were even, Wilford reined in his horse; James stopped the buggy. "There was trouble at the house last night," Wilford said. "Somebody set fire to both houses, and Mr. Olaf has been shot."

Helga gave a start. "Oh my God! Where is he?"

"He's with the doctor in town. He's alive, thanks mostly to Little Deer, who stayed with him the entire night and kept him from bleeding to death. I'm sorry about your houses. They ain't much left except ashes."

Kate had to fight back the tears of rage and sorrow. "They didn't wait long to strike back," she said. "This is Covington's work, or Palmer working for him."

"I'm going back to the farm," Wilford said. "Little Deer is there alone. And I want to see if I can pick up the tracks of the people who burned your houses. Maybe if I had stayed around last night instead of riding up into the mountains, I could have stopped them."

"Wasn't your fight," James replied. "Besides, you might have got shot, just like Olaf. We appreciate everything you and Little Deer did to help us."

"I want to go to La Grande and see about Olaf," Helga said.

"Of course," James said. He turned the buggy around, and they started toward La Grande while Wilford rode back toward the farmstead. When they reached town, Helga directed him to the doctor's office. When James stopped the buggy, she jumped down and ran toward the office, tears streaming down her broad face. Inside, she found Olaf lying on a bed near the window being tended by a young lady with long, dark hair and wearing a white apron.

The doctor got up from his desk when Helga entered with Kate and James following. "You this man's wife?"

"Yes. I pray that he will be all right."

"He'll be laid up for a time, but he's in good hands with Ingrid. She's a great nurse and will take good care of him."

A look of relief spread across Helga's face. She walked over and looked down at her husband. He was asleep, so she went over to Kate and James, who were now in the office. "I'm going to stay here with Olaf. This young lady is a fine nurse, I'm sure, but I've been tending to this man for a long time. Nobody knows him like I do."

Kate gave Helga an embrace. "We'll all hope and pray he'll be all right," Kate said. "We'll come back and check on you from time to time."

The doctor protested, but Helga held her ground until he relented and let her stay.

James and Kate left Helga with her husband and started back toward the farm. He placed his hand over Kate's and tried to be reassuring but knew he was coming up short. Wilford's description left no doubt what they would find, and through it all, the children sat in the back and said nothing.

From the meadow, they got their first look at the destruction. Kate's heart sank. Their home, the one Uncle Lewis had worked on for a year, had been destroyed in one night. "Uncle Lewis worked hard to build this place. Now it's been destroyed by a bunch of greedy, ruthless men," she fumed.

James put his arm around her and said, "What was built can be rebuilt. The spirit that built this place out of nothing but raw wilderness cannot be defeated by this wanton act of violence. We just need to be thankful that no one was killed."

"You're right about that," she said softly.

"You know, Kate, as I watched you talking to the settlers yesterday and hearing about how you put together that freight line last fall, I think there's a lot of your uncle's spirit in you."

"I don't know," she sighed. "I try to stay strong, but it's so hard when things like this keep happening."

"I know," he said. "I spent four long years trying to survive the war. I know what a struggle it can be. We've got to stay strong."

James remembered the strength of his own family, his father's determination to stand up and be strong the day of his departure. Now, he would need his father's strength to help Kate through this ordeal.

"You know, the motive behind this was to get rid of the people they see as their enemies, people who can thwart their plans," Kate said. "Fortunately for us, they happened to choose a night most of us were gone. When they find out, they'll be back again."

*   *   *

They spent the night in what remained of the barn, sleeping on makeshift beds. After the war and spending so many nights sleeping on the ground during his trip to Oregon, James was accustomed to such accommodations. That aside, he felt his family's suffering and hated to see them reduced to living so crudely.

*   *   *

The next morning, they prepared breakfast over a campfire James built in the yard. All they had to cook was a ham they found in the cellar. Their flour, coffee, and other food had been destroyed.

After breakfast, James was standing out in the yard talking to Wilford, who had just returned from his tracking mission. When he looked across the meadow, he saw a large contingent coming toward them. "They're coming back," James said.

"I don't think so," Wilford replied.

A large number of settlers descended on their front yard. Their neighbor, Mr. Grigg, was leading the group. "We heard what happened. We're here to help you rebuild your house," Hiram said. "There'll be more arriving shortly."

Within an hour, fifteen families had arrived, many carrying saws and other woodworking tools.

"I was a carpenter in Missouri," one of the men said.

A large man with a dark beard stepped out in front of the others. Kate remembered his name as Kenton.

"Let's get organized," Mr. Kenton said. "There's a sawmill up at Oro Dell. We can have one crew cutting timber, another hauling the logs down to the mill, and another hauling the lumber up here where another crew will start building. We can get this building up in a few days."

Following Mr. Kenton's suggestion, they organized into teams. Mr. Grigg took over, cutting the logs in the nearby forest. Aaron Worth took the responsibility for hauling logs down to the mill, Mr. Kenton oversaw hauling lumber from the sawmill to the farm, and a man named Samuel Witson took charge of the carpenters. All James and Kate could do was stand and look on with awe as the building process got underway.

Wilford called James to one side. "I been checking out those tracks the raiders left behind. While you're getting your house put up, I'm gonna follow them all the way and see where they wind up."

"Be careful," James said. "These are dangerous people."

*   *   *

The first load of lumber arrived at noon two days later. The men started erecting the frame for the new house. He wasn't a carpenter, but James found a hammer and joined in. They would assemble an entire wall then hoist it into place.

James left the decision to Kate as to how they would rebuild. This had been her uncle's property; the shape of the new house should be up to her. She decided that instead of rebuilding both houses, they could combine the two into one. There would be an addition to the main house for Olaf and Helga.

The work went on at a feverish pace. First, there was the weather to contend with. Their luck held; there was no rain while they worked. The men would toil until dark; in turn, the women cooked over fires in the yard. To feed all of them, James and Kate went to La Grande and bought a wagon load of supplies.

By the end of the week, the walls and floor were in place. Next, they started working on the roof. By the end of the following week, the house was essentially completed, except for the inside work, which James and Kate would do. They had a large house in place, an addition for Olaf and Helga, and a covered porch in front.

Kate was astounded that the house had gone up in such a short time. Feeling humbled, she searched for a way to thank all the people. Her efforts came up short; there was no way to express the gratitude she felt. She tried, but one of the men said, "It's us that owes you for what you and your uncle done for us. It's the least we could do."

*   *   *

They had a house but not furniture, so they made do the first night by sleeping on the floor. It was a bit uncomfortable, but most importantly, they had a roof over their heads again.

"We'll go to La Grande and maybe on to Portland to refurnish," James said.

*   *   *

Wilford rode into the yard a few days later as James, Kate, James Junior, and a hired man were unloading furniture and a wood stove from a wagon. It was the last of several loads of household supplies they had purchased. "I found them," Wilford said. "They're holed up in a pine forest about a five-hour ride from here. I followed them from here across the valley to a shack near the mountains, then out to their camp. I don't know who owns the shack, but they got lamp oil inside. I 'spect that's what they used to burn your houses."

"Let's take a look," James said.

Following the raider's trail, James rode with Wilford out across the river to a shack at the foothills of the Blue Mountains. It was a flimsy affair made of pine slabs, located at the base of a small hill. The roof was made of tar paper that had torn loose in several places and was flapping around in the wind. The door was unlocked. Inside, James found two cans containing lamp oil.

"You're right; that's probably what they used to burn us out," James said. "We need to find out who owns this place."

After leaving the shack, Wilford led him to the edge of a pine forest. "They holed up about two miles from here in these pines."

"There's probably too many for the two of us," James said. "We need to get the sheriff."

"From what I been hearin', I don't think the sheriff is gonna help you," Wilford replied.

"I guess you're right. They were out to get us that night because they see us as a threat to stop them from getting the settler's land. The word is probably out by now that they failed. Sooner or later, they're gonna try again. Let's get over to La Grande."

The sun was setting when James and Wilford reached La Grande. After getting directions from a man on the street, they tied their horses to a hitching rail on Main Street. They walked down the wooden sidewalk to the end of the street, then across the freight yard to the office of E. G. Covington. Although it was late, they found the freight owner inside. He looked up when James and Wilford stepped through the door. "We're closed for the day."

"I'm not here for business," James said. "Freight business will be the subject of my visit, however."

A scowl formed on Covington's face. "Who are you, and what do you want?"

"I'm James McKane, and this is Wilford Johnson. I believe you and my wife have had a few conversations about this problem already."

"You're the husband of that meddling woman Lewis Harrington brought up here. I thought you were dead."

"I imagine you did. Did you mean recently, or further back?"

"I don't know what you're talking about," Covington said.

"Well, I was mistakenly reported to have been killed in the late war. That was an honest mistake resulting from the chaos of the situation. There was also the little matter at Harrington Farms recently that I suspect was intended to make me and all my family casualties. I guess you wouldn't know anything about that."

"It's all news to me."

"Well, think about this, Mr. Covington. We've found a legal way to get around the freight agreement you have with the settlers. I think you already know about it, but I'm reminding you again, just in case."

Covington chuckled. "How do you plan to do that?"

"Harrington Farms is buying all the crops and doing all the hauling. My wife started the plan last fall. It worked well."

"I already know about her fool plan, but I don't take it very serious. You don't have the wagons and horses to keep up that operation. You'll go broke soon enough. Your wife was lucky last year, but such luck won't last."

"Maybe, but don't count on it."

E. G. Covington's demeanor changed. He looked up at James with a cold, hard glare. "Let me tell you a few things, my friend. I've been operating up here ever since the British were still in Oregon, and I'm still around. I know more about this country and what it takes to do business here than you or your kin will ever know."

"Times change, Mr. Covington."

"I'm a determined man who will not be done in by the likes of you or those hicks Lewis Harrington brought up here. Harrington came to me 'cause he needed help to pull off that scheme of his. When things didn't go right for him, he tried to shift the blame to me."

"Your motives are clear to me," James said. "You're just like the Yankee profiteers descending on the South, looking for a way to make some quick money. I've seen enough of that. We're not going to back down from you. I hope that's clear."

James walked out of the office with Wilford following, ignoring Covington's cold glare. "Let's stop by the courthouse," James said when they were out on the street.

"I'm going to wait out front," Wilford said when they reached the courthouse.

James had only been in the bottom floor of the courthouse where the newspaper offices were located. He assumed the county offices must be on the second floor. He went inside and down the narrow hall to the stairs. Upstairs, he found the sheriff dozing at his desk. He woke when James closed the door. "Something I can do for you, mister?"

"I want to report that someone burned down two houses out at Harrington Farms and shot the overseer," James said.

"I heard about that from the doc, but I wonder why you waited so long to come and report it yourself."

"Why? It doesn't look much like you plan on doing anything about it."

"I'd be careful about making remarks like that. Me and a deputy were out there a few days ago and took a look around."

"And what did you find?"

"We found a few tracks but lost them in the foothills. Indians, I suspect."

"For your information, Sheriff, I have a tracker who was able to follow them all the way through the foothills to an old shack at the edge of the mountains. I don't know who owns that shack, but I plan to find out."

"Let me give you some advice about taking the law into your own hands. That don't set too well around here."

"Then I suggest you go take a look for yourself," James said. "If you do your job, I won't have to do it for you."

"Where is this shack located?"

James described the property. "Do you know who owns it?" he asked.

"No. That's an isolated area, and there's no proof that the shack owner was the one who attacked your place. I say it's Indians. A band of Paiutes attacked a stockman just south of the valley a few days ago."

"The men who actually attacked the house are holed in some pines not far from that shack. You could go out and round them up."

"I could. But without any proof they were the ones who attacked your place, it would be a waste of time."

"Their tracks lead from Harrington Farms out to that shack," James said. "How much proof do you need?"

"More than that, I'm afraid."

There was no point arguing with the sheriff; James turned to leave. As he opened the door, the sheriff asked, "Who are you, mister, and what your connection to Harrington Farms is?"

"I'm James McKane, Kate McKane's husband."

"You don't say?"

James left the courthouse and found Wilford still waiting in front. "No luck with the sheriff, I take it?" Wilford said.

"Not much."

It was well into the evening when they reached home. Kate was waiting on the porch. "Where have you been?" she demanded. "We've got enough problems without the two of you disappearing."

James dismounted and explained about the shack, the visit with Covington, and the sheriff. "I see what you're up against trying to deal with the local sheriff. I don't know if he's on Covington's payroll if he's afraid of Covington, or just doesn't care."

"I don't know either. Come into the house and have some supper."

While they were eating some fried chicken that Kate had saved for them, James talked some more about the visit with E. G. Covington. "He's plenty worked up now. They failed in their try to get rid of us, and it's just a matter of time until they try again. The freight line you started last fall is eating at Mr. Covington; he's not going to stand by and let it go on. The only thing we can do is be on our guard and be ready for them next time."

"I don't want any more violence," Kate said.

"None of us do. I've seen my share already with the war and the troubles Wilford and I had getting up here, but I don't see how this can be resolved any other way."

* * *

Wilford found James on the front porch the next morning. "I been thinking about those fellas holed up out in the woods," he said. "They had surprise the last time. You can't let 'em do that again. I know where they are and can keep an eye on them until they make their move. If they try to move against this place, I can warn you."

"That's asking an awful lot," James replied.

"To tell the truth, I get uneasy just sittin' around a house. I'm better off out in the woods anyway."

James reluctantly agreed. It was dangerous, but if anyone could do it, Wilford would be the one. "Be careful out there."

"I will."

James explained to Kate what Wilford was planning. Like her husband, she was worried he was putting himself into harm's way. He brushed off their concerns. Since Wilford was insistent, she prepared some food for him while he was saddling his horse.

Kate and James stood in front of the house and watched Wilford riding across the meadow. Watching horse and rider disappear beyond the meadow, James reflected on how much he had come to depend on the man. At the start, he had been very reluctant to take Wilford on as a guide; now, he was totally indebted to him.

*　　*　　*

Since James's arrival, the younger children had been constantly at his side. Drew was always asking questions about the war, and Alice stared in awe at the father she could not remember from Tennessee.

James Junior turned out to be a different matter. He was quiet and actually seemed to avoid his father as much as possible. When James looked at this oldest son, the boy reminded him so much of his own father, both in appearance and manner.

They had little chance to talk during the day. The boy would go off to the fields with the hired hands, leaving only meal times for a chance for them to communicate. James would try to get up a conversation at the table, but all he could get from his son were mumbles and shakes of his head.

*　　*　　*

Enough of this, James concluded. After supper, he asked his oldest son to come out on the porch. When they were outside, the boy sat down on the front step and looked off into the distance.

James pulled a chair to the edge of the porch and sat down. "Son, we need to get to the bottom of whatever is bothering you. Ever since I arrived, you've been avoiding me. I want to know why. You know, I risked my life to find you."

The boy shook his head and continued to stare off into space. James made another attempt to get the boy to talk without success.

After several tries, James's patience gave way. "Damn it, boy, I'm your daddy, and I'm going to be treated with some respect. Do you understand?"

"Yes. I understand." Then James Junior said, "No. I don't understand. It's because you went off to war and left us that we had to leave Tennessee and come all the way up here. We've had nothing but sorrow ever since you left. I've seen Mama sitting and crying 'cause she didn't know what to do. Where were you when we needed somebody to help us?"

Without further word, the boy got up and ran into the house, leaving James stunned. During the long struggle across the frontier, he could think of little else except finding his family. He had even left his own ailing father to come up here. During the long days in the saddle, he would think of all the joy they would have when they were all together again. This he did not expect. He did not understand his oldest son's resentment toward him.

The door opened, and Kate stepped out and put a hand on his shoulder. She had overheard their conversation. "Give him some time. He's just a small boy who has seen a lot of trouble in his life and is confused. Deep down, he really does need you. Just give him a little more time."

*　　*　　*

The next day, Doctor McBrighton brought Olaf and Helga to the farm in a buggy. Helga and the doctor helped Olaf down. He walked toward the house with the aid of a cane. Before going inside, they stood and marveled at the new house. Neither of them could believe it had built so quickly. The interior had been filled with new furniture hauled in by wagon, Kate explained.

"Remember, Olaf, take it easy for a while," the doctor said. Olaf promised he would. With that, the doctor took his leave.

Kate showed them to their quarters. When they were settled in their rooms, Helga looked around and asked, "Where is Little Deer?"

"She's in the kitchen," Kate replied. "She's been learning how to make bread and pies."

Helga went to the kitchen and returned with Little Deer. The girl looked at all of them, appearing nervous. She had given up her Indian clothes and was wearing a long, red dress Kate had given her. Helga motioned for her to have a seat in one of the chairs.

"I've been thinking about this ever since I saw Olaf laid up nearly dead," Helga said. "I had to drag it out of him, but I finally got the whole story about how Little Deer pulled him out of the fire that night and tended his wound to keep him from bleeding to death."

365

Olaf looked down at the floor while his wife was talking.

"I also know about the grudge you been carrying all these years," Helga said. "This is a violent land we live in, but at the same time, there're always some good people around to make it a little better."

Helga walked over and placed her arm around Little Deer's neck. "I know you can't really believe this young woman is in any way connected to what those Indians did to you several years ago. You were lucky she was there that night, or you wouldn't be here today. Since we were never blessed with any children, I would like for her to stay with us all the time. You've got to get rid of your prejudices. I know that you're a big man who can do it."

Olaf looked up at his wife. "Yaw, I guess I've been doing some thinking myself. Maybe you are right."

Helga and Little Deer walked over to Olaf, and the three of them embraced. Helga had tears running down her cheeks. A little a trace of moisture formed in Olaf's eyes as well.

James and Kate walked over and gave each of them a pat on the back. They knew Little Deer didn't understand much of the conversation, but maybe words were not needed. Still, when Wilford returned, they would have him explain it all.

*   *   *

Olaf continued to improve. After a week in the house, he grew restless. When he mentioned going out to the fields to supervise the planting, a quick scolding from his wife put an end to the idea.

With no word from Wilford, James began to worry. Several days had passed since he went out to keep an eye on the holed-up raiders. Dealing with such dangerous men, anything could have happened. James thought about looking for Wilford. Firstly, he didn't know exactly where the man was, and secondly, he might give away Wilford's location. Best leave tracking matters to an expert, he figured.

There was a better way to put his time to use; he would try to find out who owned the shack where the lamp oil was found. He hitched up the buggy. Kate joined him, and they went to La Grande to see what they could find.

Spring was yielding to warmer and drier weather. The wild-flowers in the meadow were wilting under the onslaught of summer. The sun hung hot below the dark blue sky. But Kate had grown accustomed to the climate; now, she could even find some appreciation in it. "This country just seems to grow on you," she said. "There's always a nice view of the mountains, from about any direction."

"It does overwhelm you at times," James replied. "Ever since we hit the

Rockies late last fall, I've been amazed at this country they call the west. At times, it can be all pretty and quiet, but other times violent and unpredictable."

"I know someone that might be able to help us. Let's go over to the courthouse," Kate said when they reached La Grande.

"Not the sheriff, I hope. We're not going to get any help out of him."

"No. This person doesn't work for the county."

James drove over to the courthouse. After parking the buggy, they went inside and walked down the hallway to one of the newspaper offices. Inside, they found Howard Klaspell.

"Mr. McKane. I see you found your wife."

"I take it you two have already met," Kate said.

"Yes, we have. Thank you again for your directions," James said.

"My pleasure. Now, what can I do for you?"

"I'm trying to find the owner of some property," James explained about the shack he and Wilford had found.

"If you knew the legal description, we could find out upstairs. I've got a map of the county here if that will help."

Howard got a map out of his desk drawer and spread it out. James studied it for a few minutes. "It must be in this area," he said as he pointed to a spot on the map next to the Blue Mountains.

"That's out in an isolated location. Let's go upstairs and see what we can find out."

In the county clerk's office, Howard spoke to a young man who produced a book containing a list of registered deeds for the county. Howard opened the book and scanned the pages until he stopped and pointed to an entry. "Here it is. E. G. Covington owns a tract out there. I believe that is where that shack is located. I've heard he runs a herd of cattle out there."

Kate looked at Howard then James. "That's the proof we need to link Covington to the violence against us."

Howard shook his head. "I'm sorry, Mrs. McKane, but that might not be enough. This just indicates he owns the shack. It doesn't prove beyond a reasonable doubt he's involved. That's a remote area. Anyone could have used that shack. I want to help you, but I think you need more proof before you can get any action from the sheriff."

"That may be, but it proves we're on the right track," James said. "Covington's got a lot to lose on this deal. He's a likely suspect."

"And I need not point out to you that he can be a very dangerous man," Howard said.

"Yes, we've seen some of his handiwork already," Kate replied.

With their business finished, they went downstairs. "Thanks for your help," James said to Howard.

"My pleasure. Glad I could be of some help to you," Howard replied.

On the way back home, Kate reflected on how lucky she was to have James back. Since the loss of Uncle Lewis, she had felt so alone and overwhelmed. With her husband beside her, she felt optimistic.

The problems she inherited were many. She owned a large estate in a still untamed land. She was trying to manage both a farming business and a freight line without any business experience. Without James back in her life, she might ultimately have given up and gone back to Tennessee.

Helga and Little Deer were working in the garden behind the house when they arrived. It was bumpy at times, but Little Deer seemed to be adjusting to her new life. What's more, Olaf was coming around. Helga's powers of persuasion were strong, even with a stubborn man such as her husband. As James and Kate drove by the garden, Helga and Little Deer waved.

*   *   *

With another harvest coming up in the fall, James went over the remains of the barn, planning how to rebuild it. The sound of a horse coming into the yard interrupted him. He saw Wilford ride in and dismount.

"I got some news for you," Wilford said. "I been watching their camp up in the pines. Yesterday, I saw the dark-haired one who seems to be their leader ride out of camp. I followed him out to that shack we found. When he got to the shack, another man was waiting for him."

"What did this man look like?" James asked.

"I couldn't get close enough for a good look, but he was a big fellow. It might have been that freight owner in town."

"That sounds like Covington," James said. "We found out that shack belongs to him."

"I came in to warn you it looks like they getting ready to do something, so you best be ready."

"Yes, I suspect they are. They know they failed in that last raid. Kate's new freight line threatens Covington's business, so he's good and stirred up by now. We've got to be ready for them this time."

"I'm going back out there and keeping an eye on them, so I'll know when they make their move."

"Stay and have supper first," James said.

After supper, Wilford packed his saddlebags with supplies then rode back toward the raider's camp.

James took stock of what they had to defend themselves with. They lost some of their weapons in the fire, but James still had his pistol, the Henry, and a shotgun. Olaf had a shotgun in the barn. Wilford had a pistol with him but had never gotten around to replacing the rifle he gave to the Indians. Since Palmer was reported to have at least seven men in his gang, they would have to rely on surprise for an advantage. While James was sorting through his weapons, Kate walked up. "Why don't you go and get the sheriff?"

"We don't know when that bunch is going to hit us. Even if we did, I doubt the sheriff would come out here. He's protecting Covington, or he still believes Indians are behind these raids."

Kate sighed and sat down in a chair. The thought of a violent confrontation with Palmer and his henchmen sent chills down her spine. When was all this going to end so they could live in peace? Worse, how many more lives would be lost protecting what was rightfully theirs?

From the porch, James looked over the farmstead. They were surrounded by mostly open country, which could be used to their advantage. They could see anyone approaching. If Wilford could give them some advance warning, Palmer and his gunmen would be in for a big surprise.

*　　*　　*

The pending raid put everyone on edge. The children complained because Kate made them stay in or very close to the house.

Olaf heard of the coming raid and said, "By golly, I'm going to be ready for them this time."

"You're in no shape for a fight," Helga replied.

*　　*　　*

They didn't have long to wait. Two days later, late in the evening near sundown, Wilford rode into the yard, jumped from his horse, and ran up on the porch. "They movin' this way!" he yelled. "They'll likely hole up somewhere nearby until dark; then they'll strike."

"Get Helga, Little Deer, and the children and head for the Grigg farm," James said to Kate. "I'll hitch the buggy while you get everyone ready."

"I'll take the rest of them over, but I want to be here," she said.

"It's too dangerous, Kate."

After arguing, Kate gave in and got the others together in the yard where James had the buggy waiting. He instructed one of the hired hands to drive the buggy and the other ride along as extra protection. There was no need for them here. The two men had signed on to do farm work rather than risking their lives in a gunfight.

After kissing Kate, James helped her into the buggy with the children. Helga led a protesting Olaf out to join them. Before they could get going,

369

James Junior got up from his seat. "I want to stay and help."

"I appreciate your offer, Son, but somebody has to help take care of your mother, brother, and sister," James said. He gave James Junior a pat on the shoulder; the boy sat back down. Then James signaled the driver, and they started toward the road.

"You have any idea which direction they'll ride in from?" he asked Wilford.

"They'll probably come across the meadow."

While James was grateful for Wilford's help, at the same time, he felt guilty. This was not Wilford's fight. He was already indebted to the man for getting him up here, far more than the money he paid him. Now, he was asking him to stand in harm's way one more time. He considered just telling Wilford not to stay; warning them was sufficient. But if he had learned anything about this man, telling him to ride away wouldn't do. Wilford would stay anyway. That much James knew.

They stationed themselves at the edge of the meadow to wait. And the wait was a short one. They soon heard horses coming up the road. "They're here," he said to Wilford.

"Wait. There are only two or three horses coming. That must be somebody else," Wilford replied.

Mr. Grigg and two other nearby settlers rode across the meadow. "Kate told us what was about to happen, so I rounded up some of the others," Hiram said. "I didn't have time to get the word out to very many."

"I certainly appreciate your help, but I can't let you risk your life for this," James replied.

"The outcome of this concerns all of us," Hiram Grigg answered. "Besides, Mr. Bates here is a veteran of the recent war and can probably be of considerable help to you."

James did not argue the point. With Palmer having at least seven men, they could use all the help they could get.

They took up positions behind some small bushes at the edge of the meadow and waited. Wilford rode out a short distance to watch and warn them in case the raiders came in from another direction.

A half hour later, a rider rode up in the darkness. "It's me!" Wilford yelled. "They're coming straight toward the meadow."

They formed a line across the meadow and waited. The situation reminded James of some of the battles during the war when they would wait for the enemy to strike. On this night, he had the same fears that he always felt before the start of a battle.

The first things they spotted were the lit torches. This time, the raiders were coming to do a thorough job. James and the rest waited. Soon, they could hear their attackers talking. "Them sod busters sure got that house back up quick," one of them said.

"No matter. They won't be in shape to rebuild anything after tonight," another said.

"Quiet, you fools," another said. "You want them to hear us coming?"

James watched until he could make out the outline of the leader, the one they called they called Palmer, he assumed. When the approaching riders were about fifty feet from them, he spoke, "You boys are out of luck here."

The leader drew up with a start. "What the hell? Who are you, mister?"

"Don't matter. You and your men turn and ride out of here."

"Mister, you're getting yourself deep into something you don't want to be in."

"I'm already involved, and you're not burning out or shooting anybody this time."

Four of the eight riders were carrying torches, a mistake on their part. The light illuminated them, making them good targets. The others, harder to see in the dark, would be the real threat.

The lead rider rode up until he was in front of James. "This is the last warning you're going to get," James said. "Turn around and ride out of here." He held the Henry up in the air to drive home his argument.

The leader was undaunted. He urged his horse closer. "You people out here don't listen very well. You've interfered in certain affairs too long. Now you're gonna pay. You're just like Lewis Harrington; he wouldn't listen, and look what happened to him."

There it was, a confession to the murder of Lewis Harrington. James's anger exploded. This same bunch had burned both houses here, shot Olaf, and now admitted to killing Kate's uncle. He could contain his rage no longer. He leaned over into the man's face. "You bastards killed a man and tried to kill others over nothing but pure greed."

"And we're going to do the same to you." The leader reached for his pistol. James, now totally overcome with anger, reached out, grabbed the man, and pulled him from his horse. As the raider was falling, he grabbed James's shirt, pulling both men to the ground.

In the dark, the other riders were confused. "Palmer, what's happening?" one yelled.

"You men stay put!" Wilford yelled.

Wilford rode up to where James and Palmer were now struggling on the ground. He got down and pulled them apart. "It's over!" he yelled.

"Like hell it is!" Palmer yelled.

Unknown to the rest, Palmer had recovered his pistol. In the dark, neither Wilford nor James saw it until it was too late. The pistol fired. The bullet struck

James in the chest and sent him reeling to the ground. Wilford fired his pistol; Palmer staggered a couple of steps and fell.

The other riders tried to fire but could not pick out targets in the dark.

"Better drop those weapons!" Wilford yelled.

One of the riders fired a shot in Wilford's direction. The round sailed past him. Hiram Grigg and the others opened fire on the torch welding riders. The attackers were thrown into confusion by the outburst of gunfire. Being caught by surprise and now leaderless, they choose to retreat by turning their horses and riding off into the night.

Wilford fired some additional rounds in the direction of the fleeing raiders before racing over to James. He dropped to his knees. Blood covered James's shirt and formed a pool around him. Hiram and the others rode over.

"We got to get him to the doctor," Hiram said.

Wilford stood and let out a deep sigh. "Better do it fast. He's lost a lot of blood."

Looking at the man lying on the ground, Wilford took off his hat and walked out a short distance from the others. He and James had shared the dangers of the trail. He had saved Wilford's life the night the Sioux warrior was sneaking up on him. Moreover, James had taken the lead in getting them past the Sioux that had them cornered in a gully. If they couldn't pull James through, there would be no justice in all this.

Except for Noah Anderson, James McKane was one of the few white men Wilford had ever known who had come to treat him as an equal in all respects and even rely on him for advice. Wilford was a hard man in some ways, a product of the mountains and the way of life of a mountain man. Now, he kept his head turned away, so no one saw the tears. All that work to get up here, and now this. *If there is a just God, he has to save this man's life.*

He was distracted by the sound of a buggy racing up the road toward the meadow. The erratic driving indicated someone at the reins with little experience in handling a team: James's son, he suspected. Fearful the buggy would be wrecked, Wilford rushed out to help stop the horses. The young man pulled back on the reins, slowing the team and allowing Wilford to reach out and grab the harness. When the buggy stopped, Kate scrambled from the front seat. Wilford moved to intercept her before she reached James's body. "I'm sorry, ma'am, but he took a shot in the chest, and his hurt bad."

She began screaming. "No, no, no! He can's die! He just came back to us! He can't be taken from us again! God won't let him be taken from us again."

Kate fell on the ground, sobbing hysterically. Hiram Grigg helped her to her feet and led her toward the house. James Junior walked over to his father's body and started sobbing softly. "I'm sorry, Daddy. I'm sorry. You've got to recover. My mama can't take losing you again."

Wilford gave the boy a few minutes, then took him by the arm and led him toward the house. "I'm sorry about your daddy. He and I shared the trail on the way up here, and he saved my life a couple of times along the way. We got to pray that he recovers."

More settlers were now arriving at the farm. The word was out about the confrontation, and people were arriving to help. Some of the settlers loaded James into a wagon and started toward La Grande.

"Someone better go and get the sheriff," Hiram Grigg said.

The women tended to Kate and the rest of the family, offering them encouragement

Kate called to Olaf. "Please get me a horse saddled. I have to be with James. I can't let him die."

"No, it's too dangerous in the dark for you to go alone. I'll drive you in the buggy. I'll have one of the hired men get it ready."

Wilford called some of the men aside. "I think I might have hit one of them. I'm going to get a lantern and ride around and see if I can pick up some tracks."

"Hard to do at night," Hiram said.

"Better to work with a fresh trail," Wilford said. "If someone will go and round up the sheriff, I'll see if I can get a line on this bunch."

After getting a lantern from the house, Wilford rode around the meadow until he picked up the tracks of the fleeing raiders. By lantern light, he followed. Soon, he noticed blood on the ground. One of them was hit bad, judging from the amount of blood. It would be difficult to find the wounded man before daylight, but with such a wound, he probably wouldn't get far.

*   *   *

Sheriff Avery Benton arrived at the farm accompanied by a deputy. He found Kate McKane getting into the buggy. Her eyes were red and swollen; deep worry lines cut across her face. The sheriff dismounted. When Kate saw the sheriff, she got down from the buggy and stood in front of him.

The sheriff cast a wary eye at the distraught woman. He took off his hat and held it in front of him. "First of all, Mrs. McKane, I'm sorry, terribly sorry, about your husband. I know you think if I had done my job better, this might not have happened. The truth is, you couldn't have gotten a conviction against Covington or any of those other people based on what you knew at the time."

"Sheriff Benton, there's no use in arguing that point now. I don't know what it takes to get justice up here. They killed Uncle Lewis, and nothing was ever done about it. They burned our houses to the ground, and you insisted

Indians were to blame. Now they've shot my husband, and he may die. Just what does it take to get justice here, Mr. Benton?"

The sheriff scratched his head. "I don't know myself sometimes. I spent years in California working for the mining interests, always putting my life on the line for twenty dollars a month protecting the interests of the mine owners.

"I never thought that was justice either. I gave it up and came up here hoping things might be different, but they weren't. It was the same old story. There were always somebody's interests that needed protecting. There was always somebody wanting to get rich at somebody else's expense."

The sheriff looked at her. "I know you thought I was protecting Covington, but it wasn't me that was protecting him. It was the system of justice up there that was protecting him."

The sheriff stared down at the ground, out of words. He stood there in awkward silence for a moment, then put his hat back on and motioned for his deputy. "We'll camp out here for the night and head back in the morning at first light. We got some business in town."

*   *   *

Kate sat in a chair next to the bed where James was lying. As she listened to the ragged breathing, she was drawn back to the time when her Father-in-Law, Albert McKane, had come to the suites of rooms at the main house where her and the children lived. "It's James," said. "I've just received a report that he's been killed." Then he turned and left the room without offering her any condolences, any tenderness at all.

For a time, Kate had sat there in the room, feeling numb. She found it hard to process the terrible news. One of the house servants came in and took her newborn son, Drew. During the coming days, as the magnitude of her loss began take hold, she sank into a state of deep depression. Life began seeping out of her, leaving behind a hollow shell in its place. She would cry for a time while remembering the life she had shared with her husband; then, for a time, she would curse the hand of fate that had taken James from her. She remained in this state until the day Lewis Harrington came into her life.

Uncle Lewis' zest for life ultimately started to penetrate through the cloud of despair she was living in, and slowly life started having some meaning again. She could cherish her children again. The things around her starting to have meaning again. She could listen to the birds singing outside her window and derive pleasure from it.

Now there was no Uncle Lewis to bring her back to life. If she lost James this time, would she ever be able to face life again? Kate prayed. She prayed until the sunlight filtering the curtains on the window announced the arrival of a new day.

*   *   *

The sun was a pale patch rising over the mountains to the east when Wilford arose. He studied the tracks. The raider was still bleeding badly. He can't get very far, Wilford concluded.

In a short time, the bloody tracks branched off from the others toward a small gully. The wounded man had been abandoned by his companions. Wilford got out his pistol and rode toward the gully. A horse was standing just inside. Further inside, a man was lying face down.

There was a wound in the man's side. Wilford bent over the wounded raider and concluded the man was still alive, but barely so. He tried to stop the bleeding with rags from his saddlebags then got the man's horse. He secured the wounded man in the saddle as best he could tying him so he wouldn't fall off, then started toward La Grande.

People on the street and sidewalk stared at Wilford and the wounded man. Ignoring them, he got the raider down and carried him into the doctor's office. "Man's been wounded bad," Wilford said as he put him down on the table. He saw Kate sitting next to the bed where James was lying. "How is he, ma'am?" Wilford asked.

Kate, the exhaustion showing on her face, said. "He survived the night and Doctor McBrighton says that's a good sigh."

"I'm relieved to hear that, ma'am. He's a tough man. He'll pull through."

The doctor got up from his chair and looked at the wounded man. "You folks sure keep me busy bringing in wounded men. This one doesn't look very good, but I'll do what I can. Who is he?"

"He's part of a bunch that tried to shoot up the McKanes last night," Wilford said. "As you know, James here was wounded, and the leader of this bunch is dead. If you can pull this one through, he might be able to tell us where his friends are."

*   *   *

Wilford started back to the farm. At the edge of La Grande, he met the sheriff and his deputy. The lawmen listened passively as he told them about the wounded gunman.

"I'll check with the doc later," the sheriff said. He looked at his deputy. "Let's swing by the office and pick up Fred, then go over and pay E. G. Covington a visit."

The sheriff's lack of gratitude for bringing in the wounded raider annoyed Wilford. But that was to be expected, he supposed. The best he could hope for was that the lawman would stay true to his word and bring in Covington. The freight owner had caused more than his share of trouble and heartache; it was time for him to be held accountable.

*   *   *

The sheriff and his deputy picked up another deputy named Fred Grouse at the courthouse then proceeded to the freight office. E. G. Covington was at his desk, writing in a ledger.

"Avery. What brings you boys over here?"

"It ain't a social call."

Covington leaned back in his chair. "What's this all about?"

"I guess you can answer that better than anyone," the sheriff said.

Covington sat up with a look of anger on his face. "I don't know what you're getting at."

"There was another raid out at the Harrington's last night. It was a bloody one; three men were shot. One of them was Palmer, and he is dead."

"That's too bad, but what's it got to do with me?"

The sheriff thought for a moment. "I've been seeing this coming on for some time now, in fact, ever since Lewis Harrington brought those people up here. I hoped I wouldn't have to deal with it, but now I guess I do. I don't think there's any doubt you're the one behind all this."

Covington jumped to his feet, his face red with rage. "You see here; there's no proof I had anything to do with any of what happened out there. I made a business deal with Harrington and the others. That's all there is to it."

"Well, E. G., that's what I've always wanted to think. Too much has happened for me to believe that anymore. You were seen talking to one of those misfits out on your property a few days ago."

"I was trying to hire some men to round up stray cattle."

"Listen, I know Ellis Palmer from my days in California, and I can tell you he's not the sort that goes around hiring out to round up stray cattle. On top of that, one of his men is down at Doc McBrighton's right now, getting patched up. I suspect he can shed more light on this."

Covington walked around and stood in front of his desk, facing the sheriff and his deputies. "Let me tell you something. I know people from Salem, Portland, and all over this state. I'll see that you never hold an office around here again."

"I reckon I'm getting too old for this job anyway. In the meantime, you're under arrest for murder and arson." The sheriff motioned for the deputies to take Covington to jail.

As they were putting handcuffs on him, Covington raged at the sheriff. "You no-good excuse for a man, I'll see you in Hell for this."

"Take him and lock him up," the sheriff said.

*   *   *

People from throughout the valley came by the farm inquiring about James. "He's still alive but very weak," Kate would tell them. "But I haven't given up hope. I believe that God will spare him."

James' fate was taking a toll on the children. Kate would sit with them on the settee and try to boost their spirits. "You daddy is a strong man," she told them. "He will recover."

Alice would look at her through tear-filled eyes and say, "I don't want to lose my daddy." Kate embraced her daughter. "I know, dear, none of us wants to lose him. I thought I had lost him once. We will hope and pray until he is well again. And I will fight to see that justice is done for Uncle Lewis and your daddy."

The news spread quickly about Covington being arrested for the shooting of James McKane and the death of Lewis Harrington, the burning of two buildings at Harrington Farms, and the wounding of Olaf Hanson.

Kate felt some sense of relief that justice was finally catching up to Mr. Covington. What still disturbed her was that several members of the gang got away. She would never be able to rest until all of them were held accountable for their crimes.

Chapter 37

Pursuit of Justice

Grief, held in the back recesses of Kate's mind, welled up over her like a cloud. The void within that had been filled with James's return had opened up again like a giant chasm, pulling her into its vast reservoir of despair. He was still alive, but the doctor told her it was fifty-fifty at best. And beyond the incomprehensible despair that she might lose him again, there was the unfairness of it all. Had fate failed to destroy her by his reported loss back in Tennessee, so it sent James back into her life again to perhaps finish the task? The injustice of it all ate at her very soul. Why were such acts permitted to happen?

But there was a difference this time. This time, Kate was a stronger woman. When she thought of losing James again, the pain cut through her like a knife just as it had in Tennessee, but this time she would not retreat into a shell. The pain remained, but from deep within, she pulled up the strength to go on. Uncle Lewis rescued her the first time; this time, she would save herself if it became necessary.

A few days after the shooting at the farm, Kate had a visitor. It was a tall man with thinning black hair wearing a black suit and string necktie. He introduced himself as Michael Brand.

Kate asked him inside. He took a seat on the settee, opened a small valise, and pulled out some papers. "The court has asked me to serve as prosecutor for the case against E. G. Covington."

"I'm happy to hear that he's going to trial," Kate said.

"Well, yes, but you see, the problem is, much of the evidence against Covington is circumstantial."

"Wilford Johnson and my husband tracked the people who burned our houses out to a building on Covington's property."

"That's true, but that building is out in a remote area, so anyone could

378

have used it. That will be his line of defense."

"Wilford Johnson saw Covington talking to Palmer out at that shack."

"Again, that doesn't prove he hired them to attack your farm. Wilford Johnson only saw them from a distance and didn't know what they were talking about. You and I believe he's guilty. Unfortunately, a jury might not be so easy to convince, especially in La Grande where Covington has a lot of influence."

Kate horrified at the thought of E. G. Covington going free, lapsed into a state of despair. "What are we going to do, Mr. Brand?"

"I would like to get the trial delayed for a time to work on additional evidence, but I don't know if the judge will agree."

"Mr. Brand, I want to see these men brought to justice. I've lost too much to them already. The men who got away can provide the evidence we need to convict Covington."

"That may be true, Mrs. McKane, but we don't have them in jail. The wounded man that Wilford Johnson found died before anybody could get much of anything out of him."

"There's got to be a way," Kate said.

"I'll keep working on it. And as I said before, I'll try to get the judge to delay the trial."

Mr. Brand gathered up his papers and put them back in the valise. "I wish I could be more encouraging, but I wanted you to know the situation."

"I appreciate that, Mr. Brand. I'm not going to rest until Covington, and all those he hired to do his dirty work are brought to justice."

"Believe me, Mrs. McKane, I know how you feel. I want them convicted just as much as you do. I'll do what I can."

After bidding Kate a good day, he went out and got his horse. "You'll be hearing from me," he said as he mounted.

Kate returned to her seat on the porch, bearing the brunt of the prosecutor's words. She was so despaired by the news; she didn't hear Wilford come up to the porch. "Ma'am."

She jumped. "I'm sorry, Wilford. My mind was on something else."

"I been thinking some about the other night," he said in a low voice. "I was the one that broke up Palmer and your husband. I should have kept a closer watch on Palmer and made sure he was disarmed. I was careless letting him get hold of that pistol and shoot. I've been troubled something awful ever since."

"It wasn't your fault, Wilford; we owe you so much already. If it hadn't been for you, we wouldn't have gotten James back."

"Just the same; I've been thinking about the rest of that bunch. With their leader dead and the one that hired them in jail, I doubt they stayed around very long. Like as not, they on the run back to California, where they came from. If I strike out after them now, I might be able to catch up with them somewhere along the way and bring them back."

"You're only one man, Wilford; there must be at least six of them."

"That's true, missus, but I got surprise on my side. I got vengeance in mind also; that can make up for a lot of numbers."

"If you had some help, it might be possible. There's a good chance that Covington won't be convicted with the evidence we have now."

"Then I got to go after them. I won't be at peace with myself until I do. On the way up here, James saved me from a Sioux brave out on the prairie and again when some Sioux had us cornered in a gully. I owe you and him this."

"Is there anyone who can help you?"

"I got no time to look around for help. Besides, I can make better time traveling alone. I'm going to start tomorrow morning."

Kate didn't have an argument to overcome Wilford's determination. *Could he really bring back these men?* She wondered. Justice might just depend on it.

*   *   *

Before leaving, Wilford decided to have a talk with the sheriff about Palmer's gang. There were rumors around the valley the sheriff was acquainted with Palmer and some of his men. That being the case, he might have a line on where they would go.

White lawmen were usually suspicious of a Negro's motive, especially here in Oregon. The war had ended the state's ban on Negros, but laws didn't change people's feelings. It was only out of necessity that he made a trip to La Grande to see the sheriff.

The shooting had brought Wilford to one of the lowest points of his life. On the one hand, he had fulfilled his obligation to get James to Oregon. But that wasn't enough. Pure carelessness had allowed Palmer to get off that shot. The very thought of it was tormenting. Without some atonement for his carelessness, he would never be able to live with himself.

In La Grande, Wilford went into the courthouse and found the sheriff in his office. Avery Benton gave him a suspicious look when he stepped inside. "You that fella that came up here with James McKane?"

"That's right. I'm the one that told you about the wounded raider. Now I've got some unfinished business with that bunch."

"I doubt it'll do you much good now. I figure that bunch is on the way back to California by now. They'll head for Shasta, most likely."

"I'm going down after them," Wilford said.

"That's a pretty tall order for one man."

"That may be, but I have to do it."

"With Palmer gone, I suspect their leader will be a man named Emmett Dossett. He's a bad sort and won't hesitate to slit you from ear-to-ear if he gets a chance. Emmett's got a young nephew that's probably riding with them. I suspect he's the one they used to lure Lewis Harrington out into the foothills. I always suspected it was him, but I could never find any of that bunch. I never told the McKanes 'cause I didn't want to get their hopes up. Covington kept them well out of sight until he needed them to do a job. If you can get Emmett under control, then the others might come a little easier. Just the same, I don't envy you riding across country trying to keep that bunch from cutting your throat."

"I'm determined to bring them back," Wilford said.

"I wish you luck. You're gonna need it."

Wilford bought supplies for the trail then rode back home. The only thing he was short of was a rifle. He could have bought one in La Grande, but his mind was on James's Henry. A fine weapon it was; now, if he could just get his hands on it. Kate was in the house, helping Helga.

Wilford, always a little uncomfortable in white homes, stood just inside the kitchen. "Ma'am, I was just wondering about James's Henry rifle. I'm in need of one, and I want to inquire about borrowing it. It's a fine weapon."

"Of course. I'm sure James won't mind." Kate went into a side room, got the rifle and remaining rounds from James's possessions, and gave them to Wilford. "Please be careful out there."

"I certainly will."

*   *   *

As the sun peaked over the mountains, Wilford saddled his horse and packed his gear. The family was still asleep—all the better for him. Goodbyes made him uncomfortable.

In truth, Wilford didn't feel much in common with the people here. Over time, he and James had come to an understanding. Mrs. McKane, by all appearances, was a fair person, but being around her made him feel uneasy.

Wilford rode due south through the mining camps in Baker County. He thought about asking the miners if they had seen six white men riding through, but he rode on. A Negro inquiring about white men might get the miner's suspicions aroused. He would find their trail soon enough.

His plan carried a bit of a gamble. There were other routes out of the valley, but the south route was the quickest. After the shootout and loss of their leader, Wilford figured these men would make haste and take the easiest trail rather than the longer ones through the mountains.

His hunch paid off. The second day, he picked up the trail of six horses heading south. They were the same tracks he had seen around the farm, and they were recent. If they didn't get in a big hurry, he stood a chance of catching up to them. Once away from La Grande, they might not feel the need for haste—so he hoped.

The tracks took Wilford through dry, mountainous country then turned west. Here, the trail grew faint. But he was relentless. Wilford scoured the ground, picked up faint traces of the six, and pushed on. His persistence began to pay off; the tracks became more distinct. Not expecting anyone to be following them this far south, they were getting careless.

The country was now arid and hot; the sun beat down on him and his horse. By the time they reached the shores of a large lake, both were near exhaustion. Wilford watered his horse, rested, filled his canteens, and started out again. The trail now led southwest, across an expanse of desert.

Wilford stopped for short periods to rest himself, and his horse then pushed on. The going was slow, but he believed he was gaining on the men he pursued.

At another small lake, Wilford replenished his water supply and watered his horse. When he could find shade, he would stop and rest, then make up the time by traveling at night. In the cool night air, he could set a better pace. It was a gamble; there was the risk of his horse stepping into a hole and breaking its leg. He elected to take that chance.

The hot, dry country started giving way to forests and cooler temperatures. The distant mountains brought memories of days when he and Noah traveled here. And it gave him a good indication of where the six men were going. There was a passage through the mountains into California.

The next morning, as the dawn was breaking, there was smoke visible in the distance. The outlaws' camp, he was getting close.

In his haste, Wilford had not taken the time to devise a plan for dealing with these men once he caught up to them. Up against six, he needed surprise and luck.

An hour later, he reached the outlaw camp located at the bottom of a ravine. They were saddling up to ride and taking their time about it. Confident they had eluded any possible pursuers; they were in no hurry, a fact Wilford appreciated. All he had to do now was watch for an opportune time to make his move.

The gunmen finished saddling their horses and started off into the mountains. Wilford's familiarity with the trail they were using provided him some advantage. If he could get around them, there were places ahead where he could make his move. By mid-afternoon, he slipped past the riders and found a spot high above the trail where he could watch them approach. Late in the afternoon, the six riders reached his location and stopped to camp for the night.

"Hell, we're almost in California now," one of them said.

Wilford got a break. The outlaws were very careless by camping in a spot that left them only two ways out. On the west and east sides of the campsite, there were steep cliffs, leaving them with the choice of going on south or turning around and going back north. Wilford decided this was his best chance. He would make his move that night.

When darkness settled in, Wilford slipped through the rocks and brush to the outlaw's horses. He cut the rope line, then slapped the horses on their flanks, scattering them into the night.

The sounds woke the sleeping men. "The horses are loose!" one of them shouted.

"Scatter out and try to find them," someone commanded.

This was the opportunity Wilford was waiting for. With the men scattered, he could single out individuals without their companions knowing what was happening. From his position, in the faint campfire light, he could see the one giving orders. That must be Emmett Dossett, he concluded. *Get the leader under control first*, the sheriff had advised. That would make the others easier to handle.

His years among the Indians were paying off tonight. They had taught him how to move silently without being noticed. Like a shadow, he worked his way among the bushes until he could reach out and touch the outlaw leader. Before acting, he looked for any of the others about. Wilford raised his pistol to strike the man, but he got careless and stepped on a twig. The man started to turn.

Wilford brought the butt of the pistol down before the man could yell out to his companions. He had just finished binding and gagging the man when he heard voices. "Can't find them damn horses in the dark. I wonder how they got loose in the first place. I don't think Mavis tied that line very well."

"That's likely so," another said. "Young pup's kinda slow anyway. If it wasn't for him being Emmett's nephew, we'd be better off leaving him for the buzzards."

Wilford started to make a move for the other two when he heard more voices behind him. "We'll have to wait until morning to round up those horses."

"You two seen Emmett?" another asked.

"Naw, I ain't seen him since the horses ran off," one of them replied.

"Well, if he wants to go wandering around in the dark and break his fool neck, he can. I'm going to bed and waiting for morning," another said.

A young boy walked into camp. "I reckon them horses is scattered across South Oregon by now," one said.

One of the older men walked up to the young man, who was probably not more than fifteen. "You tie that line good?"

"Sure."

"Then how did they get away like that? I'm gonna have a talk with Emmett about you. Where in the hell is he, anyway?"

"Don't know," the young man replied.

"I guess we better take a look. Easy to fall in a hole or down a cliff out wandering around in the dark. Let's spread out and see if we can find him. Shit, this is a pretty fix with the horses scattered about and Emmett gone to boot."

While the outlaws were out of sight, Wilford decided to move Emmett further up the cliff to ensure his companions didn't find him. He grabbed the outlaw by the scruff of the neck and hustled him up the mountain. The gagged man tried to curse at him, but the rag in his mouth muffled the sound.

After securing Emmett Dossett, Wilford made his way back down the cliff to wait for the others. In a few minutes, the five straggled back into camp. "I don't see where he could get off to," the young one said.

"Maybe he found a woman out in the bushes somewhere," one replied. "I ain't worrying about him no more tonight."

"I'll tell him you said that," the young man said.

"Don't make no matter to me."

Wilford decided to wait until the rest of the gang were asleep before making another move. He waited in the dark until he could hear snores, then eased into camp. He worked his way up to where one of them was sleeping, clamped a hand over his mouth, and then shoved his pistol into the man's face. "Don't make a sound," he whispered. He tied and gagged the man.

By morning, Wilford had all the gang tied and gagged. He hauled Emmett Dossett down the cliff to join his companions. When Wilford removed the gags, the raiders let out a barrage of curses and threats. "I'll kill you when I get loose!" one of them yelled.

"I don't plan on you being loose anytime soon," Wilford said.

It took most of the morning to round up the outlaws' horses. He saddled each one and got his charges mounted.

"Who are you, and what are you planning on doing with us?" Emmett Dossett asked.

"I'm taking you back to La Grande to stand trial."

"I remember you," Emmett said. "You was riding with that McKane fella."

"That's me."

384

"Well, mister, let me remind you that there's six of us, so you gonna have a devil of a time getting us all the way back to La Grande by yourself," Emmett said.

Wilford rode up and looked straight at them. "Let me remind you varmints of something. I don't have to get back with all six of you. I only need to get back with one or two to testify at the trial. The rest of you, I can feed to the wolves. Since all of you are riffraff anyway, I doubt you'd ever be missed much. If I have any trouble with any of you, that's what I'll do feed you to the wolves."

Would his tough talk carry any weight with these desperados? Wilford didn't know. And the outlaw was right. It would be a difficult trip back with six desperate men on his hands. But whatever it took, he was going to see they were brought back to face justice. He struck the lead horse on the flank, and they started moving north.

The gunmen swore at him constantly, but Wilford remained calm. He rode at the end of the column so he could keep an eye on all of them. Occasionally, they would stop, and he would offer them a drink from his canteen.

During one of these stops, one of them tried to kick him. Wilford pulled the man down from his horse and looked at him with cold, hard eyes. "The next time you try that, I'll leave you here on the trail."

The swearing continued as they made their way north. "I'm gonna get them gags back out if you don't shut up," Wilford said.

By the third day, Wilford was nearly exhausted. He could sleep little at night, worrying about one of the men getting loose and freeing the others. He couldn't keep this up much longer. Shortly after starting out, he dozed off in the saddle and awoke to find one of the outlaws had almost freed his hands. That was it. Wilford now realized he couldn't go on alone. Ultimately, one of these desperate men would get loose and catch him off guard. Without some help, he could not get these cutthroats back to La Grande. To make matters worse, he had to put loose hobbles on the outlaws' horses to keep them from making a break. Traveling so slowly, they only covered a few miles each day.

Where would he find any help out here? First, there were very few settlements. Besides, a Negro traveling with six tied up white men would arouse too many suspicions. There had to be another way.

Wilford reflected on his options. He knew this land from his days in the mountains. Being a mountain man, he had always relied on the land to provide for his needs. What did the land have to offer him now?

He thought. The Paiutes. Paiute land was only a few hours' ride from here. He and Noah had hunted with them at one time. Of course, that was many years ago. After so long a time, there might not be anyone among them who

385

would remember him. He spoke a few words of the Paiute tongue; that might help. He decided it was his only chance.

He turned them from the course they were following and rode east. Wilford's best hope was that the band he and Noah had hunted with still lived on the same lands and that some among them would still remember him. The Northern Paiutes, he remembered, could be very unfriendly if you got on the wrong side of them.

By afternoon, Wilford was fighting to stay awake. He dozed off in the saddle and awoke to find Emmett Dossett staring at him. "You ain't going to last much longer, I judge," Emmett said. "You best let us go and get out of here. If you don't, one of us is going to get loose while you're dozing. Then, I'm gonna take pleasure in cutting you up in pieces."

Wilford was too tired to respond to the outlaw's threats. If he didn't get help soon, he might well pass out from the fatigue that consumed his entire body. Feeling numb from exhaustion, he looked through partially closed eyes and made out a group of riders to the east. He watched them approach. They had found the Paiutes or more to the point, the Indians had found them.

The gunmen looked at the Paiutes and swore. "The damn Indians are gonna lift our scalps."

"Just shut up and set easy," Wilford said.

The Indians stopped in front of them, and then one rode on out to Wilford. Using his limited knowledge of the Paiute tongue, Wilford managed to get off a greeting. The Paiute leader was a young man with long hair hanging down his back, wearing buckskin pants and carrying a rifle across his saddle. There were nine Indians in the party, all carrying rifles. Two had small game slung on back of their horses.

"Why do you come to our land?"

Wilford turned and pointed at the men behind him. "These men are murderers. I'm taking them back to La Grande for judgment."

The Indian looked at Emmett Dosset and the rest of the gang. "Most white men are murderers. What is so different about these men?"

"They seriously wounded my friend and killed another man," Wilford said. How fortunate it was the Paiute leader could also speak some English. He decided to see if he could gain some advantage with the Indians. "I once hunted with Elk Horn. He was a friend of mine."

The young warrior looked at Wilford. "Elk Horn is my grandfather. He is very old now. He stays in his lodge most of the time. You will come to my village and see him."

Relief swept over Wilford. The Paiutes weren't hostile, and with them in his company, there was less worry about the desperados escaping.

The raiders swore again. "The red devils gonna lift all our scalps."

"If you don't shut up, I'll scalp you myself," Wilford replied.

After a thirty-minute ride, they reached the Paiute camp on the bank of a small stream. The people lived in rather simple dwellings of rushes laid over a framework of poles they called wikiups. Indian women were working at cook fires in front of the lodges while some children ran about.

The Paiute leader took Wilford to a wikiup located in the center of the camp, then told him to wait while he stepped inside. When the young man reemerged, he motioned for Wilford to enter.

Wilford stepped inside. An elderly Indian dressed only in a loincloth was sitting in the back. His hair was totally white, and his bronze face was wrinkled. "My eyes now fail me," he said. "My grandson has told me you are a friend from the days when I was young, and we hunted together. I can remember only two such men. I know the days of one of them have already passed. Perhaps you are the one called Wilford."

"Yes. I was the one that hunted with you."

The old man responded to Wilford's words. "It has been a long time since the days we hunted the buffalo and the elk."

Wilford spent several hours talking to the old man about the days when he and Noah hunted with the Paiutes. When the opportunity came, Wilford explained why he came to the Paiute land with six desperate white men that he was trying to bring to justice.

The old man asked for his grandson to come into the wikiup. When the young man was inside, they talked for a time, and then he turned to Wilford. "I will honor the time when we hunted together as friends. My grandson and some of the others will go with you for a time and help you bring these men to their judgment. They cannot go all the way because there is trouble between us and the white men, but they will help."

At last, Wilford could rest. These men would meet their judgment.

Chapter 38

The Conclusion

A Week after Wilford's departure, Mr. Brand, the prosecutor, returned to the farm with some disappointing news. Kate had just returned from La Grande and visiting with James.

"How is your husband, Mrs. McKane?"

"Still very weak, but he seems a little stronger."

"I wish my news was better. I've been informed by the judge that he won't grant any delays. Covington's got some influence, and he's using it to his advantage," the prosecutor said.

"I was hoping we could delay the trial until Wilford Johnson gets back," Kate said.

"We have no way to know when that will be or if Wilford Johnson will even be successful. It doesn't give me just cause to get the trial postponed. The case will go to court in three weeks. I'm sorry. I wish I had better news."

Kate was heartbroken, even bitter, at the news. Going to trial with circumstantial evidence meant this man who had taken so much from her stood to go free. How could she go on living if that happened? Fate never seemed to be on her side.

*   *   *

For three weeks, Kate spent her time worrying, both about James and the upcoming trial. She was starting to feel more hopeful about James, but the one and only chance to make Covington pay for his crimes might be slipping away. There would be no justice for the wounding of her husband and Olaf and the murder of Uncle Lewis. *How could that be*? She kept asking herself. What kind of system would absolve a man like E. G. Covington for such horrendous crimes? One that revolved around money and power; that's what

388

it was. Often, she would fret until her self-control slipped away, and she would break down and cry.

On the morning of the trial, Olaf hitched the buggy and drove Kate to La Grande. Her intention was to stay at the boarding house in town until the trial was over. That would allow her to visit James during the evening. E. G. Covington was going to see her face every day, like it or not. He would see her on the witness stand testifying against him; every time he turned around, her stare would greet him. Being a man with little or no conscience, it probably would not bother him, but she would gain some satisfaction from it.

The trial was big news. The courthouse was surrounded by buggies, saddle horses, and wagons. Word was circulating among the crowd that a reporter from Portland would be in attendance.

Most of the upstairs floor of the courthouse, except for the sheriff's office and jail, had been converted into a makeshift courtroom. The desks of the other county officials had been pushed to one corner and chairs set up for the spectators. In front, there was a wooden desk for the judge with a gavel and Bible on top and a pitcher of water.

All the seats appeared to be taken. Kate vowed that if necessary, she would stand for the duration of the trial. "Mrs. McKane!"

Kate turned and saw Howard Klaspell near the front, motioning to her. She pushed her way over to the newspaperman. "I saved you a seat."

"Thank you so much."

Mr. Brand was sitting in front of them. E. G. Covington was sitting at a nearby table with a portly man dressed in silk shirt and wool trousers. As Kate was taking her seat, Covington looked in her direction. The twisted grin on his face forced her to look away for a moment. Then, remembering her vow, she turned and looked directly into his face. He turned away and whispered something to the man sitting next to him: his attorney, she assumed.

To the side of the judge's desk sat twelve empty chairs for the jury.

The judge made his way through the crowd and took a seat behind the desk. He was a short, gaunt man with a facial expression resembling someone biting into a green persimmon. He looked out over the crowd, then picked up the gavel and banged it on top of the desk. "I'll tolerate no nonsense in this courtroom. Anyone tries, I'll have the sheriff throw them in jail. All right, Mr. Brand, get it started."

The prosecutor stood up and read the charges against E. G. Covington. "Mr. Covington is charged with arson in that persons in his employ did set fire to two houses located on the estate known as Harrington Farms. Mr. Covington is charged with attempted murder in that persons in his employ did shoot and wound one Olaf Hanson, an employee of Harrington Farms. Mr. Covington is further charged with attempted murder in that a person in his employ and acting under his instructions did shoot one James McKane. Further, Mr. Covington is charged with murder in the first degree in that persons in his employ did murder Lewis Harrington."

The crowd stirred for a moment but settled down when the judge banged his gavel. "Start the jury selection."

The court clerk stood and read off a list of names. After each name was called, the person would come forward and sit in a chair. Mr. Brand and Covington's attorney would question each of the prospective jurors. The prosecutor tried to get some of the men disqualified based on their acquaintance with E. G. Covington. The judge overruled all of his requests.

While the jury selection was proceeding, Howard briefed Kate about the days since Covington's arrest. The old freighter had been hard at work pleading his case. His approach was to convince all who would listen that Lewis Harrington was the source of all the trouble, not him. "I'm just an honest businessman trying to make a living," he often said.

After a full morning of wrangling, a jury of twelve men was seated just before noon. The judge halted the proceeds for the noon recess, ordering everyone back at one o'clock.

Kate was so nervous; she had to forgo eating. Instead, she went to the doctor's office and clinic to visit with James. She felt he looked a little better today. His color had improved, and he ate some soup. She explained about the trial and her concerns. He looked at her and gave her hand a squeeze. "You'll get justice," he said in a very weak voice. She stayed with James until it was time to return to the courtroom.

Mr. Brand opened the trial by reading an affidavit from Wilford Johnson stating he and James McKane tracked Palmer and his gang from the Harrington farm to a shack on Covington's property. The affidavit further stated Wilford Johnson had seen Palmer and Covington near the shack just a few days before the last raid on the farm.

The defense attorney countered by pointing out the shack in question was located in a remote area and could be accessed by anyone without Mr. Covington's knowledge. The attorney pointed out that Mr. Covington had, on one occasion, met with someone at the shack with the sole purpose of hiring people to round up stray cattle. He further pointed out that Wilford Johnson had only witnessed the conversation from a distance and could not hear what was being said.

The last witness that day was Sheriff Avery Benton. Mr. Brand asked the sheriff to explain what he knew about the attacks on Harrington Farm.

"Renegade Indians was my first thought," the sheriff replied. "There had been some raids near the valley. We tried to track the raiders, but we lost the tracks."

"What happened when you went out to see about the second attack?"

"Well, it was well after dark when one of the farmers from out that way came knocking on my door. He told me about the raid and that some fellas had been shot. I got one of my deputies, and we rode out there."

"What did you find?"

"Well, when we got out there, I found out the McKane feller had been badly wounded, and another man named Ellis Palmer was dead."

"What do you know about Ellis Palmer, Sheriff?"

"I knew him and some of his gang from my days in California."

"And what was his usual line of work?"

"He was what some of the folks around the mines called an enforcer. That's just fancy talk for a hired gun. Some of the mine owners and local politicians used Palmer to protect their interests. He was a real mean man who would do most anything for a price."

"Sheriff, did you ever know of Palmer hiring out to round up cattle?"

"I never knew of him doing that kind of work."

Mr. Brand looked down at the floor for a moment. "When you heard about the shooting that night, what did you do, Sheriff?"

"I started to figure my idea about Indians was wrong. I guess deep down, I knew all along it was wrong, but I was hoping it would turn out to be the case. When I was told about Palmer being around, I was afraid someone was paying him to get rid of the people out there."

"I see. What did you do after the raid?"

"The next day, me and two of my deputies went and arrested E. G. Covington."

"No more questions, Sheriff."

The defense attorney stood up. "When you found out Ellis Palmer was involved in the farm raid, why did you suspect Mr. Covington?"

"I knew someone was paying Palmer, or he wouldn't be up here. I knew that Lewis Harrington had trouble with Covington over the new settlers, so he was the only one that had a reason for wanting to get rid of Mr. Harrington and Mrs. McKane."

"Sheriff, that seems to be based more on speculation than facts, don't you think?"

"No, I don't. I seen some of the papers Covington had persuaded the settlers to sign. It would have given him basically everything they owned if they couldn't pay their freight bills. He had a free hand to charge whatever he wanted. He was also making loans and charging interest rates those people couldn't possibly pay. I know Lewis Harrington, and later Mrs. McKane were telling the settlers not to sign these agreements. I know they started buying crops at the farm to stop Covington from carrying out his plans. I think that was what drove E. G. to do what he did. He stood to lose a lot in the long run and decided to do something about it."

"Sheriff, have you ever considered that Lewis Harrington himself might have been trying to swindle the settlers?"

"Maybe at first, after listening to some of the talk, Covington was spreading around. After a time, I reluctantly changed my views about the situation and decided the evidence pointed toward Covington. He was the one trying to ruin the settlers and realize a big gain for himself. I didn't tell the Mrs. McKane about this 'cause I didn't want to get her hopes up. I guessed I hoped it would come to an end, and I wouldn't have to do anything, but I should have known better."

"Speculation on your part, just speculation."

The trial recessed after the sheriff concluded. Kate left the courthouse feeling emotionally drained from testimony that stirred bitter memories. And there was the trial itself. The defense attorney was planting the seeds of doubt, doubts that might well sway the jury. After visiting James that evening, she had a light supper and went to bed but found it difficult to sleep that night.

*   *   *

The next day, Kate took the stand. She sat in the witness chair with her hands folded in her lap. "Mrs. McKane, please tell us what your uncle told you about the business deal with Mr. Covington," the prosecutor said.

"He explained to me about the original agreement he and John McDonald had put together with Mr. Covington. After he brought the settlers up here, he found out Mr. Covington was having them sign a different agreement. This one would put them in deep debt. It gave Covington the right to charge whatever he wanted for hauling their produce."

"Did he tell you why Mr. Covington was doing this?"

"Yes. He said it would give Mr. Covington a lot of power and influence if he owned all this land. After the railroad survey, there were rumors of a rail line being built through the valley, which would run through some of the settlers' land. A lot of the valley is public land, which can only be acquired by homesteading. Mr. Covington saw this as a means of acquiring a big portion of the area."

"So, E. G. Covington would have a substantial, long-term gain from all this?"

"Yes," Kate said.

"Objection," the defense attorney countered. "That's just the witness's opinion." The judge agreed.

"That's all," the prosecutor said.

The defense attorney got up from his seat. He glared at her. *He's trying to intimidate me*, she concluded. "Mrs. McKane, how long had you known your uncle when he brought you up here?"

"I met him for the first time when he came to Clarksville, Tennessee that spring."

"So you really didn't know that much about your uncle or what kind of man he really was; is that true?"

"I found out quick enough that he was an honest and caring man," she replied. "He took in me and my children and helped me get over my grief."

"But you were never really involved with him as far as his business was concerned; is that right?"

"No. That was all set up before I came up here."

"The fact is, Mrs. McKane, you really didn't know that much about your uncle at all."

"I knew enough," she replied. The questions were starting to annoy her.

The defense attorney picked up a sheet of paper and handed it to her. "Have you ever seen this document before?"

The paper contained a list of what appeared to be stockholders in a mining company. One of the names was Lewis Harrington.

"I've never seen this before," Kate said.

"Mrs. McKane. Do you know how your uncle financed his land and the experiments he and John McDonald were involved with?"

"Well, no, I really didn't know that much about his early life, but he did mention something about being in California for a time."

The prosecutor was now on his feet. "I object to these questions. They are not relevant. Mr. Harrington's past business dealings have nothing to do with this case."

The defense attorney countered. "Mr. Harrington's past conduct, we believe, led to the current problems with Mr. Covington and to Mr. Covington being falsely accused of these crimes."

"All right, go ahead," the judge said.

"Mrs. McKane, your uncle got most of the money he used to buy land here in Oregon from his mining interests in California."

"That may be," she replied.

"The mine in question had a number of problems concerning ownership. At one point, there was violence between the owners of the mine. I submit that this is where Palmer got involved and that Lewis Harrington was the one who brought Palmer in to help protect his interests here. Palmer worked for the mining interests in California. That's where he and Lewis Harrington got involved with each other. I think they had a disagreement after Palmer arrived, and that led to Palmer attacking the farm."

Mr. Brand responded angrily. "There is no proof Mr. Harrington ever had any contact with Ellis Palmer in California. The fact that both of them were once in the same state is totally unrelated to the current case. Mr. Harrington initially had no need of anyone to protect his interests. He trusted E. G. Covington and his other partners.

"It was not until he found out Covington was changing the freight agreements and peddling his high-interest loans that Mr. Harrington needed any help protecting his interests or the interests of the people he brought up here."

The judge banged the gavel. "You are out of order, Mr. Brand. If this happens again, I'll have you removed from the courtroom and thrown in jail. And Mr. Gils, I'll remind you not to make allegations you can't prove."

With order restored, testimony continued. Mr. Gils continued to try and cast Lewis Harrington as the real culprit in the partnership, but Kate held her ground, insisting that her uncle never tried to do anything dishonest.

Kate spent most of the morning testifying about the problems between the settlers and E. G. Covington. Covington's attorney continued to insist the real problem was Lewis Harrington trying to break their agreement and not the actions of Mr. Covington. She was hurt and angry at his accusations but kept her composure.

During the noon recess, Mr. Brand accompanied Kate to a small eatery on Main Street. "You've got to hand it to Covington; he found a good attorney," the prosecutor said as they were eating.

"But he can't prove all those accusations he's making."

"He doesn't have to. He's creating doubts in the minds of the jurors. Our case is somewhat shaky already. The jury is probably leaning toward acquitting Covington."

That probability took Kate's appetite. She couldn't bear the thought he might go free. That just could not be permitted to happen.

Mr. Brand finished his presentation that afternoon. The defense attorney only called a couple of local businessmen who testified that E. G. Covington was an honest man. With their testimony concluded, the defense rested.

The dejected look on Mr. Brand's face said it all. He was expecting to lose the case and unleash her worst nightmare. Kate hung her head and felt the tears forming.

The judge banged his gavel and was preparing to send the jurors out to deliberate when a deputy sheriff made his way through the crowd to Sheriff Benton. He bent down and whispered in the sheriff's ear. Then the sheriff talked in low tones to the prosecuting attorney. Mr. Brand got up and addressed the judge. "Your honor, some additional witnesses to this case have just turned up. I request permission to put these people on the stand."

The judge gave him a stern look. "This is a very irregular procedure. You had an opportunity to present your case."

"Your honor, these witnesses had fled and were unavailable when the trial started. I've just been informed they are now back in La Grande. I request a recess to question these people."

"I'll give you until tomorrow morning, and that's all."

Wondering what was going on, Kate got up from her seat and made her way out of the courthouse. There, she did a double-take; Wilford was standing in front. Behind him were six men, now all in handcuffs, being guarded by sheriff's deputies?

Seeing Kate, Wilford walked up to her. "Ma'am, here is part of the contingent of gentlemen that came calling on your place a few times. You got to pardon their appearance. They been traveling hard these past few days so they could get here in time."

Kate was stunned. "Wilford, I can't believe you could bring all these men back by yourself."

"I ran into some good help along the way."

Sheriff Benton led the outlaws upstairs and put them in cells. Afterward, the sheriff and Mr. Brand talked about how they would question them.

"The young one probably lured Lewis Harrington out to where the rest could get at him," the sheriff said. "He's your best bet. He's the youngest and probably the most scared of the bunch. The rest are hard cases and will be tough to break."

The sheriff got Mavis Dossett out of his cell and led him to a room down-stairs. They sat him in a chair, and then Mr. Brand looked at the young man.

"Son, I guess you know you're likely to hang for your part in this."

The young man glared back at him. "I ain't tellin' you anything."

"If I was you, I'd think differently," Mr. Brand said. "You were seen leaving with Lewis Harrington that afternoon. That's enough to get you hanged. We know you were riding with Palmer and his bunch the night James McKane was shot, and Palmer was killed, so there's another reason for you to swing. You're going to be meeting your maker face-to-face if you don't cooperate with me. You ever see a man hang? It's not pleasant; I can tell you that."

They pounded at the young man until his mettle began to wane. As the questioning went on, his arrogance ebbed and eroded away.

*　　*　　*

The next morning, the judge seated himself behind the desk and looked at Mr. Brand. "I hope you've got some pertinent information."

"Your honor, I believe we do."

A deputy sheriff led a nervous Mavis Dossett through the crowd. The young man glanced at E. G. Covington before sitting down.

Covington's face paled when he saw the young man being led into the courtroom. His arrogance had been replaced by concern.

The defense attorney put up a number of objections; all quickly waved aside by the judge. "Get on with it, prosecutor."

The prosecutor stared down at the young man. "Did you go with Palmer and the others to the Harrington place the night James McKane and Palmer were shot?"

"Yes."

"And what was the reason you and the rest of Palmer's gang went out there that night?"

"Palmer told us Mr. Covington wanted us to go out and put a stop to what they were doing."

Covington jumped to his feet, his face red with rage. "You lying little bastard. I don't even know you."

"You old fool, I'm not hanging for you!" Mavis Dossett yelled back.

The judge banged his gavel hard on the desk. "Order here. I'll tolerate no more of these outbreaks. Mr. Gils, keep your client under order, or I'll have both of you arrested."

With ordered restored, the questioning continued. "Did you ever see Palmer and Covington talking together?" Mr. Brand asked.

"Lots of times. Sometimes, he would come out to our camp with orders for us. Other times, Palmer would ride over and meet him at an old shack. Then, Palmer would come back and tell the rest of us."

"Did he ever send you and the others out to burn the Harrington houses?"

"Yeah. Covington came out to the camp and told us the McKane woman was turning the settlers against his plans. He wanted her stopped. He also said she was taking away some of his freight business. He said we were to go out and burn the houses down and make sure no one got out alive. He said Indians would get the blame for it."

"Do you remember who shot the foreman, Olaf Hanson?"

"Palmer did that."

"What about the last raid out there?"

"Palmer went and met Mr. Covington at the shack again. He came back and told us we missed the first time. He said that Covington wanted a thorough job this time. We were to wipe out the entire bunch. Somehow, they found out we was coming and were waiting for us when we got there."

A hush fell over the courtroom. E. G. Covington suddenly jumped up from his seat and lunged toward the witness chair. "I'll kill you with my bare hands."

The deputies, with help from some men sitting up front, grabbed E. G. Covington and pulled him back to his chair.

"Put him in chains!" the judge yelled.

The sheriff and his deputies shackled Covington and the questioning continued. After Mavis Dossett finished his testimony, the jury took only a few minutes to find E. G. Covington guilty of the charges against him. The old freighter stood and trembled as the judge sentenced him to twenty years in prison.

Tears of relief, tears of joy, they all flowed from Kate when the sentence was imposed. Justice delayed was better than no justice, she concluded. It was a victory, but the sentence was still disappointing. "He was responsible for the death of one man and wounding two others," she told Mr. Brand.

"That is true, Mrs. McKane, but we were lucky to get a conviction at all," Mr. Brand replied. "For a man his age, twenty years rotting in prison is a sentence worse than death in some ways."

*   *   *

That evening, Kate was waiting in front of the boarding house when Olaf arrived with the buggy to pick her up. The doctor had informed her that James would soon be able to come home. With that and the problems with Covington now over, she could dare to relax. Now she could get on with trying to build the dream that her uncle had started. As she looked out at the mountains and the late spring countryside, she felt a measure of peace within herself. Today, she could actually smile again.

Helga and Little Deer had a meal of roasted venison and homemade bread waiting for them. Kate embraced both of the women then the children. She told them about the trial and how Wilford's daring apprehension of the gang led to a conviction of the man who wounded their father and killed their uncle.

When they were seated, Olaf said a special blessing. "Lord, we give thanks for all our blessings. We are most thankful for the deliverance of justice to those who murdered Mr. Harrington and shot Mr. McKane. We thank you for helping Wilford Johnson in his mission to return those responsible and for bringing justice to all those who suffered from this violence. Amen."

When the meal was finished, Kate helped with the dishes and cleaning the kitchen. She was pleased at the progress Little Deer was making in adjusting to her new life. The girl knew a few words of English and was becoming a very good cook. Better, Olaf's prejudice toward the girl had abated. "She seems to be learning fast," he remarked.

*   *   *

397

The next morning, Wilford was especially quiet during breakfast. When the meal was over, he got up and announced that it was time for him to be starting back to Missouri.

"Wilford, I thought you liked it here in the mountains," Kate said.

"Yes, ma'am, I do. That is, I used to like it, but it's all changing now. Now they's farms and towns everywhere. It just ain't like it used to be. I want to go back to my place out on the prairie, sit on my porch, and look back this way and remember how it used to be, back when a man could roam up here wild and free."

Kate knew she could never repay Wilford for all he had done for them. He had helped her husband find his way up here. He had single-handedly gone after six desperate men responsible for the near-fatal wounding of James, Olaf, and the murder of Uncle Lewis so they could be brought to justice. It was a debt that could never be repaid.

Wilford excused himself and went to the corral, and saddled his horse. Then he brought it back to the house and collected his gear. He was storing it all in his saddlebags when Kate walked out, followed by the rest of her family, Olaf, Helga, and Little Deer.

"Wilford, I know my husband paid you for your services in guiding him up here, but I feel like I should pay you again for all your help since you been here, especially for bringing that gang of killers back to convict Covington."

"To tell you the truth, ma'am, like I told you before, I feel like I owed that to you."

"Well, Mr. Johnson, we'll never forget you. If you ever need a place to go, you'll always be welcome here."

"I thank you for that."

All of them gathered around to see Wilford off. Olaf shook his hand. "Good luck, my friend."

Little Deer and Wilford spoke in Blackfoot for a short time; everyone else came over and said goodbye.

Kate extended her hand. "Goodbye and God bless you," she said.

"Thank you, ma'am."

Wilford urged his horse out of the yard and rode across the meadow. Just before reaching the road, he turned and waved his hand. They all waved back. "Will he ever come back, Mama?" Drew asked.

"I hope so, Son, I hope so."

*   *   *

Later in the morning, Doctor Brighton had brought James home in a buggy. Kate and Olaf helped him down from the buggy. "Wilford left for his home in Missouri this morning," Kate said.

"I know," James replied. "He stopped by to see me."

For a time, James, supported by Olaf and Kate, stood and looked around the farm. "I can't tell you how good it is to see this place again," he said. "The doctor told me I was near death when they brought me to his office. He said he didn't think I would last the night."

Kate, her eyes fill with tears, said, "A lot of people have been praying for you, especially me."

James placed his hand over hers. "It looks like your prayers have been answered. And let's hope this violence is over and we can live our lives in peace."

"There must not ever be a dull moment out here," the doctor said. "You drug me out in a blizzard last winter and brought me three gunshot victims to tend. I do hope you people will find a way to live in peace out here."

"We intend to do just that," Kate replied.

"Stay off your feet until you get your strength back," the doctor said to James. "Now I need to get back to my office."

That afternoon, Kate walked up the hill to where Uncle Lewis was buried. Using a walking stick provided by Olaf, James walked slowly beside her. They said a small prayer then lingered for a time, recalling memories of times past, of plans and disappointments, and giving thanks for all their blessings. "We, and especially you, have endured a lot, but we survived, and we are stronger for it," James said. "Your uncle started this place, and we must see that his dream will live on."

Going back to the house, the mountains caught Kate's attention. The majestic peaks glowed in the late afternoon sun. As they paused to enjoy the beauty, Kate was beginning to better understand why Uncle Lewis loved this land so much, this place the Indian people called "Lochow Lochow," the "Lovely Little Forest." They had endured much here, yet there was so much to appreciate in this lovely place. There was a raw beauty here. Things sometimes came hard, and that made one appreciate it all the more.

Living in this land produced a love that even suffering and hardship could not suppress. To those who became a part of this land, they were part of the majesty of it all, just like the towering mountains that overlooked the valley. Kate and James had paid a high price to claim their part. Now it was their home and would always be so. Kate felt like they were part of the dream her uncle had started, and it filled her with joy.

THE END

Author's Note

This is a work of historical fiction, and to that end, I have endeavored to keep the story historically feasible. There is, however, at least one instance where I have strayed away from history a bit. This occurs in Chapter 29, where the frontier doctor performs an appendectomy to save the life of a young boy. The first such operation was performed in London in 1735; however, the operation was not performed in the United States until 1885. That would have made the frontier doctor about twenty years ahead of his time.

Of course, if the doctor was well-read, he might have known about the procedure from medical literature and been willing to try it in a life or death situation. A frontier doctor likely would have had some surgical tools. In 1865, Ether and chloroform were available for use as anesthetics.